Penhaligon's Gift

Terri Nixon

piatkus

PIATKUS

First published in Great Britain in 2018 by Piatkus

1 3 5 7 9 10 8 6 4 2

A CIP catalogue record for this book
is available from the British Library.

ISBN 978-0-349-41879-7

Typeset in Caslon by M Rules
Printed and bound in Great Britain by
Clays Ltd, Elcograf S.p.A.

Papers used by Piatkus are from well-managed forests
and other responsible sources.

Piatkus
An imprint of
Little, Brown Book Group
Carmelite House
50 Victoria Embankment
London EC4Y 0DZ

An Hachette UK Company
www.hachette.co.uk

www.littlebrown.co.uk

Terri   1965. At the age of nine she moved with her family to a small village on the fringe of Bodmin Moor, where she discovered a love of writing that has stayed with her ever since.

Since publishing in paperback (through independent small press BeWrite) in 2002, Terri has appeared in both print and online fiction collections, and published *Maid of Oaklands Manor* with Piatkus in 2013.

Also by Terri Nixon

The Penhaligon Saga

Penhaligon's Attic
Penhaligon's Pride

The Oaklands Manor trilogy

Maid of Oaklands Manor
Evie's Choice
Kitty's War

For my great-niece Zoey-Jane Rose: in a world filled with strong women, you have already shown us how your resilience and determination will shape your life . . . and that of everyone lucky enough to be part of it.

Dramatis Personae

Anna Penhaligon: formerly Anna Garvey. She arrived in Caernoweth to take up the inheritance of the local pub. She and her daughter had left Ireland in the wake of the death of a local banker's son, killed accidentally by Mairead when he had attacked her on a deserted beach. To protect her daughter, Anna said it was she who'd killed him, and the authorities in Ireland were informed that she herself had died at sea. Anna was almost killed during a terrifying summer storm, and she now lives with the Penhaligons, and has recently found out she is pregnant.

Matthew Penhaligon: a recovering alcoholic, and a lifelong fisherman who was forced to take a job as a miner following the death of Roland, his friend and skipper, when the trawler on which he worked was left to the skipper's son James. Matthew was caught up in an underground explosion at Wheal Furzy, and badly injured. Later he and James rebuilt their friendship, and James sold the trawler, the *Pride of Porthstennack*, to

Matthew, who is gradually regaining his health and is now able to do limited work in the industry he loves.

Freya Penhaligon: Matthew's daughter. She was washed off the Porthstennack harbour wall as a child, and nearly drowned, and is only just beginning to lose her subsequent fear of the sea. Her mother Isabel took her to live in London and attend private school there, but she returned to Caernoweth after several years and now works in the struggling family bookshop, Penhaligon's Attic. She became close to a visiting author and historian, Tristan MacKenzie, and, despite their disagreements over whether he should publish certain findings, they soon realised they were in love. Tristan had to leave Caernoweth, to attend to family business, and neither expected him to return, until Freya received a telegram on Christmas Eve.

Tristan MacKenzie: Author and historian originally from Honiton in Devon. He is researching the English Civil War period, and the discovery of a set of journals has led him to Caernoweth, where he has discovered the town has a much darker history than anyone had believed. Falling in love with Freya put him in a difficult position, due to her insistence that revealing the truth would have a devastating effect on her family. They had just overcome this conflict with his professional integrity, when he was called away to America to deal with a family crisis.

Mairead Casey: Anna's daughter, who suffers from mild epilepsy that takes the form of absence seizures. Clever and complicated, with a head for figures, she helped Freya turn the shop around and they soon became close; Freya is the person in whom Mairead confided the truth about the murder in Ireland. Mairead spent some time away, getting to know family she had never previously met, and is now blossoming and finding her confidence around strangers.

James Fry: a former friend of Matthew's, and the only son of popular fisherman Roland. He left Caernoweth at seventeen to train as an architect, and originally returned to try and set up his own business in town. He is now using his stone mason's skills to help rebuild the parts of Porthstennack that had been destroyed in the storm, but still dreams of starting his own architecture business.

Isabel Webb: Freya's mother, a wealthy Spanish stowaway who Matthew met in Plymouth, and who fell for the romantic notion of life with a handsome sailor. Sadly the reality of Matthew's difficult existence did not measure up, and after the accident that almost claimed her daughter's life, she and Freya left Caernoweth. Isabel later married a politician and moved to America, allowing Freya to return to live with her father.

Lucy Batten: youngest daughter at Pencarrack House. She has been obsessed with dance and theatre all her life, and is determined to find a career that will let her indulge her passion. She became friendly with Tristan's research assistant, Teddy, and there is an undeniable but unspoken spark between them. Lucy finds herself constantly expected to care for her sister's son, Harry, who has a habit of running wild at every opportunity.

Various townspeople, including:

Esther Trevellick: she and her husband worked for Anna at the Tin Streamer's Arms, until Joe's recent death. Now Esther lives and works there with her eldest grandson, Alan, and her youngest grandson Tommy lives with them and works at Wheal Furzy.

Ellen Scoble: the first person to approach Anna as a friend. A widow with a young son, she is struggling to make ends meet, and works as a bal maiden at Wheal Furzy.

Doctor Andrew Bartholomew: initially disapproving of Anna, but was so taken by the way she turned the town around and created a sense of community, that he was the one who suggested he produce a false death certificate in order to protect her.

Susan Gale: his housekeeper. An inquisitive woman, and grandmother to three unruly youngsters.

Nancy Gilbert: a young widow who now lives in the house that used to be the home of the Penhaligons before Isabel left. She has four children: Gerald, Joseph, Tory and Matty. She works at her parents' farm and has not bothered to hide either her attraction to Matthew, or her mistrust of Anna.

The Battens: Pencarrack House overlooks the town and is the home of Charles, who owns several of the town's properties and businesses; his son Hugh, who has formed an attachment to Freya Penhaligon; his two daughters, Dorothy and Lucy, and Dorothy's illegitimate and adventuresome eleven-year-old son, Harry.

Arric: The pub's cat. Found as a kitten by Joe Trevellick, by the side of the road, he terrorises the hens and takes every opportunity to show Anna who really owns the Tinner's Arms.

Chapter One

March 1911. Penhaligon's Attic, Caernoweth

The clock's hands inched onward, almost as if they didn't care that today was special. Didn't care that, at eleven o'clock this morning, the coach from Bodmin would roll into the courtyard of the Caernoweth Hotel, just as it did twice every day, only this time everything would change. Eleven o'clock was now only fifty minutes away, and after seven months of waiting, fifty minutes was both too long and nowhere near long enough.

Freya Penhaligon smoothed her dress for the hundredth time, and took a deep breath, trying to let it out slowly and give her heart a chance to settle down. She tugged at the tiny frills on the ends of her sleeves, as if Tristan would notice they weren't lying evenly and climb straight back onto the coach again.

Her stepsister stopped writing, laid down her pen, and

shook her head. 'Stop fussing, you're grand! He'll be the one hoping to live up to expectation.'

'What if he remembers me prettier than I am?' Freya blurted, and winced at how shallow it sounded.

'And what if he does? I imagine he likes you for a little more than the way your face is arranged. If he didn't he wouldn't be making the journey all the way down here, on the off-chance he might still fancy you.'

'I suppose you're right.'

'Of course I'm right. And it could be the other way about anyway – can you remember *him* clearly?'

'Sort of. But I keep seeing him the way he looked when I first met him, all puffy-eyed and grim-tempered. *That* picture's as vivid as anything.'

'And you still fell for him despite all that, don't forget.' Mairead picked up her pen again. 'And I know a fella in love when I see one.'

'You weren't here when we were fighting about those journals,' Freya pointed out, 'you'd already left for Ireland by then. He was so stubborn.'

'But he realised it eventually, didn't he? And he took your side in the end, he chose you over his principles. Doesn't that tell you all you need to know?'

'It should, I know.' Freya placed her hands over her stomach as if she could calm the flutters just by pressing there. Hers and Tristan's history was a short but intense one: hesitant friendship, followed quickly by acceptance of their deeper feelings, their discovery of the one thing that might part them, and their determination not to let it. But in the end it had been something outside the control of either that had driven

2

him back to America, and both had truly believed that what they'd found together was gone forever. But now, after months of delays and disappointments, he was finally coming home.

'It's been a long time,' Mairead said, more gently, 'and a great deal's happened since you saw him.'

Freya nodded. There had been the awful storm last August, and the worry over Anna's injuries, not to mention the devastation of so many homes in Porthstennack, and the resulting disruption in town. Then there was the crushing disappointment of Tristan's letter, explaining he had been further detained in America after all, and urging her to seek happiness elsewhere.

Worse than all of that, and leaving a cold, empty place in their newly crowded home, Grandpa Robert had been reunited with his beloved Grace during the bitterly cold January just past, a little under a year since his stroke. Papá had steeled himself for it, but it had still hit him hard when it had happened, particularly since they had only recently buried the simmering resentments that had kept them from truly knowing one another over the years. Only the news of Anna's pregnancy had been able to lift everyone's spirits.

Freya looked once more at the grandfather clock; if she walked very slowly, perhaps stopped to talk to someone on the way—

'Of course, that clock might be running slow,' Mairead mused. Freya's eyes shot wide, and Mairead grinned. 'It's not, don't worry!'

Freya tilted her hat, using the glass front of the clock as a mirror, and eyed her stepsister's reflection. 'I can never tell if you're being serious.'

'And you probably never will.'

'I liked you better before you discovered a sense of humour.'

'You did not.'

'No,' Freya agreed, and tried to imitate Mairead's accent. 'I did not!'

'Go on, then.' Mairead leaned on the shop's counter. 'Away and meet your man. I think you'll probably recognise him, there can't be too many devastatingly handsome young men coming to town, after all.'

'Devastatingly?'

'Well, passing attractive,' Mairead amended. 'Hurry now, if he thinks you've forgotten him he'll be back on that coach before you can blink.'

'Mairead!' Freya straightened her shoulders, and resisted the urge to tug at her sleeves again. This was Tristan. She loved him.

And in a little under an hour she would remember why.

Freya stood in her old spot by the stables to await the arrival of the coach. Self-conscious in her Sunday best, she tried to avoid catching the eye of her supervisor, who was scurrying from back door to laundry – particularly since the Caernoweth hotel seemed to be so strangely busy for a Tuesday mid-morning. But her very stillness drew Fiona Tremar's eye, and she stopped in surprise.

'Don't lounge about, get changed into your uniform. Or aren't you still doing extra shifts?'

Freya shook her head, pulling herself upright. 'I'm not working today, Miss. Nor tomorrow. I'm just waiting for the coach.'

'All right for some,' Miss Tremar grumbled. Her glance travelled over Freya's hat and dress, and she sniffed. 'We've got a right busy time coming up, so they do say. Something about a new building the Battens are involved in. Likely all the rooms'll be filled.' With another cross look at Freya she vanished into the laundry shed, and Freya turned as she heard the sound of the approaching coach.

Her nerves were still strung tight, but now the sensation was accompanied by warmth, and a swelling excitement. The first few people alighted, standing around in small groups with those who had come to meet them, and Freya had to stand on tip-toe to peer past them, but finally she saw him. Dark wavy hair, and an open, friendly face that drew the eye, contrasted as it was with the stern straightness of his eyebrows. The smile wasn't there now, but when it came it would light the world around him – he couldn't help but make people smile back. How could she have forgotten that?

She watched him descend the few steps to the ground, rolling his shoulders in a familiar gesture to ease the stiffness of travel, and she crossed her fingers in hope that he would be just as pleased to see her; those seven months sat between them like a foreign land. She seized what remained of her courage, and stepped forward about to call out, then froze.

He couldn't have been expecting her to have come up today; if he had been he would have instantly scanned the crowds for her, and he would have found her smiling and excited. Instead he turned to help someone down from the carriage: a woman, staring down at her feet so all Freya could see was the top of her rather-too-large hat. Short but shapely, and extremely well dressed, the woman grasped Tristan's hand as she concentrated on placing her boots carefully on the narrow steps and allowed him to guide her to solid ground. This was no mere fellow-traveller, someone with whom Tristan had engaged in polite conversation on the dull journey from Bodmin; he was looking down at her and laughing, maybe even teasing her in that gentle way he had. Freya's heart stuck, and struggled to find a beat again, and she twisted this way and that, seeking an escape from the crowd that wouldn't draw attention to herself. Finding none, she turned hopelessly back to the scene by the coach, to see that Tristan had been cornered by one of his fellow-travellers, and had stepped aside and released the woman's hand. His companion lifted her hat brim away from her face and peered around, and Freya didn't know whether to laugh in relief, or cry with joy.

'Mama?'

Tristan was locked in conversation, and as Freya hurried towards the coach she didn't know who to greet first, but Mama took the decision out of her hands by coming to meet her.

'*Mi tesoro!*' she whispered against Freya's cheek. 'It has been too long!' She held Freya at arm's length and studied her. 'I am so sorry to have missed your birthday, and by only a few days, too! You have grown into such a beauty.'

Freya blushed. From the corner of her eye she saw Tristan absently stroking one of the horses while he chatted, and thought for one moment that her heart would actually burst with the delight of these two people being here. Mama released her and moved aside. 'Go and greet him,' she said in a low voice, and smiled. 'He told me you would be at work today, he will be as delighted as I am to see you. I will wait over here.'

Freya squeezed her hand, and went to where Tristan was bidding farewell to his new friend.

'You might have to hurry,' he was saying, 'they might have been sold by now.'

'And they'll give good insight on the land *around* the fort?'

'I'm certain of it.'

'Then I'll call in this very afternoon. Thank you.'

Tristan shook the man's hand, and turned, and Freya's breath stopped, her fear returning in a rush as their eyes met. His friendly smile had fallen away, and for a moment they looked at one another in silence. He stood close enough to touch, but he didn't reach out. What if he *had* changed, and no longer wanted her near him? What if he had come back merely out of courtesy, to break things off gently, and in person? He had tried to end things by a letter before, so perhaps this time he wanted to be sure it was over.

Tristan studied her face, and Freya, keeping her own gaze somewhere around his chin, could feel the prickle of sweat along her hairline. Her fingers itched to reach for his, and she kept them firmly curled into her gloveless palms. The last thing she wanted was to make him uncomfortable, and to feel him trying to extricate himself from an unwanted embrace; better never to touch him again, than that. They had been too long apart, too much had happened ... They were different people now.

'There you are.' His voice was quiet, contented, and she couldn't speak for the relief that thundered through her. He bent his head to hers, and the touch of his lips awoke everything that had been gently slumbering these past months. As he folded her against him everything else faded,

7

and Freya became lost in the breathless joy of knowing he still loved her. It didn't matter that people were looking at them, and she didn't care whether or not there was disapproval on their faces, Tristan was here.

When they parted he was smiling, and she could feel the restless movement of his thumb against her jaw, as if he was still testing the reality of her.

'Welcome back,' she said, surprised to hear her own voice sounding relatively normal.

'Hmm. As welcomes go, that was almost worth the wait. Will you welcome me again later?'

Freya laughed. 'Of course. It's only polite, after all.'

'I look forward to it.' Day-to-day necessities had no place here, but Tristan looked reluctantly at the coach. 'I suppose I ought to collect our luggage before it ends up back in Bodmin.'

'Left to Mama, it probably would,' Freya agreed. 'She appears to have forgotten all about it.'

'Go and talk to her, I'll join you in a minute.'

Rejoining her mother, Freya belatedly asked, 'Why didn't you tell us you were coming?'

'I wanted to surprise you. I think I was the one who was more surprised, though.' She gestured at Tristan, coming towards them with their cases. 'Imagine my astonishment when I learned why this particular young man was coming here?'

'How *did* you come to talk to one another, anyway?'

'We played a game on board the *Mauretania* on the last night of the voyage, and the teams were chosen by our different destinations. We spoke of many things on the journey. He is a very impressive and accomplished person, I think.'

Freya smiled, trying not to look too proud. 'I did tell you about him when I wrote.'

'Yes, but you never said he was quite so handsome.'

Tristan put the cases down beside them and cocked an eyebrow at Freya. 'You didn't? Might I ask why not?'

'Because I'd forgotten that part. All I could remember was that you had a face like a street-wrestler – a losing one – and that you were furious with me.' Her voice softened. 'And by the time I realised neither of those things mattered, everything else did.'

'Oh, you two are so sweet!' Mama caught each of them by the hand. 'Now, I must check in, and rest a while. I will come to the shop later, when your Papá is home.' She looked at the hotel with a little frown. 'Do you know, all the years I lived in this town, I used to dream of staying here.'

'Why *are* you here?'

Mama put on a little half-smiling pout. 'Are you not happy to see me?'

'You know I am! But why now?'

'It's the perfect time for a little vacation. Henry, my husband,' she added to Tristan, 'has business that has taken him across to the West Coast. I found myself with a lot of time on my hands, and a daughter I miss horribly.' She squeezed Freya's hand. 'I was so sorry to hear of Robert's passing. Matthew must be devastated.'

'He was. We all were,' Freya said quietly. 'None of us expected Grandpa to go so suddenly like that.'

'And your stepmother?' There was an undeniable edge to her voice as she asked, but Freya ignored it.

'She and Grandpa were great friends, after a bit of a difficult start.'

'Yes, you told me how she was there when he had his stroke.'

'She pretended to be a nurse, just so he'd let her help him. He could be a cantankerous sort, but he trusted her.'

They fell silent, each with their own memories of Robert Penhaligon, who had never really taken to his son's first wife the way he had taken to Anna, and made no secret of it. Nevertheless Mama's sorrow seemed genuine, even if it was probably more for Papá's sake.

As if hearing the thought as it crossed Freya's mind, Mama spoke again. 'Freya, tell me the truth now. How is Matthew? He is able to work again?'

'Yes. He's healed well. And being back on the boats has lifted his spirits.' Freya hadn't told her about Anna's pregnancy, and didn't feel it was her place to do so. She would find out soon enough. 'He's almost back to being able to do everything he could before, but now and again his arm gives him too much pain, and he has to let Ern Bolitho take over.'

'I'm glad he has someone to help,' Mama said. 'I always liked Mr Bolitho.' She stifled a yawn, and Tristan picked up the cases again.

'Let me carry this in for you.'

'Are you staying here too?' Freya asked him, watching Mama lead the way into the hotel. She lowered her voice. 'It's very expensive. I'm sure if we ask in town someone will have a room. James Fry is in your old room at Doctor Bartholomew's, but—'

'It's only until Friday morning, I can afford it until then.'

Freya stopped, her heart sinking. Tristan was halfway over the step, and turned back. 'Aren't you coming in?'

'Friday?' Her voice came out small and disappointed. 'Can't you stay a little longer?'

'Do you want me to?'

Freya felt words bubbling up that had no place in such a respectable environment, then she saw the glint in his eyes. 'I could bear it,' she said dryly. 'Just about.'

He grinned. 'Come on. I'll get checked in, then I'll explain.'

At the desk, Mama had joined the short queue of new arrivals. She turned to greet Freya and Tristan as they came in, but a frown creased her brow, and Freya twisted to follow her gaze; Hugh Batten and his older sister Dorothy were stepping over the threshold into the hotel's busy lobby. They must be here to greet guests, something to do with that building project Miss Tremar had mentioned, but even so it was odd to see them together without Harry to bond them; they were not the closest of siblings. Hugh was much closer to his younger sister Lucy. Freya wished, for a moment, she had not told her mother of Hugh's advances during the storm last year, but there was nothing to be gained by dwelling on that now. She just hoped Mama wouldn't cause a scene.

Hugh caught sight of Freya, and his face lightened until he also saw Tristan. Then he arranged his expression into one of polite welcome. 'Mr MacKenzie. Freya.'

Freya felt Tristan tense beside her, at the casual use of her first name, but he didn't know how closely she and Hugh had worked together in the storm, and how that night had broken down more than physical fences. Once he did, he would understand.

'It's nice to see you, Hugh,' she said, with real warmth. 'And you of course, Miss Batten.' She nodded at Dorothy with a more detached politeness, then seized the chance to put the past where it belonged. 'Hugh, I'd like you to meet my mother, Isabel.'

Mama's eyes passed over a tight-featured Dorothy on their way to Hugh, and then she smiled. 'I've heard many a kind word spoken about you, Mr Batten.'

'Likewise,' Hugh murmured, and took Mama's hand. 'How lovely to meet you properly at last.'

In a brief moment of muted memory, Freya recalled the first time she had met Hugh, when he had nearly knocked her off the pavement outside the civic offices. She'd been surprised to learn that he knew who Mama was, after all he'd have been only twelve when the two of them had left town on the same coach as his sister. It was strange to think of her eight-year-old self, staring out of the window and trying to capture the memory of her home, and how her tired and sad gaze would have slid, unseeing, past the boy with whom she was destined to share such a fear-filled night years later.

'Back to work on the journals a bit more, are you?' Dorothy said to Tristan, tugging Freya's attention back to the present. She too put out her hand, and Tristan gave it a brief shake.

'Teddy Kempton will be joining me shortly,' he said. 'So, with your kind permission, yes please. We'd very much like to continue our research.'

'Mr Batten?' A loud voice cut across the lobby, and the same man to whom Tristan had been speaking at the coach strode towards them. Hugh and Dorothy straightened at the sight of him, but Dorothy stepped back, allowing Hugh to move forward.

'Go on then,' she muttered. 'Better not let him know he's dealing with a woman, after all.'

'I will call on you later, *mi tesoro*.' Mama kissed Freya's cheek, and took her leave before their little group could grow any bigger. As she left she shot a dark look at the Battens, though they were too busy exchanging irritated glances with each other to notice.

Freya drew Tristan away to the desk so he could book himself in. 'Who is he?' she asked, gesturing at the newcomer.

'His name's Pagett. He's here to discuss a joint purchase of Caernoweth Fort with the Battens, but he was expecting Charles. He won't want to deal with Miss Batten.'

'Well Hugh has absolutely no idea about the family business,' Freya said. 'If he's got to convince Mr Pagett he's in charge, he's going to be doing an awful lot of playacting.'

'I'm sure he'll be quite good at that.' Tristan gave his name to the receptionist, and Freya's spirits dropped as she heard the young man confirming Tristan was only staying until Friday; distracted by the unexpected arrival of Hugh and Dorothy Batten, it had slipped her mind. The formalities observed, Tristan left his case in the lobby, and took Freya's arm in his as they walked out into the noon sunshine.

'It must have been quite a shock to see your mother like that.'

'It was the best kind of shock I could have wished for,' she smiled. 'But I don't know how Anna will feel. Or Papá, come to that. Anyway, what were you saying about Friday?'

'Yes, I hadn't really thought about how it might affect Anna. How is she?'

'She's well.' Freya shook at his arm, growing impatient. 'Friday?'

'I gather one of the teachers from the free school is getting married?'

13

'Tristan!'

He laughed. 'No, this time it's connected, I promise. Miss Trethewey, I think?'

'Yes, she's marrying James Rowe. Why?'

'Her cottage belongs to the Pencarrack Estate, and Teddy has been negotiating a nice little rental agreement for us both when she moves into her marital home. With Lucy Batten's very willing help, of course.'

Freya stopped dead, her heart picking up a quick, light beat. 'You'll be *living* here?'

'For a while. Until the book's finished, at least. Teddy will probably leave then.'

But Freya, much as she liked Teddy, wasn't interested in his plans at this moment. 'And what about you?'

'I think I'd like to stay.' He bent and kissed Freya's cheek. 'I think I'd like that quite a lot, actually.'

'So would I.' Freya's smile grew wider. They began to walk again, and the feel of his hand in hers was as familiar again now as if he'd never been away.

'The cottage has a little bit of land at the back,' he said. 'Part of Priddy Farm. That means I can bring Bill.'

'Bill?'

'Haven't I told you about Bill?'

'I'm assuming he's not a colleague, or a friend, since you plan on keeping him in a field.'

'Oh, he's a friend,' Tristan assured her. 'The best of friends. He's about sixteen hands, and a little bit chunkier than he ought to be, but some good, regular exercise will soon put him right.'

'Will you teach me to ride?'

'You can't ride?' Tristan affected a shocked look, and Freya pulled a face.

'I grew up in London,' she reminded him. 'There was no need to learn.'

'Then yes, I'll teach you to ride. If you'll do something for me.'

'Let's see. Bring biscuits twice daily? Take in your laundry? Stock your book when it comes out?'

'Marry me.' He stopped walking, and it took a moment for his words to sink in, and even then Freya thought he was joking, but as he pulled her back to stand before him, a tremble started low in the pit of her stomach; he meant it, his expression was unmistakeable; nervousness, hope, anxious eyes staring into hers, those dark brows almost meeting in the middle as he willed her towards the only possible reply.

She nodded slowly, unable to form even such a simple word, and before she could shake herself out of the temporary inability, he threw his head back and let out a yell. 'She said yes!'

'She's trying to, at least!' Freya laughed. She looked around to see if anyone was paying attention, but only a couple of people were within earshot and gave them distracted smiles, before returning to their own troubles, affairs, and particular joys. Were any of them as excited as she was? Were *any* of them having a day when every single breath they took was perfumed with happiness? Her heart was so full it ached, and the future suddenly spread out before her, strewn with delights and secret passions.

'I'm so excited, I can hardly speak.'

'Me too.' He gave her a sideways, suddenly suspicious look.

She sighed. 'To think … I shall learn to ride a *horse*!'

15

Tristan growled, and she relented, leaning against him with a laugh. 'Is this our happy ever after, then?'

'It ought to be. We've been through enough to have earned it, haven't we?' He kissed her, and the press of his body against hers made her dizzy all over again, this time wishing they were alone. Somewhere quiet. Her hands stole up to his jaw, and slid around the back of his neck, making him a willing prisoner.

When they parted they were both breathing hard, and Freya rested against him, feeling the heavy thump of his heart beneath her cheek. 'Freya MacKenzie,' she murmured, and smiled as she heard the low chuckle above her head.

'I like the sound of that.'

'Good, because you can't change your mind now.' Freya stood back and held out her hand. 'Let's go and see the cottage you're going to be living in.'

'*We're* going to be living in,' he reminded her. 'Once we're married, of course.'

'Then I definitely want to go.'

'Let me just take my case to my room first.'

He retrieved his case from the check-in desk, and Freya found a comfortable chair in the lounge area, to sit and wait, and daydream about becoming Mrs Tristan MacKenzie. The lobby had emptied quite quickly, with the new arrivals finding their rooms, and those who'd been awaiting their chance to board the coach moving outside. The town was busier than it had ever been, with more and more people discovering the pleasures of somewhere so close to both moorland and sea, and now the railway had so many more branch lines to the coast … If the fort was really to be sold, then it was more likely to be rebuilt as an hotel than restored to its former state, as a museum. Her thoughts were interrupted by the approach of familiar voices, as Hugh and Dorothy walked past.

'You might look more pleased, Dorothy.'

'Yes. You did a good job.'

'*Something's* bothering you, though. What is it? Not that old nonsense about not being allowed to discuss the purchase yourself? I thought you—'

'No. Not that.'

'It must be the full moon coming then. Should I expect eccentric behaviour until it passes?'

Freya peeked out from behind the wing of her comfy chair, to see Dorothy facing the staircase, ignoring her brother's joke and looking thoughtful and even a little worried.

Hugh put a hand on her back to guide her towards the door. 'Stop worrying. Pagett's had a long journey, he's bound to be tired. Give him a day or so to revive, and by then Father will be home. Sorry, but you know it's true.' This last was in response to Dorothy whipping her head around to glare at him. 'But you'll be able to sit in on the meetings, at least.'

'I told you, it's not that . . . Never mind. Right, I'm not going straight back home, I have to call in at Wheal Furzy first. Captain Able has something he wants to discuss.'

She shrugged off her brother's arm and crossed the threshold without looking back. Hugh stood still a moment longer, but when the elevator's cage rattled open to reveal a smiling, relaxed Tristan, he too left. Freya rose, straightened her skirt, and went to greet her fiancé. The Battens and their various grievances had no place in her thoughts, especially not today.

Chapter Two

The Tin Streamer's Arms

Anna nudged the cat away from the store room. 'Move along, you little pest.' Arric eyed her for a moment, and she could almost hear him say, 'In my own good time, thank you.' Then he sauntered off down the passage, as if it had been his decision all along, and sat blinking up at the door to the yard. Anna obliged.

'Go on then. And leave the hens alone.' She was about to go back in when she saw a figure standing rather nervously by the gate; a woman, dressed like gentry, carrying a dainty but impractical basket. She exhibited an effortless, regal poise, despite her hesitation, and she was also strikingly beautiful, not to mention familiar. Her resemblance to Freya was remarkable.

Anna felt a lurch in her stomach that had nothing to do with the restless child inside her.

'Mrs Webb?'

The woman appeared surprised to be recognised, but spoke in a charmingly accented voice. 'Please, you must call me Isabel.' She came through the gate and up the path. Small, but curvaceous, dark-eyed, exotic ... Cradled in Matthew's arms, the contrast must have been stunning, with his height, his blond hair, his breadth of shoulder and roughness of dress—

' ... Not too much of an imposition?'

'I'm sorry?' Anna gave her head a little shake, and the vision thankfully disappeared.

'I said I would like to talk.'

'About what?'

Isabel had heard the hint of suspicion, and she gave Anna a faint smile. 'About my daughter, of course.'

Anna coloured, feeling foolish. 'Yes. Of course. Come up to Penhaligon's Attic. It's just up—'

'I know.'

'You'll also know Matthew is working then, and won't be there.'

'Yes.' It was Isabel's turn to flush. On her it was delicate and shy, and it made Anna feel like a big, clumsy bully.

'I've some things to finish up here,' she said, in a more friendly voice, 'but my daughter will make you a cup of tea while you're waiting.'

'If it's quite all right, I will wait and walk with you.' Isabel gazed around the yard, and Anna watched for a sign of distaste, but there was none. Instead a cloud of memory came across the smooth-skinned face. 'I won't come inside though, if you don't mind.'

Anna didn't need to ask why. All the nights Isabel must have spent down at Hawthorn Cottage, alone except for a demanding baby daughter, knowing the child's father was up here, drinking away his earnings. No wonder she had searched so hard for a better life for her and Freya.

But Matthew was a different man now. His uncertain past was nothing but a dark memory, and Anna no longer feared any setback might return him into the arms of Bacchus. Had Isabel realised what she'd lost, and come back to reclaim him? As deeply as Anna believed in the strength of their relationship, it would be difficult for any red-blooded man to resist such charms. Particularly when he'd known her so intimately, and they shared such a precious gift as a daughter.

Her hand stole to her own midriff, and for the first time Isabel seemed to notice the swelling there, beneath the grubby apron. Her face changed subtly; her expression sharpened, and the eyes that rose to meet Anna's were no longer soft and shining.

'Congratulations,' she said slowly. 'Matthew always wanted another child. Alas for us it was not to be. He must be very happy.'

'He is.'

'Are you perhaps hoping for a boy this time? I know Matthew would—'

'I'll only be a few minutes,' Anna broke in, in growing irritation. 'Meanwhile, why don't you wait out the front? I'll meet you there.'

Without waiting for a reply she turned to go back indoors, but not before she noticed Arric winding around Isabel's skirts. Isabel stooped to pet him and it came as no surprise whatsoever to see that, instead of hissing and stalking off, Arric nudged the slender hand in blissful acceptance.

'Traitor,' Anna whispered.

At Penhaligon's Attic, Mairead was taking the money for one of the local history books that had been donated by Doctor Bartholomew last year. The buyer had the appearance of a businessman, and seemed in a hurry, but doffed his hat to them as he passed on his way out.

'Ladies. Good afternoon, Mrs Webb.'

'Mr Pagett. We travelled down together this morning,' Isabel said, when he'd gone. 'I think he is a buildings man, but anyway Tristan told him about some books he might find useful.'

'You've met Tristan as well, then?'

'Oh, yes! What a lovely young man. And perfect for Freya.'

'I'm glad you're home, Mother,' Mairead said. 'I have to go out, and I didn't want to close up.'

'Out? Where? Wait a moment, let me at least introduce you. This is Freya's mother.'

Mairead's eyebrows shot up, then she looked more closely at their visitor. 'Oh, yes, I see the resemblance.'

'It's nice to meet you at last, Mar . . . Mairead?' Isabel stumbled over the unfamiliar name, but her wide smile made her apologies for her. 'Freya has written of you of course.'

Mairead shook the outstretched hand, but only briefly; she still hesitated over physical contact with strangers. 'It's nice to meet you, as well, Mrs Webb.'

'Oh, please, you must call me Isabel.'

'Where are you going?' Anna asked.

'I don't want to tell you yet.'

'Ah,' Isabel put in with a secretive smile. 'A young man, I expect.'

Mairead turned to her, frowning. 'Why?'

'You are a very pretty girl,' Isabel stammered, evidently nonplussed by the blunt response.

'That doesn't mean I don't have other things to do.'

Anna bit her lip in an effort not to laugh at the look on Isabel's face. It wouldn't have been at all fair; the woman had been nothing but polite and courteous.

Mairead seemed eager to leave, and Anna didn't press her on where she was going; she knew better than to try and drag an answer from her daughter when she had that closed-down manner. The door swung shut behind her, and Anna turned back to Isabel but her polite offer of tea died before it reached her lips. The visitor was standing very still, in the middle of the small shop area, and her gaze was fixed on the shelf behind the counter. Anna followed the direction of it, and saw Freya's prized model boat, the *Lady Penhaligon*, complete with its newly fixed sails and masthead, and freshly painted hull.

'She still has it ...' Isabel murmured. 'I cannot believe it. But it looks a little different, I think? What happened to it?'

'It fell.' There was no sense in telling her it had been smashed against the wall, in a fit of betrayed fury, by Juliet Carne.

'It was months in the making,' Isabel said, moving closer to peer up at it. 'The nights he spent ...' She shook her head, and blinked quickly, but not before Anna saw the glisten in her eyes. 'She kept it all through her time in London, even when she was at St Catherine's.'

'She'll have wanted to remember her father, no doubt.' Anna hadn't intended the words to sound accusatory; she, of all people, could not condemn the woman for taking her child away to a place of safety. 'I just meant, at school she'd have missed—'

'It's quite all right. I know what you meant.' Isabel looked around the shop. 'I didn't come here often when I lived at Hawthorn Cottage, Grace had little love for me.'

'I never knew Grace.'

'She was wonderful with Freya, and with me she was ... polite. Kind, even, most of the time. Robert, on the other hand ...' Isabel gave a half smile. 'One always knew where they fit into Robert's views, and it was usually somewhere below the delights of getting one's fingers caught in a drawer.'

'He was hard work,' Anna agreed, encouraged by the unexpected flash of wry humour, 'but he cared well enough for his family.'

'Which was why I was not a favourite. He never trusted me to make Matthew happy, and in the end he was right, wasn't he?'

Anna's heart softened towards her. 'You gave him a beautiful, kind daughter, Isabel. Of course you made him happy.'

'I feel that he was the one who gave Freya to me,' Isabel admitted. 'And I repaid him by stealing her away. Ah! This town!' She wiped a finger beneath her eye, and shook her head. 'I must learn to put all my memories in the right places, must I not?'

Anna didn't know what to say, so she remained quiet while

Isabel patted her hair into place and recovered herself, and then offered tea, which Isabel declined. 'I must not trouble you for too long. I wanted to talk about Freya.' She followed Anna into the kitchen, still gazing around with a bemused sort of nostalgia. 'I'd forgotten there was no sitting room. It's peculiar for me to be here, you know, after all this time.'

'I imagine it must be. Do sit down.'

Isabel did so. 'Matthew and his father were at odds for a good while. It's nice to know they were reconciled at the end.'

'Yes. Anyway, Freya will be thrilled to see you. She often—'

'We've already met, at the hotel when the coach came in. As I said, I travelled down with her young man.'

'Of course. He's a lovely lad, right enough.' Anna took some potatoes from the sack and put them in the sink. She had no idea what to say now, so she busied herself with rummaging in the drawer for the small knife.

'I like your accent,' Isabel said. 'It is not like the others here.'

'Thank you. I'm from Ireland.'

'Ah. I remember now.' She paused. 'It seems Matthew has a liking for the exotic.'

There she went again! Anna attacked the first potato, more savagely than was warranted. 'I thought you wanted to talk about Freya,' she said, with some asperity.

'How is he?' Isabel blurted the question, before collecting herself. 'I mean, of course Freya has told me he's healed, but when I think about what had happened in that awful mine ...' She shuddered. 'I could not believe he was put in such danger, and so far below ground.'

Anna remembered that feeling all too well. 'It was a horrible shock, and he was dreadfully ill afterwards with an infection.

24

But he's strong and healthy – well, you already know that. Most importantly, he's happy in his work again.'

'Good.' Isabel seemed to relax then, for the first time. Anna silently scolded herself for painting the woman in her own mind as shallow and predatory; she'd captured Matthew's heart once, and he was not the type to be swayed by beauty alone, otherwise Nancy Gilbert would have hooked him back into Hawthorn Cottage months ago. Isabel had been a fierce, sparky young stowaway when Matthew had found her, and in order to have remained hidden on board ship for so long she must also possess courage, resilience and sharp intelligence.

Nowadays she was the picture of well-bred aristocracy. Her hands were linked on the table before her, and she gave Anna a friendly smile as she continued to look around the kitchen, plucking memories from the various objects that Anna knew had been there since Grace's time. Then she gave a small exclamation, and withdrew a tattered notebook from her basket.

'I brought this. For Freya. She asked me about it a while ago, but it slipped my mind.'

Anna wiped her hands on the towel and took the book, and her heart leapt. 'Matthew's stories,' she breathed, and sat down to glance through the pages of close, neat handwriting. She looked up at Isabel, gratitude swamping her suspicions. 'Thank you! You'll make her enormously happy. It should come from you, though.' She tried not to sound too hopeful as she added, 'Unless you're not staying?'

'I am staying a while,' Isabel said, taking back the book without argument. The way she ran her hand across the cover did not go unnoticed. 'Where is Freya now, do you know?'

Anna shook her head. 'She's taken a holiday from work, so I expect she and Tristan have gone for a walk. Are you sure I can't fetch you a cup of tea?'

'Quite sure.' Isabel paused. 'I heard what happened to Juliet Carne. Such a terrible shame. I remember her as a little girl, she reminded me a bit of me at that age, a certain ... freedom of spirit, I liked to call it. My Papá had other words though.' The ghost of a smile drifted across her face at the memories. 'I'm glad Freya had you to turn to, when Juliet died. You must have been a great strength to her when I could not be.'

But in that she was wrong. The poor girl had actually had no one: Mairead had been in Ireland; Matthew in hospital, Grandpa Robert with him; Tristan had been called back to America, Teddy to Plymouth ... There had been no one on whom to unburden herself except Anna, and Anna was the one person she'd believed she couldn't trust.

'Freya tells me there is a little boy who sometimes visits,' Isabel said, breaking the silence. 'Boys always like story book adventures, perhaps he would enjoy Matthew's tales.'

'That'll be young Harry. Harry Batten, that is, from Pencarrack. His real name's Henry.'

'I did not know there were children at the big house.'

'He was born in London apparently. I gather there was a scandal attached to his mother, Dorothy, at the time.'

'No doubt,' Isabel murmured. 'And the boy is allowed to come into town?'

Anna gave a little laugh. 'To tell the truth they're hard pressed to stop him. He goes to boarding school in Plymouth now, so we don't see him so often. But I'm sure Freya would like to read to him next time he comes in, particularly now she has that book.'

'Is he away at school now?'

'I think he's due back in a couple of weeks, for the Easter holiday.'

'That is good then, he will have these stories to occupy him.'

'How long are you staying for?'

'I'm not sure. Did you say Easter is soon? What date is it this year?'

'I believe Easter Sunday falls on the sixteenth of April.'

'Then I shall probably stay until after that. My husband will be away until at least May.'

Anna hoped her smile didn't look false. That was a long time indeed, to spend in a town like Caernoweth, unless there was a very good reason to be here. And much as she knew Isabel did love her daughter, she didn't believe for one minute that Freya was the sole reason she'd come back.

Isabel rose from her seat. 'I have troubled you long enough, I will call again when Freya is home.'

They both looked towards the shop as the bell jangled. 'That's more likely to be her than a customer,' Anna said. 'Wait a while.' She went into the shop, and sure enough Freya and Tristan were taking off their coats, and both seemed consumed with an air of excitement.

Freya kissed Anna on the cheek. 'Is Papá home yet?'

'No, but your mother is here.' She accepted a kiss from Tristan too. 'It's lovely to see you again.'

'It's good to see you, too. Freya told me about the accident, of course. I'm so glad to see you're fully recovered.'

Throughout this polite speech, Anna noted the way his

27

attention followed Freya as she took their coats into the hall to hang them up; it seemed the girl's fears had all been for nothing, there was no mistaking the devotion on *that* young man's face.

He and Freya joined Isabel in the kitchen, and Anna moved around the bookshop, straightening the odd book, listening to the joyful exclamation that presumably greeted the sight of the precious book of children's stories. She was smiling to herself, picturing Freya reading them to Harry Batten, when she heard the house door open; Matthew hated coming in through the shop: stinking and usually soaked through, he always had. The first time they'd met he'd been yelling from the depths of a dirty blue Guernsey jumper, as he'd fought to peel it off the moment he'd arrived home. How things had moved on, in such a short time.

She waited until she heard him climb the stairs to their bedroom, and when she followed him she found him removing his shirt ready to wash.

'I heard talking in the kitchen,' he said. 'He's here, then?'

'He is.'

Matthew nodded. 'Good thing too. If he hadn't shown his face this time I'd have been after his blood.' He turned to pour water from the jug into the bowl on the dresser, and Anna studied him from behind. The smaller scars from the explosion were fading. The worst ones, where the infection had taken hold, were still painful even after all this time, and Anna picked up a pot of cold cream, ready to massage it when he had finished washing.

'There's something else.'

'Oh?' He patted himself down with the towel, then hung it around his neck while he crossed to where she stood. 'What's

28

that?' He then proceeded to make it impossible to answer, and she was happy to let him.

When the kiss broke, he grinned down at her. 'You were saying?'

'Was I?' Anna smiled back, threw the pot of cream onto the bed, and looped her hands around his waist. She kissed his neck, and felt his fingers tangle in her hair and gently pull her head back so he could kiss her again.

'I believe so.' His lips travelled over her jaw and down to her collar bone, and he eased the neck of her blouse away so he could reach further down, his breath warming her skin.

Anna didn't want to spoil the moment, she didn't want to give him cause to feel anything except what he was clearly feeling now. For a moment she considered keeping him up here until Isabel left, but that would achieve nothing. Nothing except a few more minutes of utter bliss in his arms. She took them, but eventually she drew back, and sighed.

He frowned. 'What is it?'

'We have another visitor.'

'Do we?'

'It's Isabel.'

She'd been prepared for his hands to drop away from her, as if Isabel herself had come into the room, but it didn't happen. Instead he groaned, and his head sagged onto her shoulder before he dragged himself upright again.

'What the blue bloody blazes does she want?'

'Matthew!' Anna couldn't help laughing. 'She's come from *America*! She's not just popped up from Porthstennack!'

'Well *you* weren't too keen to tell me she was here,' he pointed out.

'That's a fair point. Anyway she's brought something quite precious with her, but I'll let Freya tell you about that.' She picked up the cream again. 'Turn around, I'll do this, then leave you to get dressed and respectable before you come down.'

'I wish I hadn't come home early now,' Matthew grumbled, turning obediently to lean down and brace his hands on the dressing table. 'I thought it'd be nice to welcome the MacKenzie lad, but if I'd known—'

'Hush,' Anna said. 'She's not here forever.' She scooped out some of the cold cream and, with gentle fingertips, spread it over the scar that marked the deepest of the wounds and smoothed it into the tight, sore skin. With her other hand she stroked the back of his neck.

Finally she kissed him between the shoulder blades. 'There, you're done.'

'More's the pity.'

She sympathised with his sentiments, it would have been glorious to simply fall into their bed, right now, and give in to the seemingly never-diminishing need she had for him.

'I'll go and tell them you're on your way,' she said instead.

He laid one hand gently on the swell of their child. 'Are you all right? Not too tired?'

'Not at all.' She placed her hand over his, willing the baby to move, but, as usual, it was apparently waiting until she was alone, or asleep. 'I'll see you in a few minutes.'

'I'll be down d'rectly.' The look on his face as she left said, loud and clear, *Don't worry*, and for the length of time it took to descend the staircase and walk down the short passage to the kitchen, she took comfort from that silent entreaty. But when she pushed open the kitchen door, and saw Isabel's excited expression melt into disappointment at sight of her, Anna knew it wasn't Matthew she needed to worry about.

* * *

James Fry put the letter on the little hall table and took his coat from the peg. He might have guessed that the next moment, drawn by the sound of his feet on the stairs, Mrs Gale would appear from the kitchen. She picked up the letter without invitation, and squinted at it, while James tried to curb his irritation; having rented Doctor Bartholomew's attic room for the past six months he was becoming used to the housekeeper's harmless but unapologetic interest in the lives of others, but this was an important letter and he winced as he saw a wet thumb-mark appear on the paper.

'Lut-yens,' she read aloud. 'Who's that, when he's home?'

'An architect.' James gently but pointedly plucked the envelope from her wet hands, before she could smudge the ink. 'I'm off to post this, then I'm going down to 'Stennack. I shan't be back for tea.'

'Father's cottage ready for movin' back in then?'

'Not quite, but almost.' And if this letter bore the fruit for which he desperately hoped, the pleasure of living there would belong to someone else. 'Good afternoon, Mrs Gale.'

He hurried out, before she could think of anything else to ask. It hadn't escaped his attention that she'd referred to the cottage on Paddle Lane as his father's, and she was right; it hadn't really felt like home since he'd moved back, and after

Roland's death, and then Juliet's last year, it felt even less so. Now the future had, at last, given him something to smile about. He patted the envelope in his pocket, and his smile widened as he saw a familiar figure, her long-legged determined stride carrying her quickly towards the junction with Priddy Lane.

'Mairead!'

She turned, and her rather set expression smoothed out. 'I haven't seen you for a day or two.'

'No, I've been busy at the cottage.'

'How is it now?'

'Almost done. It's taken longer than I'd hoped.'

'Not surprising,' she said, 'since you spent a good long while helping others with their own houses. I hope they've told you how grateful they are.'

'Let's just say I've eaten more pasties these past few months than is good for my waistline.' He patted his stomach. 'As for my own house, there's still some work to finish in the back bedroom, and I've been waiting for more limestone to make the plaster. But now I have it so I can get that done in a few days.'

'Are you going there today?'

'For a little while.'

'In that case you're going the wrong way,' she pointed out helpfully.

He rolled his eyes, smiling. 'Nothing slips by you. I'm going to post this letter first.' A little burst of excitement made him add, 'It could be the changing of everything for me.'

'Oh?'

'There's a new place being built, up Widecombe way, near

Okehampton. In Devon,' he added, seeing her blank look. 'The architect is Edwin Lutyens, who is, quite frankly, a genius. And,' he grinned, 'it's a castle.'

'A *castle*!'

'A real, honest-to-goodness castle. I'm hoping to secure a job there.'

Mairead's face clouded. 'I thought you wanted your own business? Wasn't that what selling the *Pride* to Matthew was all about?'

'Not entirely, but yes, a good part of it. The main reason I was trying to get the cottage fixed up was so I could rent it out and use the income to rent a premises of my own.' She was looking strangely boot-faced, and he sighed. 'Mairead, you were the one who reminded me what I want out of life, or have you forgotten already? It's partly because of you that I did sell the *Pride*.'

'Well then, what's changed? Don't you want your own business anymore?' Her blunt interrogation had its usual effect of making him question his own motives, and he gave it some thought before he answered.

'Yes, I do. But I can't pass up an opportunity like this. A couple of years working under someone like Mr Lutyens would put some real weight behind my own experience, and besides, I've spent nearly all the boat money on Pa's house. I need to earn some capital.'

'And in what capacity will you be giving this man your experience?'

'Whatever's offered, if anything.' James favoured her with a wry smile. 'I'll be honest with you, I'll do whatever I have to, to get on that build. If I rise in the ranks, so much the better.'

'You will.' Mairead Casey wasn't given to empty compliments and platitudes; whatever came out of her mouth, she believed it.

She looked as if she wanted to talk a little longer, but kept glancing down Priddy Lane as if something, or someone, were calling her.

'I've got to go,' she said. 'Will I come and find you after? We haven't had a chat in a good while.'

'No, we haven't. I'll see you a bit later then.'

He continued up towards the pillar box fixed to the lamp outside Kessell's, belatedly realising he'd been so wrapped up in his own news he hadn't even asked her what she was doing. She was dressed in her Sunday best, too. Perhaps she was meeting a man? Not that it was any business of his, and she'd soon tell him as much. He remembered that first meeting at Penhaligon's Attic, when she had sent him out to stand in the road. James, who had practically grown up in the shop, had felt like a burglary risk at worst, an annoyance at best.

He gave a soft snort of laughter as he dropped the letter into the slot in the pillar box, and noticed that the squirming sensation of nervousness had vanished. He had written that letter awash in a sea of self-doubt, sweating over it, rewriting it several times from scratch. He had also turned out the letter Charles Trubshaw had written to him last year, offering him the chance of work up in Manchester, and read it over and over again, before slipping it into the envelope along with his reference letters, and addressing the whole to Edwin Lutyens. But did it say what he wanted it to say? Did it complement his application, or would it appear nothing more than a desperate grasping gesture? Twice he had got as far as the lamp box, then quickly withdrawn the letter before it had fallen from his fingers, certain there was more he could do. Then a two-minute chat with Mairead, and the letter was gone. He'd left everything familiar behind once before, when he'd taken Shaw's apprenticeship, but this time there was one big difference: there was no family to miss. Only friends. The new, the mended, and the sweetly unexpected.

Chapter Three

Pencarrack House

The house was utterly quiet. Lucy Batten sat up in bed with her knees raised, her arms wrapped around them, her keen ear listening for any sounds that would at least indicate morning was not far off, but there was nothing yet. No clanking of buckets from the kitchen, drifting up through the open windows or the back staircase, no birds singing.

Although everyone would have been sleeping anyway, it still felt abnormally still. As if the house itself were waiting with as much eagerness as Lucy for the arrival of Teddy Kempton tomorrow. Or rather today ... Lucy leaned over and twitched at her heavy curtain, but the dark sky gave her no clues. She ought to have accepted Hugh's invitation to his friend's party, at least then she'd have come home tired enough to have slept right through.

She sighed and pushed back the covers. It might help

to have a snifter of something and read a while, it certainly couldn't hurt to try, anyway. She wrapped her thin robe a little tighter, and went down to the sitting room, still trying to calm the leaping anticipation that was keeping her so wakeful. While Tristan had been away in America, she and Teddy had written long letters to one another, letters which had, in the comfortable distance between Caernoweth and Plymouth, quickly become bold and flirtatious on her part, and earnest and hopeful on his. Now, thanks to her casually telling him about the school teacher getting married, he would be living just down the road, and spending a great deal of time here, in this house, reading the old Batten journals in the gallery.

Lucy grinned to herself, as she crossed to where the decanter sat on the side table. If she hadn't initially been so keen on keeping Tristan MacKenzie around, she wouldn't have suggested they look at those diaries, and would never have realised it wasn't Tristan that drew her under his spell at all, but his unassuming and shy, but brilliant, research assistant: Edward. Teddy. Mr Kempton, with his earnest manner, his fascinating light blue eyes, and the touch that had nearly melted the back of her dress when he'd helped her to her feet after their collision. An outraged gazelle, he'd called her then – it still made her smile.

She rubbed her temple where the bruise had been, then unstopped the decanter and sniffed at the contents – probably brandy, she wasn't too familiar with spirits. She shrugged and poured some into the nearest glass. As she raised it to her lips she heard the front door click open, then shut, and she looked at the clock on the mantel; almost three o'clock.

'Hugh?' she called in a low voice. When there was no

answer she replaced her glass and went out into the hall. Her brother stood with one foot on the lowest stair, one hand on the bannister, the other rubbing his hair so it stood up in spikes all over his head.

'How was the party?' she asked.

'Deadly. Should have come, you would have livened it up a bit.' His voice was slurred, and he was evidently struggling to focus.

'It looks as though you had a decent enough time,' Lucy pointed out. 'You're completely blotto.'

'What of it?' Hugh scowled, completely missing the intended humour in Lucy's words.

Irritation took over, and Lucy glared back. 'You know, you're going to have to snap out of this at some point.'

'Snap out of what?' Hugh abandoned his stairway ambitions, and joined Lucy in the sitting room. 'I've had a drink. Nothing to snap out of. In fact I think I'll have another.' He picked up the glass Lucy had left on the table, and shook his head. 'Who on earth drinks brandy from a whisky tumbler?'

'You do, apparently,' Lucy said archly, then adopted a softer tone. 'Hugh, I mean it. The Penhaligon girl has chosen someone else, I've heard they're even engaged. You have to accept it now.'

'I accepted it ages ago. Hard to argue, when you kiss a girl and she just ... *looks* at you afterwards.' He refilled the glass and raised it. 'To true love.'

'Darling, you know I adore you when you're funny-drunk, but really, you *have* to pack it in. Even Dorothy's noticed, and she's likely to tell Father.'

'And what if she does?'

Lucy sighed and sat down. At least this was taking her mind off the long wait for Teddy. 'He's going to have to put his foot down, you know that. It doesn't matter too much what Dorothy or I do—'

'Oh, but Dorothy's a shining example of perfection. *Now* she is, anyway.' Hugh sat opposite, in their father's chair, and rolled the whisky glass between his hands, frowning down at the dark liquid. 'You know as well as I do what she was like before she had Harry.'

'But even if she went back to her old ways it wouldn't bother Father too much. He'd kick up a bit of a fuss, but he wouldn't have to try and clip her wings.'

'Whereas me?' Hugh looked up, and it took a moment for his crossing eyes to meet hers. 'I have to behave myself, do I? Why is that, pray?'

'Because you're the—'

'Heir to Pencarrack, yes. Actually I'm not.' He mimicked her stunned expression, then smiled, a little tightly. 'Remember that storm last year? Of course you do. Well, before Collings fixed the roof I had a loose tile above my bedroom. Rattling like I don't know what in that high wind. I came downstairs to sleep instead. You found me in here, remember?'

Lucy nodded. 'Just before we went out.'

'I was wide awake so I had a little poke around the library. It was probably on my mind that, sooner or later, I'd have to learn something about the businesses, and in the meantime it would be the most likely thing to send me off to the land of Nod.'

He waited for Lucy to smile, but she couldn't. 'Anyway,' he went on, 'you always said I was a nosy parker. Turns out you're right. I had a little glance at Father's will. It was right there in the top drawer, I didn't even have to go hunting for it.' He finished the drink in one gulp. 'Dorothy is going to get it all. I mean, I knew she was angling for the mines, but apparently our dear Father has decided she's to have the quarry, and the house as well. Rather rum, I thought.'

Lucy sat in shocked silence while his words sank in. It wasn't simply that they'd assumed, with Hugh being the only boy, but Father had actually *said*, out loud and more than once, that Hugh would inherit the house, the businesses, the mines and all that came from them . . . everything, with the exception of a couple of smaller properties and some personal items.

'Do you think Dorothy knows?' she managed at last.

Hugh snorted into his empty whisky tumbler. 'Oh, I'd say so, wouldn't you?' He pushed himself unsteadily to his feet. 'So, you see? I can get roaring drunk, marry who I please, and Father won't bat an eyelid.'

'But why have they lied?' Lucy stood too. 'Why didn't they say from the start that it would go to the eldest child, and not the son?'

'God knows. I only wish I'd found out before that MacKenzie bloke arrived.' Hugh made his weaving way across the room. 'If I'd known from the off that I was free to marry outside my stupid social class, I'd have whisked the delectable Miss Penhaligon away when we first met.'

'Could it be a mistake?' What kind of mistake, Lucy couldn't imagine, but it was chilling to think their father and sister had lied to them about something so important.

'See for yourself.' Hugh waved vaguely towards the hallway. 'Library desk. Right hand side, top drawer. At least it was, last year.'

'Are you going to tell him you know about it?'

'Not on your life.' Hugh smiled, but it was an empty, sad kind of smile. 'I'm having far too much fun holding the upper hand, and watching the old bastard squirm whenever I mention my inheritance.'

'*Fun* is going out riding on a windy day,' Lucy said tightly, 'or going to parties. This is not fun. You have to tell him.'

'No! And you mustn't either. Promise now.'

'You've kept this to yourself for . . .' she counted quickly on her fingers, 'seven *months*!'

'And I'll keep it to myself until the day Father dies, and the truth comes out. Then everyone who hopes for a reaction they can gossip about will be extremely disappointed.' He started across the hall to the stairs again, then turned back. 'Promise me,' he repeated.

Lucy glared at him for a moment, then said reluctantly, 'I promise.'

'Good girl.' For a moment a hint of his old smile was there, affectionate and sweet. Then it was gone, and he climbed the stairs with the dragging feet of an old man. Or a very drunk one.

Lucy looked towards the library. If only she'd stayed tucked up in bed, she wouldn't have been burdened with this too, but now she had to see for herself. A minute later she was closing the library door behind her, shutting out the rest of the house.

The desk stood in front of the window; Father and Dorothy both used it, which meant of course Dorothy knew. Father wouldn't leave something like that in an unlocked drawer, unless the only other person likely to find it was already aware of its contents. The drawer squeaked as she pulled it open,

41

and she winced, but really, she wasn't doing anything awful, after all.

She moved the table lamp closer so she could see properly, but it didn't seem as if anything as important and private as a last will and testament was here any longer. She moved aside some paperwork, and her eye was caught by the word 'Fort' on one of them, so she pulled it out and angled it beneath the light to read. It appeared to be some kind of draft proposal for a business partnership, between her father and someone called Pagett. Lucy squinted; it looked very much as if the two of them had put in an application for the purchase and renovation of the lovely old fort by the sea, but not for repair or restoration. Instead the plan seemed to be to turn it into a high-class hotel, pandering especially to the elite when they travelled down to take the sea air. This must be what all the buzz and fuss was about, over at the hotel; lots of visiting businessmen and suppliers, presumably. And where exactly was the money coming from for such an ambitious project?

Lucy returned to bed, with the unsettling feeling that Hugh might have had a narrow escape after all.

* * *

'Have you picked up the keys to Priddy Lane yet?'

Ambling thoughtfully back to the hotel after doing just that, Tristan hadn't noticed Freya crossing the road on her way to work, and was startled to hear her voice so close. 'I've just got back from Pencarrack now. And paid the first month's rent at the same time.'

'Are you looking forward to it?'

'I'll say. The hotel's all very nice, but there's nothing to beat the peace and quiet of your own little study, and a kettle within easy reach.'

He looked down at her as she walked beside him, and she turned her face up to him, smiling. The dark glossy hair that curled on her forehead made her eyes appear even darker, her long eyelashes made the shine deeper, and as for that lovely mouth ... He pulled her to a halt, silencing her half-hearted protest with a firm kiss.

She drew back after a moment, and glanced around the courtyard nervously. 'If Miss Tremar or Mrs Bone see me I'll be for the high jump.' She extricated herself from his embrace, though with evident reluctance.

'Stay off work today,' he urged, on a whim. 'Help me move in. *I'll* pay you!'

'I can't! Besides, it's not only about the money. If I don't come in, someone else'll have to do my work, and that's not fair is it?'

He studied her for a moment, then sighed. 'I wish you weren't so ... so ...'

'Goody two-shoes?'

'I was going to say conscientious, but have it your way.'

'In any case, tomorrow is my last day here.'

'Last day?'

'Mairead is taking over Miss Trethewey's position at Priddy Lane school, which means I'm going to be working full-time at the shop. So you see, you're not the only one to have benefited from Miss Trethewey's upcoming marriage.'

'I assume Mr Rowe will benefit as well.' Tristan winked before remembering he wasn't talking to Teddy. He touched

Freya's fiercely flushing cheek and changed the subject, not sure which of them was more embarrassed. 'I've only met Mairead a couple of times, but I can see she'd be a formidable teacher.'

'She won't stand any nonsense, that's for sure,' Freya said, relaxing again. 'She didn't tell anyone about the interview, not even Anna, until she found out she had the job. She starts on Monday. I can't wait to get started as a proper shopkeeper. I've got so many ideas!'

He smiled. 'You and Penhaligon's Attic were made for one another. You'll make your grandmother proud.'

'I hope so. She loved it so much.' She gave Tristan a sudden, narrow-eyed look. 'Will you expect me to stop working after *we're* married?'

'As if I could make you do anything you didn't want to. You'd be bored out of your glorious mind sitting at home in Priddy Lane, even if I was in the next room writing. And who would take care of the family business? Besides, your father would have my hide if I so much as mentioned it.'

'He would.' There was unmistakeable relief in her smile, though he suspected she wouldn't have given in easily to any other response. And she'd have won, too.

'I'm just glad you can stop working at that beastly hotel now.'

'You said it was nice!'

'As a guest, it's adequate, certainly. But I've never enjoyed the thought of you doing all those things you hate, and for other people.'

'Like laundry?'

'Like laundry,' he agreed. 'That, I might have objected

to, and you can be sure I'd have looked for a way to put an end to it.'

'So I'll just be doing *your* laundry then? And your cooking, and cleaning?'

He opened and closed his mouth for a moment, not sure what to say, then noticed the gleam in her eyes.

'Miss Penhaligon, you're a horror,' he said, and kissed her again.

'On the subject of horror,' Freya said, 'my supervisor Mrs Bone will be watching the clock and looking for an excuse to dock my wages.' She demonstrated how much she still cared about that by wrapping her arms around his waist, and laying her head on his chest. He felt the press of her soft breasts through his waistcoat, and his heart thumped with a mixture of longing and affection. Half of him wanted to lead her up over the moors somewhere quiet, and take her, body and soul, beneath the warm spring sky, and the other half wanted to sit down with her in a crowded room and just watch her shine.

He settled for another kiss, and stored away the memory of how fresh it tasted, and how enthusiastically returned, before reluctantly letting her go, with a promise to call on her at home later.

It was mid-afternoon before Teddy arrived. Tristan had taken his bags down to Priddy Lane, and was now back in the hotel lobby near the open door, awaiting the arrival of his friend, his car and the rest of his belongings from Plymouth. There was a newspaper on the table, and he picked it up, interested to note that his old landlord, Doctor Bartholomew, was chasing a parliamentary seat in the upcoming by-election, but before he could read the details he heard the familiar sound of his treasured Austin, and the wheels crunching over the gravel outside. He went out into the courtyard, where Teddy was climbing out of the bright red car, acknowledging the impressed gaze of bystanders with a suitably aloof look. Tristan grinned, letting his friend have his moment of glory for a while longer before going over.

Teddy shook Tristan's hand warmly. 'It's good to see you again, old man. How did you leave things in Vermont?'

'Better. Not perfect, but easier at least.' Tristan reached into his waistcoat pocket and withdrew the keys to the cottage. He jingled them in front of Teddy's eyes. 'Come on, our new home awaits.'

'Just a moment,' Teddy said. 'I have a note for you, from your stepmother. It's all right,' he added quickly, in response to Tristan's look of dismay. 'She's not asking you to go back to the mill, she simply wanted you to know she and the girls are safe.'

'Safe?'

'After the fire. The church,' he clarified, seeing Tristan's confusion. 'In Honiton.'

Tristan's stomach lurched. 'Not St Michael's?'

'Afraid so.'

'What happened?'

'The sexton apparently spotted it, last Sunday morning when he went in to get ready for the morning service. They think it was a spark from the heating furnace. Anyway, it started in the roof, and he raised the alarm and it seems more or less everyone turned out to help.'

'Was anyone hurt?'

'Luckily, no. And a good many of the contents were saved, thanks to the townspeople.' He handed Tristan the note. 'I'm surprised you hadn't heard.'

'It seems it's easier to get news of what's happening halfway across the world than what's happening a county away.' Tristan glanced at the note, then tucked it into his pocket. 'Well, I'm glad it was confined to the church, sad as that is.'

'It could have been much worse,' Teddy agreed. 'Be sure and pass on my good wishes, when you write back, won't you?'

'I will. Meanwhile,' Tristan walked around to the passenger side of his car, 'jump to it, lots to do.'

The remainder of the afternoon was spent packing away the things Teddy had brought with him, the work punctuated with Teddy's questions about the situation in America, though Tristan suspected his friend was only asking in an attempt to take his own mind off Miss Batten. They were discussing the best place for the picture of Smeaton's Tower that had hung in his Plymouth office, when he decided it was time to share the news.

'By the way, when do you suppose I can fetch Bill?'

'As soon as you like. I thought I could drive you up, you could see him onto the train, and we'll drive back down to meet it. You don't mind riding from Bodmin, do you?'

'On the contrary.' Tristan stretched his aching arms out in front of him, and then rolled his shoulders. 'It'll be good to get back in the saddle again.'

'Didn't you ride while you were away?'

'A little, but it's not the same. Slow plodding down the trail to the mill, and back again. Try and get one of those horses to do more than canter and they'd be more likely to buck you off. I've missed riding Bill, and when he comes off the train he'll be as keen to get in a good gallop as I am.' He gave Teddy a sidelong look, then added casually, 'We could take Freya up with us.'

Teddy picked up the painting and held it against the wall. 'Good idea. It'd be nice for her to meet your stepmother, and your sisters.'

'Indeed. Particularly as we're to be married.'

'Well, yes, it's only ... ' Teddy put the painting down, very carefully, on the sofa. 'Did you say—'

'Married, yes.'

'Good God! And we've been talking nonsense for the past three hours?' Teddy came over and grasped Tristan by the shoulders, giving him a shake before letting out a joyful laugh and slapping him on the back. 'This is wonderful news!'

'I thought so,' Tristan agreed. 'She'll be here in a little while, so we can put it to her about a trip up to Honiton.' He raised an eyebrow as an idea took him. 'Perhaps you'd like to ask Miss Batten, too?'

Teddy stilled, and Tristan could almost see his mind leaping ahead, to how to broach the subject, which words to choose, and how to react if she declined. 'Why not?' Teddy said at last. 'She might enjoy it, and she and Freya are almost of an age. They'll probably get along quite nicely.'

'Then it's settled. We'll go on Sunday.' Tristan picked up the painting himself. 'Now, stand over there and tell me if it's straight.' As he pressed the painting to the wall, and Teddy passed by him, he could see the gleam of excitement in his friend's eyes; Lucy would be sure to say yes, and Teddy would be almost as thrilled as Tristan had been when Freya had failed to utter that same tiny word. The world, and particularly Caernoweth, was becoming a brighter, more hopeful place every day.

Chapter Four

Honiton, Devon

Freya accepted Tristan's hand to climb down from the car. Her head was still spinning, despite the length of time she'd had in which to get used to the sensation of travelling at speed along the roads, and her knees didn't feel quite settled enough in their sockets to keep her upright. But she managed not to fall over, and tried not to show her intense relief at finding the road beneath her boots steady and solid.

'Well, what do you think of her?' Tristan asked, a little anxiously. She opened her mouth to tell him what would make him happy, but he smiled and shook his head.

'Never mind. We'll take the train back with Bill.' He glanced at Teddy and Lucy in the back seat. 'They'll be as pleased as you.'

'Are you sure?'

'Of course. I'll ride back from Bodmin, but Teddy can meet you there and drive you back.'

'Thank you.' Freya relaxed against him. She'd have to get used to the car sometime, but at least her day wouldn't be marred by the knowledge that she would have to endure so much of that awful, sick sensation again. She could taste the fuel, smell it on her, and the combination of that, and the rumbling and rattling of the car's wheels on the uneven road, had made her sure more than once that she would actually be ill.

Lucy Batten, on the other hand, was well used to it already, and she jumped down, laughing. 'What a splendid motor! Father's would never go that fast. On second thoughts, it might if you were driving it, Tristan!' She stared at the house where they'd stopped. 'Gosh, is this it?'

Freya looked at it for the first time too, and swallowed hard. The house was by no means comparable with some of the grand houses she'd seen in London, but it was no rural cottage either. Sitting here, on the edge of town, it took up the space of two of the larger Caernoweth houses, and the garden was a riot of colour, inviting passers-by to stop and admire it. She'd had no idea Tristan's family were wealthy, and her nerves took another leap.

'It's not mine,' Tristan said, 'it belongs to my stepmother's family. When Catherine brought us back from America as children, this is where we moved to.'

'Right, come along.' Teddy held out his hand to Lucy. 'Let's leave these two to their afternoon tea, and go and explore. There are some lovely houses around about. We'll start at the Tracey Estate.' He struck a pose, and declaimed, 'Will no one rid me of this turbulent priest!'

'What?' Lucy asked, still smiling.

'Legend has it Sir William de Tracy – different spelling,

51

interestingly – was one of the knights who clobbered Thomas à Becket. The Tracey estate is rather beautiful though.'

'It's quite a walk,' Tristan said. He looked down at Lucy's shoes, and caught Teddy's sheepish glance. 'Go on, then, take the car.'

Teddy beamed. 'We'll call in when we're back, and then we can all walk to the church if you like?'

Tristan's own smile faltered and he glanced at Freya. 'I don't know. It's just going to be a burned-out shell, isn't it?'

'I'd still like to see it, if you don't mind?'

'Tristan's right,' Teddy put in. 'It'll be smelly and dirty, and probably quite depressing.'

Lucy also seemed to note Tristan's reluctance, and wrinkled her nose obligingly. 'Well, in that case I would be quite happy to miss out.'

Freya frowned, but did not pursue the point. 'A walk somewhere would be nice, though. The rest of the town seems very pretty from what I've seen.' She didn't add that it would be a good excuse to leave early, if things didn't go well with Tristan's family after all.

Tristan nodded. 'If we have time, then. We've already eaten up a lot of the day with travel.'

'We won't be long,' Teddy promised. He and Lucy got back into the car, and Tristan held out his arm.

'Are you ready?'

Freya took a deep breath. 'I think so.'

'Then, soon-to-be Mrs Tristan MacKenzie, come and meet your new family.'

'Do they know?' Freya hung back for a moment. 'That we're engaged, I mean?'

'No. I thought it would be nice to tell them together.'

Freya nodded. 'All right, then.' She took a step onto the path, but pulled up short again. 'Who will be here?'

'My stepmother, Catherine; my sister, Sophie; half-sister, Janet; and possibly Catherine's mother. One or two staff you probably won't even see. Don't worry!' He tugged her gently onwards. 'They're all quite normal and nice. Even Elaine.'

'Who's Elaine?'

'Mrs Scott, Catherine's mother. Sweetheart, listen. You're here because I love you. Remember that.'

Freya looked up at him, and her hand tightened on his arm, but in a decisive way now, rather than a nervous one. 'I'm being an idiot,' she admitted. 'Come on.'

Freya relaxed further as they stepped into the small entrance hall, which was neat, but not particularly grand. The stairs were carpeted in a rich crimson, but worn in places, and the many pictures on the walls were watercolours of what were probably local places, painted with varying degrees of talent. Even the mat was threadbare in the middle, and missing pieces of fringe off the sides.

A door opened at the end of the hall, and a little girl of around six or seven appeared. Her eyes flew wide at the sight of them, and she gave a shriek of joy that scattered the last of Freya's fears.

'Mother! Tristan is here! And he's got a *lady* with him!'

'See? Lady Penhaligon!' Tristan murmured, and Freya's own smile found its way back onto her face just as a second door opened to reveal a handsome woman, dressed in gardening clothes and clutching a pair of shears.

'Tristan!' The woman put the shears on the table and, in

53

between hushing the little girl and hugging her stepson, she introduced herself to Freya.

'Tristan has told us all about you,' she said, 'the girl from the bookshop, yes?'

'Yes. My name's—'

'Freya!' the child blurted. 'Mother told us so!'

'Janet!' Catherine remonstrated, but mildly. 'Go and find Sophie, and tell her we have guests. How long are you here for? Shall I have some tea sent in?'

Without waiting for a reply, she poked her head into the room from which Janet had emerged, and called for tea and cakes to be sent to the sitting room. Then she peeled off her gardening gloves. 'There, a perfect excuse to leave that for another day, and now I can shake your hand.'

'The garden's beautiful, Mrs MacKenzie,' Freya ventured, following her into the sitting room. 'Do you do much of it yourself?'

'All of it,' Catherine said, with unmistakeable pride. 'William – Tristan's father – keeps trying to hire me a gardener, but they'd never get it the way I want it, not in a month of Sundays.'

Tristan took the big chair near the window, while Freya found herself occupying a small two-seater settee next to the irrepressible Janet MacKenzie. The little girl was fascinated by Freya's hair, and kept beaming up at her when, at Catherine's insistence, she removed her hat. Freya couldn't help smiling back, not only grateful, but with an already flowering affection.

'How old are you, Janet?'

'Six,' the girl said. 'Sophie's thirteen, but she's not nearly as grown up as I am.'

'Is she coming down?' Catherine asked.

'I told her to,' Janet said, thereby neatly absolving herself of any further duties as far as her sister was concerned. 'How long *are* you here for?' she asked Tristan.

'Only an hour or two. We'll need to be in good time to catch the last train.'

A girl appeared in the doorway, smiling at Tristan. 'An hour's not nearly long enough.'

'Sophie!' Tristan rose to his feet. 'Freya, this is my other sister. Sophie, I'd like you to meet Freya Penhaligon.'

'Ever so pleased,' Sophie said, nodding at Freya. She was very like her brother in the way they held themselves; square-shouldered and tall; even at thirteen Freya could see she would be a beautiful woman one day, and one who knew her worth. Her hair, if it hadn't been tamed by ribbons, would undoubtedly have been the same curly mass as Tristan's, and her eyes, though a more muted green, were ringed with the same thick lashes. Her dark eyebrows were every bit as straight and stern, too – on her it had the effect of contrasting with the delicacy of her features, and she was already a strikingly pretty girl.

She held out a hand to Freya, who shook it, relieved beyond belief that Tristan's family was so warm and welcoming. 'It's a delight to meet you.'

Sophie sat next to her stepmother on the settee opposite and settled her hands in her lap, the picture of a well-bred young lady. For a few minutes, while they waited for tea to arrive, Catherine asked Tristan about the family business. He gave her all the news of the paper mill that his father had asked him to, which even Freya knew was not all of it. Catherine didn't appear to be aware of any gaps, and Tristan kept his report flowing, evidently used to skimming over the less savoury aspects of the business.

Throughout this discussion Sophie's gaze kept straying to Freya. It wasn't a hostile look, but neither was it wholehearted acceptance like Janet's; rather it was the same reserved politeness she had shown as they'd been introduced. Freya reminded herself she was changing the shape of this family, and was bound to be initially met with reservation, but it was unsettling nevertheless.

Eventually Catherine seemed to realise her anxious questions were excluding their guest, and she apologised. 'Tell me more about yourself, dear,' she said. 'A bookshop? How interesting.'

Freya could tell Catherine considered it anything but, and catching Tristan's eye she saw the flash of laughter he was struggling to keep in. She determinedly turned away from him, and gave Catherine and the girls a brief history of the shop, and how it had once been Yorke's Emporium.

'All manner of knick-knacks and treasures, from picture-frames to glassware, riding tack, and even old boat parts.'

'That sounds much more exciting than books,' Janet said, and immediately blushed as Sophie shot her a look.

Freya smiled. 'My own stepsister feels the same. But I like stories, so I love being surrounded by books.' She nearly went on to explain about Papá's stories, but in the first place it would open up too many questions about him and Mama, and in the second she still felt a very private attachment to them. Mama's suggestion she read them to the little Batten boy had been surprising and unexpectedly sweet, but they were hers for a little while longer at least. So she kept that to herself, and sipped

56

her rapidly cooling tea, trying not to glance too obviously at the wall clock.

'Teddy's here too,' Tristan said. 'We're going for a short walk after he's taken his guest to Tracey.'

'I do like Teddy,' Catherine said with approval. 'It's a shame you can't stay longer, we never have time for a nice natter anymore, and he's so interesting.'

'We have to be sure we're in time for the last train,' Tristan explained again.

'Don't you have your car?' Sophie asked, disappointment pulling those straight, dark eyebrows down. 'I was hoping you'd take me for a spin.'

'Teddy's taken it to the estate, but I'll take you for a very quick ride if we have time.'

Catherine was puzzled. 'If you have the car why do you have to worry about the time?'

'Ah, yes.' Tristan hesitated, and Freya suddenly couldn't look at anyone. 'Teddy's driving back. We're taking Bill on the train.'

'Taking Bill?' Sophie sat upright, and her gaze swivelled to Freya again. 'Are you expecting to stay in Cornwall for long then?'

'Forever,' Tristan said, his voice gentle. 'We're getting married.'

Sophie's cup rattled in her saucer, and she replaced it quickly on the side table. 'Really? Congratulations.'

'Oh, my goodness!' Catherine stood up and came over to hold her hands out to Freya. 'My dear, I can't tell you how delighted I am!'

Janet wrapped her hands around Freya's arm and hugged it

so tightly Freya broke into a laugh, though it was a nervously shaky one. 'I'm so relieved you're pleased.'

'Pleased? You're an absolute delight!' Catherine returned to her seat, and fixed her stepson with a wide smile. 'Tell me all your plans!'

'We haven't really made any yet,' he admitted, shooting Freya a glance that said, quite clearly, *I told you so!* 'Teddy and I will be sharing the rent on a cottage at the bottom of town, and then, when the book's finished and Teddy moves on, Freya and I will tie the knot and make it our marital home.'

'And is Freya happy about that?' Catherine asked. 'Having grown up in London, my dear, would you be content living the rest of your life tucked away down there?'

'I wouldn't mind living in a hole in the ground, as long as it was with Tristan.' Freya was surprised at how readily the words sprang to her lips, as true as they were; she had expected to stumble and stutter, and try to justify the choices Tristan had made.

'A very good answer,' Catherine said with a little smile. 'And an honest one, I can see that.'

A rap at the door prevented further observations on the news, and they waited while Catherine's housemaid answered it. A moment later Teddy and Lucy came in, and greetings and introductions were made once more. Sophie stared at Lucy in open awe, and almost curtseyed as they were introduced. She flushed with pleasure at the bright, familiar way Lucy spoke to her, and after the formalities were completed, retreated to her settee, her entire attention focused on the pretty blonde with the fine manners and the easy smile. Lucy gushed her praises of the lace Janet thrust under her nose, and of the delicate porcelain in which her tea was presented to her, and Freya hid a smile as she considered that perhaps even the porcelain wasn't enough, and that Tristan's stepmother wished she had a velvet cushion as well.

In the ensuing melee Tristan rose from his seat, and came to perch on the arm of the settee next to Freya. His hand found hers, and she met his eyes with a slightly blurred smile.

'I love you,' he murmured. 'I can't believe how lucky I am.'

Freya caught sight of Sophie's face, half-turned away from her and very still. The girl didn't respond to Teddy's chatter with more than a perfunctory smile, even when he trotted out what was evidently an old, well-worn question: 'And when are you going to marry *me*, Miss Sophie?'

After a moment he cleared his throat, embarrassed, and moved away from her. 'Now,' he said, as soon as a pause presented itself, 'we'll have to get a move on, if you want to take Bill back tonight, I don't know that there's time for a walk after all.'

'You can stay for the night,' Janet said. 'Can't they, Mother?'

'Oh yes,' Sophie said, brightening. 'Miss Batten, do stay.'

'We don't have room for everyone,' Catherine pointed out, and Sophie subsided again.

Janet lifted pleading eyes to her mother. 'Just Tristan and Freya then?'

Freya's heart sank. She wanted to stretch her legs, get some fresh air, then go home. She could hardly wait to step off the train at Bodmin. But she could see the idea appealed to Tristan, and it was his family after all; considering how long he'd been away, the visit had been rather rushed. The question and response flew silently between them: *I'm so sorry, would you mind too much? No, it would be lovely.*

'I'll call in to Penhaligon's Attic as soon as we're back,' Teddy offered, 'and let your father know you're safe. Don't worry, I'll make it perfectly clear you're staying with family. I'm sure Anna wouldn't mind looking after the shop until you get home, but if there's any kind of problem I'll do it myself. Then I'll come and meet you from the station tomorrow.'

'Oh, no need,' Freya said, trying to sound enthusiastic. 'I can take the coach back from Bodmin, I've done it before.'

'Excellent! Then we'll stay. Which gives us plenty of time.' Tristan pulled Freya to her feet. 'Who's coming for a walk?'

'Me!' Janet jumped up and seized Freya's other hand.

'Sophie?' Tristan prompted

She looked from him to Lucy, and half-rose, then her gaze swivelled to Freya. 'No, thank you,' she said. 'But have a nice time.'

Catherine stayed behind to work in the garden, and so the five others went out into the lane. Teddy and Lucy strode ahead, and Janet scampered after them, leaving Tristan and Freya to bring up the rear, hand in hand, but with a cloud dimming the edges of Freya's happiness.

'Sophie doesn't like me,' she said at last.

'She doesn't know you,' Tristan pointed out. 'She's at a difficult age, though she's not normally shy. I'm sure she'll come out of her shell before the end of this evening.'

'Perhaps it'll be good to stay then,' Freya conceded, after a moment's thought. 'At least we'll have a better chance to get to know one another.'

'What makes you think she doesn't like you, anyway? She seemed perfectly friendly, to me.'

'She was, at first, but didn't you see her face when you said we're to be married?'

'Ah.' Tristan put his arm around her shoulder and drew her against his side. 'It's not you she doesn't like, then, it's that you're whisking me away to live in foreign parts.'

'She's welcome to come and stay whenever she likes,' Freya said, hoping he was right. 'Make sure she knows that, if it will help settle her mind.'

'I will. You'll see, as soon as she realises we're not moving to the other side of the world, she'll be back to her usual happy self.'

'Happy?'

'Oh, yes. You see Janet there?' He nodded at where Janet was skipping between Teddy and Lucy, holding a hand each. 'Sophie was the same when she was little. We're quite close, I think it comes of us being left here without Dad, when he went back to the States. When I left to go to university Sophie didn't speak to me for a month.'

Freya laughed. 'I'm relieved it's not me.'

'How could it be?' Tristan stopped in the road and turned her to face him. His hands looped over her shoulders and his mouth dipped to hers, and for a long, sweet moment she let the rest of the world drift away.

'Let the poor girl breathe!' Teddy called, and Freya felt Tristan's mouth widen in a smile.

'Do you want to breathe?' he whispered against her lips. She shook her head, mute, and he kissed her again, ignoring Teddy's exaggerated sighs of impatience.

'Leave them alone, Kempton!' Lucy laughed, and as Freya opened her eyes again she saw the two of them drawing Janet away up the hill. Tristan's closeness was playing havoc with Freya's heartbeat, and it took a moment to come back to the realisation that she was standing in the middle of the road in broad daylight, but eventually she took a deep breath and stepped away.

'We can't be too long. You've promised to take Sophie for a drive, remember?'

'Hmm. And then we still have to load Bill's things into the car.' Tristan looked up to the sky; it wouldn't be long before the shadows began gathering. 'Do you think we ought to just leave Teddy and Lucy to it, then?'

'Perhaps.'

'What about your walk?'

'We could always go later, after they've left.'

Tristan smiled down at her. 'A twilight stroll does have a certain appeal,' he murmured. 'Just the two of us.' His hand found hers. 'And if there's a chance of repeating what just happened, so much the better.'

'I'm not promising that,' Freya said, giving him a prim look that convinced neither of them.

Tristan laughed, and signalled to Teddy that he and Freya were turning back. 'Don't be too long,' he called. 'I'll need your help with Bill's stuff.'

Teddy raised a hand in acknowledgement, and when Janet elected to continue the walk, Tristan and Freya returned to the house. Sophie's delight was evident, as was her satisfaction when Freya turned down the offer of joining them on their spin. Even if the thought of it hadn't made Freya queasy all over again, she wouldn't have gone with them for all the tea in China, and she waved them off with a deep sense of relief and went indoors to wait.

It had been a long day, and she was dozing comfortably in the big chair by the window when they returned. Sophie went straight upstairs, and Tristan came to perch on the arm of Freya's chair.

'She'll be all right. We had a little talk.'

Freya pulled herself upright. 'Did you? What did she say?'

'That she knows she was a bit of a rotter earlier, but that she actually likes you and hopes you aren't too cross with her.'

'Of course I'm not! Did you tell her I understand?'

'Naturally. She might not come out and apologise directly, she's still a thirteen-year-old girl, after all.' He grinned. 'But you can be sure she won't give you a rough ride about stealing me away, at least.'

'Oh, that's such a relief!' Freya slumped again. 'Thank you.'

'Right,' Tristan held out his hand, 'Time to get those two love birds back on the road.' She allowed him to pull her to her feet and lead her outside again, where the day's colours were already becoming more muted, and where the shadows lay longer on the path. Despite her tiredness, and the little waves of envy she felt for Lucy and Teddy returning to Caernoweth, she couldn't deny the thrill as she realised her new life was beginning now, with the simple moving of a horse from one county to the next; the sooner this day was over, the sooner it would all begin in earnest.

Tristan and Teddy went up to the stables, to fetch everything they could carry of Bill's, leaving Freya and Lucy alone. Lucy glanced around to ensure she wasn't overheard, then said, in a low, conspiratorial voice, 'You and Hugh could never have been what you and Tristan clearly are. I see that now.'

Freya flushed. 'You knew about that, then?'

'Darling, Hugh hasn't been himself for months. It's not your fault,' she added quickly, as Freya opened her mouth to apologise yet again. 'I mean, when I heard your chap had gone, that he wasn't coming back, and that you *still* didn't consider Hugh, I must confess I did wonder. Why on earth would you hold on to something so hopeless? But now I've seen you together...' she trailed off and gave Freya a tiny smile. 'Well, I understand, that's all. And I don't blame you for not wanting to cover up the memories.'

'That's exactly it. Do you think Hugh will understand too?'

'My brother has other worries just now,' Lucy said, and her expression darkened. 'Not that he no longer wishes things were different, but... Anyway, they're coming back, let's help.'

Freya followed her gaze, to where Tristan and Teddy were approaching from the back of the house, laden with saddle, harness, and boxes of grooming equipment. She saw the way Lucy's face brightened again, and how she brushed Teddy's arm as she passed him on her way to the stable to bring more, and she smiled for the sweet, shy young man she had grown so fond of. Her mind briefly snagged on what could be bothering the usually carefree, fun-loving Hugh Batten, but the sound of Tristan's voice, drifting across from the car, banished the curiosity; Hugh was none of her business, this man was. And she couldn't be happier.

Chapter Five

Early on Sunday morning Anna glanced at Isabel as she watched her daughter and three virtual strangers driving off towards the rising sun. The woman's face was a study in mixed emotions, but uppermost was worry; it was to be expected, although she had only become concerned when Freya told her Teddy and his young lady friend were to go with them.

'There's no cause to fret,' Anna said, touching Isabel's arm. 'Teddy's not some foolhardy lad out for dangerous fun. He's a sensible young man.'

'Yes. Of course.' Isabel gave her a faint smile. The two of them had shared no more than a few brief conversations since Isabel's arrival, but so far Anna was hopeful that the time might pass pleasantly enough until Freya's mother returned to America.

'I ought to get on,' Anna said, when Tristan's motor had rounded the bend at the top of town, and carried Freya and the others out of sight. Matthew had left early, despite it being a Sunday, to take advantage of the continuing mild weather. 'What are you doing today?'

Isabel squinted at the sky. 'I thought I might go down to the beach. I think it will be another nice day when it warms up a little, and since I'm halfway there already ... ' She caught Anna's expression, and smiled wider. 'Don't worry, I am not chasing after what is no longer mine.'

Anna felt the heat in her cheeks. 'I didn't think you were. I very much doubt you would see him, in any case, he'll have sailed on the tide this morning.'

'I know. It was ever the case.'

Anna silently scolded herself for steering the conversation in a direction with which Isabel would always be more familiar. 'Enjoy your walk,' she said, and pushed open the door to Penhaligon's Attic, wondering why she didn't believe Isabel for one moment when it came to Matthew. She looked out of the window, where Isabel's demure, exotic beauty stood in contrast to the still-grey light of early morning, seemingly waiting for the rising sun to touch her and bring all her astonishing colour to life. Threat or not, the day of her departure could not come a moment too soon, then life for all of them could return to normal. They had the birth to look forward to, and a wedding to plan ... Anna paused on her way to the kitchen, and gave a groan – what if Isabel now decided to stay until Freya was wed? Tristan had indicated Teddy would be staying at least until the summer, so that would push the plans forward towards August and beyond. It was entirely possible, then, that Isabel would be here for another six months at least. Six months!

With Mairead down at Porthstennack helping James, it was mid-afternoon by the time Anna had finished the laundry and hung it out to dry in the back garden. She checked the beef pudding she'd put on to boil, and then locked up the shop. It was odd, and sad, to see this house and shop in darkness during the day; she felt Robert's loss quite keenly at moments like this, and sent a little thought Heaven-wards to him as she walked down to the pub. His gruff presence and rare but infectious laugh was easy to recall, and the memory of it never failed to make her smile. *You in't no bleddy nurse ...*

In the Tinner's Arms Esther was running a cloth over the rail by the bar, removing smuts left by chimney smoke, and her grandson Alan was rolling a full barrel up the passage ready for the evening opening. Anna couldn't help a little smile as she thought back to the day she and Mairead had arrived; dirt, grime, grease and darkness everywhere. No care taken over anything, the chimney unswept, the floor likewise. How things had changed.

Anna went down to the store room to take an inventory, shooing Arric aside when he got between her and the door. As she counted, and checked, and made notes, she became aware that the conversation between Alan and his grandmother had altered, and now included a third voice.

She frowned, hoping it wasn't someone insisting they open early, and rose to find out what was happening, but before she had gone a couple of steps across the store room, Esther appeared.

'I'm sorry, Miz Garvey ... Miz Penhaligon, but there's a gen'leman insisting on talking to Miss Casey.'

'Mairead? Why? Who is it?'

'He won't give a name, says he wants to surprise her. We told 'im she don't work here no more, but t'idn't goin' in.' She tapped her temple.

'She's out for the day,' Anna said, a gnawing fear beginning in the pit of her stomach. Who would be searching for Mairead? The police? Someone from home? 'Does he have an accent?' she asked, trying to keep her voice steady.

'Matter of fact, he do, a bit. Not so strong as yours, but the same.'

'So he's from Ireland.'

'I reckon. D'you want me to tell 'im she'll be back at the shop come teatime?'

'No!' Anna took a deep breath, and straightened her apron. Her mind whirred into action. If it was the police she couldn't go and talk to them, but neither could she entirely trust Esther to correctly pass along any message. She toyed with the idea of somehow appearing with a scarf over her face, claiming some illness, then shook the idea away as foolishness. But she could do the next best thing.

'Go back and tell him I'll be there shortly,' she said at last. 'And whatever you do, don't get my name wrong again. Please!'

'No, of course.' Esther seemed to realise what was causing Anna such concern, and her voice turned earnest. 'He don't look like a policeman, if that's any 'elp.'

Anna wanted to laugh, but her insides were wound too tight. 'I'm sure he doesn't. But we can't take that chance, can we? Tell him I won't be a moment.'

Esther went to deliver the message, and Anna waited until the door to the pub had clicked shut, before following. Her hands clenched and unclenched, focusing her mind, and her nerves, and her heart wanted to climb out through her mouth as she called through the door.

'I'm Mrs Pen'aligon, the manager. How can I help you?' Mairead had said she was getting good at the accent, but never had it mattered so much, or sounded so wrong.

'I'm looking for Miss Casey. I was told she lived here.'

Esther was right, the voice was unmistakeably Irish. And also vaguely familiar. Anna searched her memory with increasing panic. Was it Liam Cassidy's father? Or his brother? Her own solicitor?

'Not no more,' she called. 'She'm livin' elsewhere now.'

'Then do you have a room I could use?'

'We'm not a coaching inn.'

The voice grew impatient. 'Mrs Penhaligon, I don't enjoy talking through doors. Are you going to come in?'

'I'll be in ... d'rectly,' Anna said, wincing even as she spoke. 'No coach out on a Sunday night, but there's an 'otel top of town.'

The voice took on a despondent note. 'I can't afford that. Do you know of any lodging houses? Since Mairead's not here I'd only need the one night.' He certainly didn't sound as if he was going to force the issue, and he used her daughter's given name with comfortable familiarity ...

Anna hadn't even realised she'd stooped a little, in her attempt to adopt a different persona, and now she gasped and snapped upright, her heart racing. 'What's your name?' But the familiarity slipped into place, and even before he spoke again she knew.

'Keir Garvey. I'm Miss Casey's cousin, once removed.'

Anna leaned against the wall, one hand pressed to her chest, tears springing to her eyes. Keir! Her beloved, long-missed cousin. Here in Caernoweth! But he believed her dead – disgraced and drowned – just as the rest of her family did.

She gradually became aware the silence had stretched, and she heard Keir muttering something to Esther about walking to the railway station instead of waiting for tomorrow's coach. Suddenly the thought that he might leave without knowing she was alive was the biggest horror Anna could think of. Of all the people who might have come here to seek out Mairead, Keir was the one she had always known, without hesitation, that she could trust.

'Are you travelling alone, Mr Garvey?' she managed, hearing the new, slightly strangled note in her own voice. 'No other . . . cousins, or aunts or uncles?'

He gave a soft laugh, and now the familiarity of it wrapped warm arms around Anna; how could she ever have mistaken him for anyone else? 'No,' he said. 'No one.'

Anna's heart was thumping heavily, and her hand shook as she placed it on the door to push it open. The last time she'd seen Keir Garvey he'd been sixteen years old, and she fifteen. He'd be thirty-five now, and when he stood upright from where he'd been lounging with one elbow on the bar, playing with the brim of his hat held between two large hands, he blocked out nearly all the light from the little window behind him.

Anna blinked up at the face that turned to her, blandly polite; bright blue eyes passing over her face without recognition, the features that had never been handsome, but now had a maturity and strength that drew the eye as surely as the broad, twisting scar that ran the length of his jaw. She didn't speak, sure she would burst into tears if she tried.

Keir opened his mouth, to enquire again, perhaps, after alternative rooms, but his face suddenly lost all expression and he passed a hand across his eyes, squeezing them tightly shut for a second. When he opened them again they were brighter than ever.

'Anna?' he whispered. 'Christ, is ... is it you?'

She nodded, vaguely aware of Esther, open-mouthed and staring, but the rest of her attention was on her cousin, who was rubbing his face hard, as if he didn't trust his own senses.

At last she moved out from behind the bar to stand in front of him. 'I've missed you,' she said simply, and a moment later she was swept off her feet and squeezed tight, until she gave a yelp, and he put her back down with the utmost care.

He took her hands. 'I can't believe it. Not only alive, but pregnant?'

'You can't tell anyone,' Anna said in a rush. 'Not Uncle Colm nor Aunt Oonagh, and not even Maeve.'

He shook his head, as if it went without saying. 'I need to hear everything,' he said. 'Are you ...' he glanced at Esther, and turning back to Anna he mouthed, *hiding out from the law*?

'Esther,' Anna said, 'you and Alan will be all right for a couple of hours, won't you?'

Esther nodded. Her gaze kept sliding between Anna and the newcomer, and Anna realised the rumour mill would begin turning very quickly unless she put the woman straight.

'This truly is my cousin. It's all right, he can be trusted.' It was Keir's turn to look baffled, but Anna took his hand. 'Come with me. I'll explain. It'll make sense, I promise.'

*

Much later, Keir sat back in his chair in the kitchen at Penhaligon's Attic, his tea untouched, his hair in disarray where he'd constantly run his hands through it in growing amazement.

'So . . . you trust *all* these people here. In this one town?'

Anna shook her head. 'Not everyone has any clue any of this went on.' She gave him a wry smile. 'Besides, you wouldn't know it at first, but even here people have their own lives, and no time or inclination to get involved in others. Mairead and I have settled, and people seem to like us here. Most just know me as Matthew's wife, and the woman who runs the pub.'

'And your husband? Is he part of the act, too?'

'Matthew?' Anna smiled, her heart expanding at the thought of him. 'No. He's real enough.'

'The love of your life?' Keir raised a cynical eyebrow.

'And why would you look like that?'

'Because I remember when you said the same about Finn Casey.'

'That was different.'

'Yes. You were fifteen. *Fifteen*, Anna!'

'The church allowed it. And besides, he was a good man, even then.'

'He was over ten years your senior. No wonder Da was furious.'

'He didn't stop me though, did he?'

Keir snorted. 'As if he could've. He hated it, you know that. He thought you'd come running home before a year was out, but I could have told him you're too bloody stubborn.' He sobered. 'And those miscarriages—'

'Don't.' Anna shook her head. 'Mairead put all that in the past. And now I have this little one to think of.'

'Finn shouldn't have allowed you to become pregnant again, so soon after losing the first.'

'Keir, please.' Anna stretched across the table and put her hand over his. 'I know it's been eating away at you, it's bound to, we've never had the chance to talk about it. But now I have Matthew, and Mairead, and Matthew's daughter ... I'm so happy here. And today,' she laughed, still incredulous, 'today I go to work, and instead of dirty glasses and towels I find *you*!'

'And I still have nowhere to stay,' he reminded her. 'Can I sleep on your settee until I find somewhere?'

'We haven't got one.'

'You haven't *got* one?'

'What used to be the front room is the shop now. We don't need a settee, we're quite happy to sit in here and talk, when we have time. At least it's always warm.'

'That's grand, right enough,' Keir said, 'but it leaves me in the lurch a bit.'

'Not at all.' Anna took his cup and poured the cold tea away. 'We've a spare room for a while. Until the baby's born at least, and for a short while after, while it sleeps in with us.'

'Won't Matthew mind?'

Anna poured fresh tea, and favoured him with a little smile. 'Matthew has heard all about you; he'll be so delighted to meet you, he'd probably offer you our own bed.' She sat back down and lifted her cup. 'Here's to long-lost cousins.'

'To you and me.' Keir raised his own cup and tilted it towards her. 'And to our new lives in Caernoweth.'

'What?' She put her cup down quickly before she could spill her tea. 'You're staying?'

'You haven't asked me why I came, yet,' he reminded her.

'Then perhaps you ought to tell me.'

Keir clasped his large hands in front of him on the table. 'To cut a long story not nearly short enough, there was nothing left for me in New Zealand, so I went home – only to find there's really nothing for me there, either. Maeve has her own life, Da's not interested in an errant son who can't keep ... Never mind. Anyway, after what happened to you, or what I thought had happened, when I realised I'd missed Mairead's visit I wanted to come and talk to her.'

'I don't believe you.'

'Don't you?' Keir kept his famously fierce gaze on her, and Anna began to wonder if she'd been wrong, but then his eyes cut away, and he sighed. 'All right. Look, Da's as furious with me as he was with you.'

'Why?'

'You know I went out there for the gold, with my friend's family.'

'Arthur someone-or-other. Walsh, was it? You wrote that his father's health stopped him and his son from working the mines.'

He nodded. 'It's the drills. Made the work faster, but raised much more dust. Anyway, I left too, and Arthur and I bought half-shares in a farm that was going under.'

'That was about the last I heard from you,' Anna said, trying not to sound accusing.

'I know, I'm sorry. It was a mad time, and I got all caught up in it. Eventually Arthur got married. Jane. Gorgeous girl, but very demanding. We didn't get on.'

His flush told Anna a different story, and she shook her head. 'Again, I don't believe you.'

'It's true. Sort of. We didn't get along at all. But there was … something. Between us.' He cleared his throat. 'I don't know. Anyway, she treated me like hired help, and I couldn't stand the sound of her voice. But still Mr Walsh – Arthur's da – caught us one day, and threatened to tell Arthur if I didn't clear out and give my share of the farm to his son.'

'And you gave it up, just like that?' Anna could hardly believe it, yet here he was.

'I didn't want him hurt. He was – still is – my best friend.'

'And?'

Keir sighed. 'We worked hard, and we could shear sheep with the best of them, but we weren't businessmen, and we were struggling to make enough to live on. Basically we made a proper mess of it all. Truth of it is, I was glad to leave.'

'And what about Arthur's wife?'

Keir's face reflected something close to real emotion, for the first time since he'd begun talking about his own life, but he only shrugged. 'What about her?'

'You left your business, your home, your friend, and a woman who clearly meant something to you – despite what you say,' she added, as he started to argue – 'to make a new life *here*?'

'It wasn't my intention to stay, I only wanted to get at the truth about you. To see if Mairead could tell me something different to what I was hearing.' He shook his head. 'I never once believed you capable of murder.'

'But you're wrong, aren't you? I did kill Liam Cassidy.'

'It wasn't murder. It was self-defence.'

'They'd still have hanged me.'

'Yes.' He fell silent and chewed the inside of his lip, before coming to what looked like a difficult decision. 'A minute ago you looked me in the eye and said you didn't believe me.'

'And I was right not to.'

'Now I'm saying the same thing to you.' Keir propped his chin on his fists, the picture of patience.

Anna's chest tightened. 'What do you mean?'

'We grew up together, Anna. I know you better than anyone alive, I always have. It was Mairead, wasn't it, who killed that boy? Not you.'

Anna couldn't speak for a moment, then she swallowed hard. 'Why are you saying that?'

'Look, tell me if I've got this wrong, but when you heard me in the pub, asking after her, your first thought was, *is she in danger from this person?*'

'How can you possibly know what my—'

'You didn't say where I might find her, or where she lived. It wasn't until I used her first name that you thought perhaps I didn't pose any threat. But,' he shrugged, 'how could I do that, unless she had something I could threaten her with?'

'It was instinctive, it's had to be. It doesn't mean anything.' She remembered who she was speaking to then, and sighed, her eyes on his. 'Yes, it was Mairead.'

'You know you can trust me,' he said, reaching for her hands again. 'God, I still can't believe you're alive. The times I've wept for you.'

'I wish I could have told you, of all people, the truth, but it was too dangerous.'

A silence fell between them, and Anna could see him picking over the intervening years since they'd last seen one another. So many questions remained, but for now there was only one that really mattered.

'So you're staying?' she asked. 'Here in Caernoweth, I mean?'

'If I can get work.' Keir picked up his tea again. 'Know of anything I can ask after?'

'Priddy Farm might have some labouring work.'

'Pretty Farm?' He raised an amused eyebrow. 'Never seen a farm I'd describe like that.'

'*Priddy*. I think it was called Pridham's Farm in the old days. Or there's the tannery.'

'I saw an engine-house chimney as I was passing the top of town,' he said. 'Heard the stamps. My experience could come in useful there. Copper, is it?'

'Tin.' But Anna didn't want him at Wheal Furzy, with the memory of the explosion still so fresh. 'I could ask Matthew if he's got any casual work available on the boats.'

Keir shuddered. 'No thanks, I had my fill of the high seas on the way back from New Zealand. I'd rather take my chances at the farm. And I'll take you up on the offer of a few nights in your spare room, thanks.'

'It's yours for as long as you need it,' Anna said. 'And now I'm away back to the Tinner's.'

'And I'm for a sleep,' Keir said. 'So show me the room, and I'll catch forty winks so I'm at least presentable when I meet my young cousin. Where is she, by the way?' He looked around, as if he expected to see her emerging from the woodwork.

'She's down at Porthstennack, helping a friend. She'll be back by teatime.' Anna stood, and folded her arms, resting them on her stomach, and feeling the comforting and predictable reaction from the baby. 'So, since Matthew's been at work all day, and Mairead's been working too, I think the least you can do in return for bed and board is to spare either of them the need to cook your meal.' She nodded at the range. 'I put a beef pudding on to boil before I left this lunchtime, so all you have to do is prepare the vegetables to go with it.'

Keir pulled a face. It was so like his fifteen-year-old reaction to instruction from his mother, that Anna laughed. 'Matthew *loves* his vegetables,' she warned, wondering what Matthew would make of that, 'so see to it that he has the most on his plate.'

'I've been walking all morning,' he grumbled. 'Besides, that's women's work. What of the other girl you mentioned, can't she do it?'

'Freya's away for the day. Where did you walk from?'

'I used all but the last of my money for the train, and then got a ride a few more miles after Bodmin. After that,' he gestured at his feet. 'Shanks's mare.'

'Well that can't be helped.' Anna opened the back door and pointed to the basket of vegetables she kept in the porch. 'And in this house there's not much to choose between women's work and men's. We all do our bit.' She smiled to take the sting from her words. 'Keir, I can't even tell you how—'

'All right!' He waved it away. 'Don't get all soft on me now. The bossy Anna is the one I thought I'd lost forever, it's grand to see her back.'

Anna left a note for him to give to Mairead, to ease what would surely be a difficult meeting, then she went back to work with a light heart, and a strangely surreal sense of having dreamed the entire afternoon.

Chapter Six

Honiton

Teddy and Lucy left a little after five o'clock on Sunday evening. The family waved them off, Sophie looking particularly wistful, and Freya battling a surprisingly strong envy; was it possible to feel homesick after only one day?

'Come on,' Tristan said, when the car was out of sight. 'Let's go indoors and have something warm to drink.'

But despite Tristan's assurances Freya wasn't quite ready for Sophie yet, and besides, she and Tristan hadn't been alone all day. 'Shall we go for that walk first?'

'Good idea. I'll take you to see Bill, while it's still daylight. If you don't mind a bit of mud, that is?'

Freya gave him a withering look. 'I might have grown up in the city, but I'm still a country girl.'

They walked around the back of the house and down the lane to the field gate, where Tristan climbed onto the lowest bar, and leaned over to peer along the hedge. He put two fingers to his mouth and whistled, a piercing sound in the quiet spring evening, and it echoed down the lane. There came a low, whickering sound from somewhere out of sight, and a moment later two pricked ears came into view, followed by a long brown face with a white star.

Bill was one of the bigger horses of Freya's limited experience. She was familiar enough with John Rodda's pony, but Bill was different; a striking, powerful and quite frightening animal close-to. Tristan clearly didn't think so, and she took courage from the easy affection on his face, as he rubbed Bill's nose and murmured endearments. She inched forwards, and as soon as Tristan was aware of her approaching he twisted and held out his hand.

'Come and meet him.'

She lifted her skirt and climbed up beside him, feeling safer as soon as his arm went around her waist. Bill tossed his head at sight of her, and she stilled, her heart thumping, but he soon settled again, and allowed her to run a hand down the coarse hair of his nose, and then to pat his neck. The muscles bunched and flexed beneath the glossy brown coat, and he shifted on his white-socked feet, impatient to be away again.

'Can you imagine riding him?' Tristan asked with a grin. He gave Bill an encouraging slap on the flank and sent him trotting off.

'Not in a hundred years,' she confessed, taking his hand and jumping down. 'How old were you when you started?'

'I learned in America when I was ten. So you'll probably see people looking a bit appalled at my riding style once I get Bill out and about in Cornwall.'

'Do you ride like a Wild West rancher, then?' Freya rather liked the sound of that.

'Not quite. I have my own sort of mish-mashed style. Other people ... ' He broke off, and waited a moment, then went on, 'Most other people think it's dreadful.'

'But not everyone?'

'No.' He smiled, but it looked as if it hurt a little. 'Not everyone.'

Caroline. The name flashed into Freya's mind, and she swallowed hard and dismissed the little shooting pain in her chest: Caroline was gone.

'Sophie rides brilliantly,' Tristan said. 'Bill worships her. She's been our saviour while I'm away, exercising him, grooming him, generally keeping his fitness up.'

'I can't imagine her doing all that,' Freya confessed. 'She's so young. And she's dressed beautifully today.'

'In your honour only,' he said. 'Come on, we'd better get back.' He drew her away from the gate. 'Catherine will be holding tea until we get there, and Janet's likely to be making a nuisance of herself out of sheer boredom.'

'She's very sweet,' Freya said with a smile. 'I like her a lot.'

'And she likes you.' He glanced down at their linked hands, and gave them a little shake. 'You mustn't worry about Sophie. I told you, she's a bit shocked, that's all. It'll pass soon enough.'

'We'll have to start off by inviting her down to stay,' Freya said. 'We have a spare room at home, it'll be the nursery one day, but we have until June at least.'

'Then that's what we'll do. Before she has a chance to upset you again.'

'She didn't really upset me,' Freya began, but Tristan stopped.

'Yes, she did. I'm not blind, I saw your face.' He bent and kissed her. 'That's to remind you why we're here. Just keep saying to yourself: *Freya MacKenzie*. Has a nice ring to it, doesn't it?'

'Speaking of nice rings ...' Freya gazed demurely up at him, and he grinned.

'I will buy one, I promise. In the meantime I could make you one.' He reached down to the grass verge and plucked a primrose, and twisted the stem around Freya's finger. 'There.'

'Perfect!' Freya tried to keep it in place, but it sprang open again, so she threaded it through the button-hole of her coat instead.

Back at Mrs Scott's house, they discovered the owner had returned in their absence, and was waiting to meet them before changing for dinner. A delicately boned lady with a wide smile, she exclaimed her joy at seeing Tristan, insisted on being called Elaine, and whisked Freya off for a tour of her daughter's garden. During dinner the talk was lively and friendly, and even Sophie unbent a little, and asked questions about where Bill would live.

'He'll share the field with some of the farmer's horses, so he won't be lonely. There's a lean-to shed for when it rains. I've arranged winter stabling for him at the same farm.'

'Can I come and ride him?'

'Of course! You know you don't have to ask. We were only saying earlier how it would be nice for you to come and visit. Freya's sister Mairead is only a few years older than you. I'm sure you'd all get along famously.'

It sounded to Freya as though he was trying too hard, but Sophie was nodding and seemed much happier. She even smiled at Freya.

'How old *are* you?'

'Sophie!' Elaine shot her granddaughter an appalled look, then Freya an apologetic one.

'I don't mind,' Freya said. 'I turned twenty last week.'

'Tristan is twenty-seven,' Janet put in, but fell silent under her grandmother's warning eye.

'Would you like to come up and see my bedroom after dinner, Freya?' Sophie asked, a little shyly. 'I've had some new curtains put up. They match my quilt.'

Freya tried not to show surprise at the gesture. 'I'd love to, thank you.'

After dinner Sophie led Freya up the red-carpeted stairs. Janet started to follow, but Sophie shook her head. 'You don't need to see it, silly! Go and talk to Tristan. Tell him all about school or something.'

'I'm learning lace,' Janet said to Freya. 'It's ever so hard.'

'Tell Tristan about it,' Sophie repeated, and rolled her eyes at Freya. 'Little sisters are so tiresome, aren't they?'

Freya didn't know what to say; on the one hand having a sister was still a novelty, and Mairead was her best friend now anyway, but on the other, Sophie was making such an effort to be friendly that she didn't want to openly disagree. She just gave her a sympathetic smile, and spoke to Janet in her most friendly voice.

'I love the sound of lace-making, it looks so complicated. I'd like to hear all about it too, a bit later.'

Janet pouted and went back into the sitting room, and Freya

followed Sophie along the passage to a white-painted door. Once inside Sophie's room she gave the new curtains due attention and admiration, although they were a little too floral and bright for her conservative taste, and was about to make a grateful escape when Sophie sat on her bed, and indicated Freya should take the chair by the dressing table.

'He won't marry you, you know.'

Freya's mouth dried up, and she couldn't think of a single response. She just sat quietly, waiting for Tristan's sister to get off her chest whatever had been pressing on it all evening.

'He can't,' Sophie went on. 'He doesn't love you. He loves Caroline Hamilton.' She traced a finger along the pattern on the quilt, her eyes cast down, and Freya was reminded that she was still a child. It was the only thing that kept her from leaving the room in that instant.

'I know about Caroline,' she said instead. 'Tristan has told me how deeply he loved her.'

'*Still* loves her.'

'That might be true.' Although it hurt to consider it. 'But he also told me she's . . . no longer with us.'

'She died,' Sophie said bluntly, 'he didn't stop loving her. And she was *our* friend, too.'

Freya heard desolation in her tone, and moved to sit next to her. 'That must make it very difficult for you all. I'm so sorry.'

'She was cleverer than you. And *much* prettier.'

Freya recoiled at this sudden display of spite. 'Whether or not that's the case,' she began, in a tighter voice, 'your brother and I—'

'He wants an excuse to move away from here. From the memories.'

'Then why didn't he stay in America?'

'He doesn't want to be *that* far away from us, Plymouth was perfect.'

'You don't know anything about it,' Freya pointed out, growing angry now. 'Tristan and I have had some difficulties, but we've overcome them.'

'He and Caroline *never* argued.'

'I'm sure that's not true, either.'

'It is! She knew all about history, and they used to talk for hours. When they did disagree it was over something they were both learning about, and they'd be laughing while they did it. Did you laugh when you had your "difficulties"?'

Freya's ever-helpful memory supplied the image of the two of them standing on the moor, her shouting at Tristan for not understanding, and Tristan yelling about how Caroline would never have tried to make him go against his principles. Of course she wouldn't have, not if she was a scholar of history too.

'It's none of your business,' she said, and stood up, all her good intentions fled. 'I came here to admire your room, not to be told a pack of lies by a spoilt little girl.'

'That church.' Sophie rose too, her face devoid of all expression as she looked at Freya from an almost equal height. 'The burned one. Do you know why Tristan didn't want to go?'

'I think I can guess,' Freya said. 'May I go now, please?'

'They were to be married there. Caroline loved it. She wanted to live here in Honiton, with Tristan, for the rest of her life.'

'And that makes her a better person than me?' Freya spoke through tight lips. 'Because of where she wants to live?' She subsided with an effort, and tried once more. 'Sophie,

I understand, I truly do. But Cornwall isn't so far away, and there's even a beach down—'

'I don't care about your stupid beach!' Sophie lowered her voice. 'He still loves Caroline. She was worth ten of you and he knows it. You won't make him happy, and he knows that too, deep down.'

She jerked open the bedroom door and stood aside, waiting for Freya to pass. Bubbling with resentment Freya avoided her fierce green stare as she left the room, and bit down on her tongue to stop herself from speaking again; she had nothing pleasant left to say. Tomorrow, and home, could not come soon enough.

* * *

Penhaligon's Attic

The slamming of the door was absorbed effortlessly into Keir's dream. He slumbered on, staring at the door of the farmhouse he and Arthur had been so excited to own such a short time ago, now shut firmly in his face and thankfully hiding the white, angry face of Arthur's wife. The voices, however, filtered through the fog of exhausted sleep, and by the time the kitchen door opened he had half-woken, though his head still lay pillowed on his forearm.

'What the bloody hell is this?'

Keir jerked upright, his skin stinging as it peeled away from the rough material of his jacket, and felt thin drool sliding down his chin. He wiped it away, and turned to see a

tall man in the doorway, his arm outstretched to prevent who-
ever was behind him from entering. Instead of answering,
Keir tried to look past the man, who could only be Matthew
Penhaligon.

'Mairead? Is that you?' The shadowy figure in the doorway
did not reply, but Penhaligon took a step closer, and Keir saw
both fists were curled, ready. 'Easy now! My name's Keir
Garvey. I'm cousin to Anna.' Keir pushed back his chair and
reached for the note Anna had left. Penhaligon snatched it
from his fingers, and pointed to the chair, into which Keir
subsided again with no small amount of gratitude. While
Penhaligon read, Keir tried to get a better look at his cousin,
who, he could see now, was quite tall, and slender, and with a
very familiar, direct look in her moss-green eyes as she stared
back at him. She was a young Anna, and he felt a lump in
his throat.

Penhaligon handed the note to his stepdaughter, and kept
himself between her and Keir as he moved further into the
room. 'She doesn't say much. But she says I'm to trust you.'

'Then you should.'

Penhaligon glared at him. 'I'll decide that.' His glower
made his eyes look almost purple, and his scruffy half-
beard gave him an added air of ferocity. Unpredictable, Keir
decided, and made up his mind to tread warily around this
one. He wasn't entirely convinced by what Anna had told
him, and if Penhaligon was reserving judgement on him, then
he was at least equally determined to do the same. Bossy or
not, Anna had been a vulnerable woman when she arrived,
with an even more vulnerable daughter. Ripe prey for a man
such as this.

Mairead came in properly, her eyes averted, and he could see she was dusted down with what looked like flour. She washed her hands at the sink, and put on her apron, then took up the vegetable knife he had abandoned.

Keir softened his voice, remembering what he'd been told about her. 'I missed you when you came over, Mairead. I'm sorry I did.'

The girl visibly relaxed. 'So am I. Mother talks about you all the time.' She pointed the knife at the vegetable basket. 'She's got you working, I see.'

Keir grinned. 'She always could.'

'Looked more like you were sleeping, when I came in,' Penhaligon observed, his voice still hard. 'Mairead, give him back the knife.'

'I don't mind—'

'You need to go and change,' he reminded her, more gently, and she nodded and removed her apron.

'Anna says you were helping a friend,' Keir said, reluctant to lose this buffer between himself and Penhaligon so soon. 'Does she work in a bakery?'

Mairead blinked, surprised, then looked down at her white-dusted dress. She smiled. 'No, he's rebuilding his house. We've been making plaster today.'

He? Keir was determined not to appear shocked, but he shot a quick look at Penhaligon to gauge his own reaction. Not a flicker; clearly things in Caernoweth were done a little differently to back home. Or maybe that was just Mairead.

The moment she had left the room, he went back to slicing carrots, aware of Penhaligon prowling the room restlessly, and waiting for him to speak. He didn't have to wait long.

'Why are you here, Garvey? Oh, I know what Anna's note says, that you came to find Mairead. But you have to admit it's a bit out of the blue.'

'It's the truth,' Keir said.

'I thought you lived in New Zealand? Long way to come, just to visit a niece you've never met.'

'Cousin,' Keir pointed out quietly. 'Once removed. And I'd already left New Zealand before I decided to come here.'

'Still.' Penhaligon dragged out a chair, and sat down. 'How do we know there's no other reason?'

'Such as what?'

Penhaligon shrugged. 'Sent by the police? Or Finn Casey?'

Keir put down the knife, keeping a rein on his temper with difficulty. 'Mr Penhaligon, you have no understanding of the relationship Anna and I shared, growing up, so I'll forgive that. *She* trusts me, and that's all I care about.' He pushed the small pile of peelings aside, and fixed Penhaligon with a steady look. 'Come to think of it, I should be the one questioning you, don't you think?'

'This is my house, Garvey, Anna is my wife.'

'And she and Mairead are my family.'

'I wasn't aware this was a contest, but you're the one who's just appeared without advance warning. Why no letter?'

'I left home in a hurry.' Keir could see the conversation drifting in a direction he'd prefer to stay away from. 'The thing is, you're how old? Thirty-seven? Thirty-eight?'

'Why?'

'Well, you're intelligent, clearly. Educated. If you bothered to wash and shave you'd be quite respectable-looking, you have your own businesses ... and yet you're oddly unattached.

Until you meet a beautiful, desperate woman, with her own pub, and you're suddenly ready for marriage.'

'It wasn't like that,' Penhaligon said, his eyes glinting. 'You said I've no idea about you and Anna, but I could say the same about her and me.'

'But a *pub*? What man would turn that down?'

'This one,' Penhaligon said coldly. 'Now if you don't want me to throw you out of that bloody door you'd better come up with a damned good reason why I should let you stay.'

'Throw me out?' Keir asked, smiling. He stood up, and Penhaligon stood too, and Keir noted they weren't that much different in height after all, and although Keir was burlier, he could see the corded strength in the man's forearms, and noted the set of the square shoulders.

Penhaligon returned the faintly mocking smile, but it was tempered with tiredness. 'Sit down, Garvey. The last thing Anna wants is for us to get off to a bad start.'

Keir hesitated, but Penhaligon didn't wait for him to give in first, he sank back into his seat and picked up the vegetable knife himself. Watching his practised, capable hands making short work of a knobbly potato, Keir allowed himself to relax a little. 'You've done that before,' he observed, as a way of breaking the ice.

'We all pitch in in this house.'

'So Anna said.'

'She also says you're planning to stay.'

'I am, if I can get work. It's all right,' he hurried on, seeing Penhaligon's frown, 'I'm not asking you. I'm going to try at the farm down the road.'

Penhaligon grunted, and selected another potato. Keir took the opportunity to study him more closely, and saw a faint grimace on his face as he eased a stiffness in his right shoulder. The long fingers gripped the knife and worked it with what looked almost like an artist's touch; those hands were used to fine work, as well as hard labour, by the looks of them.

'Are you widowed or separated?' Keir asked, still curious as to why Penhaligon had been unattached for so long.

'What does it matter?' Penhaligon fixed him with a narrow-eyed look, then shrugged. 'Freya's mother is still alive. She's in town, actually.'

'Why did you separate?'

'None of your business.'

'It is if—'

'For goodness sake!' Both men turned to see Mairead in the doorway, looking from one to the other with a look of exasperation. 'Matthew, I'd expected better manners from you, and Mr Garvey? You clearly don't hold Mother in very high regard if you don't think her own charms were enough to win Matthew over!'

'Of course I do!'

'Then why are you questioning him so closely?' Mairead shook her head. 'I ought to knock your two heads together!'

Keir's mouth dropped open, and Penhaligon's twitched, and Mairead began clearing the table, while the two men each struggled to find the original thread of their suspicions. The reason for the Penhaligons' separation might not be Keir's business, he acknowledged, but there was one thing he kept coming back to.

'How am I supposed to believe you weren't swayed at least a little bit by the fact that Anna inherited a pub? Surely it's every fella's dream?'

Mairead stopped sweeping peelings into the compost bucket, and Keir saw her exchange a look with Penhaligon. Neither spoke for a moment, and then, to Keir's surprise, Mairead, passing Penhaligon's chair on her way to the back door, squeezed his shoulder. As far as Keir was concerned that alone might have put an immediate end to his misgivings, but Penhaligon turned back to him and nodded.

'All right. If it'll set your mind at rest.' He sat forward, his hands clasped on the table, and a muscle jumping in his jaw, and Keir could feel his own body tensing again as he waited.

'You think Anna inheriting the Tinner's was sugar added to the mix,' Penhaligon said quietly. 'One more reason she'd be the perfect wife. It was actually the opposite. It was the hardest obstacle I had to overcome, once I knew I loved her.'

Keir listened as Penhaligon told him bluntly, and without drama, about his struggle against the hold that drink had had over him all his adult life. As he described what had happened last year, when he'd thought Anna was leaving and had turned to the nearest bottle of rum, Keir's reservations flooded back. No wonder he had been reluctant to reveal the reason behind the collapse of his marriage.

'You see?' Mairead said, when Penhaligon had fallen silent. 'That proves it's Mother he loves.'

'But how do we know he can be trusted, when the first sign of difficulty might send him spinning back into his old ways again?'

'He's been tested since then,' Mairead said. 'Severely. And he's not wavered an inch.'

'If your cousin took me at my own word, I'd probably think less of him,' Penhaligon admitted. 'After all, I have Anna's assurance, he doesn't.' He stood up. 'But, Garvey, you're sitting at *my* table, preparing to eat my food, cooked by my wife and stepdaughter. I don't have to explain anything more to you, and if you intend to stay here you'd best make sure I don't have any reason to doubt you.'

'What sort of reason?'

'Such as I don't believe for one minute your story about coming here to find Mairead. At least I don't believe that's all of it. If I find out that you're hiding something that could hurt anyone I care about,' he leaned down, bracing his fists on the table, 'I'll have your hide nailed over my front door.'

He withdrew, leaving Keir not as shaken as he no doubt hoped, but thoughtful. It was true, he hadn't told either of them the full story, and he didn't know if he ever could, not if he wanted to keep Anna's respect. He'd been on the verge of telling her earlier, almost persuaded by her gentle pressuring, but looking at the swell of her stomach, seeing her happiness now and remembering her grief at the loss of her first child, he couldn't. Arthur's wife would have had her own baby by now, and there was no way of telling whether it was his or Arthur's . . . nevertheless, he knew. And regret was a merciless lesson when it was too late.

* * *

Honiton

On Monday morning Sophie was just as she had been at dinner the previous night; shy, polite, affectionate towards her family and deferential towards Freya, though now Freya noticed the tight line of her lips and a dullness in her expression. But there was nothing to be gained by drawing Tristan's attention to the discord, his frequent warm smiles and secret touches put Sophie's jealousy where it belonged. Freya had only to endure it a short while longer in any case, while they said their goodbyes, then she and Tristan would lead Bill to the station together, load him onto the train, and they could all set off back home.

Catherine helped her into her coat. 'Will you be busy today, dear?'

'No,' Freya admitted. 'The shop hasn't been too successful lately. But I'm excited to be taking it over full-time.'

'Freya's full of wonderful plans,' Tristan said, heaving the spare saddle onto his shoulder in readiness for his ride from Bodmin. 'I have a feeling Penhaligon's Attic is going to be on the lips of people from Land's End to John O'Groats, before too long.'

Freya laughed, but Sophie spoke up earnestly. 'Oh, I'm sure of it. After all, now she can pour all her time into the little place, and be a real shop-keeper.'

Tristan smiled, clearly missing the point that Freya was not the great scholar his former love had been. 'It might be little but it's a treasure-trove of past glories. I could quite happily get lost in there.'

'Ah, *now* we know why you're marrying her,' Sophie said, with just enough of a teasing note in her voice that the others laughed, but Freya only smiled.

'He's marrying me for my biscuits, actually,' she said, hoping she had successfully hidden the sudden pain behind the joke.

'And why are *you* marrying *him*?' Sophie asked. Her eyes met Freya's, challenging her.

Freya took Tristan's hand, and stared back. 'Because he has nice hair.'

In the laughter that followed, Freya gripped Tristan's hand so tightly he glanced down at her in surprise, but she didn't loosen her hold. They made their final farewells, Janet bouncing up and down and begging, to no avail, to be allowed to go to the field with them, and then started down the lane to fetch Bill.

The train journey was a haven of peace after the turmoil of the previous evening. They talked quietly, and dozed, and at each station Tristan went back to check on Bill. Freya stared out of the window at the countryside rolling by, and the towns through which they passed, and when they reached Plymouth she found herself peering more carefully, as if she might see her young friend Emily Parker. Emily actually lived on the very edge of Dartmoor, and not in the city itself, but it was nice to think she was close by; Emily was such a sweet girl ... so unlike Sophie, who was only a couple of years younger, but might have been a different species altogether.

'What was that look for?' Tristan returned to his seat, and Freya found a quick smile for him.

'Nothing. How's Bill?'

'Getting restless,' he admitted. 'Actually, I was thinking of taking him off soon, and starting the ride back from the next station instead. Would you be all right?'

'Of course.' Freya could see the poorly concealed eagerness, and it made her smile though she had her doubts that Bill was the slightest bit troubled. 'That's a very good idea.'

'I'll give you the fare for the coach,' Tristan added, pressing her hand. 'And only if you're sure—'

'Tristan, really, it's quite all right!'

He relaxed. 'Thank you.'

'Did you think you had to ask permission?'

'I thought you might be wary, travelling alone,' he said. 'I wouldn't want that.'

'I hadn't even considered it,' she said truthfully.

'That's good. Only Caro ...' he stopped, and flushed.

Freya removed her hand from his, in case she clenched her fingers. 'It's all right,' she repeated, and turned back to the window.

'Freya ...' He reached around to bring her face back to his. 'I told you how I felt about Caroline. It doesn't lessen what I feel for you, in fact it's helped me understand it.'

Freya forced a smile. 'I'm sorry.' It didn't seem to be enough to dispel the sudden tension, so she went on, 'Perhaps you'll tell me more about her?'

He looked at her doubtfully. 'You don't have to say that.'

'I mean it. Later. When we're home.'

'I like the sound of *when we're home*,' he said, and kissed her forehead.

'Do you?'

'Why say that? You know I do.'

'It's just ... your house in Honiton. It's so lovely, and your family all adore you. It'll be hard to give up.'

'I've spent more time away from there than I have staying there,' he said. 'First university in London, then New York, Plymouth ... And New England, of course. I love my family, particularly my sisters, but I'm not so deeply rooted as they want me to be.' It was the closest he'd come to admitting any kind of difference among the MacKenzies, and Freya took it as an encouraging sign; perhaps she ought to tell him about Sophie after all, so he'd at least be prepared if she ever accepted their invitation to visit.

'Of course,' he went on. 'they're bound to miss a brotherly presence in the house, but they'll be glad I'm happy.'

Freya bit down on the words that had sprung to her lips, and swallowed a sigh. It didn't matter now, anyway; they were on their way home.

Tristan got off at Liskeard Station, and before the train pulled away again Freya could see him leading a very frisky Bill up the platform; it clearly wasn't an excuse after all, and that made her feel better, despite what she'd told him. The saddle was on the ground, but it would be a while before Bill was ready to have it put on his back. Tristan turned at the sound of the whistle, and waved to Freya, but his attention was quickly dragged back to calming the horse in order to tack him up ready for the long ride home.

Freya sat back in her seat, missing the warmth of him next to her already. She steered her thoughts determinedly away from Sophie MacKenzie, and onto Penhaligon's Attic. There was no rule that said it must remain a bookshop; books had never really sold well in Caernoweth, but if she combined it with a sort of buy and sell second-hand shop then the townspeople would benefit too. It would be run on a similar basis to the Widows' Guild, only for everyone. She could bake Granny Grace's biscuits and sell those ...

She closed her eyes, lulled by the slow rocking motion of the train, half awake and half asleep, thinking and musing, and drifting off now and again into a light doze. She was brought awake by a slamming sound, and blinked out of the window at the station sign. Bodmin already! She scrambled to her feet, her heart thumping, and fumbled with the door of her carriage but it only rattled and would not budge. At the sound of the station-master's whistle, she let out a cry of dismay.

The train began moving, very slowly, past the passengers who'd alighted from the first-class carriage nearer the front. Freya gave another shout, and the nearest passenger realised what had happened and leapt to grab the door handle. He pulled it open, and seized Freya's hand, pulling her free of the train to land in an awkward, stumbling confusion among him and his surprised friends.

'Hey, Miss!' he laughed, helping her upright again. 'That's a heck of an entrance.'

Freya brushed down her skirts, and turned a grateful smile on him, then she caught sight of one of his companions, and gave an inward groan. He stepped forward, his own smile polite and forced.

'Good morning, Miss Penhaligon.'

'Mr Batten.' She shook his hand, disappointed at the return to formality between them, but determined to uphold it if that was his wish.

'This is Peter Boden,' Hugh said, indicating Freya's saviour. 'American, if you hadn't guessed. He's engaged to a friend of the family. Lives in London now, and down for what he quaintly terms a bachelor party, at Caernoweth Hotel.'

'Thank you so much, Mr Boden,' she said. 'I think I've heard Lucy mention you.'

'Lucy?' Mr Boden turned to Hugh, an eyebrow raised. 'Your sister Lucy? Why'd she be talking about me?'

'She's obsessed with dancing,' Hugh explained. 'Desperate for her turn on the stage, and ever since the Brownsworth party she's been dropping your name into every conversation.' He looked at Freya. 'How did you two get talking?'

'We went for a drive yesterday,' Freya said. 'Up to Honiton.'

'I thought Father was using the car to ferry Pagett about.'

'We took Tristan's.'

'Ah.' Hugh's expression clouded as the rest of her words registered. 'Yesterday, eh? Overnight stay.'

Freya wished she hadn't brought the subject up. 'We're going to miss the coach if we stand around here nattering,' she said, and thankfully conversation halted as they hurried to where the coach stood waiting.

Freya sat opposite Hugh as they swayed their way back to Caernoweth. Unsettled by the air of tension she engaged Peter Boden in a lively conversation about London, and a few places they both knew, but was uncomfortably aware of Hugh's gaze burning across the narrow space between them.

Before too long they were rolling into the courtyard at the Caernoweth Hotel. Hugh climbed down and offered her his hand and, swept up in the relief of being home, she took it, and on impulse kissed him lightly on the cheek as she reached the ground.

His whispered voice cut through her distraction. 'Don't be cruel, darling.'

Jolted, she looked up to see him smiling, though still a little tightly. 'I don't mean to be,' she murmured back. 'But we *are* still friends, aren't we?'

'Always.' He pressed her hand, then sketched a brief, half-bow and stepped back into his group of friends, whereupon they vanished into the hotel.

Freya took a deep breath, and turned towards the road, but was stopped by a voice that rose above the diminishing noises of a busy arrival.

'Freya, wait!'

Mama hurried across the courtyard, throwing a suspicious look towards the lobby and the bachelor party. She hooked her arm through Freya's. 'I'll walk to the shop with you, and you can tell me all about Devon.'

By the time they reached Penhaligon's Attic she had told Mama a little about the MacKenzie family home, Tristan's stepmother and grandmother, and his two sisters, but she hadn't mentioned Sophie's skilfully applied animosity – knowing Mama she would hop straight onto the next train and give the girl a piece of her mind. It was an amusing and comforting thought, but it would achieve nothing; it would be pointless to bring that single niggling part of her Honiton experience back to Caernoweth.

Anna greeted her with a welcoming smile. 'Good to have you back. How was it?'

'Wonderful! Tristan's family are all lovely, and they adore him, of course.' Freya peered more closely at Anna, who had the appearance of a woman fighting to hold in some news of her own. 'What's happened? You look fit to burst.'

'I've someone I'd like you to meet,' Anna said. She spared Mama a quick glance. 'Both of you, I suppose, since we're all family.' She called through to the kitchen, 'Come and meet Matthew's daughter!'

There came the sound of chair legs scraping the stone floor, and Freya exchanged a puzzled look with her mother, before turning her attention back to the door. The man who came through it was about Papá's age, perhaps a year or two younger, with a shock of black hair, and bright blue eyes. He was possibly the tallest man Freya had ever seen, and powerfully built, with a scarred chin, and a smile that transformed his quite plain face into something so appealing she couldn't help but smile back. His teeth were strong and white, contrasting with the unmistakeable, deeply tanned look of a man who has spent his life out of doors, in sun as well as wind.

'This is my cousin, Keir Garvey,' Anna said. 'Keir, this is Freya, and her mother Mrs Webb.'

Mr Garvey stepped up and took both Freya's hands in his, and his smile widened even further. 'Freya. Thank you for allowing me into your home.' His voice was deep and soft, his accent an odd mixture of Irish and something else. He turned to Mama, and Freya waited for the inevitable admiration to cross his face, but he merely bowed, and uttered a polite greeting. Mama, on the other hand, was staring at him with unabashed fascination.

Freya didn't know how to address him, or what to say, but she found she was still smiling despite her astonishment. She looked at Anna, who smiled back as if she still couldn't believe it herself.

'I hope you don't mind, I've offered him Robert's room for a day or two, until he finds lodgings in town.'

Freya found her voice. 'Of course I don't mind. It'll be wonderful to get to know you, Mr Garvey. Anna has mentioned you often.'

'The first thing you'll learn is that I'm not Mr Garvey. I'm Keir.'

'Keir.' Freya tried out the unfamiliar name. 'I look forward to hearing all about New Zealand, Keir.'

'He and your da are already firm friends,' Anna said. 'I left them to their own devices while I was at work last night, and by the time I came home they were finishing each other's sentences, and laughing at things I'd no notion of what they meant.'

Keir grinned. 'Hardly, but we're working on it. Anyway, I'm hoping to get a job at the farm down the road. If I'm lucky I'll get a lodging there too, so I'll be out from under your feet before too long.'

'Right then,' Anna said, 'I must away to the pub now or Esther'll be up here, wanting to know why I'm late. It still feels as if she's the one in charge.'

'How was Mairead this morning?' Freya asked, tugging off her coat. 'Nervous about the new job?'

'Not at all. Champing at the bit, in fact. Which reminds me, where's your man and his horse?'

'He's riding from Liskeard,' Freya said, and explained why he'd taken Bill off early.

Anna nodded. 'Good for them both, I'd say. Keir's a keen horseman, too.'

'Tristan will be thrilled to meet you, Keir,' Freya said. 'He's never been to New Zealand, but he's travelled a lot, and spent time in America recently for his family's business. He did a lot of riding while he was there.'

'He's a rancher?'

'No, an historian.' Freya chuckled at Keir's expression, and shook her head. 'I'll explain properly later.'

'Please do! Wait for me, Anna, I'll walk as far as the pub with you. You can point me in the direction of the farm.'

The cousins said their goodbyes and left, and then Freya and her mother were alone in the shop. Freya's simple pleasure at her first proper day in charge was slightly marred, but she told herself she ought to enjoy Mama's company while she could. 'Would you like some tea?' she asked, going to the kitchen.

'Yes, please. And then ...' Mama hesitated. 'Then I'd like you to tell me all about those people you were with yesterday.'

'Tristan's family? I've told you all there is to know, really.'

'Not them. That Mr Kempton, and the Batten girl.' Mama followed her into the kitchen, and stood with her arms folded while Freya opened the tea caddy.

'They're nice people. Quite safe to be with. There's not much more to say. Teddy's a research assistant, Lucy doesn't do anything, as far as I know, but apparently she's very interested in the theatre. Dance, particularly.'

'Did you talk much?'

'It was hard to, in the car, and when we got to Honiton they went off for a walk together.'

Mama pursed her lips. 'Are you friends?'

'With Teddy, yes. Lucy I don't know very well. But I think we could be, someday. She seems very nice, and helped out a lot in the storm last year.'

'She's gentry, and a long way from your station in life,' Mama said shortly. 'She's probably laughing at you.'

Freya stared, hurt. 'She's not like that.'

'They're all like that.' Mama came over, and put her arms

around Freya. 'I don't want to sound cruel, *mi tesoro*, but I have experience of what it's like when the wrong people mix. I don't want you to be the subject of gossip or jokes among those people.' She hugged Freya a little tighter, then released her. 'Let them alone in their big house.'

'Mama—'

'And now, I think I will go back to the hotel and rest. I didn't sleep at all well last night, knowing you were not coming home.'

'What about your tea?' But in truth Freya was glad she was going; the injustices of the past two days were beginning to turn what should be a wonderful memory, into something that tasted decidedly sour.

'I will come and see you again soon.' Mama touched her hand. 'I'm sorry if I have upset you. I would not do that for the world. But your Papá has clearly not taught you these lessons, and so I must. Stay with your own people.'

'Like you did, you mean?' The words were out before Freya could bite them back, but Mama only smiled.

'I learned my lesson, did I not? I cannot say I have regrets, because had I not broken free I would never have met my Viking, and had you. But yes, I have learned.'

Freya frowned. 'Is all this coming out because you saw Hugh and I were travelling in the same coach today?'

Mama's lips were drawn into a thin line. 'Perhaps. I saw you kissing him.'

'I wasn't—'

'Learn from me,' Mama said gently. 'Now I will go and find some sleep, and I'm sure my mood will be sweeter when I wake.'

Exasperated, Freya watched her go, wondering why some otherwise perfectly nice people felt the determination to spoil the simplest pleasures of others. Then she took her tea through to the shop, feeling her spirits lift again as she looked around her new domain. None of that mattered now. Penhaligon's Attic was about to be reborn.

Chapter Seven

Pencarrack House

With Father due home later today, there was an air of expect-
ancy hanging over the house that Lucy could never quite
fathom; after all, he would simply closet himself away with
Dorothy until he'd caught up on all the business news, after
which he would be nothing more than a shadowy presence
around the estate. But he'd always had the knack, despite his
unimposing form and quiet manner, of putting people on their
guard and creating a kind of worried tension.

Lucy went in to breakfast, where Dorothy was already finishing her usual half-grapefruit and a cup of strong coffee, and
perused the small selection on the sideboard.

'Have you seen Hugh this morning?' Dorothy asked.

'Good morning to you, too, sister dear.'

Dorothy sighed. 'Good morning. I trust you slept well?'

Lucy chose a poached egg and some toast, and sat opposite.

'Very, thank you.' She noted the tight-lipped impatience with a little smile. 'The nights are so mild at the moment, aren't they?' Then she relented. 'In answer to your question, I haven't seen Hugh yet, no. He's probably fallen asleep on someone's couch at the hotel.'

'Fallen asleep? Whatever are you talking about?'

'It was Peter Boden's stag party last night. You know, Heather's chap. The theatre manager.'

'Right. At the hotel, you say?' Dorothy rose, patting at her lips with her napkin.

'Yes, why?'

'Father isn't due home until this evening, and Mr Pagett has requested one more meeting this lunchtime, before we exchange draft contracts.'

'It's going ahead then? The purchase of the fort?'

'The purchase has already been agreed,' Dorothy said. 'It's the building work we're wrangling over now. We need a reliable local man to oversee it, and Pagett has had no luck finding one. He's on the verge of calling in a London company, which would hardly make it worth our while investing, since the profits would be cut so much.'

'What about James Fry?'

'Who?' Dorothy stopped halfway to the door.

'James Fry. He's living back here now, after working up in Dorset with some architect or other. I forget the name.'

'And how do you know him?'

'Does it matter?'

'Of course it matters!'

'I met him on a coach, last year.'

'Did you have a carry-on with him?'

'Dorothy!' Lucy almost dropped her butter knife in astonishment at the assumption. 'No, I did not! We saw each other once or twice socially, that's all!'

'Good. Well then, I'll tell Mr Pagett we have someone to contact, that ought to keep him happy for a short while, then I can discuss this Mr Fry with Father, tonight.'

'You probably know him, actually,' Lucy said. 'He grew up here, he's your sort of age, and he was friendly with Matthew Penhaligon.'

'Penhaligon?' Dorothy frowned. 'Oh, yes. The chap who came a cropper in the explosion last year.' Lucy wondered if it was her imagination, or whether Dorothy's patchy memory really was feigned. Perhaps she still felt the guilt more deeply than she wanted to let on; she'd been fairly dismissive at the time.

'Anyway,' Dorothy went on, 'we'll discuss it later, but I have to find Hugh just now. If you see him, send him back to the hotel and tell him I'll meet him in the lobby.'

'It's so silly that Mr Pagett won't take you seriously,' Lucy said, with a rare flicker of sympathy. 'He really ought to.'

'Oh, he will,' Dorothy gave her a grim smile. 'Eventually, whether he wants to or not, he'll have to.'

* * *

Priddy Farm, Porthstennack

Getting a job proved easier than Keir had dared to hope; one look at the size of him silenced any doubts Stan Pawley might have had about employing a stranger, and they shook hands within five minutes. Keir hardly even had to cite his experience on the New Zealand farm.

'I can certainly use you,' Pawley said. 'We're doing up the loft above the stable, it'll be ready in another couple of weeks or so. Rent'll come off your wage, if the place suits.'

'That'd be grand,' Keir said. 'I've a room with my cousin a while longer yet.'

'Your cousin bein' Anna Penhaligon, that right?'

'That's right.' It was strange hearing that name applied to her, but immeasurably more welcome than 'Anna Casey' had ever been.

'She'm all right, tell the truth,' Stan said, though his expression said he still couldn't quite work out why. 'Pub's a different place, anyway. Clean for starters!' He gave a wheezy laugh. 'And John Rodda did say the Widows' Guild've saved a packet by 'er lettin' it out to 'em for free.'

'I wouldn't know anything about that. Anyway, I'd like to get started today. Is that all right?'

'You'm keen!' Stan huffed his breathless laugh again. 'Come on, boy, let's get you stuck in.'

Three hours later, with the stable cleaned out and fresh straw put down, Keir left the fork standing against the wall, and went out into the yard to sluice away the sweat. He knelt on the dusty ground by the water trough, and brought handfuls of ice-cold water to his face, pondering on the twists and turns that had led him here, living under the same roof as Anna again. Only now they were supposed to be the adults, and the ones the youngsters looked to for guidance ... He hoped Anna was better at that than he was, for their sakes.

'You're new.'

The low voice stopped him as he wiped the water away with his sleeve, and he found himself looking at the most exquisite face he had ever seen. He stood up slowly, and, watching him with a speculative, curious expression, and a determined jut to her finely shaped chin, the woman let her gaze rove over him, unchecked by embarrassment. Or even politeness. The hair that escaped her hat was a light, golden blonde, her neck was long and slender, and her body neatly encased in a grubby work dress that nevertheless flattered what promised to be a breath-taking form beneath it. She favoured him with a sudden, bewitching smile.

'You're a big lad, aren't you?' she said softly. 'What's your name?'

He cleared his dry throat. 'Keir Garvey.'

Her expression faltered, then the smile returned. 'Related to 'er that runs the pub?'

'Cousins.'

The woman put down the basket of eggs she was carrying, and glanced around, then came closer. 'I'm Nancy.' She looked up at him, small white teeth nipping at her lower lip, and her hand crept out and brushed across his bare forearm. Each hair responded individually, and he felt a familiar shooting sensation in his groin. He didn't speak.

'Strong,' she mused. 'Hard worker, I'd say.' Her gaze flicked to the stable, and she reached out a long finger and plucked a piece of straw that was stuck to Keir's shirt. Brushing the material flat again, she let her hand linger on his chest. 'That's some impressive muscles you've got there.' She spread her fingers so that the tip of her thumb rubbed across his nipple.

110

Her eyes were a very light, icy blue, and they were opened wide, but by no means innocent.

Keir summoned his self-control and removed her hand. 'If you'll excuse me, I've got work to finish.'

She stooped to pick up the egg basket again. 'Don't let me stop you.' Her voice was smooth, and although her accent was very much of the region, and he was growing used to it on others, on her it sounded almost exotic. 'Don't know if you've seen it, Keir Garvey, but there's a nice loft in that stable.'

He stared, not sure if she was mocking him. He wasn't the least bit handsome, and some people saw his size and his easy smile, and made the mistake of thinking him simple. Maybe she was having some fun at his expense, and would go back to her friends the minute he showed a response, to share the details of another conquest.

'Don't look like that!' she laughed, and now she sounded much more natural. 'Are you scared of me or something?'

'Not at all.' He'd had more than his share of brief, sweet encounters, on many a sunny afternoon, but never with such a bold creature as this; he didn't know whether to be flattered, or amused, or to play along with the impression she clearly had of him as some brawny simpleton she could use at will. He almost chose the latter, but his pride stopped him. Instead he lowered his voice, and leaned in close as if to tell a secret.

'I have to ask,' he murmured, amused to see how she reacted to his nearness, standing rigid and raising her chin. The tables weren't precisely turned, but the direction of the teasing had shifted. 'What kind of woman comes up to a man she doesn't even know and suggests … what you've suggested?'

Nancy shifted the basket onto her arm, and stretched out

her free hand until the finger touched his hip. 'The kind who in't afraid to say what she wants.' She gave all her attention to drawing slow circles on the rough material. 'The kind who's been properly wed, and known a man's touch.' Now she raised her eyes to his again. 'Just because that man is in the ground, it don't stop her from wantin' to feel it again.'

'I'm sorry for your loss, Mrs ... Nancy,' Keir said, straightening away from her. 'But I'm sure you'll understand, this is my first day here.' He had been hoping his blunt refusal might result in her embarrassment, but she just nodded and gave him a thoughtful look.

'Then I'll come and find you tomorrow, when it in't your first day.' As her hand left his hip she let it drift across him, lingering, and a smile crossed her face as she felt the hardening shape of him beneath his trousers. 'Nice to meet you, Keir Garvey.'

He didn't reply, but as he watched her walk away across the yard he wondered if he hadn't lost his mind. The woman was beautiful, willing, and experienced ... and he had turned her away. He gave a short laugh. Anyone who knew him from his life in New Zealand would have refused to believe it. When he was safely in the stable, out of sight, he adjusted his trousers to account for the effect she had had on him,

God only knew what would happen tomorrow, but he was at least certain of one thing: this was turning out to be an interesting job after all.

Chapter Eight

The weather was turning decidedly chilly. The wind off the sea was stronger today, and Tristan slowed Bill to a walk, letting him pick his own careful way through the gorse bushes that flanked Polworra Quarry. A day's rest on Tuesday had done them both good, but this morning's gallop across the top of Caernoweth, and out to the fort, had been even better. Ambling now down the rough track that led past Wheal Furzy, he felt Bill tense beneath him at the increasingly loud noise of the tin stamps, frightening after his previously quiet life in Honiton.

'Sorry, old lad,' he murmured, 'but you have to get used to it.' He patted Bill's lathered neck in sympathy. 'Just a bit further, then we'll call in at Pencarrack and see how Teddy's getting on, what do you say?' Bill huffed and tossed his head, still skittish, but he settled down as he realised the sound was falling away behind them the further they went, and Tristan relaxed into the saddle again and loosened his grip on the reins.

They crossed the road at the top of town, and within a couple of minutes arrived at the perimeter of Pencarrack House. Tristan turned Bill to follow the walled track that led around the back of the property and once more gave him his head, and the horse gathered his muscles and loped into a canter.

A sloping strip of long grass marked the edge of the Serth Valley, and they slowed again as the pathway narrowed, bringing them closer to it. Teddy's rough translation of the name was 'head of a rocky mass', and Tristan already knew that *serth* translated as 'steep', or 'abrupt'. He rose in his stirrups and peered down the valley; devoid of the trees and shrubs that grew in abundance at bizarre angles from the two facing sides, the ground fell away steeply here, in a tumble of sharp, unforgiving granite. He shuddered. No wonder there was such a big hedge encircling Pencarrack, especially with a youngster living here.

He set his mind to remembering where he'd seen the stables on his previous visit; he had a feeling they were on the same side as the wing that housed the library and the gallery so he started for the rear gateway, but before he reached it he heard a high-pitched shout, followed by a scream of laughter, and a group of children erupted from behind the hedge. Bill gave a shrill whinny and sidestepped, and jerked his head, wrenching at the reins and sending a hot flash of friction across Tristan's palms. Then he reared, and came down again with a thump hard enough to send his startled rider sliding from the saddle.

Tristan landed with a body-numbing crack that brought his teeth together and sent a hot flow of blood into his mouth, whether from lips or tongue he had no idea. The air was driven from his lungs, and he managed a single shallow breath before he bounced over onto his back and realised he was still sliding. From the corner of his eye he saw the edge of the valley coming closer, and the memory of the rocks below sent a spike of horror through him and he jammed his heels into the ground, trying to slow his progress before gravity had its deadly way. The long grasses whipped into his face, and he was aware of a stabbing pain in his hip, but all he could think about was the sharp peaks of granite that waited to tear him to pieces.

He jerked to a sudden stop, and realised someone had seized both the back of his shirt and the upper arm nearest to it. His collar pulled tight across his throat, but he didn't care; he was moving again, with painful, short, jerking motions, but at least it was away from the edge of the valley. Whoever had caught him was joined by other small hands, high voices raised in panic, and he helped as far as he could, digging his heels harder into the ground, and pushing himself back up the slope. Then at last he was still.

He lay staring up at the sky for a minute, trying to find enough breath to speak. His left ribcage and hip were on fire … He squinted down the length of his body, dreading what he might see, but there was no blood, although the tiniest movement sent bursts of pain through him from shoulder to knee. He closed his eyes against the brightness of the sky, and listened to the youthful accusations and demands, and finally one of them said something useful.

'Go to the big 'ouse, Gerald! You'm the oldest!'

'It's 'Arry's fault, he should go!'

'I'm not supposed to be playing out!'

Tristan wanted to growl at them to stop arguing and bloody well *do* something, but he could summon neither the strength nor the breath. Somewhere close by he heard a whicker, and then a familiar velvet nose pushed itself into his limp hand.

'Good boy,' he muttered, his eyes still tightly closed. 'Good lad.'

When he awoke it was to see a stranger's face looking down at him. He couldn't feel his body, and sent a silent prayer of thanks skywards for that, before the sensations flooded back and he heard a thick groan coming from his own tight throat.

'Get on, boy. You'm gunna be all right. Nothin' broken, I don't reckon.'

'Brace yourself,' another voice warned, from somewhere on his other side. 'We'm gunna lift . . . now!'

There was a disorientating sensation of leaving solid ground and Tristan only then realised he'd already been lifted onto a blanket while unconscious, and his rescuers now gripped the makeshift stretcher by the four corners.

'Steady.' This from the man by his head. 'Slow and easy does it. Hold on, boy, you'm on yer way, now.'

The childish voices from before spoke up too, with the notable exception of one; Harry Batten had presumably made himself scarce, and with good reason.

'We're that sorry, sir!'

'We never meant no 'arm!'

'Shut up, Tory, you're the one who screamed!'

'I never! Tell him, Bobby!'

Tristan prised his eyelids open with an effort. Bill was not within his limited sphere of vision, and he tried to speak, to ask if he was all right, but the children's arguing was too loud and the swaying sensation was making him feel sick. Besides, he could still taste blood, and the side of his tongue was already swelling up.

The man by his feet spoke up. 'You there. Bring Mr MacKenzie's horse 'round the stables. And you, the Gilbert girl? Fetch the doctor up, tell him 'tis urgent. The rest of you, get off to school before I report you to your head!'

'Or Constable Couch, for trespass,' the other added in a sinister voice, and Tristan drifted away again, this time to the sound of adult chuckling.

'You were lucky,' Doctor Bartholomew said, some time later. 'By all accounts you could have been killed today.'

'So I gather,' Tristan croaked. His mouth was dry, and he gratefully accepted a glass of water, wincing as the liquid ran over his swollen tongue, but glad of the cooling sensation. Every movement hurt something, and he tried not to yelp as he leaned over to replace the glass on the bedside cabinet. But knowing nothing was broken came as a huge relief, and he told himself to stop being such a weakling.

'It'll still be painful for a good bit, yet,' the doctor cautioned. 'The shoulder will probably stiffen over time. Put a cold cloth on it once you're home, to reduce inflammation. If you can get hold of some ice, so much the better.'

Tristan nodded, knowing there was little chance of that. 'By the way, have you seen Teddy?'

'No, why?' Bartholomew began packing the unused coils of bandage back into his bag.

'Only that he's here working on some research, and I'll probably need his help to get home.'

'Research?'

'You remember I was working on your family's old journals, when I was staying in your spare room last year?'

'Yes, of course.'

'It appears there's an historical connection between your family and the Battens.'

'Hardly surprising.' Bartholomew snapped his bag shut. 'Both families have been around forever, they're bound to have crossed paths.'

'Actually the Battens haven't been around nearly as long as you'd think,' Tristan said, drawing himself carefully to a more upright position. 'And we're still uncovering the details, but if it does turn out you're related, it might help with the by-election.'

Bartholomew's interest was piqued. 'Indeed. Bring it all to me, won't you? When you've found out what it's all about?'

'We will,' Tristan promised. 'We'd only just found it when I was called to America though, so there's a long way to go.'

The door opened a crack, and Teddy poked his head around. 'All decent, old man?' he asked, his casual voice belied by the concern on his face. 'How is he, doctor?'

'No broken bones. A slight sprain to the ankle, some bruising to the hip and ribs.'

'And an evil mark on his neck,' Teddy noted, frowning.

'Comes of being dragged by the collar,' Tristan said, 'but I'd rather that than the alternative. Have you seen that valley wall?' He stood up shakily, favouring his left leg, and accepted help to slip his shirt back on after Bartholomew's examination. His fingers refused to function on the buttons, and when he looked at his right hand he saw the welt left by the snapping, sliding rein, and sighed.

'Poor old Bill.'

'He can stay in our stable as long as he likes,' Lucy said. She'd followed Teddy, but waited outside the room until Tristan was clothed. 'You're the poor old thing, Tristan. How's the pain?'

'Pretty impressive, as far as pain goes,' Tristan said with a wry smile. It was a relief to be up and about again, boosted by the knowledge of his close escape. The thought of those rocks still made his stomach churn. 'I'll see if Anna's cousin wouldn't mind fetching Bill, if that's all right? He's used to horses.'

'Of course.' Lucy patted his good arm. 'Collings is waiting to drive you home.'

'It's not far,' he protested, but half-heartedly; he could feel a sweat popping up along his brow already, and any weight at all on his left foot made him want to sit down again and stay there.

'It's far enough,' Bartholomew said. 'You're still in shock, I'd advise you to accept the help that's offered. I'll drop a pair of crutches around this evening, as soon as I get back home. You'll only want them for a day or two.'

'How's the research going?' Tristan asked Teddy, mostly to take his mind off the urge to lie down, or vomit, or both.

Teddy looked from him to the doctor, and his voice was hesitant. 'It's . . . ticking along quite nicely.'

'Boys,' Lucy spoke up. 'You can discuss this later, surely? Collings is waiting with the motor.'

'Has anyone spoken to Freya?' Tristan asked, accepting Teddy's supporting hand beneath his elbow.

'Not unless one of those blasted children told her,' the doctor said, then his frown cleared. 'How's Mrs Penhaligon going on, by the way?'

'Quite well, I think.'

'She must have only a couple of months left before her confinement.'

Tristan blew out a breath, and it carried a tiny sound of discomfort. Even talking was starting to become a struggle. 'Yes.'

'When her time's due, Mrs Gale will be pleased to help.'

'Yes.'

'I mean, with her history—'

'Doctor!' Lucy took his arm and steered him towards the door. 'Do let him go, there's a dear. We'll be sure to pass on your kindest regards to Anna, and we'll take care of Tristan, but you've said yourself he ought to go home now.'

'I suppose you'll want to be waited on, hand and foot,' Teddy grumbled to Tristan.

'Of course.'

Teddy shook his head. 'Some people will do anything to avoid washing the dishes.'

Settled in the back of Charles Batten's Silver Ghost, Tristan stole a sidelong glance at Teddy, and saw he was still troubled.

'If you're thinking about what happened to Caroline, you needn't. This isn't the same.'

'No, not that. Though having said that, only by the grace of the Almighty. Tristan, you really ought to be more—'

'Then are you worried about sharing what we've found with Bartholomew?'

Teddy was silent for a moment, then he sighed. 'You promised Freya you wouldn't.'

'No,' Tristan pointed out, 'I promised her I wouldn't *publish*. She knows I still want to get at the full story. Don't you think the doctor deserves to know, if anyone does?'

'And what if *he* decides to publish it? Writes a memoir or some such thing? Especially if he's elected to Parliament.'

'I very much doubt he'll do that.' Tristan winced as the car rolled over a bump, and, suddenly aware who was driving them, he gave Teddy a warning look. 'We'll discuss it at home.'

His entire left side, from neck to ankle, ached abominably, and he dreaded the moment when the car stopped at Priddy Lane and he'd be forced to move. They slowed at the junction, above which towered the statue of Malcolm Penworthy, and Collings peered down the narrow lane on their right with a frown.

'Can I drive right through?'

'No,' Tristan said, 'the road turns into a grassy mud bath just past the houses, and ends at the school. But it's all right, we'll walk from here, thank you.'

He and Teddy climbed from the car and watched, with occasional flinches and indrawn breaths, as Collings finally managed to turn the Silver Ghost around at the widest part of the road. He barely missed clipping the memorial as he went, but as far as Tristan was concerned it would be only fitting to see the whole bloody thing brought down.

'Come on, old man,' Teddy said. 'Let's get you indoors.'

'Will you go and see Freya for me? And talk to Mr Garvey about collecting Bill?'

'Are you trying to avoid discussing what Bartholomew should and shouldn't be told?'

'Maybe.' Tristan swallowed. 'I feel a bit ill, to be honest. We will talk about it later though, I promise.'

But even as Teddy helped him down the lane, and then settled him with a cold wet cloth and a cup of tea, his mind picked over the discoveries they had made about Malcolm Penworthy; how the dark side of his story was caught up in the violent and unlawful death of young Sarah Trevellick ... And how that had only been the beginning.

* * *

Lucy watched her father's car out of sight before going back into the house. Dorothy was coming out of the sitting room, her face a study in deep thought, but when she caught sight of Lucy the distracted look was replaced by a cross one.

'That school matron needs disciplining; she's obviously no good at spotting malingerers. Poorly indeed! Harry should never have been allowed home, he must have sneaked out the minute he arrived.'

'Probably.'

'Well he's not to leave the house again until after the date his school term would have ended. Please see to it he knows that.'

Lucy almost pointed out yet again that she was neither parent nor nanny, but in the end she just nodded. 'I'll try.'

'On another subject, did you say you and Mr Fry had a walk-out?'

'Why do you keep ... No I didn't. Why?'

'Father's going to send for him.' Dorothy shook her head. 'Thank goodness *he's* home. Relying on Hugh has been even more tiresome than facing Mr Pagett's indifference.'

'Tiresome? He's your brother, not your employee!'

'You must have noticed his antics are becoming all the talk, and for the worst possible reasons.'

'What antics?'

Dorothy sighed. 'You're spending all your free time with that research bloke these days, instead of your real friends, or you'd know. At Mr Boden's stag party, your brother got outrageously—'

'*My* brother?'

'—outrageously drunk, and was sick on the stairs, after which he passed out, as you suspected, in one of his friends' rooms.'

'I assume you found him though, in time for your meeting with Mr Pagett?'

'I did. He stood there looking green, and barely spoke a word.'

'Which is as you like it,' Lucy observed, 'otherwise how would you get your own words in?' She turned to go upstairs. 'Honestly, Dorothy, you are horrid to him. Leave him alone.'

'And last night,' Dorothy went on, raising her voice, 'he spent the evening playing card games with that same bunch of idiots, and lost jolly nearly his entire month's allowance.'

Lucy stopped. 'As you say, *his* allowance.'

'He's becoming unmanageable.'

'Don't be so bossy. You're not his mother.'

'You asked for details,' Dorothy pointed out. 'I merely said he was being tiresome.'

Lucy shook her head and continued up towards the gallery, but Dorothy's exasperated voice stopped her in her tracks again. 'If Hugh isn't careful, Father's going to have to come down *very* hard on him, and then where will that leave him?'

'Precisely where he is now!' The angry words were out before Lucy could stop them, and Dorothy quickly joined her on the staircase.

'What's that supposed to mean?'

'Never mind.'

'Lucy!'

'All right!' Lucy glared. 'I promised I'd say nothing, but the fact is, Hugh knows he's not going to inherit Pencarrack. That you're getting it all.' She watched her sister carefully, hoping to see some sign of surprise, but there was only a faint flush on Dorothy's otherwise expressionless face.

'Does he indeed?'

'So he's got nothing to lose, has he? Why shouldn't he drown his sorrows?'

'Because he's still a Batten, that's why.'

'Why *are* you getting it all?' Lucy asked. 'I mean, I know you work hard and everything, but why is Father throwing Hugh over like this?'

'Hugh has no interest whatsoever in the mines, or any of our other enterprises.'

'He was ready to learn! That's how he discovered the truth, by going through the things in the library.'

'I've been working with Father since Harry was born,' Dorothy reminded her. 'Hugh deciding now that he might have a little snoop around, and satisfy his curiosity, is just insulting. He shouldn't have assumed he'd inherit just because he's male.'

'He didn't assume. I've heard Father say it myself. Was that simply to keep Hugh on the straight and narrow?'

'It's worked until now,' Dorothy said coolly. Then she sighed. 'Look, it's not as awful as all that. He'll still have plenty of money, and he'll get properties on the estate.'

'Can you imagine how humiliated he's going to be when it becomes public?' Lucy shook her head. 'My best guess is that he's hoping people will think Father has disinherited him because of bad behaviour, rather than because of you worming your spiteful, selfish way into the business and pushing him out.'

Dorothy hesitated. 'If I tell you something, you must promise to keep it to yourself.'

'All right.'

'I mean it!' Dorothy grabbed at Lucy's arm. 'You *have* to keep this secret better than you kept Hugh's. I'm not even certain that telling you is the sensible thing, but it might help you to understand.'

'All right!'

'Not here. Come to my room.' Dorothy pushed past her, and led the way up the stairs. Lucy followed, her heart tripping uncomfortably fast; little secrets had a way of becoming big, festering ones, and she wasn't sure she wanted to hear this one after all.

Dorothy seemed to have gathered herself by the time she ushered Lucy into her room and closed the door. Unlike Lucy's own bedroom, this one was more like an office; the dressing table held only the barest hint of femininity; a silver hairbrush and mirror set, a few hairpins pushed into a neat pile, a single spray-bottle of perfume. The rest of the space was taken up with notebooks and pens, and an ink pot stood where Lucy might have expected to see a jewellery box. Dorothy had never been one for adornment beyond the necessary, even in her wilder days.

'Well?' Lucy sat down and folded her arms.

'You must promise not to tell Hugh,' Dorothy insisted.

Lucy faltered, on the verge of speaking her mind, and possibly ruining her sister's willingness to impart a confidence. 'All right,' she said reluctantly. 'I promise.'

Dorothy sat on her bed, laced her hands together on her lap, and took a deep breath. 'The thing is, Father has, for some time now, had doubts. About Hugh.'

'Yes, but he'd soon have settled—'

'Not about his suitability. About . . . his parentage.'

Lucy couldn't think of a single thing to say, but the silence swelled between them until she had to speak. 'Doubts? What kind of doubts? Why?'

'It's not my story to tell.'

'Story!' Lucy stood up, too agitated to sit still. 'This isn't a play! You're talking about our brother! And, and . . . Our *mother*!'

Dorothy winced. 'Hush! Do you think that hasn't gone through my mind a hundred times?' She rose too, and went to the window to stare down over the valley. 'I had no idea either, and I only recently discovered Father had changed his will. Of *course* I pummelled him for a reason!'

Lucy made a sceptical sound. 'And he told you Mother had been unfaithful?'

'Yes.'

'Did he say who with?'

Dorothy shook her head. 'I didn't ask. He was too distraught, even after all that time.'

'But he's certain enough that *you're* his child.' Lucy hadn't meant to sound quite so scathing, but Dorothy's lips tightened.

'I think that's obvious. And Harry will, of course, inherit from me one day, which will put everything back in order.'

'If that's his aim, why doesn't he leave it all to Harry right away?'

'Oh, you can be sure he tried that.' Dorothy gave her a tight smile. 'But he needs someone to run it, not merely own it. As I pointed out to him.'

Despite everything, Lucy felt a trace of admiration. Dorothy would have countered Father's suggestion with a hard-nosed one of her own, and there would have been no getting out of it; if Charles Batten wanted the family business to go to his only certain male heir, it would first have to go through that boy's mother.

'So you'll keep your promise after all then?' Dorothy said.

'What do you mean, *after all*?'

'Oh, Lucy. Do you really think I can't read you like one of those books you and Kempton are so obsessed with? You had no intention of keeping anything from Hugh!'

'But you told me anyway.'

'I thought, once you heard the truth, you'd understand why it would be cruel to tell him. After all, no one's certain, and he could very well be as much a Batten as you and I.'

'But Father couldn't take the risk.'

'Quite so.'

Lucy sighed and held out a hand to Dorothy. 'I'll keep the promise.' This time she meant it.

Dorothy shook her hand, firmly, but with an unusually affectionate squeeze. 'You're far more sensible than you let on. I know I can trust you.'

'For Hugh's sake,' Lucy clarified. 'And you have to promise to stop being beastly to him. And,' she added quickly, 'don't let Father know both his secrets are out, whatever you do.'

'I won't.'

Lucy went to the gallery, hoping to immerse herself in taking notes from the book Teddy had left for her, but, still distracted by this startling revelation she only spent one or two minutes glancing over the passages he had marked, before making her way back to her own room. As she crossed the top of the stairs again she looked down into the hall, and saw Dorothy moving, with urgent steps, towards the library. She watched, open-mouthed and betrayed, as Dorothy's voice wafted up the stairs. 'Father? I'm glad you're still here. There's something you ought to know.'

Chapter Nine

The Tinner's Arms

Teddy's early appearance in the pub, particularly without Tristan, came as a surprise. He looked tired and drawn, and his usual open, friendly face was pale.

'Whatever's the matter?' Anna said in alarm. 'Do you need to sit down a minute?'

'No. Thank you,' he said. 'I was hoping you could tell me where to find your cousin.'

'He's working at Priddy Farm.' Anna peered at him closely. 'Has something happened?'

'Yes, but I'm led to understand I'm worrying over nothing.'

'You'll have to be more precise than that,' Anna said, cautiously relieved. 'I've never learned the art of mind-reading.'

'Tristan's had a spill.'

'A spill?'

'As I understand it there was a bit of . . . rather rambunctious play between some of the local children, up at Pencarrack, and Bill was a bit startled by it. Freya's gone down to the cottage now, but she's asked if you wouldn't mind covering the shop for a short time.'

'Of course. I'll go now. Why were you asking after Keir?'

'I need to arrange to collect Bill from the Pencarrack stables.'

'Well he'll be working just now, and won't be able to do anything. You can tell Freya we'll make arrangements for the horse later, and that she's not to worry.'

Teddy thanked her and left, and Anna went in search of Esther, and found her rummaging in the cupboard under the stairs. 'I'm going up to the shop,' she said. 'Freya's had to— Whatever are you looking for?'

'Little Nippers,' Esther said, from the depths of the cupboard. 'Joe did put some in 'ere last summer.'

'Little what?'

Esther emerged backwards, blowing a stray lock of wispy grey hair from her eyes. 'Mousetraps.'

Anna pulled a face. 'We've mice in here? I thought Arric kept them at bay.'

'He've gone wanderin',' Esther said glumly. 'Most likely he'll be back, when he'm bored, but in the meantime it's up to us, and I'm jiggered if I can find they traps.'

'I'll have a search around at home, see if we've got any.' Matthew and James had brought down all manner of junk from the attic, before the conversion had begun; it was in the stone-built outhouse in the back garden now, but there might be something useful there.

'Maybe we'll get Ripper at the next guild meetin',' Esther muttered, sounding doubtful. A recent widow herself, she had taken a great deal of persuading to join the Widows' Guild, but the ever-persistent Ellen had finally convinced her to swallow her pride. It occurred to Anna now that it had been too long since she and Ellen had sat down together just to chat, busy as they both were, and if Anna went down to visit her she might even pick up some tips at the same time, since Ellen was in regular need of Ripper herself. The thought of having to take the infamous mouser into her property gave Anna the shudders, but it might be the only answer; the hens would not react well to having vermin scurrying around the houses, and they might stop laying altogether.

Penhaligon's Attic was predictably quiet that afternoon, but as Anna glanced idly through the ledger she was pleased to see an encouraging list of orders, largely from schools; the extra money would be useful when the baby came.

'You're not to go expecting riches and treats,' she cautioned her bump, out loud. 'Milk for as long as I'm able, then bread and water until you're at least twenty.' She smoothed her hand over her stomach, feeling a little push in response, and smiled. 'All right, maybe you can have butter on your bread at Christmas.'

'Oh!' With the door open to let in the freshening spring breeze, Isabel had stepped quietly into the shop unnoticed. 'I'm so sorry to disturb you, I was expecting Freya.'

'She's had to go out.' Anna told her of Tristan's accident, and Isabel frowned.

'But he's a practised horseman, surely? How did it happen?'

'Apparently some children were playing up by Pencarrack, with the lad who lives there. You remember I told you about him?'

'Yes, I remember. But he is home from school already? I thought you said it would be Easter.'

'Teddy tells me he came home early, due to some kind of illness.'

Isabel looked alarmed. 'Illness?'

'Don't worry,' Anna said, faintly amused at the strong reaction, 'it was one of those magical illnesses that miraculously disappears once the child is allowed home.'

'That is good.' Isabel relaxed. 'I hate to hear of sick children. Ever since Freya, you know ... And of course Matthew's poor little sister.'

Anna could have kicked herself. 'Yes, of course. Anyway, I think the children just startled Tristan's horse, they meant no harm by it.'

'I see.' Isabel looked around, clearly wanting to stay and wait for Freya, but reluctant to invite herself. The thought of sitting down and making idle, polite conversation with Matthew's former lover held no stronger appeal now than it had a week ago, but Anna had a better idea.

'Would you think it awfully rude of me to ask a small favour of you, since you're here?'

Isabel glanced at the door, the instinctive, wistful turn towards escape, before manners reasserted themselves. 'Not at all, I'd be pleased to help.'

'Would you mind watching the shop for a few minutes? I wanted to search for something in the outhouse, while we have the light. I'll not be long.'

Isabel's smile was one of unmistakeable relief. 'Of course, take as long as you must.'

*

Everything from the attic had been put into the outhouse in a hurry, once work converting the attic had begun, but from what Anna could remember the fastidious James had curtailed Matthew's tendency to simply throw it all in there and be damned. As a result, things should be stacked reasonably neatly, and it shouldn't take too much time to search.

She pulled open the door and sighed. Matthew's impatience had evidently won out after all, towards the end of the job; the smaller items, which were all he could manage one-handed, had started off being stacked neatly, but the ones closest to the top were placed haphazardly and likely to tumble the moment she moved anything. Except one box.

It stood to one side of the messiest pile, and as a result it drew Anna's eye as she blinked against the task ahead. Eager to put off rummaging in this mess for a moment, at least, she reached for the smallish box, and saw why it had been placed more carefully than the rest; printed across the box's lid in smudged charcoal, was 'Grace'. The hand was as neat as the writing on the side of the *Lady Penhaligon*, not Robert's usual hurried scrawl. Written with love.

Anna lifted the lid. Inside were a few letters, bound in blue ribbon; a shawl; a hairbrush; a small jewellery-box; and something soft, wrapped in thin paper. Anna peeled the paper away and caught her breath; it was a christening gown, in beautiful ivory silk. Her first thought was that it was Matthew's, and that they might use it for their own child, then she hesitated. It was quite likely to have been more recently used for his little sister. Anna replaced the lid thoughtfully, and put the box back where she'd found it. The last thing she wanted to do, now that life had settled down, was raise sad memories.

After a further search, during which she knocked over a pile of books, and twisted her ankle trying to avoid breaking a grubby floral ewer and bowl set, Anna finally unearthed two dusty, but thankfully unused, spring-loaded mousetraps. She put them into her apron pocket, brushed down her cobwebby skirts and prepared to leave the outhouse, but her attention was pulled back to Grace Penhaligon's rather sad little box of personal effects, and she lifted it down again – she could always talk to Freya first, and test the waters, before broaching the subject with Matthew.

Isabel had decided against waiting after all. 'I think Freya will be busy for quite some while, looking after her young man,' she said. 'I will call in later this evening instead, and hope to catch her then. What did you find?' She nodded at the box Anna had left on the counter.

'A few bits and pieces. Nothing of importance.' Anna had no wish to revive any memories of their happier days as a young family, nor to be reminded again of how much longer Isabel had known the Penhaligon family. Isabel eyed her thoughtfully, but pulled on her gloves and left without questioning further.

Mairead came in from work shortly afterwards, looking more tired than usual. She perked up as her gaze too fell on the counter. 'What's in the box?'

Anna opened it. 'Some of Matthew's mother's things. I want to ask him if he'd mind us using this beautiful christening gown for our own little one. Isn't it gorgeous?' She lifted out the paper-wrapped garment, but Mairead leaned forward.

'What about that velvet box, what's in there?'

'Some of Grace's jewellery, I assume.' Anna unwrapped the gown and laid it on the counter. 'What do you think?'

'Very pretty.' Mairead sounded doubtful, and when Anna waited, she sighed. 'You haven't even thought about the fact that you're a Catholic and he's a Wesleyan, have you?'

'Of course I have. But I've not been devout since before you were born, and with all the secrets this family's holding on to I can't see one more would make a difference. Accepted into the church, is accepted into the church.'

'All right, so.' Mairead shrugged. 'It's a pretty gown, anyway. Was it his, do you think, or Freya's?'

'I hadn't even thought it might be Freya's.' Now Anna was doubly glad she hadn't shown Isabel. 'I'd thought it might have been his wee sister's though.'

'Now you mention it, that's more likely. I'd be surprised if Freya's even baptised.'

'What makes you say that?' Anna began folding the paper gently around the christening gown again.

'Isabel's Spanish, so she's almost sure to be Catholic, and when the subject of inter-faith baptism came up, can you honestly see *that* woman giving in?'

'Like me, you mean?' Anna's voice tightened.

Mairead shook her head. 'You're not giving in either, you're doing what's best for your family. Whatever you or I believe, or don't believe, isn't important.'

Anna subsided. 'You're right. Look, my emotions are bouncing around all over the place, let's just get tea started, shall we? I can ask Matthew about the gown and the jewellery box later.'

'The box will be for Freya anyway, won't it?' Mairead threw over her shoulder as she went to the kitchen. 'Grandmothers always like to pass on their jewellery. Aunt Oonagh said she'll leave me her emerald set when she goes.'

Anna flinched. 'There's no need to be so blunt about it.' She put the gown back in the box, and replaced the lid. 'How was school today, anyway?'

'It went well enough. A couple of the older ones were pushing their luck a little. And your friend's boy, Eddie Scoble, caused something of a stir.'

Anna put the box under the counter, and followed her to the kitchen. 'A stir?'

'He fell asleep right there at his desk. The others thought it was hilarious.'

'They would,' Anna agreed. 'But are you sure he wasn't messing around? Trying to make his friends laugh?'

'Quite sure. He'd the dribble on his chin and everything. When he woke up he didn't know where he was. Got quite upset to find the others poking fun, I found him fighting one of the other lads over it after lunch.'

'That doesn't sound like Eddie.' Anna sat at the table with a little grunt of discomfort, and poured milk into her cup. 'Has he done it before?'

'It's only my third day,' Mairead pointed out. 'But the headmaster seemed surprised to see him when I took them both along to his room. Not at all surprised about Bertie Gale though, he seems to be going the way of his older brother.'

Anna thought about Susan Gale. 'I don't know the mother that well, but looking at the grandmother . . . ' Then she heard herself, and shook her head. 'And hark at me, gossiping away just like her.'

'You're a real Caernoweth resident now,' Mairead said, and although she smiled, Anna couldn't ignore a twinge of unease; to be a real resident of the town was one thing, but there were

136

better examples to follow, and if she wanted to continue to keep her family safe she would be wise to remember that.

* * *

No. 5 Priddy Lane

Freya wrung the last of the water out of the cloth, before handing it to Tristan to replace the rapidly drying one tucked beneath his shirt. 'I'll have to go soon, they'll be waiting tea. But I'll try and come down before breakfast.'

'I'll keep an eye on him,' Teddy promised.

'I'll be all right by tomorrow,' Tristan said. He was looking a great deal better already, the colour had returned to his face, and although he still winced when he moved, he was smiling more readily, and his breathing was quite normal. 'I considered writing to Sophie and inviting her down next week. What do you think?'

Freya's heart sank. 'So soon?'

'I thought the sooner the better. Give her less time to build up the wrong picture of Caernoweth in her head. Once she sees the town, and gets to know you properly, she'll love you almost as much as I do.'

Freya couldn't help a smile at that, and Tristan pressed his advantage. 'Besides, some help with Bill would be useful since I won't be riding for a week or two.'

'Well I can't argue with that, can I?' Freya sighed. Then she relented. 'I'm sorry, you're right. She can't stay here with you and Teddy though, so tell her she's welcome to stay at

Penhaligon's Attic. She can have my room, and I'll bunk in with Mairead for a few days.'

'Thank you, darling.' Tristan drew her close for a kiss. 'You'll see, the two of you will be firm friends before you know it. I'll tell her to come on Monday.'

'In the meantime, don't try to do too much,' Freya fixed him with a stern look. 'How are things going anyway, with the journals?'

There was no answer, but a quick glance passed between the two men and Freya frowned. 'When you left for America you were about to tell me something important. I think you ought to tell me now.'

'Come on, old man,' Teddy prompted gently.

'Yes, old man, come on,' Freya said, only half-joking. 'I can see you've found something, and if it concerns Anna, it concerns me.'

'We have.' Tristan sighed, and shifted in his seat. 'You'd better sit down for a few minutes.' He waited until Freya had dragged a chair over beside him. 'You knew about Malcolm Penworthy's ... passion for the Trevellick girl?'

'Sarah, the healer, yes.'

'Bartholomew's diary says Sarah was treating Penworthy at Bartholomew's cottage.'

'Sarah's brother would usually come with her,' Teddy put in. 'He'd wait by the gate until she'd finished, then walk her home again. But that particular night he'd been called to someone else's aid. He planned to return via Bartholomew's house to collect Sarah, but instead he was arrested by Penworthy and falsely accused of murder.'

'Falsely?'

'It appears Penworthy pushed himself on the girl more forcefully than usual, and she'd fought back. Somehow or other, she died. We don't know how.'

'Bartholomew heard it happen, and when he went outside to find Penworthy,' Tristan's voice was loaded with disgust, 'he had been trying to dig a hole.'

'Oh, the poor girl.'

'Sebastian interrupted him, and once Penworthy instigated the arrest he was hanged within the week.'

Freya was unable to sit still any longer, and she rose to pace the room. 'But the Trevellicks were persecuted for centuries after that. They lost everything!'

'That isn't all we've found,' Teddy said. 'Bartholomew took his own life shortly afterwards, and we think Pencarrack House was gifted to his son, Daniel. A much smaller place back in those days, of course.'

'Why his son?'

'Bartholomew was blinded at the battle of Stratton Hill, remember? The later diaries were dictated through Daniel, and it's reasonable to suppose that, after the death of his father, the boy went to Penworthy with what he knew.'

But Freya couldn't fathom it. 'Why on earth would the man get his son to note all this down? You'd think he'd have wanted to keep it secret as much as Penworthy did. That he'd have carried it to his grave.'

'We wondered the same,' Tristan said. 'But having talked about it we think it was probably some form of insurance. Penworthy didn't know about the diaries at that point. Bartholomew would have wanted his son to have had some protection, and so armed him with everything he knew.'

'And Penworthy gave him a house? It doesn't make any sense.'

'Ostensibly in recompense for Blind John's death, the last act of kindness for an old friend. All perfectly innocent, and even rather touching. I'm sure the title deeds will bear that out. In reality, it was protection for Penworthy.'

Teddy spoke up again. 'The name Batten derives from Bartholomew, when you follow it right back, via the name Battle, which is quite ... ' Catching himself wandering off into one of his favourite topics, he waved the details away. 'The point is, the very first Pencarrack journal was penned by someone named D. Batten.'

'And the transfer deed would tell you that the "D" was Daniel?'

Teddy nodded. 'But Daniel was, and is, a very common name, so that in itself proves nothing. We would need something solid that links the two families, to be certain, but the handwriting is uncannily similar.'

'That's what I was going to tell you,' Tristan added, 'just before I got the letter from Catherine that Father needed me in Vermont. It's enough to link them in *our* minds, but not quite enough to make it official.'

'We know Penworthy was also wounded at Stratton Hill,' Teddy went on, 'so in his business he'd have welcomed someone with a steady hand, a strong back, and a proven instinct for keeping quiet.'

Freya looked from one to the other. 'So Daniel worked for Penworthy as what, a foreman? A farm manager? What *was* Penworthy's business?'

Tristan hesitated. 'You know the reputation Cornwall has earned, particularly during the seventeenth century.'

'Smuggling?'

'Not only that.' His face betrayed his reluctance, but he went on. 'In 1646 Batten noted that one of his first tasks was to organise a gathering down on the shore, around the headland from Porthstennack. It was just after the last Royalist stronghold had fallen, and the event was in honour of the men who'd fought and died for the king. Over a hundred people gathered, and were fed and entertained at Penworthy's expense.'

'That sounds like the act of a generous man.'

'And so he was. No one's disputing that. He himself didn't stay beyond the toast to the king, it seems he wanted them all to relax. What do you know of Barbary pirates?'

His question was so unexpected that Freya just looked blankly at him for a moment. 'Pirates? Like the privateers?'

'No. Nor like the jolly souls gallivanting all over the stage, singing about Modern Major Generals.' Tristan's voice turned hard. 'I'm talking about slavers.' Jolted as much by his tone as by his words, Freya still stared at him, mute. 'For instance,' he went on, 'back in 1645, hundreds of men, women and children were stolen from along the Cornish coast and shipped off to Africa. And that wasn't anywhere near the first time, nor the last.' He held up a hand. 'It's well documented, and part of what I was going to be investigating before I even heard about the books you'd been given.'

Freya's own voice came out barely more than a whisper. 'And this gathering you were talking about, at Porthstennack, the year after?'

'Out of all those people, only around twenty remained on the beach by the end of that night. Entire families were missing. I already knew that much, from previous research, I just hadn't connected it to Malcolm Penworthy at that point.'

'Are you saying *all* those people were captured and stolen away, in one night? How could someone as well known as Penworthy get away with such a thing as that?'

'With a good deal of co-operation, by keeping himself out of the way, and by holding himself above reproach by everyone. Who would suspect him, when he gifted the survivors with the deeds to their homes?'

'It says as much in the journal,' Teddy put in quietly. 'Penworthy was so convincingly devastated that even Batten himself questioned it for a long time. But we're reaching the part in the journals now where his mind is starting to wander. He's expressing guilt without direction. Remorse with no focus. He's keeping his secrets so far, but they're certainly affecting his mind.'

'Can't you read ahead, and find the answers sooner?'

Tristan shrugged. 'What would be the point? We can't change any of it.'

'Besides,' Teddy said, 'anything of this nature should be read in sequence. What we think we know will always colour the way we interpret what we read.'

'In this case it was helpful, to a point,' Tristan admitted. 'I knew about the other attacks, so when I read all this veiled nonsense Batten has written, I could see through it to what it meant.'

Teddy nodded. 'But if we let impatience get the better of us we could easily deduce a wrong conclusion from some later comment. The context might have changed, or anything.'

'I'm certain the truth, about Batten at least, will out before we're much farther in,' Tristan added. 'And it's likely your ancestors were victims, just as Anna's was the perpetrator.'

'Penhaligon's Attic has been in my grandmother's family for generations,' Freya said slowly. 'We always assumed the land was bought fair and square. Do you think it might actually have been given to them by Penworthy?'

'Stephen Penhaligon was a friend of Bartholomew's, and probably of his son's too, so it's likely. Particularly as Stephen died fighting alongside him. Unfortunately that means it's also likely other members of your family were sold overseas.'

Freya stared in dismay. 'Then those who were left benefited from what happened. From Penworthy's crimes. My home and my business are as tainted as Pencarrack House.'

Tristan took her hand and squeezed it. 'It's not tainted at all. Your family weren't to blame for taking some compensation for the dreadful things that had happened to them. They were owed it.'

'But would he have earned enough money by selling slaves, to make it worthwhile giving up all that rent, and others besides?'

'Without a doubt,' Teddy said. 'It wasn't just that one incident, the journals are full of them. There was also the more recognised version of smuggling, of course, there are references to "tasks" and "undertakings", from the Lizard up as far as Trethkellis. And there's a place just along from the fort, where a small boat can come ashore in relative safety at low tide. A few trips before the tide turns, and no one's any the wiser but Penworthy's a lot richer.'

'And so is Batten,' Tristan added.

'On what?'

'Rum, tobacco, silks. All kinds of things. And people, of course. Young Batten seems as obsessed with keeping an accurate diary as his father was. As I said, much of it is disguised as legitimate business, but once you've chipped through the surface language it's staring you in the face.'

Freya shook her head. 'If you do find the two families are connected, what will you do?'

'The Battens probably already know where their wealth came from, but Doctor Bartholomew has a right to learn the truth, too. Smuggling's one thing, but illegal slavers are something else entirely.'

'But there's no sense in burdening him, surely?' Freya removed her hand from his, disappointed in his reply though not surprised, and crossed to stare out of the window.

'He already knows there might be a link between the two families,' Tristan pointed out. He asked me to tell him what we find out. And since he's standing in the by-election, that connection might be helpful. No one else would know it's a *bad* thing that joins them.'

'We'd know. And so would he. And if it gets out—'

'It won't.'

'What about Lucy? She's helping with the notes, isn't she?' Freya turned to Teddy. 'She might let something slip.'

Teddy's jaw tightened and he wouldn't look at Tristan. 'I've been giving her harmless passages to transcribe,' he said, with a discernible edge to his voice. 'Household accounts, dinners, social engagements, land acquisitions. That type of thing.'

'So you've been using her, but lying to her.'

'No!' Tristan glared at Teddy, this was clearly a source of tension between them too. 'It's all still valuable information on our social history, things that people will want to read about. Freya, we've talked about this. I don't want to go back to that tired old argument, but please . . . can we just accept that I *have* to find out what truly happened? Uncovering the past is my job. More than that, it's my passion.'

'I know.'

He tried to rise, to go to her, but his muscles had evidently stiffened through sitting, and he slumped back in his chair.

Freya hurried back to his side. 'Keep still, you idiot!' She sat on the arm of his chair and took his hand. 'Look, for a historian I just don't think you fully understand the pride this town takes in its heritage.'

'I'm starting to,' he muttered, and shifted in his seat. 'You still have my word, I won't publish any of these findings.'

Freya replaced his hand on the arm rest, and rose to go home. 'Good.'

'But if Bartholomew asks again, I'm telling him.'

'Even if it destroys him?'

'It won't.'

'I hope you're right,' she said, studying him thoughtfully. 'And I hope you know a lot more than I think you do.'

* * *

Pencarrack House

The library clock seemed to be getting louder the longer the silence went on. James eyed the two people in front of him, fighting the urge to speak first; Charles Batten had been the one to summon him here, let him state his reasons. So far the man had simply gestured to a chair, then he and his daughter had both retreated behind the large desk and, ever since, Charles had been engrossed in reading something. Dorothy had occupied herself staring at the desk top. Extremely rude, both of them, James decided. Well, he wasn't putting up with this kind of treatment.

Just as he was about to declare his annoyance and take his leave, Charles Batten replaced the paperwork he'd been studying, and finally gave his guest his attention. 'You have your credentials, I take it?'

James blinked. 'Credentials? No, the letter didn't say anything about that. Mr Batten, why did you ask me here? I'm a busy man.' His own firmness surprised him, but he had to keep reminding himself that the Battens were not rulers over him or his home. He owed them nothing.

His tone seemed to take Charles aback too, and he coloured a little, but whether through embarrassment or anger it was impossible to tell. His manner was as quiet and understated as ever, and his tone was measured. 'I asked you here on the recommendation of Miss Batten,' he gestured to his daughter, 'who tells me you trained in your craft under a noted architect in Dorset.'

'Yes, Richard Shaw. I worked under him at Bryanston House as a stone mason, then as an apprentice architect.' James's heart began to beat faster, but he managed to keep the sudden excitement out of his voice. 'Why do you ask?'

'I have a position opening up, Mr Fry. Not as an architect, you understand, but an overseer of building work.'

'I see.' James automatically glanced around the room in which they sat, but Charles shook his head.

146

'Not part of the Pencarrack Estate. A new project, in alliance with Pagetts. You have heard of them?'

'Of course. They're becoming quite a name in the development of hotels.'

'Quite so. Together we have purchased the remains of the old fort overlooking the cliff.'

James kept his voice calm. 'Go on.' From the moment of his return to Porthstennack he had dreamed of working on such a project, and he made a mental note to curb any further displays of irritation in case it jeopardised anything.

'The plans are drawn up,' Charles warned again, 'so, to be clear, you would not be contributing in any creative way to what's already been decided. You would simply be the eyes and ears of the architect already hired by Pagett. And my eyes and ears also, of course.'

Dorothy shifted slightly in her seat. The tiniest of movements, but it drew Charles's eye. 'I mean *ours*.'

James eyed Dorothy with fresh interest; he knew she had a hand in the management of various other Batten concerns, such as Wheal Furzy and Polworra, but it seemed she was involved in Caernoweth Fort, too. For a split second he thought about bestowing his most brilliant smile on her, but decided it would do more harm than good; she was not someone to be swayed by overt flattery, he remembered that from their youth.

'It's very good of you to consider me for the position,' he said, now alternating his gaze between both Battens equally. 'I assume it's dependent on my written credentials?'

'Naturally,' Charles said, gathering papers together in readiness for the end of this short meeting. 'You can bring them this afternoon. Leave them with the housekeeper, and we'll write to you when we've made our decision.'

'I'm afraid I don't have them.' James hoped his desperation wasn't apparent. 'I've sent them to Edwin Lutyens in support of an application to work for him.'

'Work for him where?'

'He's building a castle in Devon. I'm expecting to hear any day now, whether or not I've been successful, along with the return of my references and a personal letter from Charles Trubshaw.'

James hadn't intended his explanation to sound like a bargaining speech, but Batten and his daughter exchanged a frown.

'And is that position in your preferred field of architecture?' Dorothy asked, getting right to the heart of it.

'No, Miss Batten. But as I said, I'm also a trained stone mason. I hope to be taken on in some capacity of that nature.'

'Would you accept that position over this one, if you were given this opportunity?'

'It would depend on which terms are more favourable.' James could hardly believe he was speaking those words aloud, after spending so long fighting to keep his father's business going. The money he'd made from the sale of the *Pride of Porthstennack* was running out fast now, and here was a lifeline, but was it a strong enough one to risk passing up work at Castle Drogo?

Abruptly worried his confidence was taking him down a rapidly narrowing path, he backed up a little. 'If I were lucky enough to be given the choice, I would naturally prefer to stay in town.'

'Naturally?' Dorothy sat forward. 'I would have expected someone who's had a taste of the wider world to be quite keen to further expand their horizons. You must have wanted that once.'

'It's different now,' James said quietly. 'I have ... friends here. I didn't, then.'

'What about family?'

'I had only my father. He encouraged me to accept the apprenticeship offered.'

'And now?'

'He died last year.'

'And what have you been doing since then?'

He told her about the fishing boat, and its subsequent sale to a much better qualified and enthusiastic skipper, and about the repairs he was helping with, on the cottages destroyed by last year's storm. Dorothy sat back again, her curiosity apparently satisfied. 'Father, when does Mr Pagett want the work on the hotel to begin?'

'Mid-April. We'd need to have someone in position within a week.'

'If you can't produce your credentials by Tuesday, Mr Fry, we'll have to withdraw the offer. You do understand?' Dorothy rose to her feet and held out her hand. 'I hope to hear from you before then.'

James stood, and shook her hand, bemused as much by her suddenly dominant manner as by this swift turn in his fortunes. 'I hope so too, Miss Batten. Mr Batten. Thank you.'

Outside in the bright sunlight, he had to stop and think back over the astonishing twenty minutes that had passed since his arrival at Pencarrack House. It didn't seem real.

He took a deep breath and straightened his waistcoat; both opportunities might come to nothing, but even if that were the case, he'd lost nothing, but gained a day or two of hope and excitement. And if he'd learned anything over the past year it was that hope and excitement could always be found again, if you looked hard enough.

Chapter Ten

Penhaligon's Attic

Keir finished lacing his boot, and stood up straight in time to see Anna lifting the last of the dinner plates from the washing-up water.

'You're working too hard,' he said. 'Surely one of the girls could have done that?'

'Or you could have,' she pointed out.

It was taking a little getting used to, how everyone here pitched in with all the jobs, and he gave her an apologetic look, glad Matthew was out. They had, after a week, started to relax a little more in one another's company, though there was still caution on both sides and Matthew would have been quick to pick up on Keir's neglect of his duties. But then, if Matthew had been here, he'd probably have done the dishes himself, Keir thought, and sighed.

'Freya and Mairead are both busy today anyway,' Anna

said. 'Right, that's me done, I've got to go and get the Tinner's ready for the meeting.'

'Does your man work every Sunday?' Keir asked, banging his boot heel against the floor to settle it more comfortably.

'Not every week, but while the weather's good. What are you doing this afternoon, besides kicking our home to pieces?'

Keir grinned. 'Sorry. I've something to attend to at the farm, a little mending job. I thought it'd be easier to do it while most of the workers are away home.' He glanced at her from the corner of his eye, and saw an expression he remembered all too well from childhood. Even then she'd been able to see through him. 'I have, so!'

'And after that? A little stroll to the beach, perhaps? Or would you be stopping off at the home of a certain young widow?'

'Oh, you've heard about that, have you?' It was no secret he was walking out with Nancy Gilbert, but the swift way word flew around this part of the world still took him by surprise. 'Perhaps I will be, yes. Do you have an objection?'

'On the contrary.' Anna dried her hands and draped the towel on the rail of the kitchen range. 'While she's sinking her hooks into you, she's keeping them out of Matthew.'

'I thought Isabel was your worry there?' Keir was surprised by a mild pang of jealousy. 'Sure, Matthew's a good-looking fella, but not every woman's going to—'

'I know!' Anna laughed. 'Calm yourself! Anyway that was before you came along. Mrs Gilbert evidently has a liking for the tall, strong type.'

Keir bit back a comment about a particular one of Nancy's former bedfellows; that man was anything *but* the tall, strong type ... nor, he suspected, was he quite as 'former' as she claimed. But he didn't want to spoil the day with dark thoughts when the afternoon stretched ahead, and a half-hour spent in the barn fixing one of the stalls was a small price to pay for the glorious time he and Nancy had had breaking it.

'Anyway,' he said instead, 'I'd say she's no time to be thinking about Matthew, not with three children under her feet, and one out doing God knows what.'

'Not to mention a fifth hanging off her skirts,' Anna said with a little grin. 'Right, I'm away to the pub. Will I see you at supper?'

'I'm sure I'll have worked up an appetite,' he said, and laughed as she blushed. 'Oh, but you can pass out comments about me clutching at the widow Gilbert's skirts?'

'Go on with you.' Anna shooed him towards the door, and he left, still smiling.

The work took less time than he'd expected. When he'd hammered home the last nail, setting the broken stall back to its former state, the sun was still high, the weather mild, and there was an extremely enthusiastic lover waiting a short walk away up the hill. As he put the hammer and the spare nails back in their leather pouch he pondered the relationship; it wasn't love, nor anywhere near. They didn't really talk, or even particularly like each other very much, and there was a fierceness to Nancy's lovemaking, almost a defiance, but they struck sparks off one another in a way he'd never known ... God, and wasn't *that* a lie? Keir straightened, as the realisation hit; it was just like it had been with Arthur's wife.

What the hell was he doing? Had he learned nothing from his stupidity? Then again, did he want to? He picked up the bag and glanced back once more at the newly fixed stall, and couldn't help smiling as he remembered Nancy pushing him back against the wooden rail, her hungry mouth already open ready to fasten onto his. The creak; the splitting sound; the relief and breathlessness as he'd landed with Nancy on top of him. He'd wanted to laugh then, and share the absurdity of it with her, but she was already kissing him, her agile fingers tugging the shirt out of his trousers—

'Oi!'

Keir stopped in the process of pushing the bolt across the barn door, and turned to see three men striding across the yard towards him. He recognised one of them, the other two he'd never met, but he assumed were field workers. Those two hung back, but Alfie Nancarrow had no qualms in squaring up. He stopped less than two feet away.

'What's in the bag?'

Keir glanced down, surprised. But the accusatory tone lit the spark of defiance he'd always had trouble keeping in check and, instead of answering, he shrugged. 'What's it to you?'

'Stuff's been goin' missin',' put in another of the men.

'What stuff?'

'Food, mostly.'

'Eggs,' Nancarrow added. 'A lot of 'em.'

'And you think I've a load of eggs in this bag?' Keir almost laughed, but something about Nancarrow's face stopped him. 'I've not been stealing your precious eggs.'

'Then who has?'

'How would I know? I've not even been here a week!'

154

'Right. And when did stuff start going missing?'

Keir's eyes narrowed; this was starting to look grim. 'Look,' he said in as reasonable a tone as he could manage. 'I don't know why you think I've had anything to do with—'

'What's in the bag?' Nancarrow repeated.

'Tools!' Keir wrenched back the flap of the leather pouch and showed him. 'See?'

'What are you doing with them?'

'Mending a f . . . mending a stall! Go in there and see if I'm not telling the truth!' Keir stepped back and gestured to the barn. 'Last stall on the left. You'll see brand new shiny nails and everything.'

'Oh, we will.' Nancarrow's voice was soft, but his expression wasn't. 'Why are you here on a Sunday?'

Keir sighed. 'Because *I* broke the stall, so I thought I should fix it on my own time.' It was the truth, but it sounded lame, even to him.

The shorter of the two other men spoke up. 'Not because you thought you'd have plenty of time to look around and take whatever strikes your fancy?'

'There's nothing here I'd want.' Keir went to move past him, but was stopped by a strong hand planted in the centre of his chest. He was too surprised to do anything except obey.

'I still say you've been stealing,' Nancarrow said. 'Maybe not today, but since you've been here, the lay has halved most days. Explain that.'

'I don't have to.' Keir's anger was starting to burn. 'I don't have to explain a bloody thing. Not to you.'

'You do if you want to keep this job. Farmer Pawley relies on me to keep order.'

155

'Those hen-houses are in full view of the farmhouse! Do you honestly think no one would have seen someone like me foraging around there?'

'They'm not goin' missin' from the 'ouses,' the taller man said. 'They'm goin' from the lime cask.'

'The *what* cask?' Bafflement took over for a moment. 'What's that?'

Nancarrow sniffed. 'I thought you was a farmer before you worked here?'

'I worked on a sheep farm,' Keir pointed out tightly, not liking the suspicious tone. 'Had nothing to do with poultry.'

'Anyway, 'tidn't only eggs,' Nancarrow went on. 'It's been all sorts. Cabbage from the garden, spring onions, milk … A whole lot went missing yesterday evening. Where were you?'

'Mind your own business,' Keir said, his voice tight, 'and get out of my way.'

'Not until you own what you've taken.' Nancarrow moved to block Keir's path, walking backwards as Keir kept moving. 'Come on. The money'd be docked from your wages, but at least you'd keep your job.'

'I've taken nothing!' Keir shoved at Nancarrow's shoulder, and sent the man stumbling to the side with the unexpected force of it. Instantly the two others stepped in, and as he feinted to go around them the tool bag was ripped from his hands, and a moment later it swung around to hit him between the shoulder blades. He pitched forward onto his hands and knees and a boot hooked up beneath him, catching him below the breastbone. Struggling to breathe, Keir's vision darkened and another kick took him in the side, pushing him over to lie, gasping and shocked, in the dust of the farm yard. How could a day so full of promise have turned into this? Almost as bad as the unwarranted attack was his failure to realise it was going to happen, and to be ready for it.

'I've taken nothing!' he shouted, furious with himself as much as with them. He scuffled out of reach of any enthusiastic boot that might be coming his way, and stood up. He felt his right hand curling naturally into a fist, and experienced a bitter relief that now, at last, he was prepared to defend himself. 'If any one of you wants to take me on, let's do it. But three on one makes you cowards in my book.'

'Tell the truth, Garvey.' Nancarrow stepped up to Keir again, indicating he would be the one, should it come to a real fight. 'Admit you've been taking what's not yours, and we'll put it straight.'

'You sound so reasonable,' Keir said, allowing a tight little smile. 'But you're wrong. I've no need to steal, I wouldn't know where to take anything to make it pay, and in any case I'm no thief. Now, what are you going to do about that?'

Nancarrow studied him for a moment, and in that look Keir noted the sharpness of the man's mind. Here was no bull-headed, hit-first-ask-later ruffian; there was shrewdness in that gaze, and no shortage of intelligent appraisal.

'All right,' Nancarrow said at last. 'I believe you din't take no eggs.'

Keir's tone was laden with sarcasm. 'Well, hallelujah for that—'

'But,' Nancarrow held up a hand, 'we all know who you've been havin' a walk-out with. And we also know no one would so much as blink if they seen *her* goin' to the lime cask. Or the garden, or the hen-houses.' His smile was a thin line that didn't find his eyes. 'You've been puttin' her up to it, that's what I reckon.'

Keir's estimation of the man plummeted again. 'Why would Nancy steal from her own father? And even if she *was* taking a few eggs, is it stealing if it's family?'

'It is if she's passin' the profit on to you,' Nancarrow said. 'Her pa already gives her what he can afford to give. If you've persuaded her that's not enough, you don't deserve to take his wage, and he'll want you gone. Which is nothin' compared to how the honest workers will look on it.'

Keir sighed. 'All right, I'll help you find out who's responsible if I can, but I swear to you, and I'll swear to Farmer Pawley, that I've not been stealing. Nor have I had others do it on my behalf,' he added quickly.

Nancarrow eyed him, his expression bland. 'If we find out otherwise, Garvey, you'll be sorry. I promise you that.' He stepped aside, and Keir walked away, keeping his hands deliberately relaxed and resisting the urge to push his way past. It still felt like Alfie Nancarrow had won.

At Hawthorn Cottage, Nancy was already waiting by the gate, a new, light, and expensive-looking shawl across her shoulders. 'Tory's got charge of the younger kids,' she said. 'Gerald's out.' She squinted up at Keir. 'You all right? You seem a bit out of sorts.'

'What's a lime cask?'

Nancy blinked. 'Well, it's more like a bucket really, for eggs. You cover them in lime water, and that way they keep longer. Why?'

'Where's it kept?'

'On Pa's farm? In the outhouse alongside the kitchens. What on Earth are you askin' about that for?'

'Nothing.' Keir put an arm around her and they began to walk down the lane towards the beach. They'd come this way once or twice before, but never made it as far as Porthstennack and today was no exception.

A little while later, they lay hidden in the cowslips in the field opposite Priddy Farm, their clothes tossed to one side, their bodies relishing the prickle of the grasses and the brush of the breeze. Their lovemaking had, as always, left them both breathless, and it was a while before either spoke. A quiet lay over the field, and Keir's heartbeat sounded loud in his own ears, punctuated by the soft panting of the woman at his side.

He cleared his throat. 'How was your evening?'

The panting ceased, and was replaced by a faintly puzzled laugh, as Nancy rose on her elbow and looked down at him. 'What?'

'Did the kids behave? Did you sleep?'

'Keir Garvey, what *has* got into you?' Nancy trailed one finger down his chest. 'Why would you want to know how I spent a Saturday evening?'

He gave her a faint smile. 'I just thought ... we don't have conversations. I'd like to.'

'I'm sure we can find something more interesting to talk about. Like where you got this?' She touched a reddened spot on his side that seemed very likely to bruise overnight. Someone's boot had left an impressive mark.

'Fell against the stall while I was fixing it.' He didn't know why the lie had risen so smoothly to his lips, but he was starting to dislike the suspicion that was growing in his mind.

'Ah. The stall.' Nancy bent her head to Keir's chest, and blew gently before flicking her tongue across his nipple. Then she looked up, and smiled slowly. 'We'll have to test your handiwork sometime.'

Where did she get the money for that shawl? 'Were you home?'

'Last night?' Nancy's teasing vanished, and she sat up and linked her arms around her raised knees. 'Why are you so keen to know, anyhow? What's it to do with you?'

For a second he considered telling her, but the sight of her golden hair falling softly down her curved back, and the perfection of her skin in the sunlight, made him reluctant to ruin the afternoon to no good purpose.

'Nothing,' he said, and sat up beside her, his arm sliding around her waist. He brushed her hair aside and fastened his teeth gently in her earlobe, then whispered, 'I was just making conversation. Come here.'

Her light blue eyes scanned his face for a moment, then her smile returned. 'So soon?'

'Always.'

Nancy twisted towards him and pushed him back to the ground. He had time to reluctantly admit she probably was behind the thefts from the farm, and to wonder what he was going to do about it, then she leaned down and ran her tongue along his collar bone. All the while her hands were busy on him, stroking, pressing, encircling ... and then nothing else mattered.

* * *

160

The Tinner's Arms

Esther and her two grandsons were out for the afternoon, so it was left to Anna to prepare the pub for the arrival of the women of the Widows' Guild. Feeling the heat, and uncomfortable in her seventh month of pregnancy, she did the minimum possible to escape the sharp, critical eye of Alice Packem, and unlocked the door just as Ellen Scoble arrived. Ellen looked thinner than ever, but she gave Anna her usual bright smile, and asked how she was feeling, while she shed her coat.

Anna confessed to a little discomfort, and, mindful of Mairead's recent concerns, she asked after little Eddie. 'My daughter says he seems tired at school,' she said, taking Ellen's coat and laying it along the newly polished bar top. 'I hope he's not sickening for something? I know he suffers from a chesty cough.'

'He's well enough.' Ellen seemed disinclined to take the conversation further. 'How is Freya's young man doing? I 'eard he came a cropper up Pencarrack.'

'He's mending,' Anna said. 'Freya's taking good care of him.'

'I'm sure she is. When will they wed?'

'We don't have a date ... Ellen, what are you doing? That can go with your coat.'

Ellen paused in the act of placing her scarf on the table where the exchanges would usually go. She flushed slightly. 'No. It's my offering.'

'But it's the one Ned bought for you, isn't it? That Christmas before he—'

'Nah, that's a different one.' Ellen waved a dismissive hand. 'Besides, it's nearly summer. Now, let's get these chairs put 'round. No, you stay there, I'll do it.'

Anna obediently stood back and let Ellen busy herself, noting how her friend's eyes continually cut to the table with its lonely offering. It was definitely the same scarf; there was even the faint residual stain of Anna's own blood, from when it had been wrapped around her head after the accident last year. Why would Ellen have lied about something like that? It was up to her if she wanted to exchange it, after all.

The wooden box carrying the renowned mouser, Ripper, caused a stir as always, and the smell of freshly baked bread set mouths watering throughout the short meeting, but when the time came for the ladies to queue up and make their choices, Anna was more interested in which of them chose the scarf – it was Martha Rodda. She watched Ellen pretending interest and amusement in the tussle over Ripper, between Little Alice and Ern Bolitho's mother, and made up her mind to find out what was going on when Ellen stayed for her usual cup of tea after the meeting.

But Ellen left uncharacteristically early, with her loaf of bread and pat of fresh butter. 'Can't stay an' chat this time, Eddie's doin' some garden chores. I ought to go and make sure he ain't chopped his toes off with the spade.'

'Take care, Ellen.' Anna gave her a hug, noticing that although Ellen returned it with a cheerful smile, her attention was back on Martha, who was folding the scarf into a small square. As soon as Ellen had left, Anna took Martha to one side. 'Can I offer you something for that?' She gestured at Martha's pocket.

'For the scarf? I like it. It'll come good in the winter.'

'Yes, but ... it's the one Ned gave Ellen not long before he died.'

'Oh.' Martha looked troubled. 'Why'd she give it up, then?'

'I think she must be in difficulties,' Anna said. 'She's not been herself for a while. Let me give you something else?'

'Like what?'

'What do you need?'

'Eggs. Farmer Pawley've had a run of bad lays this week, he couldn't give me my usual.'

'Ah, we don't have any spare, either. The hens are a bit troubled by rats since the cat went off. Anything else?'

'Get on, then.' Martha took the scarf from her pocket and pressed it into Anna's hands. 'Take it back to the girl. I don't want nothin'. I'm fortunate, see? I'm married again.'

Anna took the scarf, and thanked her.

'It's nice Ellen's got a real friend lookin' out for her,' Martha said. 'She's a good girl.'

'She's always been very kind to me. I'm sure she'll be grateful to you for this.'

She had planned on giving the scarf back to Ellen the next time they met; it wouldn't be needed for months yet, after all, but Martha's words weighed on her; in truth she'd been so caught up with her own life and family, she hadn't been much of a real friend at all. So she waited until the last of the women had left, then began the slow walk down to Ellen's house.

When she got there she was surprised and frustrated to find the house locked up, and no sign of anyone at home. Eddie was certainly not digging over the garden, and there was no washing out to dry as there was in every other garden today. Anna frowned, and went to the window, cupping her hands around her eyes to cut the reflection of the sun. She peered in, but there was no movement and no sound. Definitely no one home. Perhaps Ellen and Eddie had gone to the beach? Even so, it was unusual to find any of these houses locked.

Anna glanced up at the sky; the light was changing, it would soon grow chilly as evening drew in. But there was still time for a quick walk down to the shore, on the off-chance her friend was there. If not, she would post the scarf back through the letter-box, and answer Ellen's questions later.

The beach was busy enough, but there was no sign of Ellen and her son. Several people were working today, and Anna's heart gave a little leap of pleasure to see the *Pride of Porthstennack* moored in its usual place, bumping against the harbour wall, rising and falling with the swell. Anna climbed the steps, holding her skirt high to avoid sweeping the wet stone with it, and went down to the boat.

Matthew emerged onto the deck from below, and when he saw her his face went through an amusing selection of expressions, from pleasure, to worry, to exasperation, and finally back to the slow smile that crept inside her and stayed there.

'What do you think you're doing, you daft woman?' He jumped from the deck onto the harbour wall, and took her face in his hands. 'It's slippery as hell here, and you in your condition!'

'I'm perfectly fine,' she soothed. 'How much longer will you be working?'

'We're all but finished. Another ten minutes maybe. Will you wait and let me walk back with you?'

'I was hoping you'd say that.'

'Good. Sit down there,' he pointed to a low capstan a short way up the harbour wall, 'and don't move.'

'I wouldn't dare.' Anna caught at his shirt as he went to walk away, and he stopped, looked at her for a moment, drew a deep, theatrical sigh, and then kissed her with a thoroughness that left her laughing and breathless.

'Now do as you're told,' he said, and his grin made her want to grab his hand and make him do it all over again. But she let him go, and contented herself with watching him work.

After the terrible year they'd had, it was a joy to see him immersed in the life he loved again. His right arm was still a little stiff, and now and again he stopped what he was doing and gave it a squeeze or a rub, but the strength in his shoulders, the flash of sunlight that turned his dark-blond hair bright, and the dextrous movement of his hands, all gave him the appearance of a man in his twenties rather than the swiftly approaching forty.

Anna was so taken with watching him, and allowing herself the anticipation of feeling his arms close around her in their bed that night, that she almost missed the figure clambering over the rocks towards the road. Eddie Scoble. She half-rose, ready to call out, but there was no sign of Ellen, and she caught sight of Matthew and remembered his admonition … he'd used a joking voice, but the worry had been real. The very last thing she ought to be doing was hurrying over wet rocks, just to ask a boy where his mother was.

So she stayed put on her capstan, her hands folded on her lap, and eventually Matthew came over. The waning sunlight was still bright enough over the sea to make her squint against it, as he held out his hand to her and drew her to her feet, and she put her arm around his waist, heedless of the damp of his shirt.

'Carry me up the hill?' she asked plaintively. 'I'm only a little whale, after all.'

'Ah, *that's* why you waited.'

'Of course. You don't think it's because I want to spend time alone with you, do you?'

'The thought never crossed my mind.' Matthew shook his head. 'You might vaguely remember I got blown up last year? So I'm sorry to say I won't be transporting any whales, no matter how little, up this bloody hill.'

'Ah, you're just being mean.' Anna tightened her grip around him, then settled for taking his hand. 'Come on then. You can at least help me down these steps.'

On the way through the village, she called in at Ellen's house again, and this time Eddie was there.

'Ma's not home,' he said, taking the scarf. 'She's up with Granny Donithorn.' He inserted himself between the door and the jamb, making it clear Anna was not welcome to come in and wait. 'I'll tell her she left this behind.'

Anna almost corrected him, but bit back the words. 'Yes, thank you,' she said, instead. 'I hope your Granny's well.'

She waved as she went back down the short path to where Matthew waited, but when the door closed and hid the solemn-faced little boy, the question wouldn't go away: why was Ellen lying?

Chapter Eleven

Monday March 27th 1911

James Fry propped his chin on his hands, and stared at the table until his heartbeat settled again. The choice that had haunted his dreams, that he had hardly dared hope for, was now a reality: an interview – declared in the letter as a mere formality – for a foreman's position at Castle Drogo, or a similar position, on a decidedly less certain project, here in Caernoweth. There was no real difficulty in this decision; the Devon-based build would be run by a known and skilled firm, its architect a man James respected above most others, the Caernoweth project little safer than a leap off a cliff in the dark. And he had certainly never expected to be offered a position as high as foreman.

Still, courtesy dictated he tell the Battens face-to-face, so he donned hat and coat, and put the letter and its attendant paperwork into his pocket. It wouldn't hurt to show the Battens the reason he was turning down their offer – who knew when he might be glad of an amicable relationship with the biggest landowners in the area?

Drawing almost level with the Caernoweth Hotel, he saw Freya's mother crossing the courtyard. Her return had been the talk of the Tinner's, but she had tended to keep to herself at the hotel, and this was the first time he'd laid eyes on her in almost twenty years. It was an odd moment, and he found himself hoping she hadn't seen him.

'James? James Fry?' Isabel peered closer, and her face split into a bright, welcoming smile. 'It *is* you! Wait a moment!'

At this distance, and in her summer hat and fashionable skirt, she could have passed for the seventeen-year-old girl Matt had been so proud to show off, but as she came closer James could see the footprints of time and care across her face. She was more beautiful now than she had ever been.

'Isabel!' He took her proffered hands and squeezed them. 'I'd heard you were back.'

'Likewise,' she said, and stretched up to kiss his cheek. 'We missed you when you left, you know, Matthew and I.'

'And I missed you both, too.' It wasn't wholly untrue, although there had been a widening gulf between them even then. James fell silent, trying to remember the last time they had spoken, and if there had been harsh words. But if there had been, they were not part of this new life.

Isabel clearly thought the same, and didn't mention the rift. 'I heard about Roland,' she said quietly, instead. 'I'm so very sorry. He was a lovely, kind man.'

'Thank you. A lot of people thought so.'

'He was so very good to . . . ' she caught herself and stopped, but James shook his head.

'It's all right, Matt and I have mended our fences. Pa was only as kind to him as Robert and Grace Penhaligon were to me.'

'I'm glad. Anyway, where are you off to today, so very smart and serious?'

'Pencarrack House. I have a message for Mr Batten.'

'Oh! That sounds like fun. Can I come, too?' She linked her arm through his, and James laughed; she hadn't changed after all.

'If you like.'

'I do like. It's always nice to see how the privileged in different places live. Lead on, Mr Fry.' Isabel folded her hands on his arm and they continued the short walk, talking more easily now.

'I am glad you and Matthew are friends again,' she said as they drew near the manor house grounds. 'You were always so close.'

'He owns Pa's boat now, although you probably know that.'

'Yes. I understand his new wife made it possible to buy it from you.'

James didn't want to get into a conversation about that, so he altered the direction slightly. 'She and Freya get on very well.' He'd intended it to be comforting; that Freya's mother should know her daughter was in good hands when she herself could not be there. But he could see his mistake in the way Isabel stiffened.

'Yes,' she said. 'I have seen this for myself.'

'I'm sorry, I didn't mean—'

'And what of her own daughter? The one with the strange name, and peculiar manner?'

It was James's turn to draw back. 'Peculiar?'

'Perhaps that is a little harsh. Very ... abrupt, I think?'

'She's honest,' James said. 'If that's peculiar I think more people should strive to be odd.'

Isabel stopped, and looked up at him. 'I was not insulting her,' she said. 'You know her well, this Marie?'

'Mairead,' James corrected. 'We're reasonably friendly.'

'Very young, to be teaching children.'

'Yes. But wise beyond her years, I think.'

'She ought to learn some manners, *I* think.'

'She's perfectly well-mannered.'

'Then you clearly don't know her as well as you think you do!' Isabel gave a light, teasing laugh, and began walking again, drawing James with her. 'No, I'm sure she is perfectly pleasant, and *honest*, as you say, but Heaven help those poor children!'

'What do you mean?'

'Can you imagine taking lessons from a girl who doesn't know when to keep her thoughts to herself?' Isabel shook her head, the floppy brim of her white hat dancing in the sunlight. 'But I'm being cruel, forgive me. Freya cares deeply for her, so I know she must be a good person. I just think she has a lot to learn when it comes to social graces. What chance has she of finding a nice young man, otherwise?'

They had reached the top of the Battens' drive, and James gently removed her arm from his, glad of the excuse to cut the conversation short. 'I'm here on business, so it's best we don't arrive like a couple on a social call.'

'Then I will wait in the hall, and we can walk back to town together. I'd like to hear more of people I used to know, like

Mr and Mrs Cornish, and Farmer Pawley. I understand his younger daughter and her husband have our old house?'

'Yes. She's a widow now, though, these past three years.' James raised his hand to the bell. 'I shan't be long.'

Isabel kept looking around her, as if she was expecting to be ejected from the grounds before she'd set foot in the house. James wanted to tell her not to wait for him, but no good reason came to mind and he hoped she might become nervous enough to change her mind and leave; if she kept talking about Mairead the way she had been, he might easily lose his temper.

He was still pondering the depth of his annoyance when Mrs Andrews, the housekeeper, opened the door. Her startled gaze fell on Isabel first, then her attention shifted to James, who gave her his best smile and removed his hat.

'Good morning. Mr James Fry. Is Mr Batten at home?'

'He is.' She looked enquiringly at Isabel. 'Is he expecting you both?'

'Oh, I'm just here for the walk,' Isabel said. 'No need to trouble Mr Batten on my account.'

Mrs Andrews stood back and gestured them both inside. 'I'll tell him you're here, Mr Fry.'

The two of them stood in silence. Isabel kept her attention on the stairs, and with no further conversation forthcoming, James contented himself with studying the carved wooden stair rail, and the intricately sculpted plaster on the high ceiling. He was having a bet with himself that it was the work of an Italian craftsman, when Mrs Andrews returned.

'Master said to take the papers from you, and see you're not kept.'

'I'm not handing over my papers. I'd like to talk to him, if I may?'

As the housekeeper vanished again, Isabel turned to James. 'What papers?'

'My credentials. Mr Batten has offered me a job on a building project, but I've found something better.'

'In Caernoweth?'

'No, near Okehampton.'

'Quite so,' Isabel shrugged. 'Who would want to spend their days in a small town, when the world awaits?'

'It's hardly the world,' James pointed out with a smile. 'Both jobs are good. I can't believe how lucky I am to have the choice, after the way things have been.' He paused, then went on, 'Pardon me saying, but you've chosen to come back and spend a longish while here, there must be something in town to keep you.'

'Of course there is. I have *family* here!'

'Family.' His voice came out flat. 'Yes, of course.'

'Oh,' Isabel said quickly, 'I'm sorry, I should have thought before I spoke. You must miss your poor father.'

'I do. But I have friends here, too.'

'You can always make new friends.' She nodded, her expression serious. 'No, I believe you have made the right choice.'

The library door opened again and Mrs Andrews came towards them. 'Mr Batten will see you now.'

'No need.' James reached into his pocket, and his fingers closed on the envelope, and he took a deep breath. 'Please see that Mr and Miss Batten read these carefully, and I'll await their decision by the end of tomorrow. Otherwise I'm sure they'll understand I'll have to take up the other position.'

He put the packet into the hand of the exasperated Mrs Andrews, and glanced at Isabel. 'Are you ready?'

'But I thought you—'

'I've changed my mind.' James replaced his hat. 'Thank you, Mrs Andrews, I've no doubt I'll see you again soon.'

'Gracious!' Isabel said, when they stepped out into the sunshine again and started back. 'You seem to have found an urgency you didn't have earlier.'

'Do I? I'm sorry.' James slowed his pace. 'I hadn't even realised.'

'Please, don't let me hold you up,' Isabel smiled. 'I think you have people you'd like to tell about your new job?'

'Not really, I'm just full of energy now. Actually I might walk over to the fort, and reacquaint myself with it, it's been a few years since I've been there. Would you like to come?'

'No, thank you.' Isabel pulled a delicately distasteful face. 'That place has always given me shivers.'

'Not me. Matt and I spent a lot of time there, when we were boys.'

'So I understand.' Isabel put a hand on his arm, drawing him to a stop. 'I'm so very glad you two are friends again. And I hope we can be, too?'

'Of course.'

'Good. And now I shall leave you to your trip into the past, both near and distant, and I shall spend some time walking in these beautiful grounds.' She waved a gloved hand to encompass Pencarrack. 'Far more suited to my footwear, and my temperament, I think?'

'Doubtless,' he grinned. 'Enjoy your walk.'

'And you're sure you have made the right choice?'

'Never more sure of anything in my life.' James tipped his hat to her and left her to explore the gardens of the big house. Despite his bravado, he felt faintly queasy, and his heart was hammering; leaping off the cliff in the dark was the easy part after all, now he had to hope the tide was in.

* * *

Penhaligon's Attic

Freya gave a sigh of relief as Mairead came into the kitchen. 'Thank goodness *you're* here, at least.'

'How long has all this taken?' Mairead stared around her in gratifying admiration.

'All day, with the bedrooms as well,' Freya said. 'Anna helped with a lot of it though.' She couldn't help feeling pleased as she looked around at the results of their efforts; the kitchen was scrubbed clean, from floor to ceiling, and the table set for everyone who was expected, with clean napkins by every place setting. In addition the old campaign bed had been taken from Keir's room and put up in the attic bedroom next to Mairead's, and Freya's own room swept and polished, fresh bedding put on, and wild flowers from the hedgerow near Hawthorn Cottage arranged in one of Granny Grace's favourite vases on the dresser. Before she had left for work, Anna had also unearthed Granny's matching ewer and bowl set from the outhouse, and Freya had cleaned them vigorously to remove the accumulation of dust and cobwebs. The last of the week's money had gone into preparing delicious food so that she could spend more time showing Sophie around the town, and getting to know her. Now the larder was packed with pies, jellies and bread, and the oven threw out the warm, sweet scent of the biscuits made to Granny Grace's own recipe. Then it was just a matter of waiting. And waiting.

Freya went to the window. The street was almost deserted, the shops – including Penhaligon's Attic – had closed over an hour ago and most people had already gone to their homes, or their evening jobs. 'I was beginning to think it would only be Tristan, Sophie and myself.'

'Where are they?' Mairead absently straightened a crooked napkin, then nodded, satisfied. Freya wondered if she even knew she'd done it.

'I have no idea,' she said. 'They left early enough. Teddy was driving, and he promised they'd be back here long before now. It's going to be dark soon.' Freya frowned. 'I do hope they haven't broken down.'

'Or had an accident,' Mairead said. 'Those motors can be very dangerous.'

'Mairead! Do you think I should borrow John Rodda's trap and go— oh! No need.' She smiled in relief. 'They're coming.'

'Ah right.' Mairead stood up, and seeing Freya's beady look, she took her cup to the sink to rinse it. 'I'll go and wash, while you greet your young guest.'

The sound of Tristan's car rattled to a stop outside, and Freya took a deep breath and went to the front door just in time to see Sophie's look of unguarded dismay, as she stared up at the house from her seat in the front.

Tristan allowed Teddy to help Sophie alight while he slowly crossed the pavement. He was still limping, and Freya suspected he'd been too keen to give Bartholomew's crutches back, but he was definitely improving. 'I'm so sorry,' he said in a low voice. 'Sophie insisted we stop in to see Lucy, and of course Teddy wasn't going to refuse that, either.'

'It doesn't matter, you're here now.'

'If I'd been driving I'd have—'

'I'm just relieved you're all safe.' Freya touched his cheek, noting the new, deeper lines of tiredness and pain at the corners of his eyes and mouth. 'How are you feeling?'

'Stiff, and sore,' he confessed. He turned to where Teddy was lifting Sophie's carpet bag from the back seat. 'Thanks, old man. And thanks for doing all the driving.'

'Of course,' Teddy said. 'You're in no fit state. Besides, you know how much I enjoy giving the old thing her head.' He patted the bonnet of the car as if it were a thoroughbred horse, and Freya smiled.

'Will you come in for tea, Teddy? Anna's had to leave, and Keir's still at work, so we've plenty of room at the table.'

'Don't mind if I do, thank you.' He offered Sophie his arm to walk her to the house, but she shoved her hands into her coat sleeves, as if it were cold enough to require a muff.

Freya exchanged a look with Tristan, who shrugged. 'She was unstoppable up at Pencarrack,' he murmured. 'You'd have thought she was going to her first society party, rather than a chat and a cup of cocoa with someone she barely knows.'

'Didn't I tell you?' Freya whispered back. She sighed, not liking to see the disappointment on Tristan's face. 'It's all right. I'll do my best, and if you do too, I'm sure we'll have her happy as a sand boy by the time she leaves.'

Inside, Freya took Sophie's coat, and hung it up in the hall.

'Shall I show you your room now, before tea? Then you can have a wash and change if you like.' She attempted a conspiratorial smile. 'I remember the smell and the muck on my skin after a ride in Tristan's car.'

'I like it,' Sophie said immediately. 'And so did—'

'Caroline. Yes, I had a feeling she would have.' Freya picked up Sophie's bag and hefted it up the narrow stairs. 'This way.'

Despite the coolness of Sophie's reception, she was glad she'd spent so long on the girl's room. She pressed the light switch, and watched to see if the fact that they had electricity was any consolation, but it didn't seem to be. Sophie merely trailed after her into the room, and sat down on the bed. She looked quite small, suddenly, and a little bit lost, and Freya was surprised to find herself yielding to a degree of sympathy.

'Listen,' she said, sitting down beside her. 'I know you don't like it, but I love your brother very much.' She didn't add that he loved her in return, it would only provoke an instant denial. 'And *you* love him, don't you?'

'Of course!' Sophie showed the first sign of animation since she'd arrived, but it was not the kind Freya had hoped for. 'How dare you!'

'Then,' Freya went on, keeping her voice calm, 'think about it like this. He's tired, he's in pain, and he's travelled all day to fetch you down, just so you can see why he loves this town so much. I suggest we *both* put our dislike of one another to one side, and try to make him happy.'

Sophie was clearly taken aback by that, and Freya realised it had only just occurred to her that she too might be the object of dislike, and it didn't sit well. She smothered a little smile, by biting the inside of her lower lip, hard.

'All right,' Sophie said at last.

'Good. Come down to tea when you're ready.' Freya rose and brushed down her skirt briskly. 'Are you hungry?'

'No. Lucy – that's Miss Batten to you, I suppose – made her housekeeper bring masses of sandwiches. And cake.'

'But I've been … Never mind.' Freya sighed. 'I'm sure there'll be something to take your fancy. And the food will keep, if not.'

Downstairs, Mairead had put fresh hot water on to boil, and was talking to Tristan and Teddy. Freya began removing plates of food from the larder, to the accompaniment of impressed noises from the others which soothed her ruffled feathers somewhat.

'Are you sure you're not filled up with Miss Batten's sandwiches?' She'd intended it as a playful comment on the male appetite, but was met with puzzled looks.

'Sandwiches?' Teddy asked Tristan. 'Did I miss something?'

'We had hot chocolate,' Tristan reminded her, 'I told you. No sandwiches.'

'No cake?'

'I think I'd have noticed,' Tristan said with a smile. 'I might be tired, but I'm sure I didn't *actually* doze off, during all that fascinating chatter about the theatre.'

'Lucy's very keen on dance,' Teddy said. 'Better not let her hear you dismissing it so lightly.'

As the talk moved on to Lucy Batten's ambitions in the public eye, Freya met Mairead's raised eyebrow with a little shake of her head. It didn't matter. It wasn't worth the fuss. Let the girl go hungry if she wished that badly to make a point.

By the time Sophie came into the kitchen, her hair brushed, and her skin scrubbed clean of the grime she professed to love so much, Freya was wearing a more or less genuine smile.

'You look lovely,' she said. 'Come and sit down. This is my sister, Mairead.'

'Pleased to meet you,' Mairead said, nodding from the far side of the table.

Sophie wrinkled her nose. 'What's that smell?'

'Smell?' Freya sniffed, then gave a dismayed start. 'The biscuits!'

Despite everything she couldn't suppress a giggle at the way everyone moved into action: Mairead, whose chair was nearest, leapt to her feet and opened the range; Teddy flung open the back door; and Tristan threw a protective pot holder to Freya, who dragged out the smoking tray and hurried into the back garden with it. All the while, Sophie was watching with an open mouth, as if some play was being performed for her.

When everything had calmed down, and the smeechy air had cleared, they sat down once more to the spread that had taken Freya all day, and far too much of her savings, to prepare. Sophie seemed to have forgotten all about the phantom sandwiches; distracted by Tristan's conversation about Bill, she helped herself to cold ham pie, followed by some thickly cut bread and jam, and finished with a large slice of fruit cake. During the entire meal she barely spoke two words to Freya or Mairead, but Freya didn't mind; the girl was relaxing, interested for the first time since she'd arrived, and her face had lost that stubborn, closed look.

Papá still wasn't home, although it was now fully dark out, and Tristan's exhaustion was starting to show. Seeing it, Freya gestured for him to follow her into the back porch. She checked that Teddy was still entertaining Sophie with stories he'd heard from Lucy, then she pulled the door half-closed, and spoke quietly.

'You need to go home and rest.'

'I do feel a bit off.' He drew her close and put his lips to her temple. 'I want to marry you, Miss Penhaligon. And soon.'

'Me too,' Freya whispered.

'I'll come up first thing in the morning, and make sure Sophie's behaving.'

'I'm sure she'll be all right now. Don't push yourself.'

'It's been nearly a week. I'm getting better every day.'

'Today has been a test,' Freya pointed out, 'and you look done in.'

'I know, but I'll need to take Sophie down and introduce her to Farmer Pawley tomorrow.'

'Oh, she'll love *that*!'

She felt laughter shake his body. 'He needs to know who's taking Bill out. And it might turn out to be the making of her.'

'It's hard to remember she's only a child.' Freya moved away. 'I'll try to be nicer to her.'

'You've tried from the outset,' he said, and squeezed her arm. 'I'm under no illusions, I just want her to understand how much I love you, and the best way to do that, is for her to love you too.'

'We might be waiting a long time then,' Freya said, with a little smile. 'I'll settle for her knowing I'm not trying to steal you away from her.'

'Which she'll soon come to realise.' Tristan moved ahead of her back into the kitchen, where Teddy was returning from the hall with his and Tristan's coats, and Mairead was putting the last of the leftovers back in the larder. There was no sign of Sophie. 'You must have spent a fortune on this,' he said in a low voice. 'You shouldn't have, really.'

'I'm putting everything into this week,' she admitted. 'Whatever it takes. If it means going without, once she's gone home, then that's what I'll do.'

'You're putting my sister up, I'm not going to let your family go hungry.' He reached into his waistcoat pocket, but she put a hand out to stop him.

'I'm not too proud to take some help,' she said, 'but not now.' The last thing either of them needed was for Sophie to believe Freya was chasing her brother's money, on top of everything else.

Tristan subsided. 'All right. Tomorrow.' He took his coat from Teddy. 'Where's Sophie?'

'She went to look for the lounge,' Teddy said with a grin.

Freya gave him a reproving frown. 'Didn't you tell her?'

'I thought it'd be more fun this way.' Teddy winked. 'She'll laugh about it, you'll see.'

'This time last year, perhaps,' Tristan said, shaking his head. 'Come on, let's find her and say our goodbyes.'

As he finished speaking, Sophie came back into the kitchen, eyeing the straight-backed chairs with distaste. 'I couldn't find your sitting room,' she said to Freya. 'Is it upstairs?'

'Your brother and Teddy are leaving,' Freya said. 'You'd better say goodbye, then I'll show you around.'

'Why does the hallway smell like fish?' Sophie went on.

'It's horrible. And I'm sure I saw a mouse scuttling behind the skirting board in my room.'

Freya exchanged a glance with Tristan – this was going to be a very long week.

* * *

Anna let herself into the house as quietly as she could, grateful for the comfort and peace of her own home. The pub hadn't been particularly busy, but tempers had been short, and arguments many. Even the unflappable Brian Cornish had pulled a face.

'T'idn't a full moon, is it?'

'Not for another week or so,' Anna sighed. 'Fishermen are short-tempered enough over the winter, I'd started to get used to that, but it seems to be the miners tonight.'

Brian nodded and called out, 'Here, Alan! Young Tommy said anythin' to you about troubles at Furzy?'

Alan Trevellick had muttered something about Tommy's shift being cut short two days in a row, then went to fetch a new barrel of ale. He'd been as out of sorts as the rest, tonight, and Esther had cuffed him around the ear more than once during the evening.

'Your grandpa'd be turnin' in his grave, young Alan! See you do 'im proud, boy!'

Anna had left early, rarely so grateful to escape the smoky, malty air of the Tinner's Arms, and as she slipped off her shoes in the hall she thought ahead to the bliss of laying her head on her pillow, and listening to the soft breathing of her man next to her as she drifted off into her own slumber. Her stockinged feet now silent, she was able to hear the low murmur of voices from the kitchen, and noted a faint, flickering light beneath the door. Candles, not electric. It might be an early finish for the pub, but it was still too late for Tristan's sister to be up. She paused, frowning; surely Isabel wouldn't be so shameless as to come here at night, when Anna was working? Then she heard Freya's laughter, and relaxed.

She went in, and Matthew looked up in surprise. 'You're early! I was going to walk down and meet you.' His smile faded. 'Are you all right? You look tired.'

'I'm much the better for seeing you two,' Anna said. 'I thought you'd be asleep by now.'

'We were just talking. We don't get the chance much nowadays, and once she marries her cowboy we—'

'Papá!' Freya broke in, and her laugh came again, earning an answering grin from her father. 'He's not a cowboy!'

'It's nice to see you both so relaxed,' Anna said, easing herself into her own chair. 'Particularly after the night I've had.' She grimaced. 'Sounds as if there might be layoffs coming, up at the mine. Another good reason you're out, Matthew.'

'I can think of twenty more,' Matthew agreed, 'but I hope you're wrong. Closures of even some of the levels would put a lot of good men out of work.'

'I'll leave you to talk,' Freya said, half-rising, but Anna waved her to sit again.

'You'll do no such thing. I can't tell you what a delight it is to have this time with you. Both of you. Actually, Matthew, I don't want to cause any upset, but I found something in the shed the other day, and I've been meaning to talk to you about it. It concerns Freya, too.'

Anna went into the shop and fished about under the counter; this was perhaps not the time to bring up the subject of the christening gown, but she found the jewellery box and went back to the kitchen.

'This was in a box of your mother's belongings.' She held it out to Matthew, and he took it with a little smile.

'I remember this. Ma used to take out her bits and pieces, and clean them here at the table, then put them all back in without wearing them. Pa told her she was daft, but she once wore a locket up to the Penworthy Festival, and lost it in the mud. Said she'd never risk it again.'

'Mairead said the box would probably belong to Freya now.'

'Yes, I'm sure she's right.' Matthew passed the box to Freya, who ran her fingers over the decorated lid, then lifted the catch. She took out a pair of clip earrings, and one or two small bracelets, then peered closer.

'There's an envelope,' she said. 'Lying flat along the bottom. I think it's empty, though.' She took it out. 'Julia's Gift,' she read aloud, and then glanced at her father. 'Oh, Papá, I'm sorry, this must have been for—'

'No.' He shook his head, his eyes unreadable in the flickering candle light. '*Julia's Gift* is the name of a story.'

'Was my aunt the heroine of it?'

He nodded, and took the envelope, turning it over and over in his fingers, his mind clearly in the past. 'I wrote it when I renamed my boat from *The Julia*, to *Isabel*,' he said at last. 'I felt it made up for it, in some way. I'm only surprised Ma kept the envelope.'

'Why didn't she keep the story though?' Freya asked. 'If it's as good as the others, she must have loved it.'

'I don't know about good. I wrote it when I was sober, so it wasn't as fanciful as the ones you know.' Matthew shrugged. 'Maybe she found it too painful.'

'It'll probably turn up in some other part of the house,' Anna ventured. 'Or in the shed.'

Matthew gave her a warning look. 'You're not to go poking around out there again. It's too dangerous, you might fall and no one would know for hours. Promise me?'

'I promise.' Anna smiled for him, and saw she'd eased his concern when he smiled back. 'Go on up to bed, Matthew, you'll be exhausted tomorrow.'

His eyes held hers for a moment, and in their blue depths she saw a flash of something else, which sent the blood racing a little faster in her veins. 'I'll be up shortly,' she said, putting a weight behind her words that he could easily read. 'Go on. I'll wash these cups.'

He bade his daughter goodnight, and went upstairs, leaving the two of them alone at the table. Anna picked up the envelope and started to hand it back to Freya, but as her hand travelled past the lamp on the table, she paused and peered more closely.

'It's not empty,' she mused, and got up to turn on the electric light. She slipped her fingers inside the envelope and withdrew a shabby piece of paper, much-folded, creased, and with various smudges and finger marks on it. For the size of the envelope, the paper was surprisingly small, but it quickly became obvious why it had been kept in the same place as the story.

'*Little Sister.*' The poem was short, written in the same boyish hand as the one that had so delighted her to find in

185

Grace's recipe book; Matthew had been ten years old then, and only a couple of years older when Julia had died. Anna scanned the lines, her eyes burning as she imagined the grief that had gripped this house at the loss of such a shining light.

> *I'm sorry that I broke your doll*
> *And tore your birthday dress.*
> *I'm sorry that I spilled the coal*
> *And blamed you for the mess.*
> *I'm sorry that I made you cry*
> *And wouldn't let you play,*
> *I'm sorry for the times I said*
> *You'd just get in the way.*
> *But now that I can say these things,*
> *And mean each sorry word,*
> *It's too late, and you've gone for good.*
> *They never will be heard.*

Anna passed the paper wordlessly to Freya, and picked up the cups to wash. Freya read in silence for a moment, then put the poem back in the envelope.

'I'll tell Papá about it tomorrow,' she said quietly. 'See what he wants me to do with it.'

Anna nodded and gave a tired sigh as she placed the cups upside down on the drainer. 'I'm away to my bed. Sleep well, sweetheart, I'll see you in the morning.'

Climbing the stairs she tried to summon the anticipation again, that leaping excitement and pleasure at the thought of Matthew's deft hands on her, and his lean body covering hers ... but the sadness, and the tiredness, had conspired to rob her of even that. She gathered her thoughts, ready to explain to him that she only wanted to sleep after all, and to know he was beside her, but when she went into their room she realised that wouldn't be necessary. Despite everything, as she slipped into bed beside her sleeping man she found a smile on her lips, and she pressed it gently between Matthew's shoulder blades, trusting it to find its way through to his heart.

Chapter Twelve

When Tristan called for Sophie the following morning, she was already dressed to leave the house, complete with her coat and hat, and her outdoor shoes. He had been about to praise her for her promptness when he realised it was actually a quiet but pointed insult to Freya's hospitality, and he made up his mind to teach her a little lesson in manners and patience.

Freya had also correctly interpreted Sophie's eagerness, and she gave Tristan a fierce look that partly made him feel awful, but mostly made him want to kiss that scowl right off her lovely mouth. She must have read it on his face, because a light came on behind her eyes, and although her frown deepened she was unable to maintain it for long.

He turned to Sophie. 'How did you sleep? Freya says her bed is deeply comfortable.'

'I slept well, thank you,' she said, all politeness. 'Are you ready to leave?'

'I thought I'd stay for a cup of tea and a chat, if you've no objection?'

'None at all.' Sophie's lips thinned, but she turned back. 'Did you know there's no sitting room here?'

'Of course I did.'

'And did Teddy know?'

'Ah. Yes, that was a rotten joke.'

'I'll get him back.' Sophie sighed, and took off her hat with exaggerated patience. 'Sit down, then, have your chat.' She perched on the very edge of her chair, her face showing nothing but forbearance to the whims of adults.

Freya poured Tristan's tea with greater care than was necessary. 'Are you going down to see Farmer Pawley today?'

'We are. And I thought we might go down to the beach afterwards, if you'd like that, Sophie? I could do with the exercise on this silly hip.'

'I suppose so. Nothing else to do, after all.' Sophie began drumming on the table with her fingers. 'Are you ready yet?'

Tristan's cup was halfway to his mouth. 'Don't be silly.'

'Has Teddy gone up to Pencarrack?' Freya asked, sitting down as if she had all the time in the world, and Tristan bit down on a smile. 'Yes,' he said, avoiding her eyes, 'he's making notes for me today, so I can look through them at home.'

'Notes about what?' Sophie asked. Anything to do with Pencarrack always snagged her attention.

'Just some boring old diaries,' Tristan said. 'Nothing to interest you.'

'And how's Bill enjoying life at Priddy Farm?' Freya asked. Tristan guessed that this time it was only partly as a ploy to keep Sophie waiting; largely, he suspected, it was to deflect conversation from the one thing that set them at odds.

'Keir tells me he took a lump out of someone called

Nancarrow. Sounded quite pleased, actually. Other than that he's settled in well.' He took pity on Sophie at last. 'Right, it's time I took my little sister to meet Mr Pawley ... What is it, Freya?'

She shook her head. 'Only the way you said "little sister", then. Never mind.' But the smile she gave Sophie was warmer now. 'I hope we can make your stay here a little happier, Sophie. Perhaps Teddy could drive you into Truro tomorrow. They have some lovely shops there, and a beautiful brand new cathedral with three spires.'

'I'd rather go and see Lucy.'

'Come on,' Tristan urged, not wanting to upset Freya again. 'You'll love Truro. But for now we have work to do.'

He waited until Sophie had gone ahead of him into the hall, then took the startled Freya into a firm embrace. 'I'm sorry,' he whispered against her hair.

'Don't be,' Freya said. 'Family's precious.'

'And so are you. I won't let her treat you badly, I promise.' Tristan could happily have stayed where he was until he fell asleep on his feet, but Sophie would soon be trailing back to find him if he didn't hurry, so he gave Freya one last kiss and left. Sophie would simply have to get used to the way things were now, because nothing was going to change.

Priddy Farm welcomed them with the ripe smells Tristan had become used to, but which were still largely foreign to Sophie despite her experience with horses; she wrinkled her nose at the acidic air as they picked their way across the yard in search of Keir, who had promised to take them to meet Farmer Pawley.

Tristan pointed out the field that led back up to the rear of Priddy Lane. 'I can sometimes see Bill from the back bedroom window,' he said, 'but he generally likes to stay down this end, nearer the water trough and the other horses.'

'I can't wait to ride him again,' Sophie said.

'You can take him out this afternoon, if you like.'

A sudden gleam of happiness belied the way she was exaggeratedly lifting her skirt clear of any mud kicked up by her boots. She was more like the girl he knew now, chattering non-stop, rolling her eyes at his jokes, and almost running in her eagerness to see Bill again. He felt a complicated twist of emotion as he looked at her; she was still only thirteen years old, and had been devastated by the sudden, shocking loss of her idol, Caroline. Perhaps this was just what she needed, after all.

He peered around for a sign that Keir was working nearby, but there was no one to be found, although he heard a sound from inside the stone-built outhouse. 'Come on,' he gestured to Sophie to follow him. 'There's someone in there, at least.' He leaned into the dim interior. 'Can someone help? I'm looking for Keir Garvey.'

He was still blinking and trying to become accustomed to the lack of light, when a small figure barrelled past, and knocked him sideways into the door. He uttered a low groan as the impact reawoke the pain in his side, then watched, bemused, as the small boy hurtled across the yard and out through the farm gate.

'Tristan!'

Keir strode across the field, waving, and Tristan raised a hand to return the greeting, watching with envy as Keir put one hand on the gate and leapt over it easily. As he drew closer he looked at Tristan more closely. 'You're a bit pale, are you all right?'

Tristan grimaced. 'Farmer's lad knocked me a bit. Where did Sophie go?'

'She went running that way.' Keir pointed towards the gate. 'I met her last night, incidentally. Polite, lovely manners, but not much of a talker, is she?'

Tristan would have corrected him, but at that moment Sophie reappeared at the gate, with her hat in her hands, her hair flying around her head, and her face red and angry.

'The little tyke got away!'

'You chased after him?' Tristan almost laughed, but he didn't want to wound her feelings.

Sophie frowned. 'He could have really hurt you.'

'Don't worry about me. And thank you for trying to catch him, but I'm sure he didn't mean anything.'

'That's not the point,' she said hotly, and only then caught sight of Keir's surprised face. 'Good morning, Mr Garvey.'

'Morning, Miss MacKenzie.' Keir backed away towards the stable, and jerked his head for them to follow him. 'Bill's in here, he threw a shoe yesterday. Blacksmith's coming later this afternoon. You'd better come and meet Mr Pawley afterwards, Miss MacKenzie, so he knows you're not just some ruffian horse-thief.' He grinned at her furious expression. 'Well come on, look at you! Hair all over the place. Anyone would be forgiven.'

Sophie's mouth dropped open, and Tristan readied himself, but, to his relief, she began to laugh. 'You're no squire of the manor, Mr Garvey, how do I know *you* can be trusted?'

'Ah.' Keir tapped the side of his nose. 'Tell you what, we'll let Bill decide, shall we? Come on.'

Bill's whicker of happy recognition always made Tristan smile, particularly this time as it was directed at Sophie. The horse bent his head to her hand, and snuffled at her palm which usually held a treat of some kind. She grinned, and felt in her coat pocket and brought out an apple.

'I took it from the larder this morning,' she said over her shoulder to Tristan. 'I hope Freya won't mind?'

It was an unguarded moment, and Tristan didn't want to make too much of it, so he just said, 'She won't mind a bit.'

Sophie ran her hand down Bill's neck, as far as she could reach over the stall. 'He's looking fitter than ever,' she mused. Tristan glanced at Keir, who was watching the exchange closely; it seemed he'd only been half-joking when he'd suggested letting Bill decide.

'She's been riding him since she was ten,' he said in a low voice. 'She's more familiar with him now than I am.'

Keir nodded, not taking his eyes off Sophie and Bill. 'What about grooming?'

'We don't have yard staff, so we're used to doing what needs doing.'

Keir unhooked a headcollar from its peg on the wall, and unlatched the stall. 'Come on, fella.' He slipped the headcollar over Bill's head and led the horse out, then handed the short rein to Sophie. 'Now it's your turn. You can check him over properly, make sure I've been doing *my* bit.'

Tristan stayed back, as Sophie picked up the hoof that had lost its shoe and laid it along her thigh. Heedless of the mucky smudge on her skirt, she brushed away the clinging bits of straw, examined the hoof, then let it carefully back down, before continuing her appraisal. Keir scrutinised every move, and Tristan gave a secret sigh of relief to see the approval on his face.

The meeting with Stan Pawley went equally well. 'How long'll you be out of action, lad?' he asked Tristan.

'Not much longer, I hope.' In truth, he had no idea; every time he thought he was getting back to normal he would push things too far and set himself back. His ribs still ached abominably at times, and Doctor Bartholomew had said it was due to internal bruising and swelling. The exertion of moving house hadn't helped, and jolting about on horseback was certainly not something he could consider yet.

Later, as he and Sophie wandered down the lane towards Porthstennack, he tried to broach the subject of his forthcoming marriage. What better time than when she was flushed with the success of her meeting with the farmer, and enjoying the prospect of riding her favourite horse over the coming week?

'I'm certain Freya will ask you and Janet to be her bridesmaids,' he said. That must surely appeal at least, didn't all little girls dream of that?

But Sophie would not be drawn on the subject. 'When can we go back up to Pencarrack? Lucy promised to show me some magazines she's had sent all the way from America.'

'She was probably only being polite,' he cautioned, 'she has plenty to do without entertaining other people's bored visitors.'

'Like what?'

'Well for a start she looks after her nephew when he's home from school, and he's home at the moment.'

'How old is her nephew?'

194

'Eleven, I think.'

Sophie snorted. 'Old enough to take care of himself.'

'He thinks so, too. He has something of the wanderer spirit, that's the problem.'

Sophie waved that away. 'Anyway, Lucy said it would be all right if ... There he is again!'

'What?' They had reached the narrow main street of Porthstennack now, and Tristan followed Sophie's pointing finger, in time to see the farmer's lad vanishing around the corner of Smugglers' Way. 'I should have mentioned something to Mr Pawley about him,' he muttered. 'That boy should be at school.'

Sophie's voice was grim. 'I'm going to tell him what he did to you.'

'No, leave it ... *Sophie*!' But it was too late, she had gathered her skirt and taken off down the lane at a run. Tristan hobbled faster, trying to catch her before she got herself into bother, but by the time he reached the junction with Smugglers' Way neither of them could be seen.

He sighed, and sat down to wait on the wall with one hand pressed to his throbbing side, but with his head down it was a moment before he heard the raised voices of angry children over the roar of the surf behind him. With a deep feeling of trepidation, he peered across the way and saw his sister and the farmer's boy, shoving at one another; the boy was struggling to keep hold of a lidded box that was jerking in his hands like a live thing, and, as Tristan watched, the box slipped and crashed to the ground, and the lid flew off. A small dark shape erupted from it, and flashed away up the road and out of sight.

'Now see what you've done!' the boy cried. 'I'll never get him back now!'

'Sophie!' Tristan winced as his bruised bones protested, and rather than shouting again, he made his way carefully to where Sophie now stood alone, glaring after the skinny form of the outraged boy, who had taken off after the cat.

'Little brat!' she exclaimed. Then she frowned. 'Tris, you look terrible. You should go home.'

'I've got work to do,' he reminded her. 'Let's get you back up to town, you can help Freya in the shop. No arguments,' he added firmly. 'We'll go to Truro tomorrow, then you can ride Bill in the afternoon.'

'And when will we go to Pencarrack?'

'When you've proved you can behave like a lady.'

Sophie opened her mouth to snap a reply, but settled for a mutinous look, and turned to go up the hill. As Tristan followed he wondered how long he was expected to go on being this stern, substitute father, and when he could go back to being the older brother she had adored and looked up to. When he thought of the New England paper mill, and how their father clung to it, he had the coldest suspicion that such a time would never come again.

* * *

Caernoweth Fort

James knocked a loose stone aside with his boot, and glanced across at his companion. She was examining the walls with the kind of intensity that suggested she would be the one rebuilding them, not him, and then stood back with her hands on her hips and stared upwards.

'Well?' James called. 'What do you think?'

'I think you've got your work cut out for you.' Mairead beckoned him over. 'See here. There's nothing holding it together!'

'This would have been an indoor wall when it was in use,' James pointed out. 'I'm surprised it's withstood the weather we get up here. But that just goes to show that the workmanship's made it worth saving.'

'I still can't believe you threw that other job over for this one.'

He shrugged. 'Castle, fort . . . much the same thing. At least this one's on my doorstep.' He remembered something else, then. 'Come with me.'

'It's not going to be a fort though,' she pointed out, following him across the inner courtyard. 'It's going to be a hotel.'

'It's being restored as closely as the architect can do it, so they tell me. The outside, at least.'

'Have you not seen the plans yet?'

'I've not even been told the job's mine yet,' he confessed. 'I only dropped off my references a couple of days ago. Today was the last day to accept the job or not, so I'm going over to Pencarrack as soon as I've finished here.'

Mairead hung back as James headed towards one of the few remaining complete rooms. 'I'm not going in there!'

'Come on! Where's your sense of adventure?'

'It's sitting at home with its feet up, apparently chatting with my common sense,' she said with a sigh, and reached out to take his proffered hand.

'Good, then your common sense won't be alarmed unnecessarily. It's quite safe. Matt and I used to play down there all the time.'

'*Down* there?' Mairead snatched her hand back again. 'James Fry, you want your head examined.'

'I promise I'll get that done, first thing tomorrow. Meantime,' he stepped closer, 'relax, and come exploring.'

He led her across the uneven floor, to the far side where a doorway stood empty, the stone lintel overgrown with lichen and ivy. Mairead eyed the opening, and moved closer to his side.

He spoke more gently now, after all he didn't know where her deepest fears lay, and what fed them. 'I'm not going to try and persuade you to come down if you don't want to.'

'What's down there?'

'The dungeon.'

'Is it haunted?'

He blinked. This was a question he'd often entertained in the privacy of his own thoughts, but he'd never have expected the pragmatic Mairead to ask it. 'Uh ... I don't think so. Matt used to make up stories about what might have happened there, but we never talked about ghosts.'

'But you spent a lot of time here?'

'Yes.'

'All right, then. I trust you.'

James felt an odd little squeezing sensation in his chest. 'Are you sure?'

'Are you trying to talk me out of it now? Come on, or it'll be too dark to see, and then that'll be the last chance to see a bit of your childhood, gone. The place will be overrun with builders and planners before we know it.'

That jolted him. His thoughts had centred on this dream position, handed to him without any effort on his part, and the way the hotel would look out here on the cliff. But Mairead was right; once the renovations began, one more of the happiest chapters of his childhood would be gone.

Mairead seemed to read some of this on his face, because it was her turn to give his hand a little tug. 'You and Matthew are friends again,' she reminded him. 'You don't need those old days back. Now are you going to show me this place, or not?'

They went through the doorway, and James moved ahead, down the shallow stone steps that eventually led to the huge, draughty, L-shaped space below. There were still iron bars forming cells down the long part of the L, but for all its grimness of purpose, the room delighted Mairead.

'It's so light!' She let go of James's hand, and followed the corridor to where it bent away, and from where most of the light came. Smiling, James waited, and heard her gasp of delight.

'James, look!'

'I know.' He joined her in the shorter part of the room. 'You don't realise you're walking so far underground, until you see this.'

The back wall was completely formed of rusted iron bars, bolted deeply into the granite above and below. The early evening sunlight spilled into the dungeon, and from beyond it came the sound of the tumbling, pounding tide, far below. There was a brisk breeze blowing up, and it tugged at James's hair, and Mairead's skirt, but it felt so fresh that neither of them moved away; James leaned against the bars and folded his arms, quite prepared to stay there all evening.

'We've come all the way to the cliff?' Mairead strained to peer through the bars, and down.

'*Through* the cliff,' James pointed out. 'There's absolutely no chance anyone would try to escape through here, unless there's another secret passage of course, taking you back inland. If you somehow got out through these bars, you'd fall to your death for certain. Must have been hell to work on, but then it was the prisoners who did it, so they didn't have a lot to lose back then.'

'And who'll be doing the work this time?'

'I assume they'll take local labour. There'd be no shortage of interest.'

'That'd save them having to accommodate others, I suppose. Good news for some.'

James frowned. 'What do you mean?'

'There are at least three youngsters in my class who're worried about being moved out of their homes in Furzy Row.'

'Why would they have to move?'

'Their da's too ill to work. And David Donithorn's mother's tenancy must surely be on borrowed time too, since David left. The last thing any of them need is for Mr Batten to give these houses to some visiting builder instead.'

James shook his head. 'I hadn't thought of that.'

'Hopefully it won't come to that if they use local builders.' Mairead squeezed her face against the bars, pushing her cheeks out of shape and making him grin. 'Can you see this room from down there?'

'You could, if you could get down to the cove, but there's no road. I've seen the bars from the *Pride* though, when the light's been right.'

'It's astonishing, the work this must have taken.' Mairead

followed him as he turned to go back into the main dungeon area. 'What will this part be? You know, when it's a hotel?'

'I have no idea. As soon as I've seen the plans, I'll let you know.'

'What would you make it? If you were designing it.'

James didn't hesitate. 'The honeymoon suite. Can you imagine drifting off to sleep with the sound of the sea, and the glow of moonlight, through a huge window where the bars are now? This entire underground palace, all to yourself?'

'Why, Mr Fry, you're a secret romantic!'

James looked round with exaggerated care. 'You must swear never to tell a soul.'

Mairead nodded solemnly. 'I swear.'

'Matt and I split our time between Polworra pool and here, when we were supposed to be at school. He would come up with all these wild tales of pirates, stealing children away from their beds at night.' He smiled. 'Frightened the life out of me, but I loved them anyway. I don't know where he got his ideas, but he never ran out of them.'

'A gift, I suppose. Must be nice to have.'

'But you have others.'

'Numbers, mainly,' she agreed. 'Mother thought I'd go to university, but I'm happy enough. What happened there?'

'Where?'

She pointed. 'The wall. Not the solid rock, the man-made one.'

James went over to the crumbled portion of the internal wall, where a few rocks spilled onto the floor. 'Well it can't be the weather, not down here.'

'Maybe someone was trying to escape. Or ...' Mairead's eyes gleamed. 'Maybe there *is* another hidden tunnel after all!'

James laughed. 'They didn't make much of an effort to find it, if so.' He pulled at the loose rocks. 'But I'll point this out to Charles Batten when I see him. If his architect hasn't noticed it the budget will have to be amended.'

'For such a tiny piece?'

James stared upwards, at where the wall met the ceiling. 'It might mean there's a weakness somewhere, the weight shouldn't have pushed these stones out of place otherwise.'

'Not a secret tunnel then?' Mairead said glumly. 'Forget what I said about you being a romantic.'

James crouched and reached for another stone, and gave it a small, experimental tug. It came free as easily as pulling a loose glove from his hand, and he tumbled backwards, caught off balance, and landed on his behind on the dusty floor. A chuckling Mairead leaned down to help him up, then gave an exclamation and pointed to the wall. 'There's something in there! You'd never see it if you were standing up.' She put one small hand into the gap and withdrew a wrapped package, and gave it to him.

'A book?'

'It's been well waterproofed,' she said. 'I think this is goatskin.' In response to his surprised look, she explained, 'The journals Doctor Bartholomew donated to the shop were wrapped in the same cloth.'

'Probably from around the same time then. I wonder if it's another soldier's diary? Tristan MacKenzie would be interested, if it is.'

'Ought we to take it?' Mairead frowned. 'It was obviously hidden for a reason.'

'Judging from this wrapping it's been here hundreds of

years, any purpose will have long ceased to be important. And if it wasn't intended to be read at some point, why take such care to preserve it?'

'You do have a point there,' Mairead conceded. 'Right, I've got to go back. Freya will be waiting tea, and she'll probably have made another big effort for Tristan's sister. Not that she deserves it.'

James tucked the package into the pocket of his coat. 'Why not?'

'She's got no manners.'

He remembered Isabel's assertion that Mairead suffered from the same complaint, and smothered a grin.

'It won't do to keep the little treasure waiting then,' he said. 'You ought to lead by example, after all.'

'Why don't you come to tea?' Mairead followed him up the stone steps. 'There's plenty, and you'll be something to distract her from being mean to Freya.'

He gave a little huff of laughter. 'What an appealing invitation, thank you.'

'You know what I mean.'

'Thankfully, I do, yes. Lead on, then.'

It wasn't until much later that evening, as he left the familiar, comforting warmth of Penhaligon's Attic, that he realised he'd completely forgotten to go to Pencarrack and accept the job. He stared up the hill, dismayed, and angled his pocket watch beneath the gas light: past ten o'clock. Unforgiveable to disturb the Battens at this time of night ... He would just have to pray to whichever saint looked after forgetful builders, that Dorothy Batten was more susceptible to his charms than she'd seemed.

Chapter Thirteen

Wednesday morning had dawned chilly, and Keir eyed the sullen sky with a little grimace; he didn't need to search his long experience to know it would rain later, and with some enthusiasm, no doubt. Still, there was something about being out of doors that always lifted his spirits. It didn't matter that it was overcast and grey; good exercise, hard work, and the tang of salt that freshened the air were things even the spectre of Nancy's lies couldn't sour. He would call around to Hawthorn Cottage later, and tell her she didn't have to steal anymore, that he'd make sure she didn't go short and neither would her children.

Tristan MacKenzie's horse stood contentedly tearing up grass and munching it. Keir stopped and called him over, and Bill nudged hopefully at Keir's pocket through the bars of the gate. 'Sorry, lad.' Keir patted the gleaming neck. 'I haven't got anything for you. Your young Miss is going out for the day, so you and I'll go exploring again later, what do you say?'

Bill huffed again, his breath condensing in the cool morning air, and Keir gave him one last pat before crossing the yard to begin work. He got as far as hanging his bag on the nail by the barn door before a shout sent his mood plummeting, and he saw Alfie Nancarrow coming from the direction of the house. He readied himself for further defence, both of his person and of his reputation, but something about Nancarrow's expression told him that one was unnecessary, and the other pointless.

'Stan sent me to see if you'd arrived yet.'

'Well,' Keir said, spreading his arms and fixing a pleasant smile in place. 'As you see.'

'You're to come with me.'

'Where?'

Nancarrow didn't answer. His expression was dark and closed, and he turned back towards the house. Judging from that look, it was likely to be a lot safer in the farmhouse, with Stan Pawley present, than anywhere else, so Keir took down his bag again and followed.

The farmhouse kitchen was warm, and Keir remembered the first day, when he'd called in to ask for work, and found Mrs Pawley on her knees scrubbing the stone floor. The same smell permeated the air today; a mixture of bread and carbolic soap, underlaid with the acid reek from the slurry pit, and even as he acknowledged the comforting mixture, and how much a part of his life it was, Keir sensed how close he was to losing it.

Ruth Pawley herself was visible through the half-open door to the back passageway, a bucket in her hand, and the furtive air about her of one who is not supposed to be listening, yet can't help herself.

'Sit down, lad,' Stan said. He was eyeing Keir's bag.

'There's only my crib in there, and a pair of gloves.' Keir flipped it open. 'I've not been stealing from you, Mr Pawley, I swear it.'

'But you knew what I wanted to talk to you about.'

'Of course I did.'

'Then you understand how it looks? You start here, then a few days later things start goin' missing.'

'I do understand,' Keir conceded. 'But you'd be wrong to think I had anything to do with it.'

'Then who?'

Keir hesitated. 'There was a boy yesterday, in one of the barns. I didn't see him, but he ran out, and knocked into Mr MacKenzie. By the time I arrived, Miss Sophie had chased him away.'

'A boy, eh?'

'So they said.'

'And d'you reckon t'was he, takin' what wasn't his?'

'I have no idea,' Keir said calmly. 'All I know is it wasn't me.'

'What boy d'you suppose it might have been?'

'I don't know many of the local children.'

A look passed between Nancarrow and Stan Pawley. 'Bobby Gale?' Nancarrow ventured.

'Do 'ee know Bobby?' Stan asked Keir. 'Or his young brother Bertie?'

'No, but I told you, I didn't see it happen. It might have been him.' But Keir knew it had to have been Gerald, Nancy's eldest. At fourteen, he'd not have been missed at school, if he even still attended.

'I don't b'lieve you,' Pawley said, and he sighed. 'It just don't ring true. Those Gale boys've been trouble, I'll not deny it. But they ain't never stole before.'

'I'm not saying they're stealing now,' Keir pointed out. He could feel a light sweat on his brow. 'Perhaps one of them got desperate. It's only a few eggs—'

'No, t'idn't.' Pawley's expression tightened. 'It started out like that, but in the last few days other stuff's gone. Tools. Expensive ones. Ones I can't afford to go replacin', not when things is tight like this.'

'And Bobby Gale knows the value of good tools,' Nancarrow put in. 'His pa would knock seven bells out of him, should he find out the boy been robbin' men of their means to work.'

'I never said it was *any* of the Gale family!' Keir straightened his fingers in an attempt not to thump the table. 'I'm saying it wasn't me.'

'I'm goin' to have to let you go,' Pawley said in a heavy voice. 'I don't want to, you'm a good worker. But—'

'Then let me stay! It won't happen again, I'm sure of it.' Once he told Nancy his job was at risk, she'd be sure to put a stop to Gerald's activities, and her own.

'Only way you can be sure of that, is if you know who done it.' Nancarrow had the unmistakeable glint of triumph about him, not that Keir could blame him.

'*Do* you know?' Pawley looked hard at him, and Keir wavered. If he told the truth, Nancy would lose the trust of her family, and she'd certainly never want to see him again; if he kept quiet, there was always the chance that she could speak up for him and get him his job back once her father's anger had cooled. It would be the least she owed him.

207

'No,' he said at last. 'I don't know. It's only that ... no one would risk it, surely?'

'They won't if they see we're not stupid,' Pawley agreed. 'They'll see what happens when you get found out.' He planted his hands on the table and levered himself to his feet. 'Your wage will cover some of what's lost. I'll thank you to leave my land now, Garvey. I don't want to see you here again.'

* * *

Penhaligon's Attic

Anna felt the baby shift, and she paused in her work, waiting for it to settle again. Time was really marching on now, June would be here soon, and then everything would change again. God willing it would be for the better.

A knock at the front door signalled Tristan's arrival, and as she went to let him in Anna shouted up the stairs for Sophie. 'She'll be down directly,' she said. 'I thought she'd be ready by now.'

'She would be, if we were going to visit Lucy Batten,' Tristan said with a wry smile. 'As far as she's concerned Pencarrack is the only place around here worth visiting.'

Anna shrugged. 'Understandable I suppose, being so glamorous. I'm sure she'll enjoy Truro, nevertheless.' While they waited she asked how the visit with Farmer Pawley had gone, since Sophie had been characteristically non-committal about the whole thing.

'It went very well, except for when the farmer's boy mistook himself for a charging elephant. Honestly, if it wasn't for small children erupting out of nowhere, I'd be absolutely fine.'

'And lunatics like Tom Carne, looking to lay out drunks who've jilted their sister,' Anna reminded him.

'Caernoweth seems to have it in for me, doesn't it?'

Anna gave him a sympathetic smile. 'Says a lot for what you think of Freya, that you're prepared to risk living here. Come to think of it though, the Pawleys don't have a young son, only two grown daughters. Maybe it's one of his grandchildren you saw? Nancy's got three boys.'

'Maybe.' Tristan picked up his driving gloves as Sophie came in. 'Well, young lady, are you ready at last?'

Sophie looked at him doubtfully. 'I thought we decided Teddy was going to drive?'

'Teddy has work to do. Now say goodbye, and let's go. Truro awaits!'

'Can we go to Pencarrack on the way home?'

Anna looked away quickly, biting her lips together to stifle her laughter. Tristan merely hit Sophie on the shoulder with his driving gloves, and didn't reply.

After he and his sister had gone, Anna found Freya in Sophie's bedroom stripping the bed, and she firmly took the sheet out of her hands. 'They don't need to be washed every day, sweetheart, you're not at the hotel now. I'm sure Sophie doesn't expect it. They won't be dry by tonight, anyway, it's coming in to rain this afternoon.'

'Is it?' Freya peered worriedly at the window. 'I hope Tristan will be all right.'

'He'll be grand.' Anna patted the bed beside her. 'Come and sit down a minute.'

Freya did so, and Anna put an arm around her shoulder. The girl was driving herself to exhaustion trying to make everything perfect for that ungrateful wretch, and it wasn't fair.

'She'll probably respond better to a bit of normality,' she said. 'Just go back down to the shop, let me potter around here for a few minutes and tidy things, and tonight you're to let me prepare the meal.'

'You've got the pub to run,' Freya protested.

'I can go down late for once, Esther's got Alan to help after all. Besides, if it's anything like it has been, it'll be one long string of sour tempers, and people making a single pint last all night.'

'The miners?'

Anna nodded. 'Evidently the Battens have started up a new project, and rumour has it the mine's suffering as a result. It's a worry, I know, but I wish to goodness they'd keep their arguments on the other side of the door. Or stay home and save their money.'

'I'm more worried about you. It's not good for you to be on your feet all night.'

'I sit down whenever I can,' Anna said. 'Don't worry about me.' In truth her back was a sea of aches by around nine o'clock most nights. Carrying Mairead, while being married to a well-respected doctor and living in the height of comfort, was a very different prospect to this new life of hers, but she wouldn't swap it for all the cushions in the world.

'What are you going to do today?' Freya asked.

'I'm going down to see Ellen. Is it all right if I take half that fruit cake in the blue tin?'

'Of course. Isn't Ellen working today?'

210

'Wednesdays are her late start day – once a week she works with the count house girls, cleaning the officers' underground clothes. She won't go up until after lunch, which is plenty of time for me to waddle down the hill.' She grinned at Freya's expression. 'It's all right, if I don't say it, you'll only think it!'

'I wouldn't have said "waddle", though,' Freya mused. 'Roll, maybe.'

It was good to see the smile back on her face, and Anna made a silent vow to pay attention to how much she was doing for Sophie, and to try and remove some of the burden – or to make that girl aware of it, at least. She looked around at the piles of clothes Sophie had left on the chair, and in the corner. Little madam.

'Right,' she said, levering herself off the bed with exaggerated movements. 'Off you go and open up the shop. I'll set this room to rights.'

The walk down to Porthstennack seemed to take forever today. The fresh air felt good on her skin, but the coming rain had given it a definite bite. Anna glanced at the sky, and walked a little more quickly; she wanted plenty of time to talk to Ellen before her friend had to leave for work. She shifted her basket higher up her arm, feeling the fruit cake sliding on its plate beneath the cloth cover – it would be nice to sit and chat over a cup of tea again, Ellen's house might be small, but it was always warm and welcoming, and Anna's mouth watered as she anticipated the first bite of cake. There was that to be said for having a house-guest, at least; Freya had outdone herself with her baking this week.

But the house was as still and silent as before; perhaps this time Ellen was out the back, or visiting a neighbour. Anna tried the front door, not very hopefully; when it opened she decided to put the water on the range to boil, so that by the time her friend returned, tea would be ready. She stepped over the threshold, and instantly recoiled; normally the smell of dirt and neglect might not have affected her so strongly, but in her present sensitive state it made her throat close up and her stomach roll.

'Ellen?' she called. A rustle came from the kitchen, and she went through, wrinkling her nose. Among the other smells, was that ... tom cat? 'Ellen!' There was no sign of anyone out in the small back garden, and Anna went to the range to pull the kettle across to the hot plate, and set it boiling. Frowning, she put a hand flat on the plate, as if to convince herself she was imagining things, but the metal was icy cold. She opened the squeaky door and poked around at the ash, but there wasn't even the glimmer of an ember among the grey dust. She looked more closely around her. Her heart was tripping uncomfortably fast now. What if Ellen lay upstairs in her bed, unable to move? Or ... *dead*?

Suddenly unable to shake this dreadful image, she hurried up the stairs and into the first bedroom, Eddie's. It was empty but neat, and a lot cleaner than downstairs. Ellen's room was also empty, and Anna heaved a sigh of relief, then looked again. There was only a narrow, threadbare eiderdown on the bed, no pillow, no knick-knacks on the dresser, no mirror, or brush and comb. She pulled open the wardrobe. One or two skirts and blouses, one pair of shoes ... The scarf she had returned was hooked onto the back the wardrobe door, and was the only thing that convinced Anna that Ellen still lived here.

She called to mind Eddie's room, the neatly washed, folded clothes in the cupboard, and his few toys and books stacked tidily on the dresser. The bed linen had looked quite fresh, the thick eiderdown from Ellen's bed lay doubled across it, and the curtains were tied back from clean windows. Whatever troubles she was going through, at least her son was not suffering.

Then Anna recalled Mairead's concerns at school, and amended that thought; Ellen's priorities might be in place, but that did not mean Eddie wasn't affected. She sat on Ellen's bed, her heart heavy. Everything must have been sold. Everything that wasn't absolutely vital. There was no fuel for the range, nothing had been cooked in days, and with no hot water there had been none of the usual thorough cleaning downstairs.

Tears started to Anna's eyes. *Why hadn't she realised?* Blithely going through her life, with her happy family and her baby kicking inside her, she had assumed everyone else was equally content. Work was hard for everyone, of course; times were difficult for most. She herself had fought hard enough to find her place again, but once she had, the shiny walls of her own little bubble had not allowed her to see out, to remember what it was to fear, and to weep, and to struggle through every day not knowing where your next mouthful was coming from. Listening to the arguments in the Tinner's, about the shortened shifts and potential job-losses at Wheal Furzy, she had genuinely sympathised but this brought it all crashing home. Ellen must have lost work already, maybe today she had gone up to beg for a double shift in the count house to make up for it.

The sound came from the kitchen again, and Anna rose, sniffing, and wiped her eyes on the sleeve of her blouse. She went downstairs, wondering if a rat had found its way into the pile of rubbish by the back door and shuddered, preparing herself to seize the coal shovel and have at it. Instead she stopped and stared in surprise.

'Arric?' She crouched and held out a hand. The cat blinked at her, then looked away, regal in his disinterest ... It was definitely Arric. 'Come here!' She made a sucking noise and rubbed her fingers together. 'Come!'

Arric yawned and stretched out his front legs, sticking his behind up. Then he sat down and raised his paw, and proceeded to give his face a thorough wash. The sound of the front door opening made Anna start to her feet, feeling guilty although she'd done nothing wrong.

'Ellen?'

But it was Eddie, who came into the kitchen, and looked from Anna to Arric and back again. 'You can have him back now,' he said, surprisingly calm. 'No one'll pay for 'im no more.' He tipped up a small bucket and spilled a fresh sardine and some seaweed onto the table.

'Pay for him?' Anna frowned. 'Oh, Eddie. You stole him?'

'To rent him out as a mouser, like that other one. Got a few pennies too,' he added, raising his chin in a rare show of defiance.

'But to steal from friends is unforgiveable. I'd have given you some money, if you'd asked.'

'Ma said I shouldn't. Besides, I only borrowed him.'

'You took him without asking. That's stealing.' Anna felt rotten for telling him off, especially now she realised what

214

terrible straits he and his mother were in. 'Sweetheart, I don't expect you to understand, but Esther Trevellick took comfort from having him around, since Joe was the one who found him. It was almost like he'd sort of . . . left her something.'

Eddie flushed and his eyes filled with angry tears. 'It's *your* fault, anyway!'

'What? What's my fault?'

'Why we've no money!' Eddie made as if to back out of the kitchen, but Anna was too quick for him, and seized his arm.

'Oh no, you don't! You're going to tell me exactly what you meant by that.'

'Ma said—'

'Never mind what your ma said. I'm sure she's no idea what's been going on behind her back. So?'

'All right! If it wasn't for you spoiling things, Juliet Carne would never 'ave tried to get my Uncle David back.'

Anna's jaw went slack, and she dropped his arm. 'Uncle . . . David *Donithorn*? What's that got to do with it?'

'If Aunt Ginny hadn't pushed Juliet in that pond, then she'd never have had to leave town. And Uncle David wouldn't have gone after her. Now Granny Donithorn's got no money comin' in, so Ma's been paying the rent on Furzy Lane as well as here, and Granny will have to move out of there soon anyway. I don't see my ma no more! She's always either workin', or cleanin' for Granny Donithorn!'

Eddie stopped, breathing hard, having spilled everything that had been weighing him down, and his thin frame shook as he gave in to his tears. Anna gathered him close, her own heart close to breaking.

'Oh, Eddie . . . I'm so sorry,' she whispered. After a moment

215

she felt his arms go around her too, and she stifled a sigh. Dear God, would the repercussions from that stupid, *stupid* slip never end?

'Ma says she din't want you to feel bad, so I wasn't to tell you.' Eddie sniffed and drew back. 'Don't tell her, will you? Please?'

'Of course not.' Anna smoothed his hair from his brow. 'But you must let me help you. Somehow.'

'But how?'

'I can give you a little money, for fuel, at least.'

'Ma will want to know where it came from.'

'Hmm.' Anna thought a moment. 'Where is she today?'

'At Granny's. Then she's goin' straight to work.'

'Right. Come back with me. And bring him.' She gestured to Arric, and then a thought occurred to her. 'Did you have a run-in with Tristan MacKenzie's sister yesterday?'

'Is that who it was? She's a nasty maid. She made me drop the box and I thought I'd lost the cat for good.'

'I thought so.' Anna took a deep breath. 'Why were you at the farm, Eddie?'

He looked embarrassed, and busied himself with finding the box, before throwing the sardine into it. Arric shifted his bored green gaze from Eddie to the box, and back again, and resumed cleaning.

'Eddie? The farm?'

'I made a bit of money selling a few eggs,' he muttered. 'No one'd miss them, I only took a few. Hens always lay more.'

Anna shook her head. 'My cousin got into a lot of trouble over that. Alfie Nancarrow thought he was the one stealing. And not only that, since you "borrowed" Arric here, my own

216

hens have been too upset by rats to lay anything. So you see what happens when you act without thinking?'

Eddie suddenly seemed much older than his eight years. 'Yes. I do.'

Anna felt the flush rising to her face, and sighed. 'And I'm a fine one to preach to you, aren't I?' she said quietly. 'I just wanted you to understand too. Keir was set upon, you know. They might have hurt him quite badly if he hadn't been able to look after himself. So you'd better watch yourself. You might be able to run fast, but when you're messing with a man's livelihood, he'll find a way to catch you. Promise me you'll stop stealing.'

'I can't. We need the money.' Eddie, catching the overly confident Arric unawares, scooped the cat up and dropped him into the box, slamming the lid shut in one deft movement. 'But you can have your cat back.'

'Thank you.' Anna gave him a wry smile. 'I must say you're very good at handling him. I might be able to find a job for you after all. But first, school.'

'But you said—'

'I said you could bring Arric back to the pub. You've still got schooling to attend to. But after, you're to wait for Miss Casey, and come to the shop instead of back to this empty place, all right?'

He nodded, and picked up the box. Arric scrabbled around inside it for a moment, in a half-hearted protest, but shortly the sound changed, and they heard him smacking his lips over the sardine. Anna brushed the boy's head as he passed her, and he looked up at her with wordless gratitude. She wished he wouldn't; she didn't know what she was going to do for him and for Ellen. But she'd have to think of something.

Chapter Fourteen

August 22nd 1646.

From the journal of Daniel Bartholomew:

My father is dead. At his own hand, yet Malcolm Penworthy must bear the blame for it. Tomorrow I will go to Penworthy House with the sad news, and in doing so I will make it plain that, should any ill befall me, the ugly truths that drove my father to his death will be made known to everyone. In return I will ask for enough money to take me away from this cursed place. No more than my due, as I am certain he will agree.

For their protection and mine, my father's diaries are made safe from water damage, and once I have the money they will be sent to meet my brother Robert's ship.

These pages will record Penworthy's reply in due course.

James carefully turned over the page, his fascination piqued, but the rest of the book was empty and he tossed it back onto the dresser. It slid towards the edge, and he instinctively reached out to stop it falling; mostly empty or not, it might mean something to MacKenzie and his friend, since they were reading those Bartholomew diaries even now. He caught the book by its corner, and it flopped open and a piece of paper fluttered out, from inside the back cover.

August 25th 1646

Robert,

I am sorry for the hurried nature of the note I put in with our father's diaries, and for the difficulty you must have had in finding this book. But since both have led you to find this note we must deem it a success. Should you still wish to seek me out, you will find me at a moderate lodging on the Penworthy Estate, known as Pencarrack, and living under the name Daniel Batten. A full explanation of what has passed will await you there, and you will understand why I have been reluctant to surrender my dark and shameful secrets to the vagaries of the Royal Mail.

With a brother's love, I beg your forgiveness for what you will learn.

Daniel.

James stared at the note, rereading it with growing fascination, and then, remembering his urgent schedule for the day he put both paper and book back on the dresser, and reached instead for his coat. He jumped as the door opened.

'Oh, sorry, Mr Fry,' Mrs Gale said. 'I thought you said you was goin' up Pencarrack early. Only I did think to clean in 'ere while you was out.'

'I am going up there,' James said. A strange feeling came over him as he considered the history of that place. What had happened to make Daniel Bartholomew change not only his mind, but his name too? And the house was hardly what he'd have termed a 'moderate lodging', either. 'I'll be out of your hair in a minute.'

'What's that then?' She nodded at the book. 'Looks old, so it do.'

'It is. Actually, I believe it'll be of some interest to the doctor.'

But despite her natural tendency to question, Mrs Gale had more important things to discuss than old books, and she waved a dismissive hand. 'Did 'ee hear Mrs Penhaligon's cousin got sacked?'

'No!' James stopped readying himself for his walk. 'What happened?'

'Stealin' tools, an' that. And veg. *And* eggs.' She sniffed. 'T'idn't no wonder us can't get 'em for love nor money, when they'm being sold off at market instead. Likely for twice what we do pay.'

'He seemed a decent enough bloke,' James said. 'Anna must be upset.'

'I don't think she knows yet. I only heard it from Alfie Nancarrow's missus this mornin'.'

'Well keep it to yourself,' James cautioned her. 'It might not be true, and no one'll thank you for putting it about.'

'Oh, it's true.' Mrs Gale began straightening things on James's dresser. 'She heard it from Ruth Pawley herself, who was there when Stan did the sackin'.'

'Even so.' Realising he might bump into Tristan, James picked up the book again and slipped it into his pocket, then faced Mrs Gale. 'Right. Do I look like the type of man you'd give a job to, provided he has excellent references?'

Mrs Gale eyed him critically. 'You'll do, if you straighten your tie.'

He did so, then sketched a little bow. 'I'm off then. I'll see you at teatime.'

Emerging from the library at Pencarrack, relieved after a most satisfactory meeting with Charles and Miss Batten, James was glad to see Teddy Kempton just arriving.

'I have something you might be interested in,' he said, crossing the hall. 'I found this at the fort yesterday.' He reached into his pocket for the book, 'I was going to—'

'Mr Fry!'

Dorothy Batten had followed him out, and was hurrying towards him.

'Yes, Miss Batten?'

'I wonder if you'd be so kind as to escort me over to the fort?'

'Now?'

'I have the plans here,' Dorothy said, holding them up. 'Time's running short for approving them.'

'Plans?' Teddy's face fell. 'It's true, then. The fort's being rebuilt as an hotel?'

'I'm certain they'll keep as many of the old features as they can,' James assured him.

'Can you swear to that? You're an architect, aren't you?'

'*An* architect. Not *the* architect.' But James gave him an encouraging smile. 'Look, I haven't seen these plans yet. But I'm certain no one would voluntarily destroy something with so much history. Speaking of which . . . ' He handed the book to Teddy. 'I was going to give it to Tristan, but since you're here.'

'We ought to leave now, James,' Dorothy insisted. 'Mr Pagett's arriving at teatime, and he's going to want our signature on these.'

'At least one of the lower internal walls will need looking at,' James said. He raised a distracted hand in farewell to Teddy, and followed Miss Batten out into the sunlight. 'I noticed a weakness there yesterday.'

'Then we'd better assess what needs doing, so we can inform Mr Pagett and alter the budget accordingly.' Dorothy walked ludicrously quickly, and glanced back with ill-disguised impatience. But a tiny smile lurked at the corners of her eyes; she was obviously in her element over this project, and he couldn't help smiling back. She had always been a handsome woman, and there was no harm in encouraging any attraction he might, in turn, hold for her. It certainly couldn't hurt his chances of further work, should it come up.

He slipped easily into his old, smooth tones, well-tested in the past, and, for the most part, successful. 'I'm sure you don't need my expertise to tell you what's wrong, Miss Batten.'

Her eyebrow went up. 'What I certainly don't need is any patronising nonsense from you. We hired you because we *thought* we needed an experienced man in charge. So, do we need such a man or don't we?'

He flushed. 'You definitely do.'

'And have you informed Mr Lutyens's hirers and firers that you no longer require that position?'

He recovered himself, feeling less like an idiot at this reminder that he'd been accepted by that company. 'No. I've only just been offered this one, formally,' he pointed out. 'I'd have been remarkably foolish to have burned my bridges, don't you think?'

Dorothy stopped. 'You're certainly no fool,' she said quietly. For a moment he wondered if she was mocking him, but she kept her gaze level, and there was no hint of humour there.

'No,' he agreed. 'I'm not.'

They walked more slowly then, it seemed her competitive edge had been smoothed somewhat. Talk flowed more freely between them, and was markedly less combative.

'What was that you were giving to Mr Kempton?' Dorothy asked as they drew near the fort.

'Ah! Yes, this will interest you. It was a book. I found it when I was up here yesterday.'

'What kind of book?'

'It started out as a diary, I think, but there was only about half a page. It was written by a Daniel Bartholomew, after his father died.'

'Related to the doctor?'

'I assume so. I think he believed Malcolm Penworthy to have had something to do with his father's death, although it

223

was a suicide. He wrote that he was going to visit Penworthy, and claim some kind of compensation.'

Dorothy pulled a dismissive face. 'Why on earth do you say it would interest *me*?'

James heard echoes of Mairead in that blunt tone, which was all that stopped him rising to the bait. 'It seems Daniel Bartholomew changed his name to Batten,' he said. 'This was during the Civil War period, so I assume he's an ancestor of yours.'

'Quite possibly. I gather Pencarrack goes back to that era, and before then it was part of the Penworthy estate. But no, it's of absolutely no interest to me, Mother was the one who was keen on all that kind of stuff.' She looked up at the crumbling tower that stood over them, and sighed. 'Right, let's get on with it, then.'

She led the way through to the inner courtyard, and spread the plans out on a granite slab that looked to have acted as some kind of bench. She placed a small stone on each of the corners, silently waiting for James to join her. He did so, and as her long-fingered, elegantly shaped hand pointed out features designed by Pagett's team, he realised she was leaning against him, and not only for balance. As an experiment he didn't move away, but engineered a reason to return the pressure, stretching across the plan to indicate the dungeon area.

'What will that be?' He remembered Mairead's grin as she accused him of being a romantic. 'I thought perhaps the honeymoon suite.'

'Really?' She didn't give way under the press of his shoulder against her. 'Pagett's man thinks the office. With the safe, you know.'

'My idea's better.'

Dorothy didn't look at him. 'No, it's not.'

'Have you been down there?'

She shifted, but her arm remained firmly against his. 'No.'

'Shall we?'

She was very close now, and as she finally turned her face to his he could see a tiny nervous flicker at the corner of her mouth. 'Mr Fry—'

'You came to see the place,' he pointed out in a low voice. 'Let me show it to you. There's more to the dungeon than you'd know from that.' He nodded at the plan.

They descended to the dungeon, and he heard again Mairead's gasp of delight as she looked out from the middle of the cliff face, onto the headland opposite and the crashing surf far below, and a smile touched his lips – unbidden, but Dorothy returned it.

'I remember you now,' she said. 'You and your friend Matthew. I'm older than him by a year or two, and you by about four I think. But I remember you both, neither of you were the same as most of the other boys.'

James put his hands in his pockets, sensing the shift in their relationship by that simple statement, and that this was a tipping point. 'And I remember you,' he said carefully. 'You were ... different.'

'On the outside, perhaps.' She stood still a moment longer, and then he saw something slide into place in her expression. A decision. Or a letting go, perhaps? She came over to him, and ran a hand down the buttons of his waistcoat, and he kept very still.

'We're going to be working together a lot, aren't we?' she said.

'I imagine so.' He kept his voice steady, still unsure whether she was testing him. 'I'm glad of that.'

'Good,' she breathed, moving still closer, until her lips touched his jaw. 'Don't try to pretend surprise. You're no fool, remember?'

Throwing caution to the wind, he turned his face so her lips met his, and felt her hands tighten on his waist. The jolt that ran through him took him by surprise; it had been a while since his last encounter with a woman but even so . . . The way she took control reminded him a little of Juliet Carne, too; each was appealing in her own way, and there was nothing demure or shy about either of them. They knew what they wanted, and they knew what he wanted – both of them had known that even before he did, but he caught up quickly.

Dorothy tugged at his tie, and then it was off, and flung aside, and James had to fight not to laugh as he remembered Mrs Gale's admonition that he should straighten it. Coming to his senses at the last possible moment, he caught Dorothy's shoulders and held her slightly away from him. Her face clouded over, only to clear again when she realised he was only reversing their positions. The struggle with clothing was brief, practised as they both were, and James heard a tiny sigh break free as he pushed into her.

It was quick, and uncomfortable; the rattle of the iron bars at Dorothy's back was punctuated by wordless gasps from them both, and finally a low cry that burst from his throat. She did not match it, but he saw her brows draw down and her mouth open, and a red stain crept up her throat to her face as she panted her pleasure. A woman used to secret trysts, but there was no jealousy on his part; a mutual physical need had been met. Nothing more.

They dressed in silence at first, then Dorothy spoke up, and her voice was oddly quiet.

'Can I assume you never did that with my sister?'

'No! Lucy's not like . . .' His words tailed away as he realised what he was saying, but Dorothy finished with her belt, and there was a wry little smile twisting her mouth down at the corners.

'It's all right. I know everyone remembers what I was like before . . . before Harry.'

'And not since?' He couldn't resist asking. 'I mean, you're a stylish and beautiful woman. There must have been temptations.'

She inclined her head, accepting the compliment. 'I won't deny it, there have been one or two. But on the whole, no, not since then.'

Presumably she had learned a sharp lesson from the shock of unexpectedly becoming a mother, and it was no real surprise she had let go of her rebellious side. She had channelled all that energy, with undeniable success, into the family businesses, and now she was James's boss. Certainly the most interesting boss he had ever worked under. Or against . . .

'*Now* what are you grinning about?' Dorothy's voice had regained some of its former defensive edge, and he realised it was time to set the pace for what was to come. He pulled her to him, and laced his hands in the small of her back. She looked up at him, expressionless, and he wondered if he had read her right, after all.

'Just thinking about my contract of employment,' he

murmured, and kissed her, deliberately softly. 'Does it say how often I'm to perform this particular task?'

He felt her lips curve under his as she returned the kiss, but when she broke it her tone was a warning one. 'Just don't go thinking any more about honeymoon suites.'

'I won't.'

'In that case, I'd say on a strictly ad hoc basis.'

'And you'll let me know I'm required? Or is it a two-way arrangement?'

Dorothy seemed surprised, and even touched, as if she hadn't considered he might be the one to make an advance. 'I'm open to ... negotiation,' she said at last. 'But we'll have to find alternative accommodation once the work starts here.'

'I'm sure we'll manage something.'

'Good.' She pushed away from him, and, as if someone had flicked a switch, the businesswoman came back. For the next hour they prowled every inch of the fort, making notes, discussing Pagett's plans, and calculating costs, as if nothing out of the ordinary had happened at all. Despite what he knew of her, James had to admit he found it slightly disconcerting.

'I'll have blueprints made up as soon as Pagett agrees, and counter-signs,' Dorothy said, when they had seen all they could. She removed the stones from the corners of the plan. 'We'll send word when we need you to come up to the house.'

James watched her roll the plan up, complete with the notes she had added, and just before the drawing vanished from view he noticed she had crossed out *office*, and pencilled in *Honeymoon Suite?*

* * *

The afternoon was drawing on. Keir had walked the cliffs ever since the morning's ugly scene in the farmhouse kitchen, until his feet felt likely to burst out through his boots, and now he finally started back towards Porthstennack. Trudging through the hamlet, and up the hill, his mind turned over what he might do to salvage the tattered remnants of this new life he had already come to love. A job on this new build he'd heard about, at the fort? The quarry, mine and tannery were options too ... but his reputation would go before him; no one would hire a thief, no matter how brawny he was, and willing to work for a pittance. Besides, he'd already heard dark mutterings about level closures at the mine. Whole teams laid off.

There was only one real hope: Nancy. She would be home from work soon, in time to fix tea for Tory, Joseph and Matty. Gerald would be working on the farm until late. Of course he must be the one who'd taken the tools, Nancy would never be able to get away with it. She owed Keir a word to her father at the very least. His body tightened as he remembered how she'd distracted him the last time, but before it had been a few eggs and the odd beetroot; now it was different, he'd lost both his job, and his potential home.

He couldn't go into Priddy Farm to wait for her, so he continued up to Hawthorn Cottage, and sat on the gate instead. It felt good to let his feet rest, and after a few minutes he realised he was starving and he pulled the box from his crib bag. When he saw the slice of cake Anna's stepdaughter had put in with his cheese sandwich, his anger flared; Nancy had jeopardised the whole family's reputation, not just his. He heard voices, and glanced up from his food to see Nancy, her youngest child dawdling at her side.

229

'Come on, Matty! Make haste!' She glanced up as she approached the gate, and her face brightened as she saw Keir. 'There's a sight for sore eyes.'

'Don't pretend you've not heard,' Keir said, not budging from the gate.

Nancy shrugged. 'I'm sorry you lost your job, but it don't matter none to me if you've taken a few things.'

'What?' Keir jumped down, and caught Nancy's arm. She winced, and looked down at Matty, and Keir let go at once. 'You have to go to your father and tell him!'

'Tell him what?'

'That he's made a mistake, that I deserve my job back.'

Nancy shook her head. 'I've nothin' to do with the runnin' of that farm anymore. Ma looks after Matty while I work, that's it. I left home when I married, I make my own way, and I'm not crawling back there now lookin' for favours. Not even for you.'

'Favours?' Keir fought the urge to seize her arm again. 'You've got a nerve, calling it that!'

'Listen here,' Nancy said, clearly struggling to find a reasonable tone, 'you was caught out. I can't help you. Now, are you comin' in, or no?'

'No, I'm bloody not!'

'Good. Come back when you've got a better manner about you.' Nancy elbowed him aside, and unlatched the gate. 'And *when* you can apologise, I *might* be ready to listen.'

Keir tried again, growing desperate. 'I understand you'd want to protect your own, but this is my life. I'll have to leave town!'

'Leave, then.' Nancy looked at him, her expression cool. 'I

don't need no overgrown toddler throwin' tantrums and settin' a bad example.'

'Why won't you admit it?'

'Admit what?' She frowned.

'That your boy Gerald is the tool thief. And that you stole from the farm, too.'

'I *what*?'

'Come on! That new shawl you were wearing the other day? That lie about spending Saturday night alone?'

'Get gone, Keir Garvey,' Nancy said flatly. Her face was pale. 'I don't want to see you around here no more.'

'Funny,' Keir said bleakly, 'your da said much the same thing.'

'Good sense runs in our family.' Nancy ushered Matty through into the yard, and banged the gate shut. 'Now bugger off.'

Keir watched her striding across the yard, willing her to look back, to show a crack in her suddenly hard shell. When she didn't, he found himself reaching out to unfasten the latch, to follow her, but as the door closed behind her he slammed his curled fist down on the gate and walked away.

At Penhaligon's Attic, Freya was alone in the shop and looked up, surprised. 'You're home early. Are you all right?'

'I'm surprised you've not heard,' he said. 'Where's Anna?'

'In the kitchen, I think. She's got an after-school visitor. Heard what?'

'I'll tell you in a bit, I promise. I need to talk to Anna first.' He went into the kitchen, but it was empty and the back door stood open; he could see the shadowy figure of his cousin in the garden beyond, and felt himself tighten up at the thought of telling her his news. Her after-school guest was helping her bring in the laundry, taking the dolly pegs she gave him, and putting them carefully in the basket that sat on the grass by his feet. He seemed to be about eight or nine years old, and was chattering happily enough to Anna as they worked.

Then he caught sight of Keir, and his face went slack with dismay and he turned to Anna.

'Thank you for offering tea, and for lettin' me earn a penny or two, but I 'as to go home now.'

The boy came in, sidling around the table, as if he expected Keir to cuff him around the ear if he came within reach, and Anna followed him with her basket. She looked tired, and gave a grunt of relief as she put the full basket on the table.

'Keir, this is Eddie Scoble. Ellen's son. I think he has something to tell you.'

'Ellen?'

'My friend, from Porthstennack. Tell him, Eddie, then I'll walk you home.'

Keir frowned. Anna didn't ought to be wandering up and down that awful hill. 'Tell you what, lad, I'll walk you home instead, how about that? Then you can say whatever it is you have to say.'

The boy shot a pleading look at Anna, who didn't notice. 'Grand,' she said. 'In that case, Keir, I've got something you can take with you.'

She crooked a finger at him, and he followed her into the back porch. A smallish potato sack sat in the corner, and when he hefted it he realised it was half-filled with coal. 'Since you're going to walk him back, would you mind? Ellen's kitchen range is out. Maybe you could get it started for when she gets home?'

Keir's aching feet throbbed in protest, but he nodded. Perhaps by the time he passed Hawthorn Cottage again Nancy might have calmed down, and might even be feeling the prickling of her conscience.

He set off with the boy at his side, and the small bag of coal across his back, and waited to find out what it was that Eddie had to tell him. It was several minutes before the boy spoke up.

'I'm that sorry,' he muttered.

'What, lad? Speak up.'

'I din't mean for you to get in trouble.'

Keir stopped. Eddie stopped too, his eyes wide and glistening with tears. 'Miz Penhaligon told me I should say sorry. And I am, in any case,' he added quickly.

Keir thought fast, putting the facts together. 'You?' he said, at last. '*You're* the one who stole from the farm?'

'I ... There's my ma! MA!'

Keir looked back up the hill, and saw a thin young woman coming towards them. She carried a basket, and her boots made clunking and sliding noises on the road as she came closer.

'Eddie, what are you doin' up here? Did you have to stay behind at school again?' The woman gave Keir a distracted smile. 'Is he botherin' you, sir?'

In the face of her polite enquiry Keir didn't know whether to say no, or to tell the truth. Because yes, the boy *was* bothering him. The little thief had lost him his job, his home,

233

and his woman. He was a bother, all right. Keir's patience deserted him.

'Do you have no shame, Mrs Scoble?'

Her smile dropped away. 'What do you mean?'

'Sending your son out to steal from hard-working folk.'

Mrs Scoble's voice turned hard. 'He've been at his learnin', sir.'

Keir saw little Eddie's lip tremble, and he almost relented, but then he remembered the sight of Nancy striding away from him, his accusations – his *false* accusations – causing her every bit as much hurt as this boy and his mother were causing him.

He gestured to the basket, fresh anger biting at his insides. 'What's in there? Eggs, perhaps? Or a cabbage or two? I'll bet they're not paid for, whatever they are.'

Ellen's eyes flashed. She pulled back the cover of the basket, and showed him a small pile of neatly folded clothes. 'My ma's mending.' She gestured to her son. 'Run away home, Eddie, I'll be down d'rectly.' She turned back to Keir. '*Stealing?*'

'Yes, stealing!' Keir flung the word after the boy as he picked up his feet and began to run. He looked back at Ellen, who was glaring at him. 'He told me so himself.'

'You're lying!' Ellen went to move past him. 'An' if you weren't Anna's cousin, I'd kick you right where it'd do the most good!'

'I'd like to see you try!' Keir spat the words out before he could think, and he saw the brief flicker of contempt on the young woman's face, but she didn't reply. He started walking again. 'Well, come on, then.'

'What?'

He gestured to the sack across his shoulder. 'I might be ready to commit murder, but I'm not going to make you carry this.'

'What is it?'

'Coal.'

Ellen stopped. 'Coal? What for?'

'Anna said your range had gone out. Or was that a lie you've told her, too?'

'No! Only . . . how does she know?'

'I've no idea! Do you want it, or not?'

A strange expression crossed her face, a mixture of embarrassment and relief, and her defensive tone dropped. 'Yes. Thank you. I'll pay her on Friday.'

'If that's the arrangement. I'm only the pack horse, after all.' He moved off down the hill, towards the lane down which Eddie had vanished. 'Which house is it?'

Ellen hurried along at his side. 'It's all right, I'll carry it from here.'

'You'll do no such thing. This is heavier than it looks, Anna'll have my hide.' In truth he wanted nothing more than to drop the bag in the road, and make this irresponsible woman work for herself. 'What number?'

'I said I'll take it.' Ellen folded her arms, and jerked her chin at the road. 'Go on, put it down.'

'No. What are you going to do about your boy?'

'He's done nothin' wrong. He wouldn't.'

'He *confessed*, Mrs Scoble! He told me he's been thieving from the farm.' He hesitated then, because he suddenly wasn't sure Eddie had confessed any such thing. He'd been about to, Keir was certain enough of that, but then he'd seen his mother.

Ellen had clearly read something of this on his face, because she gave a short laugh. 'He didn't, did he! I told you, he wouldn't. Now, I do thank you for carrying that there coal, and I'll thank you even more for getting back up to town an' leavin' us alone.'

Keir rolled the sack off his shoulder and dropped it onto the road. 'You're a stubborn woman, Mrs Scoble. And your son's going down a bad road. If you and his father don't do something about it, he'll be lost to you before you know it.'

Ellen blinked in dismay, and Keir had a moment's pause, but better she knew now than continue to deceive herself that her son was beyond such mischief. 'He's a thief,' he said again, firmly. 'And you need to see to it.'

'He's not,' she said, equally firmly. 'Now go away.'

Keir tried to see the funny side of being told the same thing by two women in such a short space of time, but he couldn't. Instead he had a flash of memory: Jane Walsh and a slamming, white-painted door ... Her language had been so much more extreme than either of these two had used, but then her grievance had been, too.

Quashing the memory, he waited to see if Ellen would try to pick up the sack. If she was too proud to accept a strong pair of arms when they were offered, then a little humiliation would stand her in good stead the next time some poor idiot offered help; maybe she'd learn to accept it with good grace.

She gave him a cold look, then put her basket down at the side of the road and went back to the sack, which she lifted as easily as if it had been a loaf of bread. 'Thank you again, Mr Garvey, and please give my regards to your cousin.'

She flung it over her own bony shoulder, then marched up

236

to her house and kicked open the door, while Keir stared on in astonishment. A minute later Eddie came out, scampered up the road to where his mother had left her basket, and picked it up.

'I'm that sorry, Mr Garvey,' he said again, in a low voice. 'I never thought anyone else would get in trouble.'

The little face turned up to his was earnest and open, and Keir was having trouble reconciling that look with what he'd known the boy to have done.

'The tools too?' he asked. Eddie nodded, and chewed at his lip, but said nothing.

'But what did you do with them?'

'Gave them to Bobby Gale, same as with Ma's other things we sold. He gets a ride in Mr Rodda's trap, whenever Mr Rodda goes to Truro market, and he said he'll sell them where no one'll recognise 'em, and give me a share.' Eddie sighed. 'I know he'll take most of it, but he's that much bigger'n me.'

Keir peered harder at him, his suspicions flowering. Eddie flinched, but didn't move away. 'Eddie, do your parents actually know what you've been doing?'

Eddie shook his head. 'My pa's gone, there's only me and Ma. Please, don't be mean to her no more.'

Keir spoke more quietly. 'She ought to know, Eddie. Will you tell her?'

'She'll be proper upset.'

Keir's exasperation rose again. 'I've lost my *job*, boy! And I've accused others of the very thing you've been doing, and upset them too. You'll have to go to Farmer Pawley and tell him the truth.'

Eddie paled. 'He'll beat me black and blue!'

'No, he won't. Not if I'm with you. Go and tell your mother we're going up there now.'

'Please!' Eddie hung back. 'I promise I'll go tomorrow. An' then I'll tell Ma. But . . . '

Keir waited a moment, but the boy had fallen into miserable silence. 'But what?'

Eddie's breath hitched. 'I ain't seen Ma for a day or two. I don't want to make her cry tonight.' He looked up at Keir, with brimming eyes. 'Tomorrow, I promise.'

Keir's throat was too tight for a moment, to allow him to speak. Instead he nodded, and squeezed the boy's shoulder, then made his way back up towards town, feeling wretched; on one hand his entire life had taken a hell of a battering today, on the other he'd been no better than a bully to Ellen Scoble and her son. Outside Hawthorn Cottage he paused and gathered his thoughts. He owed Nancy an apology, but he knew, even from the short time they'd been courting, that she'd be difficult to win over. She might look like an angel, but she had the spark of devilry and you never really knew what would turn her from one into the other. One thing was for certain, angel or devil, she was quite likely the most beautiful and unpredictable woman he'd ever be lucky enough to meet, let alone lie with.

'You're a fool, Keir Garvey,' he whispered. He took a deep breath and crossed the yard, rehearsing his words as he went. He let himself into the kitchen, where three of Nancy's children sat quietly finishing their tea. They looked up, unsurprised to see him, and smiled but said nothing. It was eerily quiet, in fact.

'Where's your—'

'Hush!' Tory held her finger to her lip, and went on in a whisper, 'No one's allowed to talk until he goes.'

'Who goes?'

'Shh!' The girl bent her head to her food once more. None of the three looked particularly unhappy, they simply ate their tea, cast the odd glance at one another's plates to see who was beating who, and twiddled with hair and clothes. Bored, but accustomed to being so. It was clear what was going on, and Keir had always known deep down that Nancy wasn't keeping herself for him, but it still came as a slap in the face. What made it feel worse was that this visit must have been arranged even before he'd sent her off angry, her head ringing with his accusations. This was almost certainly the giver of brand new shawls, and the reason she had lied about where she'd been on Saturday night.

Keir left Hawthorn Cottage, his spirits sinking lower with every step. She didn't need him, she didn't want him, and, as it turned out, she owed him nothing either. Everything now hung on little Eddie Scoble, and whether or not Farmer Pawley would accept his word. If he didn't, Keir's life in Caernoweth would be over before it had really begun.

Chapter Fifteen

Pencarrack House

There was a car outside, but it didn't sound like Father's. Lucy looked out of the gallery window, and, through the first drops of rain, she saw a distinctive red motor pulling to a stop.

'Tristan's here,' she said. 'I thought he was spending the day in Truro with his sister? Oh, wait . . .' she peered more closely, 'Sophie's with him.'

'Don't sound so glum,' Teddy said, bending over one of the display cases and squinting. 'She's not that awful. And she likes you.'

'I'd much rather stay up here with you, than drink tea and talk about dresses.'

'Get Harry to show her around the grounds,' Teddy suggested with a little grin.

'I hardly think they're a likely friendship, do you?' Lucy sighed and turned away from the window. 'What was in the book James gave you?'

'Just half a page, it promises more but there's nothing else.' He looked at her hopefully. 'I say, could you get your hands on property deeds?'

'Property deeds?'

'You know, conveyances and transfer documents that show root of title. From back when this was the Penworthy Estate, and Pencarrack House was just that tiny little place off the courtyard.'

'I could try, though I'd have to ask Father. It'd be far more interesting than anything I've seen from those books so far.' There was only so much one could enthuse about in a seemingly endless list of social engagements and family weddings. Lucy heard voices in the hall. 'No doubt Tristan will come right up, and you can talk about all the really interesting stuff with him.'

He laughed at the plaintive tone in her voice. 'Don't worry, they're sure to go before too long; Sophie will be off to the farm later to exercise Bill.'

'That does surprise me about her,' Lucy said. 'She really doesn't seem the type to get all mucky, and let her hair get tangled.'

'There's more to Sophie MacKenzie than meets the eye,' Teddy said. 'You'd like her if you met her when she wasn't spilling over with resentment.'

Lucy nodded. 'Perhaps. I do feel sorry for Freya—' A knock at the door interrupted her. 'Come in, Mrs Andrews!'

But it was Sophie who came in, followed by her brother. 'Your housekeeper said it was all right to come straight up,' she said. She gave Teddy a little wave across the room. 'We had a lovely time in Truro, but it started to rain.'

'And yet later, when you're out with Bill, you wouldn't

notice if someone dumped a bucket of cold water on your head,' Tristan pointed out.

'That's different,' Sophie said patiently. 'I won't be wearing my good hat, then.'

Lucy laughed. 'And a very nice hat it is, too.'

'Caroline gave it to me,' Sophie said. 'She always chooses ... *chose*, the prettiest things.'

Lucy raised an eyebrow at Tristan, who looked both embarrassed, and suddenly melancholy.

'Caroline and I were—'

'Going to get married,' Sophie supplied. 'Caroline Hamilton. Have you heard of her?'

'No, I haven't.' Lucy looked from sister to brother. 'I hadn't realised you'd been engaged before, Tristan.'

'She died,' Sophie said. 'It was horrible.'

'Oh, I'm so sorry.' Lucy put a hand on Tristan's arm. 'You must have been devastated. If you don't mind me asking, how did she die?'

'A stupid accident,' he said, his voice rough. 'She was out riding and her horse threw her. They found it dead a short way up the path from where she fell. We think it must have had a heart attack. Caroline died two days afterwards.'

'How absolutely awful.' Lucy touched Sophie's hand. 'For all of you.'

'It was.' Sophie looked at her with a strange kind of gratitude, and she wondered if perhaps people had been focusing so much on Tristan's grief that they had failed to acknowledge this little girl's.

'Would you like to come downstairs for a cup of chocolate?' she asked gently.

'I'd rather stay here a little while, with you, and Tristan and Teddy.' Sophie gazed beseechingly at her brother. 'Please, may I?'

Tristan sighed. 'We'd like nothing better, but you'd be awfully bored. And besides,' he went on, as Sophie opened her mouth to protest, 'you don't have permission to be in here. No one outside the Batten family does, except myself and Teddy.'

'I could hide if anyone came,' Sophie said. Her keen gaze swept the room, and lighted, with triumph, on the curtained alcove midway down it. 'In there! No one would see me, and you wouldn't get into trouble.'

Tristan smiled. 'Thank you for thinking of me,' he said. 'But it's not a question of being found out, is it? It's a question of what's right. Besides, I thought you enjoyed Miss Batten's company?'

'I do, that's why I thought she could stay too.'

Lucy stepped in, seeing Tristan's supply of answers running low. 'I have a new copy of *Vogue*, arrived just this morning,' she said. 'I've been waiting for you to visit before I read it.' This wasn't strictly true, she had settled down happily to it earlier, but then Teddy had arrived and there had been no contest.

Sophie looked quite gratified, and abandoned her plea. 'Yes, please, that would be lovely.'

'We'll leave the two crusty old historians to their studies, then, shall we?' Lucy held out her hand. She couldn't suppress a smile as she led the girl from the gallery; these two were about as far from crusty as it was possible to get. Teddy winked at her, and she felt the smile widen as she listened to his earnest voice following her down the landing.

'Now then, old man. I bumped into that fellow James, earlier. He found something in the old fort, I think you might like to see . . .'

As they crossed the hall to the sitting room the front door opened, letting in a stiffening breeze, a spattering of rain, and a very obviously drunk Hugh. Lucy instinctively glanced at the grandfather clock by the cloakroom. Not even five o'clock. Hugh followed her gaze with bleary eyes, and she steeled herself for a scathing comment, but it didn't come. Instead he shrugged, and went towards the library.

'Father and Dorothy are both out,' Lucy said. 'Dorothy was looking over the fort with James, and then she had a meeting with Mr Pagett, and I don't know where Father is.'

'I didn't ask, did I?' Hugh's attention shifted to Sophie. 'Your friends are getting younger and younger, Luce. Who's this?'

'This is Tristan's sister, Miss Sophie MacKenzie.'

'Ah.' Hugh nodded. 'I suppose now you mention it I can see the likeness. Very pretty.' There was an edge to his voice Lucy didn't like, but she didn't get the chance to say so. 'I suppose the perfect Mr MacKenzie is upstairs, is he?' Hugh went on. 'Pretending to do something terribly important?'

'Hugh, I think—'

'Never mind.' Hugh rattled at the library door. 'I'll be damned. It's locked.'

'What do you want in there, anyway?'

'Does it matter? I live here, don't I?' He gave the door another shove, then kicked it. Lucy winced, and saw an expression of extreme distaste on Sophie's face.

'I think I'll go and take Bill out now, after all,' the girl said, 'before the rain gets any worse. Would you please tell my brother?'

'Of course. Are you sure, though? I can ring Mrs Andrews, and she'll have hot chocolate here in two shakes of a lamb's tail.'

'No. But thank you.' Sophie took her gloves from her coat pocket, nodded briefly to Hugh, and then found a strained smile for Lucy. 'I do hope to see you again before I go back home.'

'I hope so too. Come up whenever you like.' Lucy wasn't at all sure she meant it, but was determined to try, for Tristan's sake. 'If I'm not here, you must feel free to meander around the house as you wish.'

'Except the gallery,' Sophie reminded her.

'Except the gallery.' Lucy smiled back. 'I'll tell Mrs Andrews to expect you. And watch yourself on the wet ground, if you're going riding.'

They said their polite farewells, and Lucy heard the sound of another approaching motor. This time she knew it was her father's before it appeared at the bottom of the drive, and she glanced back into the house and saw the sitting-room door swinging shut. She groaned. Hopes that Hugh would go upstairs and sleep it off were clearly misplaced.

When she went into the room, Hugh looked up from his too-familiar position at the side table, decanter in hand. 'A toast: to my enemy's enemies.'

'Hugh—'

'But wait! You're my enemy's *friend*, aren't you? Silly me.' He drank down the tumbler's contents, and refilled it. 'Not enough that you have to form an attachment to MacKenzie's research assistant, now you're playing hostess to his *sister*?'

'For Heaven's sake! Father's coming!'

'Good. It's time he and I had a chat.' Hugh's hand shook as he put the decanter back, and despite the bravado of his words, his face had turned pale.

'You mustn't,' she reminded him. 'You told me to keep it a secret, remember?' Guilt flickered as she remembered how short-lived that secret had been, but he wasn't to know that. 'Go up to your room.'

'Yes, Mummy.' Hugh gave her a crooked grin and moved to stand by the empty fireplace. 'Or rather, no, Mummy. I want to stay down here and play. Why's the library locked?'

'I don't know! Why don't you just go up—'

'No!' Hugh banged his glass down on the mantel shelf, as the door opened to admit their father. 'Ah. Here's the one with all the answers.'

'Drunk again, Hugh?' Charles's voice was calm enough, but then it always was. 'Bit early, isn't it? Still, it's good to see what you've been doing with your day.'

'And what have you been doing with *your* day?' Hugh gave him a brittle smile. 'Out collecting rent again?'

Lucy drew a sharp breath, and Charles's face tightened. 'I don't collect the rents, you know that.'

'Oh, forgive me.' Hugh took another drink. 'Perhaps you visit your tenants out of the kindness of your heart. What do you think, Luce?'

'I don't know,' she stammered. 'I'm going upstairs.'

'Yes, run along.' Hugh moved from the fireplace to the sofa, and flopped down, spilling whisky over his cuff. 'The terribly clever people await your expert opinion, no doubt with bated breath.'

'Don't be cruel,' Lucy said in a low, hurt voice. 'Just because you have nothing to do with your time, doesn't mean we all have to be the same. Why don't you come up, too? They're finding out all sorts of exciting things about our family's history.'

'Are they?' Charles paused in the act of pouring his own drink. 'I thought those books were all business accounts, parties, land acquisitions, that sort of thing.'

'They did start out like that, yes. But later ... Haven't you read them?'

He waved a hand. 'They were more your mother's interest than mine. The future's what I'm interested in, not the past.' He cleared his throat. 'But, since you bring it up, what sort of thing have they found?'

'I don't know the details,' she confessed, ignoring Hugh's little huff of amusement. 'Not yet, anyway,' she added. 'Teddy will tell me when he's ready.'

Charles shrugged. 'They've both signed an agreement that I'll be shown everything before MacKenzie attempts to publish anything. I've more important things to worry about at present.'

'Yes. Why's the library locked, Father?' Hugh sat forward again on the sofa.

'It's my office. I've every right.'

'But if I'm to take over the business, shouldn't I be allowed in, at least?' Hugh sent another glance in Lucy's direction, and despite her growing unease, she couldn't resist staying to find out what her father might say.

'There are confidential papers in there,' Charles said. 'Nothing to do with anything that might be current when you eventually take over.'

'Dorothy, you mean.'

'What?'

'When *Dorothy* takes over.' Hugh tried to stand, but that final, swiftly taken drink had struck and he could do no more than shuffle his feet. Lucy looked on in dismay as he slumped back and exclaimed on a sigh, 'Yes, Father, I know.'

Charles's expression had not changed, but then of course, he already knew Hugh had found out, thanks to Dorothy being such a sneak. 'Sober up,' he said evenly, 'then perhaps we'll talk.'

'No. Let's talk now.'

'You're in no fit state.'

'But when I am in a fit state, I'll lack the courage,' Hugh pointed out with a bitter edge to his voice. 'Do you see how it goes?' With a gargantuan effort, he found his feet and stood swaying for a moment, before drawing himself upright. 'I've known since last August, Father. I just . . . ' his voice faltered, 'I just don't know *why*.'

Charles put down his glass. 'And you won't. Not while you're likely to either sing out to the world, or pass out at any moment.'

'Tell me!' The shout echoed around the room, and Lucy flinched. Charles did not. Hugh took an unsteady step towards his father, and as the two of them faced each other, Lucy saw fear and uncertainty on Charles's face, and she frowned. Surely he must have prepared himself for this, from the moment Dorothy had gone to him?

'How did you find out?'

'I found your will, the night of the storm.' Hugh gave a short laugh. 'I'd decided it was time I learned something about the business, and instead I discovered you had no intention of passing it to me.'

'Father, you already know this,' Lucy said. Hugh's voice was filled with betrayal, and she couldn't bear to listen to it. 'Don't make him explain.'

'He already knows?' Hugh turned to her, his eyes only focusing with difficulty. 'You told him?'

'Not me, Dorothy.'

'Dorothy did no such thing,' Charles said grimly. 'I had no idea.'

'But I saw her going to you, right after . . .' Lucy hesitated, then shrugged; no use in pretending now. 'Right after I told her what Hugh had found out. I heard her telling you there was something you had to know.'

'And so she did,' Charles said tightly, 'but it had nothing to do with these two squabbling over their inheritance!'

'I can't believe you went behind my back . . . to *Dorothy*,' Hugh said, and now the betrayal was aimed at Lucy. As they both turned to scowl at her, Lucy was struck by two things; firstly that they were both seeking an alternative target for their anger, and secondly that those withering glares were identical.

She laughed in relief. 'It doesn't matter anyway, Father, you can change your will back again. Look at you! You couldn't be more obviously father and son!'

But there was no amusement in her father's face. 'You have no idea what you're talking about,' he said, his voice hard.

Hugh looked as though he wanted to be sick, and was only keeping control by the tiniest margin. 'What?' he managed.

'Don't pay any attention to her.'

'*That's* why you wrote me out of your will? Because you thought I wasn't your son?'

'I didn't write you out!' Charles went to the window, and folded his arms as he stared out over the Serth Valley. 'You'll still get properties on the estate. You'll be wealthy enough.'

'Don't . . .'

'Don't what?'

'Don't make this about greed.' Hugh sank back onto the sofa. 'Do you still think I'm someone else's bastard?'

'No, I don't.'

'But you're not changing your mind back?'

'We'll talk later.'

'Which also means "no", I take it.' Hugh shrank away from Lucy's concerned hand. 'And you can bugger off, too. You *promised*.'

'I'm sorry,' she said. 'I truly am. I didn't have any choice, Dorothy was banging on and on about your behaviour, and I was sticking up for you. She only told me the truth so I'd understand.'

'And no doubt you made a promise to her, too?' Hugh dropped his head forward into his hands. His elbow slipped from his knee and he jerked back up again, paler than ever, and now sweating. 'Good at those, aren't you?'

'Go on up to bed,' Charles said. 'I need to speak to your sister.'

Lucy tightened up at the deadly quiet voice, and part of her wished she could be the one sent away to seek the peace and comfort of sleep. She'd even have welcomed the shocking hangover that was sure to be waiting for her brother when he awoke. Anything would be better than facing that look on her father's face.

When the door had banged shut behind Hugh, Charles turned his gaze onto Lucy. 'Now, then. What, *precisely*, has Dorothy told you?'

Lucy took a deep breath, and began to talk.

* * *

By the time Anna arrived at the Tinner's it was already busy, and there was no opportunity to ease herself gently into the night's work. Preparing the family's evening meal herself had sounded like such a nice idea; a chance for everyone to get together, talk about how their day had passed, and offer sympathy or humour where it was needed.

But in the end Matthew hadn't come home from work; Freya had eaten quickly then left to visit Tristan; Mairead had stayed behind at school for a meeting with the head; Sophie had been late back, explaining blithely how her ride in the rain meant a thorough grooming session for Bill; and Keir had been understandably morose, but then disproportionately furious that Anna hadn't told him about Eddie's shenanigans ... as if she'd had the chance!

She'd been angry in her turn, and between them all they'd barely spoken two words all through the meal. It was actually a relief to leave Penhaligon's Attic and come to work, but the headache that had been pushing at her for most of the afternoon didn't dissipate. The smell of malt and beer seemed stronger tonight, creeping into the back of her throat like smoke, and the heavy, burning sensation below her ribs told her she'd eaten her meal too quickly, in her hurry to be gone.

She watched the groups of men sitting at their tables, and

couldn't suppress a little wave of apprehension; the laughter that usually drifted around, sporadic but easy, was missing tonight. Alan Trevellick had a nervous, pinched expression and young Tommy had already vanished upstairs to the room they shared.

'Bad news from Furzy,' Esther said in a low voice, as she passed Anna to go through to the store room. 'Three more levels closed off.'

'Three?' Anna bit her lip. 'Tommy's?'

'Not yet. When David Donithorn left, the level was bought up by tributers. But Tommy says that if that lode don't pay out . . .' She didn't finish, but she didn't need to. Anna's temple flared with pain and she winced and rubbed at it.

'You'm looking peaky, if you don't mind my sayin' so,' Esther said. 'Them hands is a bit swollen.'

Anna spread her fingers out. Esther was right, the reddened skin was stretched and shiny, and her plain gold wedding band looked sunk into her finger rather than wrapped around it.

'You want to go up 'ome, Missus,' Esther went on. 'Go on. We can manage.'

'I might, in a bit,' Anna said. 'I'll stay a little longer, though, and see how I feel.' She turned as the door opened, glad to see a friendly face. 'James! Your usual?'

He nodded. 'Seen Brian tonight?'

'No, I've not seen him for a few days actually. I don't blame him though, the atmosphere isn't what it could be.'

'I've noticed that.' James sat on a stool and fished in his waistcoat pocket for money. 'Any idea why?'

'Why?' The voice cut across the bar, as if someone had been waiting for that question. 'I think you'm in the best position to be tellin' us that, boy!'

James twisted in his seat. 'What? I don't even know you, do I?'

'Tobias Able. Mine captain.' Able scraped his chair back, the sound harsh in the sudden quiet of the bar. He came over to stand before James. 'I 'eard you was workin' for the Battens now.'

'I am. Or rather, I will be.'

Anna wanted to offer her congratulations at this surprising news, but this wasn't the time. She eyed Able carefully – he wasn't drunk, very few of the miners could afford to be, but a little alcohol can go a long way when fuelled by discontent, and the urging of others.

'Right then,' Able said, folding his arms, 'per'aps you'd be so kind as to let us know whether the stories are true?'

'What stories?'

'That the mine's closin'.'

James shook his head. 'I have no idea. I don't work for the mine. Surely as captain you'd be the one to find that out.' He turned back to Anna, but Able hadn't finished.

'We've heard that money supposed to go into sinkin' the new shaft, and buyin' electric drills, is bein' spent else-where instead.'

'You mean the fort?' James shrugged. 'I'm sorry. I really don't know where the money's coming from, I'm only going to be overseeing the building work.'

'Hear that?' Able looked to his fellow miners. 'We'm gunna be payin' his wages with our jobs!'

'Steady on,' Anna broke in. Her head throbbed and she closed her eyes briefly. 'That's hardly fair, now, is it?'

'Look,' James said, 'I understand how you must be feeling, but—'

'You *understand* not a thing!' For a moment Anna was certain Able was going to lash out with a fist, but after a few deep breaths he shook his head. 'You ain't got a bleddy clue, lad.'

'It's Charles Batten you should be talking to,' James insisted, 'not me. I was searching for work, like anyone else.'

'*Charles* Batten?' Able snorted. 'That goes to show you really ain't got any idea, I suppose.' He spoke slowly, with exaggerated patience. 'Charles ain't been down Furzy for weeks. This is all that stuck-up cow of a daughter's doin', that's what I think.'

James went very still, and spoke softly, so only Able and Anna could hear. 'And *I* think you ought to watch your tongue when you're talking of the people who, for the moment at least, are paying for you to sit around here and get drunk.'

'James,' Anna warned, 'please, don't—'

'Tell that to him and his cronies,' James said, and she was surprised to see the tightness in his jaw, and a flash of real anger in his eyes. He turned back to Able. 'Take your grievance to Pencarrack. And then you'd be better off going home and saving your money.' He took a drink from his own glass. 'Sounds as if you'll need it.'

'James!' Anna's own raised voice seemed to split her skull in two, and she hissed in pain.

'Oh, I will take it to the Battens,' Able said. 'And then we'll see how long that ... *woman* lasts, doin' a man's work.'

'I imagine she'll last longer than you will,' James observed, and a moment later he was pinned against the bar, with Able's fist inches from his face. Anna, her heart racing, reached across the bar, and pushed Able's hand down.

'Behave yourselves, you two! You're worse than a couple of

kids in a schoolyard.' She was about to speak further, but her vision blurred, and she blinked rapidly to clear it. By the time she could see properly again some of Able's friends had pulled him away from the bar, and from James, and steered him back to his seat.

James himself was frowning. 'Are you all right, Anna?'

'I am,' she said. 'No thanks to you, getting him all fired up like that. I'm fed up with breaking up fights in this place, and why are you always involved?'

'I was sitting here having a quiet drink,' he protested. 'He was the one looking for trouble.'

'No, he was looking for answers.'

'From the wrong person! Which I told him.' James took a long pull of his beer. 'There was no need to be so rude about Miss Batten.'

Something about the way his voice changed made Anna look at him properly. 'Is she the one who gave you the job? For which, congratulations, by the way.'

'I was interviewed by both her and her father.'

'But she's the one in charge?'

'No. At least not yet.'

'Ah.' Anna started to smile, but a new, sharper pain flared along the side of her head. 'Dear God, that's nasty.'

'Do you want me to walk you home?' James slid off his stool, frowning. 'You really don't look well.'

'It's just a headache. It'll fade, they always do.' Her back twinged in sympathy, and she sighed. 'I'll stay another half an hour, then maybe I'll go home.'

'Shall I get Matthew down, then, to help out?'

'He wasn't back from work when I left. He might call in

on his way through.' Anna dug up a smile. 'Meantime, stop poking at hornets' nests, all right?'

He grinned back. 'All right. I'm sorry.'

'It's not me you should be apologising to,' she pointed out. 'Just try to keep your temper under control until it's time to go home.'

She moved away, and pulled open the door to the passage, and the house beyond. 'Esther! Would you fetch some fresh cloths?'

A crash from behind her made her whip around, in time to see Tobias Able reel under a blow from one of the men at his table. He lunged forward and managed to return the punch before his companions pulled him away. Shouts rose from all over the pub, and James was already halfway across the room to help subdue the captain.

Anna opened her mouth to shout for Alan to come and help, but the cry never came; instead a violent cramp ripped across her belly, and she gasped and stopped dead. Her vision swam, and she clutched at the edge of the bar, and suddenly everything seemed to be happening on the other side of a thick curtain. The pain in her stomach worsened, the tight feeling grew almost unbearable, then it abruptly vanished, leaving a sense of nausea in its wake. Anna dropped to her knees, seeking some kind of privacy while she retched, and shivered, and beyond her frightening little world she could hear more crashes, and shouts, and she finally let the dizziness take her where it would.

'Anna!' A hand patted at her face, and was replaced by something cold, and she dragged in a shocked breath and opened her eyes. James was leaning over her, pressing a wet cloth to her forehead. 'I've sent Alan for the doctor. Can you stand? I'll take you through to the back room.'

Anna tried to nod, then shook her head. 'I don't know. Give me a moment.'

'What happened?'

Suddenly terrified, Anna tried to sense if there was anything amiss beneath her skirt. She managed to rub her thighs together, and let out a tiny sigh of relief; not like before . . . The cramp had gone, but she still felt horribly sick, and it seemed as if a too-bright candle was flickering on the very edge of her line of vision. She shut her eyes again.

'Is the fight over?' she muttered. 'Is anything broken?'

James gave a low laugh. 'Nice to know you're concerned about your customers.'

'I do include noses and heads in that,' Anna clarified, cracking open one eye and ascertaining that he, at least, wasn't smeared in blood. 'I feel dreadful.' She swallowed, and tasted sour vomit in the back of her throat. 'Was I sick?'

'A little bit. I'll give you some water as soon as the doctor says it's all right.' He touched her cheek, and she looked up at him again, wincing at the bright light. 'Was it the fight that did this to you? If it was, I'm sorry—'

'No, it wasn't. I was feeling bad before. You've nothing to apologise for.'

'I know I haven't,' he said. 'I was going to say, if it was, I'm only sorry I didn't make it worthwhile by planting my knuckles on the bloke's nose myself.'

Anna gave a short, breathless laugh. 'I knew there was a reason you and Matthew were friends.'

He smiled. 'Do you want me to bring a cushion to you, or will you try to stand?'

Anna gave him her arm, and he began to help her up, but as she gained her knees, another pain tore through her, and she cried out. She leaned over as far as her belly allowed, and took a few shallow breaths. A moment later she was heaving the remains of her evening meal all over her skirt. The convulsions gripped her insides and squeezed; tears poured, uncontrollable and ice-cold, down her hot cheeks; and all the while her head pounded, a hammer-blow driven by each beat of her heart.

She was vaguely aware of alarmed shouts all around her, a door slamming, and then a firm pair of hands took her shoulders and raised her head. 'Christ, Anna! What happened?'

'Matthew.' She slumped against him, and felt his arms slide around her, and his body bending to cover hers where she knelt. She let out a shaky sigh of relief. It would all be all right now.

'The doctor's here,' he whispered. 'I'm going to let him—'

'Move!' Matthew's warmth was wrenched away, and the doctor spoke again in a calmer, though tight voice. 'Anna, listen. Try to stay still, I'm just going to have a look at you.'

Anna tried to speak, but only retched again. She felt a burst of warm stickiness between her legs, and opened her mouth to scream . . .

Chapter Sixteen

Penhaligon's Attic

The group around the table was silent. Freya's attention was constantly drawn to Papá's face, so tight and pale beneath his seafarer's tan. Keir sat opposite Mairead, whose fingers were wrapping and unwrapping themselves around each other, and his face was as set as Papá's. Tristan put his hand over hers where it lay on the table, his thumb distractedly brushing her wrist. Sophie occupied the last chair. She was as still and shocked as everyone else, as they awaited news.

Freya pulled her hand away from Tristan's, suddenly unable to bear the feeling of being touched, even by him. Sophie's eyes narrowed, but Freya didn't have the energy to care. She stood up and began to pace, listening for sounds from upstairs. It was just like the day Grandpa Robert had had his stroke, only now, instead of Anna comforting her, she was the one being tended by the doctor. Again.

After last August, when they had all been convinced they had lost her to that awful head injury, they had sworn they'd never take her presence for granted again, but of course, they had; in the midst of relief, and joy, it was easy to forget the low, pulsing dread that had hung over them.

Doctor Bartholomew's feet sounded on the stairs and everyone turned to face the open doorway, Freya's hand on her father's shoulder. 'The baby is all right,' Bartholomew said, before he even reached the kitchen. 'But Anna is going to need a great deal of care, for both their sakes.'

'Oh, thank God.' Freya gestured to her chair. 'Sit down. Please.'

He did so, and directed his words to Matthew, whose eyes were very bright in the electric light. 'She is suffering from something they used to call toxaemia of pregnancy. Its proper term is pre-eclampsia. It means her blood pressure is very high, and that would account for the headache and the vomiting.' He paused, and some of the matter-of-fact confidence faded. 'As for the bleeding, I believe part of the placenta has come away from the wall of the womb.'

Matthew's head jerked up, and Mairead made a small sound of distress. 'What does that mean?' she whispered. 'Will the baby die? Will *Mother* die?'

'I think it's a small tear, since the bleeding has stopped. But she must have complete bed rest, from now until her due date.' Bartholomew looked at them all in turn. 'I need someone to be on hand constantly, to come and find me if there's more bleeding, or any further symptoms. If she continues to vomit, for instance ... ' His words trailed away, but he didn't need to finish.

'Is it all right if I ... if *we*,' Matthew amended, gesturing to Mairead, 'go up and see her now?'

Bartholomew nodded. 'Don't give her anything to be concerned about,' he warned, 'and don't let her talk too much. She needs sleep.'

'What can cause it?' Keir asked roughly, as Matthew and Mairead left the room. 'An argument?'

'Working too hard?' Freya added. 'She helped me with the rooms today, and then with the housework, and *then* had to go to work. I knew I should have—'

'No.' Bartholomew shook his head. 'None of that would have caused what happened. Problems with the development of the placenta often run in families, and there's also the fact that it's been a long time between pregnancies. But,' he added, 'neither hard work nor arguments will have helped her blood pressure. So from now on, she's to be treated like royalty. All right?'

Keir didn't reply, but pulled open the back door and went outside. Freya watched him run his hands through his hair and turn his face to the now-dark sky. Whether in remorse, or in thanks, it was impossible to tell, but he clearly felt as guilty as she did.

While she had a hundred questions to ask the doctor about what Anna had suffered, Freya couldn't think of a single one that would lessen the worry, so she said nothing. The doctor seemed ready to answer anything, but there was only a strange, bloated silence hanging over those left in the room, and he soon rose to leave.

Freya moved to show him out, but before he left he addressed Tristan. 'How's the hip?'

'Getting better, thank you. I can move it quite well now, as long as I do it slowly.'

'The ribs?'

'Still sore if I breathe in too far, or if I knock them. But a lot better.'

'Good.' Bartholomew paused again and Freya sensed he was coming to the real question. 'And how are your investigations going?'

'Slowly,' Tristan said. 'But we're putting together a great history, I think my publishers will be pleased. Still no connection between you and the Battens though, I'm sorry.'

'Ah. Oh well. I look forward to seeing your further findings.' Bartholomew nodded at them all. 'Good evening.'

When he had gone, Freya returned to sit at the table, but across from Tristan this time, instead of beside him, so she could see his face properly. 'Will he enjoy those findings?'

'Freya—'

'No! You keep making these promises to people, but you're going to have to break *some* of them!' From the corner of her eye, Freya saw Sophie shift in her seat, and made an effort to sound less annoyed. 'I mean, you've signed an agreement to tell Charles Batten whatever you find, too.'

'No, I didn't. I read that paper very carefully, and it said nothing about declaring what I've found. Only what I intend to publish.'

'That sounds familiar.' Freya's eyes held his. 'And what precisely is it that you're not going to publish?'

'The latest book, the one James found, states Daniel Bartholomew's intention to go to Malcolm Penworthy and tell him he knows everything.'

Freya drew a quick breath. 'About the murder of Sarah Trevellick?'

'He doesn't say so, specifically, but his father's journals are detailed enough. Put them together and you have a much fuller picture. It's a half-step in the right direction.'

'But there's still no connection to Batten?'

'None. Daniel simply says he'll add to the book later, when he's had his reply. He left it as a kind of insurance, tucked into the wall in the dungeon up at the fort, but nothing more was ever added to it.' Tristan sat forward, his enthusiasm bubbling up again. 'We were right, Freya. Penworthy turned that blackmail attempt around, and that was the start of the Battens' hold over this town. We can't prove it, but knowing it is enough.'

'So you're not going to reveal all that other stuff? About the pirates, and the smuggling?'

Tristan shook his head. 'Nothing specific to Batten or Penworthy. It's as you said, what would be the point? If Batten has a mind to go through the books he'll see it for himself.'

'He probably wouldn't be able to piece it together the way you have. To make the distinction between legitimate business, and the . . . the rest.'

'Perhaps not, since I'm using other sources too, to build this picture. But I'll stick to the letter of the agreement, and show him what I intend to publish, which is Penworthy's gifting of the estate to an old war comrade, and his and Batten's role in bringing the community together *after* the pirate attacks. And the later acquisition of Wheal Furzy and Polworra, of course. Caernoweth was really built from that, after all.'

'And now turning the fort into a hotel.'

'Perhaps. As an afterword, and to show the place is having a new lease of life.'

Despite it being what she wanted, Freya felt a twinge of remorse. 'I'm sorry.'

'For what?'

'For throwing cold water on everything. Making you go against what you love.'

Tristan sighed. 'You're not,' he said gently. 'Freya, I love *you*. I don't want this to come between us, and I'm doing my damnedest to make sure that doesn't happen.'

She smiled. 'Me too,' she whispered. They sat for a moment in silence, then, dreading the reply, Freya still had to ask.

'What about Blind John's story?'

'He was innocent, helpless even, and he killed himself because of the burden placed on him by Penworthy. Something like that can only reflect well on his descendants.'

'But not Penworthy's.' Freya's voice tightened again. 'Tristan, please—'

'But,' he said, reaching out his hand and covering hers, 'that was before tonight. I can't risk upsetting Anna, and if I'm honest, that's all the excuse I need to take that vile story and box it back up for good.'

'Thank you,' Freya said quietly. She thought for a moment. 'I wonder though, if there's some other way you can let Esther and her family know that Joe's ancestors weren't witches and murderers after all. Just good, honest healers. It would mean the world to her, I know it.'

'Witches?' Sophie's astonished voice cut across them, and they both turned to her. Freya had all but forgotten she was there.

'*Not* witches,' she emphasised. 'Some silly story put about by gossips in the olden days.'

'And it's time you were in bed, young lady,' Tristan added.

'I'm not at all tired. And I'm not a child.'

'Go on with you. Are you taking Bill out tomorrow?'

She nodded. 'Will you come to the farm with me?'

'I'm sorry, I've got—'

'Tristan! I came here to visit you, and I've barely seen you.'

'You spent almost all day with me in Truro today,' he reminded her. 'We could have talked a little more on our way home, but it was your choice to ignore Lucy's invitation and go riding instead.'

'Not really.' Sophie looked pleased to have another reason to put off going to bed. 'Lucy's brother spoilt it rather.'

Freya frowned. 'What do you mean? Spoilt it how?'

'He came in rotten drunk, and started kicking doors.'

'What?' That didn't sound like the Hugh Freya knew. 'Are you certain it was him?'

'Quite certain. Lucy introduced us. He was rude, and he was drunk.' She kissed Tristan's cheek. 'Goodnight.' She waited, but he didn't move from his seat. 'Aren't you going home now?'

'In a moment,' he said. 'Sleep tight.'

Sophie looked from him to Freya, and back again, and her expression darkened. 'Don't stay too long, I'm sure Freya's exhausted.'

Freya lifted her hand to her mouth to hide the smile that would only inflame things. 'Thank you for your ... *concern*,' she said. 'I'm quite well, and Tristan and I have things to discuss.'

'Your wedding, I suppose.'

Freya ignored the faintly scathing tone. 'No. Anna, actually. And how best to help her now she can't work at the pub.'

Sophie blushed, but before she could reply, the low sound of voices drifted down from upstairs, followed by the rattle of a latch. Mairead came down, some of the fear smoothed from her brow.

'Mother's sleeping now. Matthew's going to sit with her a while, then he's going down to the pub to check on things, and let them know what's happened.'

'Oh, no, he isn't!' Freya patted Tristan's arm. 'Come on, you can walk with me as far as the Tinner's, then you get off home to bed.'

'Absolutely not,' he said, standing up. 'I'll come to the pub with you. From the sounds of it, it's not a good place for a young lady tonight.'

Mairead nodded. 'All right, so. I'll tell him. Come on, Sophie,' she said on a sigh. 'Let's get you settled.'

Sophie went, without further demur, and Freya exchanged a glance with Tristan. 'She turns into a completely new person whenever Mairead's around.'

The back door opened, and, from where they now stood in the front hall, Freya peered through the kitchen to see Keir coming back in, his face creased in worry. The scar stood out, livid against his pale skin.

'I'll go and tell him she's asleep,' she said quietly. Tristan nodded, but as she walked away he caught her blouse and pulled her back. He looked at her in silence for a long moment, during which Freya could hear Anna's distraught cousin scraping back a chair to sit down, and then he pressed his lips briefly to her forehead.

'She'll be all right,' he whispered. 'Between everyone who loves her, we'll make sure of it.'

* * *

Pencarrack House

Thursday morning was as drizzly and grey as Lucy's mood. Even dancing didn't lift her spirits much, but it helped, and as she allowed her body the freedom to move, unhindered by tight-fitting day clothes, she felt some of the darkness recede. One day she would be able to do this without fear of discovery and reproof – perhaps even teach others to do the same. She smiled; perhaps that was where her ambitions lay, after all? Age needn't be such a barrier, if so.

Hungry, and still hot from the exercise, she went downstairs, reluctant to meet anyone and be asked to explain her flushed face, but to her relief she seemed to be the only person about.

In the dining room she discovered, with a sinking heart, that she was wrong about that. Dorothy looked up from a late breakfast. 'Well, aren't you the little sneak?'

'I didn't mean to,' Lucy protested, rattled at the unexpectedly direct attack. 'But you should have seen them, Dorothy! Standing together like that, there's no question at all about who is Hugh's father.'

'That isn't the point!' Dorothy dropped her grapefruit spoon, as if the very sight of Lucy had robbed her of her appetite. 'The point is, that yet again you've broken your promise.'

Lucy went to the sideboard to choose her breakfast, but her own appetite had deserted her and she only poured a cup of tea. 'I'm sick of all these secrets. Honestly, Dorothy, there needn't be any. Surely Father could split the estate evenly? Give you the mine, for instance, and Hugh the quarry. You could share the house, you probably will anyway.' She realised how that sounded, and that Dorothy had heard it too.

'Because I shan't marry, you mean? Clearly not, being so old and ugly, and with an illegitimate child trailing in my wake.'

'You're neither of those things,' Lucy said, 'and you know it. As for Harry, he's a delight. Albeit a bit of an exasperating one.' She brought her tea to the table. 'I simply meant there's plenty of room here, for both you and Hugh, *and* whoever you both marry.'

'It's a moot point anyway.' Dorothy picked up her spoon again. 'Father won't change the will, he's told me so.'

'Then he's just being . . .' Lucy looked more closely at her sister, and her eyes widened. 'That's not the real reason, is it?' Dorothy flushed and said nothing, and Lucy's temper rose. 'So much for me being a sneak! You're worse, you're a liar!'

The door opened and both of them turned, equally cross, to see the housekeeper, her gaze skipping from one to the other with ill-disguised curiosity.

'Miss Sophie MacKenzie for you, Miss.' She nodded to Lucy.

'Thank you, Mrs Andrews. Please show her into the sitting room and tell her I'll be there directly.'

'She's a bit . . . muddy, if you please.'

'Nevertheless!' Seeing the housekeeper's aggrieved look, Lucy moderated her tone. 'I'm sorry. Please do show her into the sitting room.'

When Mrs Andrews had gone Lucy looked at Dorothy. 'I don't know what you and Father have been cooking up between you, but Hugh will hear about it, you can be sure of that.'

'Leave it alone, Lucy. It has absolutely nothing to do with

you, after all.' Dorothy's words were designed to sting, but Lucy had always known Pencarrack would not be hers – unlike Hugh, she had lost nothing.

'Talk to your brother, then,' she said, her voice tight. 'He deserves to know, even if I don't.'

In the sitting room, Sophie was keeping her dirty riding clothes clear of the furniture, and instead stood by the window. 'I hope you don't mind,' she said, 'I've taken Bill around to the stables. Your lad said he'd take care of him for a little while.'

'Of course.' Lucy found a smile. 'It's nice of you to break your ride to visit us. You're welcome anytime.' She hoped she sounded sincere; she didn't dislike Sophie, but today was a poor choice for socialising.

'Actually I didn't call in to bother you with chatter,' Sophie said, sounding much older than her years. 'It's to do with Tristan. And your family diaries.'

'Then I think I ought to hear this too,' Dorothy said. She came in and closed the door behind her, taking pains to ensure it was properly latched.

Uncertainty creased Sophie's brow. 'I don't—'

'I'm Dorothy Batten. Please, do sit down, Miss MacKenzie.'

'I'm all dirty,' the girl stammered. She turned to Lucy. 'I won't take a minute of your time, I'll stand.'

'Nonsense,' Dorothy smiled. 'Those cushions are easy enough to clean.' She waved at the sofa. 'Shall I ring for tea, or chocolate? Or would you prefer lemonade?'

'Nothing, thank you.' Sophie perched on the very edge of the cushion, her body angled towards Lucy. It was clear she was uncomfortable, both physically and socially, but she took a deep breath, and blurted, 'You know I love Tristan very much, don't you?'

Lucy was taken aback. 'Yes, of course. He's your brother.'

'And I'd never do a single thing to upset him.'

'Of course not.'

'It's only that ... I like you too. You've been so kind to me. And your family is so well thought of.'

'Thank you. Sophie, whatever's the matter?' Lucy glanced past the girl to Dorothy, who had taken a chair farther back in the room. 'What's this about Tristan?'

'I think he's doing something bad. And I'm so worried he'll get into trouble.' Sophie's face worked, and a brilliant tear rolled from one green eye, so like her brother's.

'Oh, sweetheart, don't cry!' Lucy sat beside her, and put an arm around her shoulder. 'What can Tristan possibly be doing that's bad?'

'Promise me you won't tell the police!'

Lucy blinked. 'The police?'

'Tristan's lying to your father. I heard him telling Freya as much, just last night.'

Lucy drew back so she could see Sophie more clearly. 'Lying? That's not a police matter, darling, don't worry. But lying about what? The diaries?'

'He signed something, he said. To say he would tell Mr Batten everything he was going to publish.'

'Yes, of course he would have had to do that,' Lucy said. 'A family's history is a very private thing unless they choose otherwise.'

'But he's found things he's not going to tell Mr Batten

270

about,' Sophie said, wiping beneath her eye with a gloved finger. 'And I think he's going to publish them anyway.'

From the corner of her eye, Lucy saw Dorothy sit up straight. She didn't look directly at her, but she knew she'd see a deep frown if she did. 'What things?' she asked quietly. 'I'm sure it can't be—'

'Something to do with pirates, and witches.' More tears appeared, and Lucy pulled her own handkerchief from the pocket of her dress and gave it to her.

'Pirates and witches? I think he's been having a little joke with you. That's probably what comes of becoming engaged to someone who lives surrounded by story books!'

'It's not a joke, nor a story!' Sophie sniffed. 'And they said there was a murder too. Someone called Sarah.' She blew her nose. 'I might only be thirteen, but I'm not a silly child.'

'Of course not,' Lucy soothed. She exchanged a glance with Dorothy, who didn't seem quite as relieved as she ought to. 'But pirates and witches aren't things that happen in real life.'

'What about murders?'

'I suppose so, but not here. Not in Caernoweth.'

'What about in the olden days?' Sophie's eyes welled again. 'That's what Freya said.' She hesitated, then pushed on, 'She's the one who told Tristan to publish what he's found. She said everyone deserves to know the truth. He doesn't want to do it!' She took a deep, hitching breath, and looked pleadingly at Lucy, and then Dorothy. 'Mr Batten won't sack him, will he?'

'Tristan doesn't work for Father,' Lucy said. 'He works for himself. Father just gave him permission to read the books we have here.'

'And you can be sure that permission has been rescinded from this moment,' Dorothy said, standing up. 'I have the authority to do so.'

'Res ...' Sophie turned to Lucy, worried. 'What does that mean?'

'It means withdrawn,' Lucy said quietly. 'I'm so sorry.'

'And you can tell your Mr Kempton the same applies to him,' Dorothy said coldly.

'That's not fair!' Lucy sprang to her feet. 'It has nothing to do with him. If Freya Penhaligon chooses to force her fiancé into such underhand dealings, that's up to them, but don't punish Teddy.'

'They're working together, towards the same publication,' Dorothy reminded her. 'Now, tell Kempton to bring me all the notes they've made thus far. All of them,' she warned, 'I'll notice if I think something's been omitted.'

'How? You've never shown the slightest interest in the journals.'

'But there will be gaps,' Dorothy said. 'Especially if they aren't given time to fill them with false findings.' She gave her attention to Sophie, who was weeping silently once more into Lucy's handkerchief. 'Thank you for bringing this to our attention, Miss MacKenzie, your brother will understand you've done the right thing.'

'But he'll be furious!'

'He ought to be furious with Miss Penhaligon, not you,' Lucy said. 'I'll try and smooth things over.'

'Don't tell him I told you, please!'

'I won't. I promise ...' Lucy caught Dorothy's sceptical look. 'I'll try,' she amended.

'What can you tell me about this murder, Miss MacKenzie?' Dorothy came to stand in front of Sophie, her arms folded. Lucy wished she wouldn't *loom* so.

Sophie shifted in her seat under that look, and thought for a moment. 'I only know that it was to do with someone called Blind John, but that he didn't do it himself, someone else did. There's another book, you see, and it has something really important in it about your family.' She shook her head. 'They were fighting about it last night, and Tristan said they wouldn't tell the story but Freya said they ought to.'

'Never mind who said what,' Dorothy said. 'I have to speak to my father about this.'

'Will Tristan have to leave this town now?' Sophie buried her face in the handkerchief again, so her words were barely audible.

Lucy sat back down. 'There's no reason to think that,' she said. 'Why would he?'

'When he and Freya break up he's got no reasons left to stay. And besides, his house belongs to your family, doesn't it?'

'That's so,' Lucy agreed, reluctantly. 'He *will* have to find alternative accommodation, we can't rent to someone we can't trust. He might return to his rooms in Plymouth, I suppose.'

Her thoughts went to Teddy; he'd only planned on being in Caernoweth a short time anyway, and to have that cut even shorter was grossly unfair. Her heart hardened towards Freya Penhaligon; her and her so-called integrity; she wouldn't be so keen on the truth if her own family history was involved.

'What about this other book?' Dorothy asked. 'Is it the one James Fry found in the fort?'

'James.' Sophie frowned. 'I think that's the name Tristan said, yes.'

'Who else knows about it?'

'Dorothy!' Lucy shook her head. 'Stop cross-examining the poor girl! She's come here to help.'

'The doctor asked if there was any news about the research,' Sophie said. 'It was last night, when he came to tend to Anna. But Tristan didn't tell him anything.'

'Who's Anna?'

'Mrs Penhaligon. Freya's stepmother.'

'Ah, yes. The Irish woman.' Lucy had only met Anna Penhaligon once, but she'd liked her well enough. 'Is she all right?'

'I think so. Mr Penhaligon carried her home from the pub.'

Dorothy gave an incredulous laugh. 'A *drunk*?' She shook her head. 'I'd have thought Matthew could have done better.'

'Mrs Penhaligon runs the Tin Streamer's Arms,' Lucy said coldly, 'and she's pregnant.'

Dorothy subsided. 'Sorry.' She sighed, and unfolded her arms, obviously itching to go and find Father. 'Where is this new book now, do you know?'

Sophie shook her head. 'I've told you all I know. Besides, I ought to go now. Bill will be getting restless.'

'Of course. Thank you again for coming to us.' Lucy showed her out, and assured her she would not tell Tristan she'd visited. She watched until Sophie had vanished into the stable yard, and then went back to the sitting room, thinking hard, and finding those thoughts had taken an unsettling turn.

Dorothy had not gone straight to Father, after all. 'I suppose, since it's a Bartholomew book, Kempton will have put it with that set rather than ours,' she mused.

'I suppose.' Lucy frowned. 'How do you know whose it is?'

'James told me about it the other day.' Dorothy turned away briefly, but not before Lucy saw a faint blush touch her sister's cheek. Then she was all iron again. 'You're helping Kempton and MacKenzie up there, so come on, are you hiding something too? What's really in that book?'

'The only thing I've read is what we already knew. The pirate attacks along the coast around the seventeenth century. Mother had a book about it, remember? But I'm sure it was about someone called Verney, nothing to do with Penworthy, and certainly nothing to do with the Battens.'

'But you've been writing up Kempton's notes. You must know *something*.'

Lucy tried to take a deep breath, but her throat had gone tight. 'I think perhaps Teddy has been giving me a rather sanitised version to write up,' she said at last. 'He hasn't mentioned anything else to do with smuggling, nor anything like, only social occasions, births, deaths . . . stuff about Penworthy's daughter marrying a soldier and running off to Ireland. I know there's more, but they haven't told me yet.'

'And you expect me to believe that, do you?' Dorothy pulled open the door. 'I want Kempton's notes, and MacKenzie's too. You'd better turn on that charm of yours, and make sure they're in my hand by this evening. I'm going to see Father.'

'Where is he, anyway?'

'There's a meeting at the hotel, with Mr Pagett and James Fry, and one or two others, I ought to have been there twenty minutes ago myself. As soon as the business with the contracts is tied up I'm going to tell him what that wretched historian has been up to, and I think we can safely say that'll be the last we see of him.'

275

Chapter Seventeen

Caernoweth Hotel

James had never fought so hard to bite down on his tongue as during this meeting. Charles Batten's warning to him had been clear enough: *You're here to listen, Fry. Remember, you're not the designer* ... But the figures bouncing back and forth between Batten, Pagett, and Pagett's architect, were making his fingers curl beneath the table. The agreement could proceed no further until Batten's own accountant – Dorothy – arrived, and Pagett's finance manager filled the time reeling off numbers, while Batten himself demanded more details and scribbled furiously on a stack of paper in front of him.

A knock at the door announced the hotel manager – the only person permitted to interrupt the meeting – who addressed Batten. 'Someone to see you, sir. The doctor. He says it's urgent.'

Batten left the room briefly, and when he returned, his

manner had altered. James eyed him, wondering what news the doctor might have had, that had put him in such an odd, distracted mood. He didn't seem ill, but who could tell, with someone so private and reserved? He certainly wouldn't want to make any mention of it in front of his new business partners.

There was still no sign of Dorothy, and James suspected her presence would be a mere formality in any case; she had made it clear that, although her father valued her input in private, in public she was there to make up the numbers. Rather like this Pagett bloke's accountant, he thought, with grim amusement at his own joke.

He patted his coat pocket, checking he'd brought the book in which he'd written his own estimated costings, and pulled it halfway out before he noticed Batten frowning at it, and decided to leave it where it was, for now at least. *Here to listen, Fry.*

But he couldn't simply sit by without questioning this. 'Are you sure that's the *total*, for renovating the outer curtain wall?' he asked instead. 'It seems very low. Look, I've got some—'

'We've priced everything most diligently,' Pagett said, then addressed himself to Batten again. 'Once people hear my name, Charles, they're happy to undercut their rivals and give us a good price.'

'I don't doubt it.' Batten pursed his lips, and flattened the papers on the table. 'And the materials can be delivered next week?'

'Starting next week, yes. My labourers will be arriving on Wednesday the fifth, and begin work the following morning.'

'Yours?' James frowned. 'I thought you'd be using local labour.'

'There will be a certain take-up of Cornish muscle,' Pagett allowed, 'but my men are skilled, experienced builders.'

'As are those who've been building in this area for centuries,' James pointed out coolly.

'No doubt,' Pagett soothed. 'But my team know and trust one another, and they know what's expected of them.'

'And where will they live?'

Pagett looked to Batten, clearly wondering if the man was going to sit there and allow his business partner to be interrogated in this fashion, but Batten had drifted once more into his own thoughts, and did not step in to rescue him.

James smiled at Pagett. 'You do understand why I'm asking, of course? In my capacity as their works manager, I need to be sure there won't be any unrest between them and the community. And if they were likely to be taking up accommodation better suited to, say, those who work at Wheal Furzy, I'd have to caution against it.'

'You would, would you?'

'Last night I witnessed raised tensions in the pub among the miners, and your men haven't even arrived yet. Things are difficult here.'

Pagett pursed his lips. 'To answer your question,' he said at length, and in tones of strained patience, 'they'll be brought in daily at first, by special coach.'

'From where?'

'From outlying farms, where we've arranged temporary accommodation. But once they're here, they will construct a small settlement, built alongside the fort, which will be dismantled upon completion of the project.'

'Excellent.' James looked up as Dorothy came in, a leather

bag tucked beneath her arm. The men rose to their feet as one, with the exception of her father, and Dorothy nodded at them and closed the door, shutting out the noise of the hotel along with the welcome waft of fresh air. In the office, the fug of cigar smoke was turning the air blue, and it hung over the table like a London smog.

Pagett introduced his men, all politeness, but James saw a new tension in his jaw. 'Miss Batten, this is Mr Bentley, my accountant.' She accepted his outstretched hand. 'And the project's architect, Mr Rose.'

'Good morning, gentlemen.' Dorothy slid into the empty seat, and inclined her head graciously towards James. 'Mr Fry. Nice to see you again.'

'Likewise,' he murmured, and returned his gaze to the table-top, so no one could see the smile that had taken him by surprise. He forced himself to pay attention to the meeting, and was relieved to note Dorothy also questioning the costs they had been quoted.

'I'd have thought you'd be pleased at the lower price,' Bentley said. 'Do you *want* to pay more?'

'I want to be sure this isn't some kind of false economy. Do we have some kind of assurance that the quality is as we've agreed?'

'The quality?'

'Of the raw materials. And of the workmanship, of course.' Dorothy folded her hands on the table and looked at Pagett closely. 'This hotel is going to have your name attached to it, Mr Pagett, as well as ours. Are you confident that what you're supplying is not going to let either of us down, and end up costing us more?'

'Quite confident,' Pagett said. 'My dear, your father understands these things. I wouldn't worry your little head about it.' He turned a tight smile on Batten. 'The decision is yours, sir, after all. Do we sign?'

Batten took up his pen, and a moment later the deed was done. For better or worse. James tried not to let his frustration show, but he and Dorothy exchanged a look, and a silent agreement; at the first sniff of sub-standard materials, James would reject them himself. If that put the project behind, so be it.

'Father, can I have a word?' Dorothy called, as they made their way down the short corridor to the hotel lobby behind the businessmen. 'It's quite important.'

'Not just now.' Batten shook Pagett's hand one last time, and turned to James. 'I need to speak to you for a moment, Fry.'

James's spirits sank. Had he earned himself the sack already? 'Yes, sir, of course.'

Batten blinked out at the rain, and straightened his hat. 'I need you to go into Truro, and pick up the wages from the bank. Captain Able seems to be conspicuous by his absence today, and there aren't many others I'd trust. Dorothy seems to rate you.'

'Oh.' James was gratified, but a little taken aback by the request so soon. 'Of course.'

'I can't let you take the car, I'm afraid,' Batten added, 'I've promised it to Mr Pagett to take him back to the train. But the coach leaves in around ten minutes.'

James had no idea how to accomplish this task, and as Batten made ready to leave he felt a leap of mild panic. 'Which bank, and what do I do?'

'Barclay and Company. I'll telephone ahead, they'll be expecting you.' He grinned, and patted James's shoulder. 'Enjoy some leisure in town, Fry. The pay isn't distributed until tomorrow, so as long as you're back by the last coach, your time's your own. Make the most, lad.'

They emerged into the drizzle, and James pulled his coat collar higher. 'Should I take the money to the Wheal Furzy office?'

'No, bring it straight around to Pencarrack. I don't know if Captain Able will turn out to work today, and there's a safe at the house.'

Even as he spoke, the coach driver came back from taking refreshment and removed the nosebags from his horses. James looked back once more, hoping to signal Dorothy, but she was waiting for her father with increasing impatience. She was doomed to wait a little longer; as James climbed into the coach with Bentley and Rose, Charles Batten's car drew up, and swallowed up both its owner and Mr Pagett.

On the coach James fished in his pocket for his notebook, then settled back against his seat and smiled companionably at Pagett's two lesser mortals. 'Now,' he said, 'why don't I show you *my* estimates, then we can talk about where all that extra money we're saving is going to be spent.'

* * *

'Ah, the Cornish weather is just as I remember it,' Mama said, peering out of the hotel door. 'Come, *mi tesoro*, we will sit in the lounge instead.'

Freya loosened her wet hat and followed her mother

281

through the lobby, watching a group which had emerged from a narrow corridor to the side. She saw James, and Mr Batten and his eldest daughter among them, and noticed Mama was also watching them quite closely.

'You were telling me about poor Anna?' Mama said, before she could ask why. 'How is she today? Such a dreadful worry.'

'She's resting, but much better. I came up to tell you I won't be able to visit as often. You'll have to come to the shop, instead.'

Mama nodded. 'Of course. Poor Matthew must be distraught.'

'He was very shaken. Mama, where is the book of stories you brought with you? I thought you'd left it with Papá but he says not. I'd like to read it again.'

'Oh, I think it's more suited to a younger child, don't you?' Mama said. 'Why don't we take it over to the boy who lives at Pencarrack, and make his school holiday a little more exciting?'

Freya shook her head, disappointed. 'I have to go back, I can't leave Tristan too long, he has his own work to do.'

'Whereas I am as bored as can be.' Mama sighed. Then she brightened. 'I have an idea! You have spent time with the boy's ... aunt, isn't it? Why don't you arrange it with her? You can tell them *I* will come over and read to the boy.' She sat back, with a pleased look on her face. 'Then you may return to your books, your young man may return to his, and myself and Master Batten will entertain each other! It is the perfect solution, no?'

'You were the one who wanted me to break off all ties with the Battens,' Freya pointed out. '*Stay with your own kind*, you said. *Lucy's laughing at you.*'

'I was wrong. This town has different ... barriers, between its social classes. I'd forgotten that.' She leaned across and patted Freya's hand. 'Do this for me?'

'Are you so bored?' Freya couldn't help feeling a little peeved.

Mama smiled, and spoke gently. 'Come, my darling. As much as a child and a parent long to be together when they are apart, we both know I have confused things by coming back, and that neither of us really knows what to say to one another.' She gave a wry smile. 'Every time I mention Matthew it's hard to know which of you looks the most worried, you or Anna.'

'Oh, that's not true!'

'I have no designs on him, but it doesn't matter how often I say that, does it?'

'I know you haven't, Mama. Anna knows it too, deep down.'

'Perhaps, but it is *very* deep. And we mustn't upset her, especially now. So I think it best that I don't come to the shop anymore.'

'But that means we won't—'

'We will still see each other. We will have plenty of time.' She paused, and then her smile became bright and full again. 'I have decided to stay for your wedding!'

'Oh that's wonderful! But can you afford to live at this hotel for so long?'

'Henry will send funds if I ask him. He might even join me for the occasion. But we will talk about it later. As for now, will you take word to Pencarrack?'

'You're in an awful hurry.'

'Why wait? The boy must be quite bored in that big house with no playmates.'

'Dorothy's still out in the lobby, I can ask her.' Freya half-rose, but Mama stopped her.

'I've heard she has little to do with the boy's upbringing. I think you ought to go to his Aunt Lucy instead.'

Freya eyed her carefully. 'You were looking at Dorothy a bit oddly earlier.' She sat back down. 'What is it that bothers you about her, Mama?'

'I rather think *I* bother *her*,' Mama said, and sighed. Freya's mind went back to the day of hers and Tristan's arrival. There had been taut expressions, and dark glances, but Freya had assumed it was because of Hugh. Now she realised there was more to it.

'Why?' she asked. 'Is it something to do with when you lived here?'

Mama pulled a face. 'To be truthful, it was to do with her ... fondness for the local men. And your father in particular.'

Freya gaped. 'But they weren't—'

'No!' Mama dismissed the notion with a wave. 'But it was not for want of trying on Miss Batten's part.'

'But she's a lot older than him.'

'Not so much. A year or two, perhaps.' Mama's expression took on a distant look. 'You must remember, your father has always been a handsome man. Even when I first met him, at nineteen, he seemed older – he had a great deal of confidence, to go with his stature, and that is a very attractive thing in itself. Any woman would have been proud to be seen with him, even the rich ones.' She stood up, and straightened her skirts. 'Go and find Harry's Aunt Lucy, my dear. Tell her I will call around this afternoon, but don't trouble the elder Miss Batten with it.'

Freya hurried to Pencarrack, reluctantly pondering what

Mama had said about Papá and Dorothy Batten; back then he had been just a grubby Porthstennack fisherman. Drink had been as much his enemy as the empty nets he'd hauled, and the rumours about Dorothy hadn't included a taste for morose drunks, no matter how well nature had favoured them. Mama must have been mistaken, or let her jealousies get the better of her good sense, just as Anna was doing.

Lucy received her civilly enough, but there was no longer any trace of friendliness in her expression. Her face was hard and closed, and she didn't invite Freya into the sitting room, they stood in the hall instead, where Freya's eyes were drawn to the staggering range of ancient weaponry that graced the walls and alcoves: swords; axes; strange, spiked implements that made her wince to look at them . . . No wonder Tristan had been completely drawn into the Battens' history.

Harry, always curious about visitors, had come to sit on the stairs, and overheard Freya's proposal. He perked up at the idea of a whole new set of adventure stories, but Lucy shook her head.

'I don't think so. But do thank your mother for me.'

'Please, Aunt Lucy,' Harry begged.' It's still raining so I can't play out, and I've read all my books.'

'Then Uncle Hugh can buy you some more. From Truro,' Lucy added, her blue eyes cool on Freya's.

'But I want to hear Mr Penhaligon's! Freya's told me all about them.'

Lucy appeared to be battling with her usual good nature, and either it had won, or she was too tired to argue. 'Oh, very well,' she said at last. 'I shan't raise any objection when Mrs Webb arrives.'

Harry gave a hoot of triumph, and scuttled back up the stairs, and Freya held out her hand.

'Thank you. And I'm sorry for disturbing you.'

She took her leave gratefully, and it wasn't until she was halfway home that she remembered Mama's concern about Dorothy finding out, and she stopped with a sigh. Ought she to return to Pencarrack, and ask that the arrangement be kept between themselves? But the new, prickly Lucy would be just as likely to change her mind altogether, which would hardly be fair on Harry. Freya went on home, hoping Mama wouldn't be summarily turned away at the door, and imagining her reaction if she had her plans thwarted ... She grinned to herself; it was a good thing those spiked weapons were mounted so high on the walls.

Chapter Eighteen

Porthstennack

Keir's boots kicked water off the road and up over his own trousers, and the drizzle plastered his hair to his head. He swiped irritably at the water running down his face, and flicked it off his hands – at least if he'd been working today he'd likely have been in the dry somewhere, fixing something, or mucking out stables and barns. As it was, this walk down to the hamlet was an added annoyance on an already stressful day. Anna had still been pale that morning when he'd peeped in to make his overdue apologies, and he had backed out again quietly and instead headed out into the rain, to try and put things right with Farmer Pawley. But for that, he needed young Master Scoble.

He turned down the lane where he'd followed Eddie yesterday. Despite his sour mood he couldn't suppress a grin as he remembered the cross young woman kicking the door open, her sack of coal on her narrow back. A scuff mark low on the woodwork confirmed he'd found the right house and he raised his hand to knock, then belatedly remembered it was a school day, and Eddie, being the perfect little boy he was – Keir snorted – would be hard at work up at Priddy Lane.

'Ah, for crying out loud!' He gave the door a kick of his own. All this way, in the rain, for nothing. But to his surprise, Eddie's white face appeared. 'What are you doing here?' Keir demanded. 'Why aren't you at school?'

'I said I'd come with you,' Eddie said in a small voice. 'An' my ma always says if I say I'll do a thing, I ought to do it.'

'She's right about that, at least.' He stepped back, but Eddie didn't follow. 'Well? Are you coming or aren't you?'

'I'll fetch my coat,' Eddie said, pulling a face at the weather. He went back into the house, and Keir followed. He noted the clean grate, though with no fire laid ready for that night, and when he went into the kitchen he felt warmth from the range, but there was no smell of cooking, or detergent. 'Your ma at work?'

Eddie nodded. 'She says to tell you she's sorry.'

'You told her, then?'

'Yes.'

'What else did she say?'

Eddie's face crumpled, and Keir sighed; the crying of children was not his favourite sound. 'Never mind. Come on, let's get this over and done with, and then we'll both know where we stand. Once we've seen the farmer you can away up to school. Miss Casey will be after both our hides otherwise, and I don't know about you, but my young cousin has the power to scare the bejesus out of me.'

At the farm, a glimpse into the house showed him a haven of warmth and light, especially after the damp day and the silent, tense walk up from Porthstennack. Ruth Pawley eyed them suspiciously. 'Stan don't want nothin' to do with you, Mr Garvey.'

Eddie spoke up. 'He's here for me, Missus Pawley. I've got somethin' to tell the farmer.'

Ruth shrugged and led the way into the kitchen, where Stan was wrapping silk threads around hens' feathers to make fishing flies.

He put down his lump of home-made dubbing wax. 'I thought I'd told you I din't want you on my property no more.'

'I know, but this is something you ought to listen to.' Keir gave Eddie a little push forward. 'Go on, lad.'

Once Eddie started, the whole sorry tale came pouring out, and through the gulps and sobs Keir heard a story that made him tense up, filled with hot shame at the way he'd spoken to both Eddie and Ellen yesterday. He thought he'd understood poverty, but when it came to some of the choices Ellen had had to make, just to keep herself and her young son alive, he could only wonder at the so-called community in which she lived.

'Why didn't she ask her neighbours for help?' he asked. 'Surely someone would have given you something when you needed it.'

'She already took all she could,' Eddie mumbled, and sniffed. 'She won't ask for no more, on account of no one's got any spare. She says things'll pick up, and Granny Donithorn won't need her forever. ...' He turned wide eyes on Keir, as it dawned on him what his mother had meant. 'She means Granny's goin' to die, don't she?'

'No!' Keir gripped the boy's shoulder. 'She only means that your granny will find a better home. Maybe move in with other family.'

'We'm the only family she's got, and Ma's already told her to come to us and we'd fit her in, somehow.' Eddie wiped his nose on his sleeve. 'But she won't leave Furzy Row, keeps sayin' Uncle David and Aunty Ginny will be back. But they won't.'

'I don't know anything about that,' Keir said. Stan was frowning at the two of them, so he went on, 'Mr Pawley, you've heard the boy's confession. If we can work out a way of paying you for what's gone missing, will you let me have my job back?'

'And how will you pay me?' Stan asked, picking up his silk thread again and studying it. 'It's a lot of money.'

'How about if young Eddie here works for you, for nothing, over the summer?'

Stan shifted his attention back to the little boy. 'All summer?'

'And weekends,' Keir added.

'And what can you do, boy, skinny thing that you are?'

'I'm good with animals,' Eddie stammered. 'Them chickens have proper took to me—'

'Hah!' The farmer's eyes glinted. 'I'll bet they have.'

'I'll try anythin', sir,' Eddie said, in a braver voice. 'But it ain't fair to take Mr Garvey's job away.'

'I'll decide what's fair,' Stan said. He stood up at last, and put out his hand to shake Keir's. 'All right, Garvey. I'll make sure Alfie and his happy band know it wasn't you thievin' from us. You can have your job back, startin' now. As for you, young fella,' he glared at Eddie. 'You'll do as you're told, and if I get one sniff of anythin' amiss, you'll be back down the road faster'n you can spit.'

'Thank you!' Keir breathed a sigh of deep relief. 'You won't regret it.'

'See I don't.'

They went out into the yard, and the rain was coming down harder, but this time Keir greeted it with a grin. 'Get on up to school now, Eddie. And I'll get word to your ma that you'll be at Penhaligon's Attic after, so she can pick you up on her way home from work.'

'She won't be home 'til after dark,' Eddie said.

'All right then, come here to the farm instead. Find me, make yourself useful while you wait for me, and I'll take you back down when I've finished.'

'In't that the nicest thing?' Nancy, her shawl over her head, was blinking at him through the rain.

Keir bent to the boy's ear and muttered, 'Get those tools back off Bobby Gale. If he gives you any trouble tell him I sent you.' He straightened and spoke in his normal tones. 'Go on, then, lad.' Eddie left at a run, and Keir went into the barn, gesturing for Nancy to follow. 'I came to apologise to you yesterday.'

Nancy shook her head free from its makeshift hood. 'I never saw you.'

'That's because you were . . . busy.'

She flushed. 'The children never said you came by.' At least she didn't try to deny what she'd been doing. 'Anyway, nothin's stopping you now. Apologise away.'

'I'm sorry. I was wrong. I've since found it was Eddie stealing. I shouldn't have accused you, or Gerald.'

'No, you shouldn't.' She came over, her voice dropping again, and her fingers reached out to his belt. 'Anyway, no harm done. You've got your job back.'

'And where's *my* apology?' he countered, feeling himself twitch at the nearness of her, and at the sight of the raindrops on the clear, fair skin of her chest. 'I mean, you were certain I'd done it. I was as insulted as you were.'

'Then I'm sorry too.' Her hand dropped from his belt, and she caressed the front of his trousers, smiling at the predictable response. 'Well now, Mr Garvey, seems like you're not as cross with me as you pretend.'

He put one hand in the small of her back, and pulled her closer. 'And what about your other visitor?'

'What about him?'

'Are you going to drop him?'

'No. Does that matter?'

'It should.' Keir placed his other hand over her breast. The softness filled his palm, and he watched in fascination as a single raindrop travelled down from her collar bone to the top of her blouse. He bent his head to lick it away before it could be absorbed in the material, and she dropped her head back, encouraging his tongue on the slope of her breast.

'But it doesn't, does it? Because you know what I've got for you ain't made any less by what I gives to others.'

'No,' he agreed in a low voice. 'And that's all I want from you.'

She gave a chuckle, and lifted her head again. 'Good,' she breathed. Her lips locked onto his, and she grasped his hips. 'Close the door,' she whispered against his mouth.

He did so, plunging them into a strange half-light, with

stripes of daylight falling across the floor. The moment the latch went down she pulled his shirt free of the back of his trousers and slid her hands beneath his vest, and around to his stomach, her palms flat against him.

'For God's sake,' she whispered, 'hurry up!'

He twisted in her arms, and felt her short, ragged nails in the skin of his back. Her mouth was moving across his throat, her breath hot on his skin.

'Lie down,' he said, his voice hoarse.

'Orderin' me about now, are we?' she teased, stepping away and lifting her skirt so it hung over her forearms. She swayed, and the material lifted and fell, letting him glimpse the slender thighs beneath. '*I'm* not some little kid you can take under your wing, you know.'

He had taken a step towards her again, but stopped. 'What are you talking about?'

She lay back against a pile of sacking, and pulled her skirt higher. 'Gettin' all friendly with their kids so you can get on their ma's good side?'

'What's that supposed to mean?' Keir scowled. 'Eddie only came to the farm to own up to stealing.'

'All right. Don't get in a snit. Shouldn't think you'd want the likes of Ellen Scoble, anyway, why would you?' Nancy raised herself on one elbow, and in the half-light he saw her pulling at the neck of her blouse to reveal the beautiful bare breasts beneath. Always ready, that was Nancy. But he was no better, was he? Memories, never too far from the surface, of Jane Walsh, her swelling stomach and her fury at his leaving … He was in danger of repeating that mistake, and ruining yet another life.

'I don't want Ellen,' he said. 'And I never will, but there's no call for nastiness.'

'I weren't bein' nasty,' she laughed. 'Just honest. If you're looking for revenge on me and my *visitor*, you'd not pick a ragged, scrawny little bit like that, with a dirty job up the mine, and a grubby little house down 'Stennack. Nah. You've got better taste, Keir Garvey. Now come here and prove it.'

'No,' he said, surprising himself. He began tucking in his vest and shirt, his heart still pounding hard, but a calm realisation stealing over him; Nancy was not a saint, she certainly wasn't a bad person either ... She simply wasn't for him. Not anymore. Her playful but dismissive tone had chipped away at something inside him, and, after Eddie's revelations, what he'd glimpsed beneath was shameful.

'I'm sorry,' he said. 'I don't want to do this anymore.'

'I don't believe you.' She was still smiling. 'Come on, let me show you what you're missing.'

'I know what I'm missing. And maybe it's not something you can give me, after all.'

'You said this was all you wanted,' she reminded him, pulling up her blouse again. She sat up with her arms locked around her knees, her head on one side. Her voice was thoughtful. 'The only thing that's changed between then and now, is me mentionin' Ellen Scoble.'

'That had nothing to do with it. Well, maybe your choice of words did, but I promise you I don't have any fancy for Mrs Scoble.' He crouched in front of her, and fixed her eyes with his. 'You're a tonic, Nancy Gilbert. I like you a great deal. And I hope you'll still make me laugh, and make fun of me, and make me feel a little bit stupid when I get on my high horse.'

'Yes, well,' she put out a hand to be pulled to her feet. 'If you change your mind about the other stuff, you know where to find me.' She gripped his shirt and pulled his face down to hers, then looked at him searchingly before pressing her lips to his. 'This in't the end of us,' she said, when she broke the kiss. 'You only think it is.'

* * *

Truro

Picking up the wages had been a straightforward affair after all, and left James with a good two hours to spare before he needed to make his way back to the coach for Caernoweth. As always his feet had drawn him to the centre of town, and he squinted up through the fast-falling drizzle, at the towering spires of the cathedral. The last time he had stood here like this, an unassuming, bespectacled man had struck up a conversation, and almost a year later that conversation had changed James's life. Charles Trubshaw had only spoken to him for a few minutes, but the complimentary letter he'd subsequently sent, advising James to apply for the job in Levenshulme with Gerald Simpson, had quite likely helped the Battens make their decision.

This time there was no quietly spoken architect with whom to swap observations on the new cathedral; people hurried by on their errands, heads down, and the only faintly familiar face James saw was a heavy-featured, middle-aged man, who'd been travelling on the same coach from Caernoweth. He too was walking alone, but repaid James's friendly nod with a blank-eyed stare, leaving him embarrassed.

He walked on up through the town, his gaze taking in buildings to his left and right, and his mind filing away what worked, and what might be altered for the better. He'd expected to be waiting at the coach stand long before it was due, but so absorbed was he in his studies, that when he took out his pocket watch again he had to blink twice to convince himself he was reading it correctly.

He got to the coach with barely a minute to spare, and sank onto his seat gratefully, only to note the man he'd seen earlier, also late, waving at the driver to prevent him moving away without him. Suddenly uneasy, James folded his arms across his middle, checked the leather bag was still secure against his side, and, as the coach moved away on its slow, jolting ride home, he closed his eyes.

When he jerked awake, they had already pulled in to the hotel courtyard at Caernoweth, and stopped. He sat upright, smacking his lips, and pulled a face. The man who'd been sitting opposite him had already alighted, and James's heart leapt in panic, but the wages bag was still there, and still full. A young couple, just leaving their seats, gave him amused looks, and he smiled back, and shrugged, too tired to be embarrassed all over again.

The grim weather had darkened the sky prematurely, and it was growing late. His mind still full of what he'd seen in Truro, James set off to Pencarrack House, wishing he'd taken an earlier coach home after all; once away from the main road, and the hotel, it was hard to see the way clearly, even after his vision had adapted. The lights of Pencarrack pierced the darkness a short distance away, and he wondered if Dorothy was home. She might invite him to stay for a nightcap, and, aware of the sour taste in his mouth he bent down to pluck some wet grass to sweeten his breath a little. Down at this level, the noise of the wind in his ears lessened, and a tiny sound, away to his right, made him turn his head and hold his breath for a moment. When it wasn't repeated, he straightened again and let the breath out.

That was when the sky exploded.

James fell, his head ringing, his vision filled with flashing lights, and a heavy, dull pain sank into his stomach. He became aware of voices, harsh and low, another kick, and he retched, panting as his belly muscles seized up. A boot took him in the hip, and another behind the ear. He slumped, his mind spinning in terror and pain, powerless to protect himself as the blows landed. Then the ground was slipping away beneath him, and he realised he was being hauled away. Too late, he tried to detect the weight of the wages bag, but he already knew it was gone. His assailants had him by the arms, and he could feel the toes of his boots digging twin paths into the ground as he was dragged into full darkness around the side of Pencarrack House.

His face smashed into the grass as they dropped him, and he tried to curl up but he had no strength left. They had the money, why didn't they just leave him?

'Get it,' a voice rasped.

You've already got it ... He was sure he'd spoken aloud, but there was a roaring in his ears and he couldn't hear his own voice. Someone seized his shoulder and rolled him onto his back. He couldn't lift a hand to help himself, it was as if he was awake, yet dreaming. His head pounded, and two sets of hands patted him down, but this time they were seeking, not striking. He felt something wrench at his coat pocket, and then all contact ceased.

'That it?' He had no idea if it was the man from the coach, but it sounded familiar.

'Must be.'

'Right, on three . . .'

'Maybe we shouldn't—'

'Now!'

James groaned and tried to tug his arms free, but it was hopeless. As the voice counted three, the ground beneath him vanished, and he was tumbling through empty air. When he landed, all coherent thought left him. There was a single, bright flash of agony, then nothing.

Chapter Nineteen

By Friday mid-morning the rain had cleared. Lucy found Harry and his mother after a late breakfast, in the sitting room. Harry was earnestly explaining the plot of a story Mrs Webb had read to him yesterday, but Dorothy was staring into the distance, and it was clear none of it was going in, though she made appreciative noises.

'That sounds exciting,' Lucy said, sitting down next to her nephew. 'It's very kind of Mrs Webb to come over here to read to you.'

Dorothy swam back. 'Hmm?' She frowned. 'Who *is* Mrs Webb, anyway? Harry never really said.'

'Yes I did,' Harry said. 'She's the lady with the story book.'

'Yes, but who—'

'Freya Penhaligon's mother,' Lucy supplied. 'The stories are ones that Mr Penhaligon wrote for Freya when she was little.'

'Freya's . . . ' Dorothy gave a little start, and stood up. 'You mean this Mrs Webb is *Isabel Penhaligon*?'

'I thought you knew.'

'How would I? Nobody mentioned her new surname, when Hugh and I bumped into her at the hotel.' Dorothy looked at Harry, tight-lipped. 'She's not to come here again, do you hear?'

Lucy rose too. 'What on earth's the matter with you? She's perfectly nice, and Harry's enjoying the stories. At least it's keeping him in the house where we can keep an eye on him.'

'I want her to come again!' Harry looked up at his mother, and his voice rose. 'I *like* her. You can't stop her anyway, this isn't even your house, it's Grandfather's!'

'Henry George, apologise to your mother at once!' Lucy's tone stopped the boy in his tracks, and he flushed.

'I'm sorry.' He turned pleading eyes on Lucy. 'But tell her, Aunt Lucy! Mr Penhaligon's stories are truly fun!'

'We don't know if she even wants to come back,' Lucy pointed out. 'The rain's stopped and she might have other things to do. She has family to visit, after all.'

'Go to your room, Harry,' Dorothy said. '*If* Mrs Webb wants to come back, we'll discuss it then. And no sneaking off!' she called after him as he pulled open the door. 'I want to hear your feet going up those stairs.'

'Can I go in Aunt Lucy's room, and look out for the farm cart?'

'No! Little boys who have no manners do not get to choose their punishments.'

'But my room faces the wrong way!'

'The produce isn't due for another few hours,' Lucy soothed. 'Perhaps by then you'll be allowed to wait in the garden.' When he had gone she turned to her sister again. 'You're looking even more distant than usual today. What's wrong? Has Father spoken to Hugh?'

'It's nothing to do with Hugh,' Dorothy said. 'It's James, and the Furzy and Polworra wages.'

'What about them?'

'We, well Father at least, thinks he's run off with them. He went to fetch them from Truro yesterday, and no one's seen him since.'

'Perhaps he missed the last coach home?' Lucy glanced at the clock, and winced. 'And the first one back ... Look, he'll probably be back before the end of the shift.'

'What if he isn't?' Dorothy moved away to stare out of the window. 'What if Father's right? James seemed so decent.'

'And I'm sure he is. But even if he's not, that won't make it your fault. You're not the one who sent him. Try not to worry. Where is Father, anyway?'

'In the library, of course. I'd be in there with him, only Harry wanted to tell me about those infernal stories.'

'At least he wanted to talk to you.' Lucy smiled. 'That's a good thing. And good that you stayed.'

'Don't speak as if I'm the worst parent in the world!' Dorothy swung around to glare at her. 'I'm not *that* awful. We go for walks, and I help him with his school work, we actually talk quite a lot, you know!'

'I know, you're right. I'm sorry.'

'When he runs off, it's not to get away from me, it's because he's wilful, and adventuresome!'

'And because he's made friends locally,' Lucy pointed out, 'rather like his mother used to. Perhaps if you weren't so strict about that, he'd not feel the need to sneak away quite so often.'

'Perhaps. He's that bit older now, and school seems to be doing him some good, if you disregard pretending illness just to bunk off the last two weeks of term. Where are you going?'

Lucy paused, her hand on the door handle. 'I want to speak to Father about Hugh.'

'Not now!' Dorothy shook her head, as if Lucy were mentally lacking. 'It's really the worst time, with this wages thing.'

'It'll be a storm in a tea cup,' Lucy said. 'James will have stayed overnight in Truro, and overslept. You'll see.'

'I hope you're right.' Dorothy pushed past her. 'I'm going to talk to Father about it now, and see if he's heard anything.'

'I'll come with you, we can harass him together.'

But, as before, the library was locked and Dorothy frowned. 'I suppose he must have gone to fetch Pagett and his reporters from the station.'

'Reporters?'

'It's the ground-breaking later today, or had you forgotten? Well no matter, I still have work to be getting on with.' She fished a key from her pocket, and Lucy hoped Hugh wasn't somewhere watching; what a blow to know Dorothy had such easy access to everything that he'd been denied.

Once inside the library Dorothy picked up a small notebook from the table. 'I didn't realise James had shown these to Father.'

'What are they?'

'Some cost estimates we made when we were at the fort the other day. Much more realistic than the ones Pagett's come up with.' She flicked through the pages distractedly, then put the book down, and sighed. 'What time does the next Truro coach get in?'

'A little after six o'clock. What was it that you rushed off to tell Father?'

'When?'

'When you made me promise to keep his secret, and in return you promised to keep Hugh's. I saw you go scurrying into the library the minute we'd finished talking.'

Dorothy frowned, still distracted by worry about the wages, then her expression cleared. 'Oh, that!' She looked uncomfortable for a moment. 'Someone had arrived, quite unexpectedly, on the same coach as Mr Pagett, that's all. I thought Father ought to know they were here.'

Lucy tried to see past the bland expression. 'It must have been—'

'MOTHER!' Harry's panicked voice cut through Lucy's words. Startled, she and Dorothy hurried into the hall to see the boy, white-faced and halfway down the stairs. At sight of them he jumped the last few.

'There's a man! In the valley! I think he's dead!'

Heart pounding, Lucy followed Dorothy and her son out through the French windows at the back of the house, and across the rear garden. Harry ducked through a gap in the hedge, something he had evidently done often before, and Lucy and Dorothy had little choice but to follow, if they didn't want to lose him. They emerged onto the stretch of ground between house and valley, and Harry ran to the valley's edge.

'Stop!' Dorothy cried. 'You'll fall!'

'He's down here, I saw him from my window!'

Harry slithered over the edge, and disappeared from view. Lucy and Dorothy exchanged horrified glances, and hurried to the lip of the valley. Harry was scrambling between rocks, and grabbing at wind-blasted shrubs to keep his balance. Dorothy seized Lucy's arm, and pointed. 'There! Oh God, it *is* him . . .'

'Who?' Lucy squinted and followed Dorothy's finger, and among the rocks she saw a pale shape. A hand. As her focus sharpened, she saw a sleeve, and finally a glimpse of light blond hair. James. Her heart squeezed painfully tight.

Harry was scuffling sideways towards where the body lay, and Dorothy was shaking, but to Lucy's astonishment she sat down, and wriggled to the edge.

'What on earth . . . Dorothy, no! He's a better climber than you are. Look at all the practice he's had, the little monkey! Stop!' she cried, in growing desperation. 'If you fall you might take him with you.'

'Go and fetch someone.' Dorothy's foot slipped, and she cried out, then found a firmer footing. 'Go on, quick!'

'But—'

'I'm coming, my love. I'm coming,' Dorothy chanted breathlessly, and it wasn't until Lucy turned away to seek help that she realised her sister was not talking to Harry.

Chapter Twenty

Penhaligon's Attic

Tristan looked across the shop at Freya, who was bent over a book, a needle in hand, but unmoving. He too was finding it hard to concentrate, listening for sounds from above, where Doctor Bartholomew was checking Anna's progress. His pen was as still as her needle.

Eventually the doctor returned. His grim expression made Freya put down the book, and clasp her hands to stop them shaking, and Tristan's heart tightened, but Bartholomew's words were at odds with his manner.

'She's recovering well. No further bleeding.'

Freya's frown cleared at once, and she rose to go upstairs. 'Thank you!'

Bartholomew picked up his hat, but Tristan stopped him. 'Are you quite all right yourself, Doctor? You seem rather tense.'

Bartholomew was evidently wrestling with the decision to speak up. 'I found something,' he said at last. 'A link between my family and the Battens.'

Tristan shot a glance at Freya, but kept his face carefully neutral. 'That's good, isn't it?'

'It *would* be good,' Bartholomew said, 'if it weren't for the words my ancestor used.' He put a hand into his pocket, and withdrew a sheet of extremely aged and yellowed paper. 'See for yourself. "Dark and shameful secrets." And he begs forgiveness. Nothing one wants to see, in connection with one's ancestors, I'm sure you'll agree.' He sighed. 'I hesitate to show it even to you, but you've been working so hard to find this connection, I feel I owe it to you. Even though it's turned into something I'd rather not have known about.'

Tristan took the note and read it aloud. His heart sank. 'I'm so sorry. Where did you find this?'

'My housekeeper found it in James Fry's room this morning. Yesterday she told me there was a book, now this. I've already told Charles Batten about the book.' He shook his head. 'I'm not sure I should have done that, either. The past really should stay buried. If this isn't proof, I don't know what is.'

Tristan daren't look at Freya. 'Have either of you seen the book for yourself?'

'No. But this letter is a strong enough hint that it's potentially damaging, to both of us.' He took back the paper. 'I can't find James to ask him, but I'll do so when he comes home this evening.'

'James doesn't have the book,' Tristan said, 'it's locked up in the Pencarrack gallery. And there really isn't anything damning in it. Certainly nothing that could hurt either of your families.'

306

The doctor's expression froze. Then he swallowed hard. 'You knew about it already?'

'I'm sorry. It didn't seem urgent to tell you, since it didn't connect you to the Battens in any way. I would have done, though, if I'd seen that.' He gestured to the note. 'But there was *really* hardly anything at all in the book itself, you have my word.'

Bartholomew's skin was sheathed in a light sweat. 'I no longer have any faith in your *word*, Mr MacKenzie, I'm sure you'll understand. Now, if you'll excuse me.'

'Doctor—'

'Good day, Mr MacKenzie. Miss Penhaligon.'

When the shop door had swung shut, and the bell had stopped ringing, Tristan finally looked at Freya. 'I know what you're going to say.'

'No, you don't.' She came over and put her arms around him. 'I know we've disagreed on this, but you did what you felt was right. As soon as the doctor sees that book he'll realise you were telling the truth.'

'I'll take all the notes over to his house tonight,' Tristan said. 'Once he knows everything, it'll be up to him what he tells Batten.'

'Let them fight it out between them,' Freya said. 'You've done your job, and you've satisfied the historian in you. There's an end to it, at last.'

'All but.' He kissed the top of her head. 'We just have the last of Daniel's journals to check through. Future Batten generations don't seem to have had the same fanatical interest in recording everything.'

A hesitant knock sounded from above, and Freya drew

back. 'That's Anna, I practically had to force her to use Granny Grace's stick. I'll be back down in a minute.'

Tristan took out his pocket watch. 'Don't rush, I'll go up and pick up that journal, and bring it back here to make the notes. I'll bring the newest book too, so I can show Bartholomew I was telling the truth. When Teddy comes up, tell him he's got the day off.' He grinned. 'And enjoy watching him try to explain why he wants to go up to Pencarrack anyway, without saying the name *Lucy*, or turning red.'

The front door of Pencarrack House stood wide open, and he could see through to where French windows were also flung wide, looking out into the rear garden. He stepped over the threshold, and Mrs Andrews, making for the dining room with a pile of folded napkins, stopped short at the sight of him and came over.

'You're not welcome here, Mr MacKenzie. Nor your friend neither.'

Baffled, he stared at her. 'Mr Batten has given me permission—'

'It's been withdrawn. Please leave.'

'Withdrawn? I signed an agreement!' Tristan sighed; it was the doctor, it must have been. No wonder he'd beetled away so quickly. 'Can I speak to one of the Misses Batten please?'

'They're busy.' Mrs Andrews said. 'You'll have to come back later.'

'Would you allow me to at least go up and collect my notes?'

Mrs Andrews threw a glance towards the stairs. 'Mr Batten's not here to ask.'

'I'll be two shakes. Please, Mrs Andrews ... those notes

represent *months* of work.' He saw a chink in her armour and seized on it. 'Besides I'm sure someone in your position has the authority to act on Mr Batten's behalf on such a trifling matter.'

She narrowed her eyes at him, clearly seeing through his flattery, then sighed and shook her head. 'Go on, then, but be quick. And make sure no one sees you, or it'll be more than my job's worth. And yours.'

In the gallery Tristan picked up the book James had found, and put it in his pocket. Then he looked at the rows of journals he'd never now get to read. He'd told Freya his research began and ended with the English Civil War, but there was an undeniable pull towards anything that helped piece together the past. Perhaps one day he'd get access to them again.

There was no sign of his box of papers. He hunted for a few minutes, frowning; they were not where he'd left them. Hissing with frustration, he realised he'd have to approach Batten directly and ask him to return them – either that or steal them back again. He mulled over that notion; if that was his decision it would have to be now, while there was no one in the house bar one or two servants. On his way out of the room, he paused. The final journal by the hand of Daniel Batten lay inches from his grasp, and the temptation was strong to at least look at it. It would finish everything off nicely, and bury this niggling sensation of having done half a job. And it would go some small way towards making up for having his notes snatched from under his nose.

Nevertheless feeling rather like a sneak thief, Tristan unlocked the glass case and took out the book. He opened it carefully, and scanned the first few lines of the spidery handwriting, which seemed to have gone back to the way it had been when Daniel had first begun writing his father's memories:

> *November 15ᵗʰ 1698. Winstanley's lighthouse on the Eddystone rocks is now lit. It has been two years in the making, and I thank God Malcolm is in his grave these past twenty-eight years, or this, alongside the talk of a new Piracy Act, would surely put him there.*

Tristan's heart skipped; this was the first blatant reference to illegal acts he had seen in one of the Batten journals; up until now it had all been shaded and hidden, and had required some astute reading between the lines. It was certainly all open to interpretation. Batten would now be – Tristan counted quickly – around seventy years old. A very great age for the time, and it seemed his years were making him increasingly careless; his traitorous pen was drawing out the secrets he himself had so cleverly hidden.

Tristan read on, conscious that he was putting Mrs Andrews's job at risk, but helplessly drawn, as always, to these words written in another age.

> *This act, should it pass, will allow any person accused of piracy to be tried and sentenced anywhere, they will no longer require to be brought back to England. Had this been the case throughout Malcolm's active days I believe we would both be in the ground together, in paupers' graves.*

Now that sailors no longer fear the Eddystone Rocks the opportunities for a privateer are fewer. I venture there will be an end to this means of gathering wealth, and now the estate must pay its own way. I am old. My hand grows tired, my eyes likewise, but my memories are as sharp and clear as they have ever been. My son has no love of the written word, unlike that which has driven my poor father and myself. But he will do well for Pencarrack by having inherited his mother's social graces. I cannot think there will be more to tell from the pen of the man who was once Daniel Bartholomew, and was proud to be so.

Batten had lived a little longer at least; the handwriting continued for several pages the same, although the second half of the book was empty. Tristan looked at the first line again: Winstanley's lighthouse at Eddystone. He smiled as he thought back to his musings on Plymouth Hoe, where the replica of Smeaton's own Eddystone lighthouse now stood. Where he'd been standing, too, when Teddy had run up to him in a state of great excitement about the little bookshop in Caernoweth, and the diaries written by a John Bartholomew.

How much had happened, since last year. Now he was engaged to marry the young woman who ran that shop, and his future lay firmly and happily in the town that had been nothing more than a name on a sheet of paper. With the mention of that lighthouse, it felt as if everything had come in a full circle, to be closed here, within these pages.

He hefted the book thoughtfully. Far from being simply a neat tying-up of Daniel Batten's life, this book was going to address many of the questions that went, as yet, unanswered. He would post it back later. Even if he didn't take any more notes, he had to see how the story ended. He glanced out of the window again, and saw a familiar figure walking up through the garden: Teddy. Poor chap would be bewildered and upset to find he'd been banned from using the gallery too, but the news would sound better coming from Tristan, particularly if he knew there was one more book; one that would make sense of all the others. He only hoped they'd be allowed to remain in the cottage on Priddy Lane.

He limped down the stairs, and hurried through the still-deserted house, to catch Teddy before he was able to summon Mrs Andrews by ringing the bell. They met halfway up the path, but were distracted to see Keir Garvey walking around from the side of the house. He was looking cross, and puzzled, and when he saw Tristan and Teddy he broke into a jog.

'Have either of you seen a single living bloody soul around here today?'

'Only Mrs Andrews,' Tristan said.

'Ah, that was the name. Where is she? Only I've to get her to sign the paperwork.'

'What paperwork?'

Keir waved a notebook. 'Stan Pawley's decided it's time I ran the produce cart, and learned how things're done.' He grimaced. 'Still, better than lime-washing the hen-houses, I suppose. Especially with that bloody woman pretending to help but just making life ...' he shook his head, evidently exasperated. 'Never mind. Don't ask.'

312

Tristan didn't. 'And where is the cart?'

'Round the side by the kitchen. Enough stuff on there to feed an army, too. Including a whole salted pig. God knows what they want with it all.'

'I'll come in and see if I can find Mrs Andrews.' Tristan handed the diary to Teddy. 'I'm sorry, old man, it's a longish story, but we're not allowed access to the gallery anymore.'

Teddy's face fell. 'Gosh, that's a bit out of the blue.'

'Isn't it just? But take this back to the shop, and while you're waiting for me have a little look through it.'

'What about the notes? Hadn't we better take them too?'

'Someone's beaten us to it,' Tristan said, with a heavy sigh. 'I'm hoping to find them now, I'll just introduce Keir to Mrs Andrews, then I'll have a poke around the library while she's busy.'

'Have you seen Lucy?' Teddy peered hopefully past him into the house.

'No, but I'm sure she'll visit later and explain what's happened.'

Teddy left reluctantly, and Tristan turned to Keir. 'Right, let's go and see if we can find someone to sign those off for you.'

'I had to unload it all myself, too,' Keir grumbled, following him around to the side of the house. 'Nancarrow said there'd be help, but I'm blowed if I can find anyone.'

'Seems odd,' Tristan agreed. The kitchen yard was deserted, and a quick look into the kitchens themselves showed the boxes Keir had left on the big table in the centre, but no sign of anyone to unpack them. He was tempted to go straight into the library now and hunt for his notes, but Keir called out and stopped him halfway across the kitchen.

'There's a group of people out there.'

Tristan went back out into the yard, to find Keir standing by the now-open wooden door. Through it, he could see the stretch of garden, beyond which lay that awful ravine he'd come so close to falling into. Over the hedge he could see hats and bare heads bobbing, and at least one white maid's cap.

He led a hesitant Keir across the grounds. 'They can't very well give you a telling-off,' he pointed out, 'when they're the ones making themselves scarce and leaving the house unattended.'

They passed through the gate, and Mrs Andrews came to meet them. She cast a guilty glance over her shoulder. 'Did you get what you were after?'

'Not quite, but thank you.'

'And no one saw you?'

'No one. Mrs Andrews—'

'Who's this?'

'I was coming to that.' Tristan introduced Keir, who produced the paperwork.

'Come in to the kitchen,' she said, frowning. 'Tradesmen didn't ought to be marching across the lawns.'

'What's going on out here?' Tristan asked.

'Someone've been found in the valley. It's the younger Mr Fry.'

'James?' Tristan looked past her. 'Is he badly hurt?'

'Nobody knows.' She walked on towards the house, and Tristan nodded at Keir to go with her. 'I'll stay here and find out what's happened.'

He crossed the short distance between Pencarrack and the Serth Valley's steep edge, and his attention was caught by a double row of tracks scratched into the surface of the grass. Much too close together to be tyre marks, and too uneven. And they ended a short distance from the lip of the valley ... He went cold.

Both Batten sisters, Doctor Bartholomew, Collings, and a number of other servants, were all staring down the slope. Young Harry Batten was there too, dancing from foot to foot in agitation, and Tristan heard his voice clearly.

'Will he go in Grandfather's car? To hospital, I mean.'

'If he's still alive,' one of the servants allowed, and Tristan saw Dorothy blanch. 'Stand ready! Here he comes!'

Tristan joined the group and peered over the edge. Ranged down the lethal-looking slope were estate workers, who'd formed a straggling chain and passed between them a burden that seemed little more than a bloodied pile of rags, before slipping and grunting their own way back up.

They laid James on the grass, and Tristan could see blood congealing in his blond hair, matting it into dark clumps. James's coat and waistcoat were ripped and his neck was glistening crimson, from a deep tear that ran from his ear to his collar bone; no doubt the legacy of one of those wickedly sharp pieces of granite.

Dorothy beat the doctor to his side, and knelt down. She pressed her fingers below the angle of his jaw, and it seemed everyone was holding their own breath, waiting to see if James still had any. 'He's alive,' she said, in wondering tones, and lowered her head briefly to his. Then she sat up straight, and her voice shook as she cried, 'Collings? Collings!'

'Here, Miss.'

'Fetch the car, quickly. Doctor?'

Doctor Bartholomew moved forward, and Dorothy accepted her sister's hand to help her rise to her feet. She saw Tristan, and her face went tight.

'You ...' she whispered. Lucy turned and followed her gaze, and her own expression was one of betrayed fury. Tristan stared back, speechless. What the dickens was going on? A commotion from the ground tore his puzzled attention away; James was evidently clawing his way back to consciousness. His breathing had grown light and shallow, and although his eyes stayed closed, his brow creased and his lips parted in a faint gasp. Doctor Bartholomew was carefully pressing his fingers to the various places on James's body where the clothing was torn, and frowning.

'He's got a broken collar bone, and a broken leg,' he said, 'and extensive bruising. He looks to have lain here several hours, possibly all night, which means he's at risk from having been exposed to the elements. He's also likely to be suffering internal injuries. Then there's this neck wound. I can bind it for now, but he'll need stitching up. He's beyond anything else I can do for him, he needs to go to hospital.'

James opened his eyes, briefly, but enough for Tristan to see a glassy sheen covering the blue. Then they fluttered closed again, and he muttered, 'Wages.'

'They've gone,' Dorothy said softly. 'You mustn't blame yourself. James—'

'Something else.' His voice was barely audible, and Tristan moved closer, ignoring Lucy's glare.

'What else?' Dorothy asked. James tried to shake his head, but winced and stilled. One hand crept to his side, and Tristan thought he was seeking the source of his pain, but the hand brushed his coat pocket. 'They were looking for . . . something else.' He frowned, confused, and then gasped and cried out and the doctor stopped his probing.

'Don't try to talk any more,' he said. 'Collings will bring the car around directly.'

'How should we lift him into it?' Dorothy asked, and she sounded close to tears. 'It will hurt him terribly.'

'It'd hurt him worse to stay here,' the doctor pointed out, with unusual terseness. 'Where's your father gone?'

'I don't know.' She stared around blankly. 'I think he went back indoors as soon as he knew James was alive.'

Bartholomew rose quickly to his feet, his face tight. 'I have to speak to him.'

'You can't leave! You haven't finished tending James.' Dorothy's voice was filled with outrage, and her fervour was drawing more than one knowing look from those gathered around. Her forehead was smudged with James's blood, from the brief moment when she'd forgotten herself and laid her head on his. Tristan's heart went out to her; she wasn't even trying to hide her feelings anymore.

Bartholomew hesitated, then nodded. He knelt down again and opened his bag to withdraw a gauze pad, which he pressed to the ugly wound that twisted down across James's neck. Presently Collings drove Batten's car slowly across the garden, and the estate workers braced themselves to lift. When they did so, James's scream echoed across the valley, and Tristan was ready to bet there was not one person present who did not feel it in their own bones. He himself held his breath in sympathetic agony, praying for the transition from grass to car to be a quick one. Another cry choked off into a

317

groan, and then James fell silent, and a crowd of white faces looked at one another in relief. Bartholomew was hovering, ready to help, but his increasing impatience was evident in the way he kept looking back at the house. Dorothy started towards the car.

'Where are you going?' Lucy asked.

'With James, of course.'

'You can't!' Lucy lowered her voice. 'Darling, we need you here. It's the ground-breaking later, and ...' She frowned. 'Wait, Hugh can't have gone to meet Pagett, can he, if the car's here? Where is he then?'

They both jumped as Doctor Bartholomew slammed the car door and banged on it twice. The sound seemed to bring Dorothy to her senses, and she addressed the milling servants as Collings drove carefully away.

'Everyone back to work!' Then she looked at Lucy. 'Find Harry and bring him to the house. I don't like him playing out the back here, I never did. Especially not now.' She cast a hate-filled glance at the valley, and hurried after the doctor, who was marching towards the house.

Lucy glared at Tristan. 'Sophie was right,' she said, 'it's your fault. *All of it!*' She started away, then flung over her shoulder, 'And you can tell Mr Kempton the same holds for him!' She went off in search of the ever-errant Harry, leaving Tristan to follow Dorothy and the doctor.

His suspicions grew, the more he thought about what poor James had tried to say, and he could tell Dorothy was thinking the same. His blood was fizzing as he put the pieces together in his mind, and made the ugliest of pictures, and Lucy's puzzling words rattled around in his brain: *Sophie was right ...*

He caught up with Dorothy and took her arm. 'What did Sophie tell you?'

'She said you were being pushed into publishing some rubbish about us being pirates and witches!' Dorothy wrested her arm from his grasp. 'And if you ever touch me again I'll have you thrown off Pencarrack land before you can blink!'

'I'm sorry. But *pushed* into it? By whom?'

'By Miss Penhaligon, of course.'

'And that's why we've been denied access to the journals?' Tristan was glad he'd given the borrowed book to Teddy. 'No wonder the little minx has made herself scarce!'

'It's not true, then?'

'No! In fact Freya has been the one begging me to think twice. Anything I want to publish will go through your father, in any case. You were there when we signed to say so.'

'Your sister said you were planning to go against the agreement.'

'I'm not, I swear it. Dorothy, listen—'

'Miss Batten,' she corrected him. 'And all that aside, it's still your fault James was attacked.' Her voice faltered. 'It *was* the book they were after, wasn't it?' She looked at him searchingly, and he sighed; despite his best intentions, the accusations were about to fly, thanks to Sophie and the doctor between them. He felt the weight of the book in his pocket but something kept him from showing her.

'I can't say for certain, but I think so,' he said quietly.

'Even though there's nothing in it.'

'The doctor thinks otherwise, and he must have told him there was.'

'Told who?' Dorothy's tone was innocent, but Tristan saw knowledge of the truth in her clenched jaw.

'Your father must have arranged it,' he said. 'Why else would James have been sent on the wages run? It was obviously a decoy.'

'I ... I have to hear it from him.' Dorothy turned away, but didn't protest when he followed her into the house. She gestured to a decorated alcove, displaying a pair of impressive-looking, highly polished battle axes. 'Wait there. And stay out of sight, he won't unbend if he knows you're here.'

Tristan did as he was bid, and for a brief time the historian in him awoke and he studied the axes, and the words etched onto the small brass plaque on the wall: *Hand axes belonging to Cedric Penworthy. Believed to have been used against the Spanish invaders. Battle of Cornwall. 1595.*

But even these relics, of a battle he'd studied and been fascinated by, could not hold his attention for long. From where he stood, he could hear activity drifting through from the kitchens, where the farm produce was at last being put away; he heard Keir's deep voice, and laughter raised in response to whatever he was saying, and he tried to use the pleasant, everyday sounds to calm himself. But rising anger at the shocking violence visited on the innocent and unknowing James Fry soon drove him out of his hiding place and towards the library. He heard conversation coming from within, through the half-open door, and he drew back, his heart thudding, and squinted through the gap.

'Bartholomew told me about it yesterday.' Charles Batten's normally carefully modulated voice was tight. 'He called me out of the meeting, in a terrible state about it. Then I saw it, the outline of it at least, in Fry's pocket.'

'But what did you *do*?' Tristan saw her sit down suddenly, and her voice dropped. 'It's true. You sent him for the wages on purpose, didn't you? You arranged for someone to—'

'I *had* to!' Batten let out an audible sigh. 'If it's any help to you, the men I enlisted for that job are the same ones who pulled him out of the valley.'

'How can that be a help?'

'Because it means he's no longer in danger from them. I didn't intend for them to be so ... thorough about it. Just to get the satchel, for the look of the thing, but most importantly the book.' There came the sound of something thudding onto the desk. 'But see here, it wasn't even the right one.'

'I might have told you that, if you'd only asked me!' Dorothy's voice was thick with tears. 'Those are nothing but James's costings for the build! The book you want is locked away up there.' She pointed to the library ceiling. 'Besides, James says there was only a half a page written, and all it said was that the owner was going to visit Malcolm Penworthy.'

'That's *all* it said?'

'Absolutely all.'

Tristan held his breath, and moved slightly so he could see the desk, and the room's other occupant, who was tapping the book thoughtfully. 'Bartholomew came to me yesterday, certain there was some damning information that will ruin us both. I had to think quickly, I couldn't let that book fall into the hands of that blasted historian!'

'Well you were too late.'

'Clearly.' Batten glared at her. 'But there's something else, since it'll impact on your inheritance if this gets out.'

'What will?'

'If Pagett believes there's the slightest chance of scandal, he'll pull out of the deal, and we've already put more money than we have into securing this partnership.'

'*That's* what you think is important?' Dorothy leaned forward, and Tristan could hear her incredulity. 'You'll find another investor!'

'I wouldn't be so certain of that, either. Bartholomew's found a handwritten note that proves there's *something* scandalous in our joint history, and thanks to Lucy's blasé invitation to MacKenzie and his crony, whatever it is has now come to light. No doubt your mother knew of it all those years.' He frowned, and his voice lowered to a mutter. 'We must find a way to get rid of those journals without arousing suspicion.'

'Father! James might *die*!' Dorothy rose. 'If he does it'll be your fault, and I'll tell the police as much.' She started towards the door, but her father slammed his hands on the desk, and she stopped again.

'Listen to me.' Batten's voice was calmer now. 'James will be given the best possible treatment. As soon as Hugh gets back with Pagett and my car you may take it on to Truro, and make sure the infirmary knows I will pay any expenses.'

'Hugh hasn't got the car,' she said, and sniffed. 'Collings used it to take James.'

'Oh.' Her father looked nonplussed for a moment, then shrugged. 'I'll have to send a carriage for Pagett, then.'

'Father!'

'Right!' Batten was visibly gathering his thoughts again. 'As soon as *Collings* arrives, tell him to take you back to Truro. As my messenger, of course.' He had evidently noted his daughter's emotional response; he came around the desk, and took her unresponsive hands in his, and his voice softened. 'You know I'll do anything to protect what is mine, and that includes my workers. You're right, what happened was my fault, and young Fry will be properly cared for, I promise. It's the very least I can do.'

Tristan could see Dorothy wanted to believe him, and eventually she nodded and dabbed at her eyes with her sleeve. 'I think it would be a good idea for Doctor Bartholomew to come with me to Truro. Where is he?'

'I haven't seen him.'

'But he said he was coming to find you.'

'Did he? He must have changed his mind, then. Look, I have to go up to my room and change, ready for this groundbreaking ceremony as soon as Pagett arrives, so perhaps you could arrange to send the carriage to Bodmin to collect him. Then wait out the front for Collings. I'll make your apologies for you, and explain you are attending one of our workers who's had an accident.'

'I suppose the visiting press will love that,' Dorothy said, her voice tight.

'Don't go looking for cynicism where there is none,' Batten said mildly. 'I mean to right the wrong I've done Fry, you can be sure of that, and the estate men will have their wages docked heavily for taking matters into their own hands the way they did. I have no idea what came over them.'

Tristan belatedly realised they were both walking towards him, and he started guiltily and wondered if he had time to get back into his alcove.

'Mr MacKenzie.' The voice cut across the hallway, and he

turned to see Lucy coming in through the French window, her expression melting from worry to anger at the sight of him. 'I thought you were told you had no place here? Do I have to call Constable Couch?'

'I was just leaving,' he said honestly. 'Dorothy knows the truth now, that Freya and I were by no means colluding to ruin your family.'

'If you insist.'

'It's true. My sister has been stirring trouble, hoping to come between Freya and myself. But she certainly never intended to cause anyone else any upset.'

She studied him for a moment. 'All right.' She didn't sound convinced.

'Are my notes in there?' he asked, gesturing to the library, but before she could answer, Dorothy and her father came out. Charles didn't spare them so much as a glance, instead he went upstairs, almost at a run, and Dorothy locked the library door and crossed to the cloakroom. Emerging a moment later, pulling her coat on over her bloodied clothing, she looked over at Tristan.

'Return the keys to Priddy Lane by the last day of this month.'

Tristan's heart sank. 'I understand you care deeply for James, but I would never have—'

'You understand nothing, Mr MacKenzie, clearly. You're so wrapped up in the past, you don't consider that what you're doing will have *real* consequences. In the present.' She regarded him with a bleak expression as she pulled on her gloves. 'The end of the month.'

With her words hanging in the air, cold and final, she

hurried out to wait for Collings, and Tristan looked back at Lucy. 'Look, Teddy's—'

'I don't care where, or what, Teddy is.' Lucy's gaze swept the hallway. 'I'm more concerned about my nephew just now, if you'll excuse me.'

'Can I at least help you look?'

'I think you'd be better employed looking after your sister, don't you?'

'I'll give her a good talking to when she gets back.'

'It's a little late for that. She's every bit as thoughtlessly destructive as you are. God help anyone who crosses that little madam, when she's got someone like you for an example. Now I'm asking you, once more, to leave this house and never come back. You may return the keys by a messenger.'

Tristan could feel anger pulsing in his temples now. 'I'm not leaving without my notes.'

'Dorothy told me to get them for her,' Lucy said. 'I have no idea what she's done with them. They're probably in there,' she gestured at the library. 'And I don't have a key.'

'They're my property!'

'No, they're not. They're our family's business. Father might see fit to return them once he's established that you cannot use anything you've found against us.'

'The agreement works both ways.'

Lucy's voice was brittle, equally angry. 'If you don't leave, Mr MacKenzie, I will call the estate men and have you taken off the premises.'

'And thrown into the valley, like James? Yes, I'm sure your father would be only too happy to give that order.'

'What?' Lucy faltered. 'What do you mean?'

Tristan stopped; it was not his place, Lucy would find out soon enough what kind of man her father was. 'Nothing. I wish you well, Miss Batten. Please don't let what my sister and I have done, and said, colour your view of Teddy Kempton. He deserves nothing but good things.'

She did not reply, but he could feel her betrayed gaze following him all the way to the edge of the Pencarrack estate.

Chapter Twenty-one

Penhaligon's Attic

Freya knocked gently at the bedroom door, and was heartened by the brightness of Anna's response.

'Come in. *Please!*'

'Are you that bored?' Freya asked with a smile, glad to see Anna sitting up with a book in her hands. 'It must be awful to be stuck here, on such a *lovely* day.' She pulled a wry face and looked out at the prematurely darkening sky. Rain was starting to spot the glass again, and the room had that unmistakeably chilly air that comes ahead of a good downpour.

'I'd give anything to be up and about, no matter what the weather,' Anna said, and put her book down with a sigh. 'Apart from the occasional cloudburst, what's happening out there in the real world?'

'Nothing very much.' It wouldn't do to put Anna's nerves to the test, so Freya decided against telling her of Isabel's plan to stay until after the wedding. And certainly about her revelations regarding Dorothy Batten's designs on the younger Matthew. 'How are you feeling?'

'Well enough, but going slowly out of my mind. I feel so set apart from everything. Tomorrow,' she vowed, 'I'm coming downstairs.'

'I don't know what Papá will say to that,' Freya warned, but Anna gave her a fierce look, that made her smile.

'Provided he doesn't actually lock me in, I'll be down in the shop with you all day getting under your feet. How does that sound?'

'Wonderful,' Freya said, truthfully. 'You can tell me what you think of my plans for the place.'

'Who's downstairs now? Tristan?'

'No, Teddy. Tristan's gone up to Pencarrack to fetch something. Can I help you with anything?'

'No, you're grand thanks. I've washed, and done the necessary.' Anna picked up her book again. 'Now I'm getting acquainted with *Rebecca of Sunnybrook Farm*.' She looked a little shy, suddenly. 'I wonder if you'd do me a favour?'

'Anything.' Freya straightened the covers over Anna's feet, and moved towards the window, ready to draw the curtain against the encroaching evening.

'Would you mind asking Isabel if I could borrow Matthew's story book?'

'Ah.' Freya came back to the foot of the bed, her fingers playing with the bedstead. 'The thing is, Mama's reading them to Harry Batten.'

'I thought she wanted you to do that? Wasn't that why she brought it with her?'

'I thought so too. I assumed she'd left the book with Papá. But anyway, it's keeping her occupied,' she pointed out with a little smile, 'and away from the shop.'

Anna flushed. 'I didn't mean for her to feel unwanted. For your sake as much as for hers.'

'I know,' Freya said quickly. 'Really, no one thinks that. But for the time being you'll have to be content with Rebecca. Meanwhile all I can do is shut out the rain for you.'

She reached up to pull the curtain across, and her gaze fell on the street below. She paused, frowning. 'Where are they all off to?' She turned to Anna. 'There's an awful lot of people walking up the hill. The children are running.'

'Ask them.' Anna started to swing her legs off the bed, but stopped at a glare from Freya, who wrestled for a moment with the stiff latch, then pushed the window open and leaned out.

'Mrs Packem! What's going on?'

The lady looked up with an expression of mingled horror and excitement. 'There's a fire! Up at Pencarrack!'

Freya drew back, her heart hammering. 'Oh, my God . . .'

'Go to him!' Anna said immediately. 'Hurry.'

'I can't leave you!'

'Teddy is here. Go on, now!'

Freya didn't stop to pick up her coat, and, still in her house shoes, she shouted back to Teddy to stay and take care of Anna. The shops and houses fell away behind her, yet it felt as if someone was stretching the road beneath her feet, stopping her from reaching the top of the hill. She could smell smoke on the air, well before she reached the junction at the top of town, and left the slower townspeople behind as she ran, her breath sobbing in her chest.

She eventually arrived at the house, and some of the frantic urgency died away; there was certainly a fire, but as yet it was little more than smoke billowing from a broken window on the top floor of the east wing and drifting down across the fields towards the sea. That would explain how word had travelled so quickly, at least. Then, through the smoke she saw a lick of flame start up, consuming the drape, and beginning to eat its way across the top of the window frame. Was that the room where Tristan and Teddy had been working?

'Freya!' Mama was hurrying across the grass where more of the townspeople were gathering, pointing and speculating.

'Have you seen Tristan?' Freya asked with growing desperation.

Mama nodded. 'Miss Lucy said he left a short while ago, just before the fire was discovered.' Freya sagged with relief, and Mama put her arms around her. 'He is safe,' she said. 'The family is out, and the fire service has been called.'

'How did you hear about it so quickly?'

Mama showed her the book she carried. 'I was on my way over here to visit Master Batten. Did you hear there was a man badly injured in the Serth Valley this morning, also?'

'No.' But before Freya could ask who it was, she heard a small commotion in the crowd, and Lucy Batten pushed her way through.

'Henry George, you show yourself *right this instant*! I mean it! HARRY!'

Mama's gaze went to the burning room, and she seized Freya's arm in a panicky grip. 'What if he is up there?'

'Mama—'

330

'He's so *little*!'

'You said the family was all out!'

'What if I was wrong? I was only saying what I have heard!' Mama's hands twisted together and it seemed she could not tear her eyes away from the first floor window.

Lucy saw Freya, and came over, her enmity apparently suspended. 'Miss Penhaligon, Mrs Webb, have you seen Harry anywhere?'

'No, I'll help you look.' Freya put Mama's hand away from her and turned to scan the crowd. 'He's probably watching from a safe distance,' she said, as calmly as she could manage. 'When was the last time you saw him?'

'At the valley, after they'd pulled James out.'

'James? James Fry?' Freya listened in growing horror as a distracted Lucy briefly described how Harry had seen the prone body from his bedroom window, and led them to the valley. She was desperate to know more about what had happened, and how James was, but Harry's disappearance was uppermost in everyone's mind now. Mama's reaction was the most worrying ... but she wasn't as used to Harry's wandering ways as everyone else, and she had re-established her terror-grip on Freya's arm.

Lucy, who knew better than anyone how adept Harry was at disappearing, was clearly frightened, but not yet panicking.

'The boy's safe!' A voice called from the crowd. Tobias Able pushed through, and addressed Lucy. 'I turned him away from Furzy earlier, Miss, with Bobby Gale and that Gilbert girl.'

Looking at the way her mother swallowed hard, still struggling to breathe, Freya wondered at the attachment she had

331

clearly made with the boy in such a short time. As her memories played over what Mama had said about Dorothy Batten and her own father, she began to feel queasy. She lowered her voice so Lucy couldn't hear.

'Mama, why *are* you so interested in Harry?'

'Whatever do you mean?' Mama gave her an incredulous look that didn't quite convince. 'Of course we are all worried for him, including you.'

'You seemed even more worried than Lucy.' Freya hesitated, then plunged on, 'Do you know who his father is?'

Mama's expression went carefully blank, but she was saved from further explanation by the arrival of Keir, who frowned at Freya.

'Why aren't you at home with Anna?'

She chose to overlook the gruff demand. 'Don't worry, she's not alone. I came to make sure Tristan was safe.'

He cast a suddenly worried glance up at the belching smoke. 'And is he?'

'As it turns out he's not here.'

'I'll give you a lift back to the shop, then,' he said. 'Nothing we can do here, and the fire service are on their way.'

Freya was about to press Mama on the matter of Harry's father, but looking at the regret on Mama's face she wasn't sure she wanted to know for certain after all; Papá had been many things, not all of them good, but to discover he had been an adulterer, and that Mama knew ... It would be better to re-bury the knowledge after all, at least until Anna was out of danger.

'We have a lot to talk about,' she said, 'but now isn't the time.' She kissed Mama's cheek, but before she and Keir had taken more than a few steps there came a terrific crashing noise from the stables, directly downwind of the burning east wing of the house.

'The horses are spooked,' Keir said. 'We'll have to get them out into the field. You go on.'

Freya watched in admiration for a moment, wishing she had the courage to help lead the horses out into the field, then noticed one of them, a particularly skittish and distressed-looking animal, was already fully tacked up. One of the men was having difficulty holding him, despite having a bridle and reins to grab hold of, but it wasn't until Keir stepped in, and the horse calmed, that Freya saw the white star on the horse's nose and recognised Bill. For a moment she just watched, puzzled, then it hit her, and she whirled towards the house and started to run.

'Freya! FREYA!' The voice behind her came closer, and she slowed, and turned to see Lucy, eyes wide with the same realisation.

'Sophie?'

Freya nodded, her breath short. 'She'll be in the same room Tristan was working in. Where is it?'

Lucy paled. 'Oh God, the gallery! It's where the fire is. Come with me.'

'You can't go in there, Miss!' An estate worker tried to block their path, but Lucy dodged around him and, seizing Freya's wrist, she pulled her into the house, muttering in a strange, lost voice. 'Oh, Hugh, what have you done?'

'What?'

But Lucy shook her head and made no reply. Inside the house, all was eerily quiet compared to the mayhem outside;

333

here, there was no sign that anything was amiss, until an innocent-sounding tinkle of glass came from somewhere upstairs. Lucy took the stairs at a run, and Freya followed.

From about halfway up the stairs the smell of smoke was stronger, and Freya could hear a frightening crackling sound, and the occasional muted roar as something else fell victim to the flames. Lucy stopped outside a room at the end of a short corridor, and tried the handle. It turned, but the door wouldn't budge. She hammered on it with her fist.

'*Sophie!* Are you in there? Can you answer me?'

'Lucy? Oh, I'm so scared . . . ' The girl's voice was thin and croaking, and Freya's heart slithered against her ribs. She was about to shout, but Lucy held her finger to her lips and shook her head.

'Sophie, darling,' she said, in a calm voice, 'have you locked yourself in?'

'No! It wasn't me. Please, get me out!'

'We're going to try,' Lucy said, giving Freya a helpless look. She dropped her voice to a whisper. 'Even if we had a key, the wood is warped.' Then her expression cleared. 'Sophie, listen. I'm going to fetch something that might help. How close is the fire to where you are?'

'It's . . . it's between me and the window, but it's spreading across the floor towards the door, too.'

'And where are you?'

'In the place where I said I'd hide! The alcove in the middle of the room.'

'All right. Stay there if you can.' Lucy closed her eyes briefly, and nodded to Freya. 'We're going to find something to help you, so don't worry if you don't hear anything for a minute or two.' She grabbed Freya's hand again, and raced with her down the stairs.

'What did you mean about Hugh?' Freya managed, between snatched breaths. 'Tell me!'

'Isn't it obvious?' Lucy slowed to a fast walk, and now there was anger underlying the fear in her voice. 'He's nowhere to be found, is he? And he has more reason than anyone to be furious, with both Father, *and* your fiancé.'

'But surely, he wouldn't do something so awful?'

'He wouldn't have known Sophie was around, she'd have been hiding, she knows she's not supposed to be in there, and Hugh behaved horribly towards her when they met.' Lucy crossed the hallway at a run and vanished into an alcove, emerging a moment later with an axe held in her two hands. 'Can you use this?'

'Yes!' Freya seized it, but the axe head thudded to the polished floor, perilously close to her softly clad foot. She hefted it again, this time ready for its tremendous weight. 'Is there one for you?'

'There's another one but I'm getting the MiniMax.'

'The what?'

'Fire extinguisher. I'll be up right after you. Go on, and make sure Sophie's standing well back from the door.'

Lucy vanished towards the hallway at the back of the house and Freya hurried up the stairs as fast as the heavy axe allowed. Outside the gallery once more, she noticed how much louder the roaring was, and her stomach cramped in fear.

'Sophie, it's Freya! Stay in your alcove, stay back!'

There was a pause, while Freya lifted the axe as far as she could, and then as she brought it swinging around to connect

335

with the rapidly warping wood, she heard Sophie say, 'Freya?' in wondering tones. Then the axe struck, and the shock travelled up Freya's arm to her shoulder, making her cry out and almost drop the weapon again. Behind her she heard footsteps on the stairs, and then Lucy was beside her, holding something conical, and coloured a muddy red.

'In case of fire,' she panted, reading aloud and blinking at the label, 'drive in knob by hard blow against floor. Right, get that broken and we'll see if this thing actually works.'

'Stand back,' Freya shouted, and lifted the axe. Her bicep flared, but she swung the axe again, as close to the handle as she could manage.

It took two more blows before the wood splintered, and a cry of alarm came from the room beyond. Freya dropped the axe with relief, and instead put her left shoulder to work, keeping her attention on Lucy, who was eyeing the door with a fiercely determined expression. She held the MiniMax in a grip that looked capable of anything.

The door burst inwards, and Freya felt the breath go out of her, replaced by scorching heat that seemed to shrivel her lungs into useless lumps inside her chest. She reeled back from the flames that leapt up the jamb, and heard the extinguisher strike the floor as Lucy followed the instructions. A second later a jet of white hissed past her head, and Lucy stepped forward to aim it more carefully.

With time to draw some cool air, Freya was able to see into the gallery, and her heart flipped slowly over as she realised that everything was utterly, hopelessly, destroyed. There was no likelihood of anything surviving this blaze, and no certainty of getting Sophie out alive.

'Sophie!' she shouted, and threw her arm up in front of her face to block out the worst of the heat. The fire extinguisher was still hissing, but it had slowed somewhat. There was nothing for it; she exchanged a split-second glance with Lucy, whose blonde hair was stuck all over her face with sweat, and who looked back at her with terrified realisation, and then she plunged into the room.

The flames were, as Sophie had said, spreading across the floor, between the glass cabinets and the door. There was a strong smell of spilled paraffin mingled with the belching black smoke from the leather-covered books, and midway down the room, on the left, was the curtained alcove. Sophie was peering out, dressed in her riding clothes, and holding her skirts as far off the floor as she could.

'Come to me!' Freya croaked, trying not to breathe too deeply. The smoke was one thing, but the heat flashed into the back of her throat and it felt as though someone was rubbing her flesh raw with glass paper. She held out her hand, but Sophie looked at the leaping flames, so close to Freya's feet, and shrank back, shaking her head.

'I can't!'

'You must!' Freya edged closer, eyeing the floor with dread, and wishing she'd at least taken the time to change out of her house shoes before she came out. At least Sophie had boots on. 'We're all right yet for a few minutes,' she said, as calmly as she could, and not at all sure that was true. The glass cabinets were blazing, and the paraffin lamp lay on its side halfway down the double row, recognisable only for the brighter glow of it against the burning cabinets. The carpet between them was now being rapidly consumed, and had even disappeared in places.

'Run through quickly!' Freya said. 'Take my hand, and I promise we'll be out of here in two shakes!'

'No!'

'For Tristan!' Freya took a breath and coughed so hard she was convinced she would see blood on her sleeve, but there was none. 'Think how devastated he would be. And little Janet, too.'

'It's all my fault!' Sophie cried harder, and then her sobs turned to coughs, but she edged out and took two tentative steps before one of the cabinets beside her collapsed with a crash, and a splintering sound, and she cried out and backed into the alcove again.

Freya slumped in despair. 'You're not safe in there, Sophie! I know it feels as if you are, but . . . ' Her gaze swept the ceiling, wondering with a sudden dread if there were gas pipes above it. 'You *have* to be brave!'

'I *can't*!' Sophie's voice rose to a scream. Freya glanced downwards at the floorboards, now alive with small flames, and at her thin house shoes.

'Stop!' Lucy's voice came too late, as Freya took her first step, but a second later she felt something cold and wet on her feet, and realised that, unable to take her place in time, Lucy had instead aimed the last gasp of the MiniMax at the floor. Freya plunged on until she was standing before the alcove, where the fire had not yet reached. The floor felt blessedly normal beneath her stinging feet.

She reached out for Sophie's hand. 'Come on,' she urged. 'You'll be all right, you're wearing boots.' If worst came to absolute worst, she could at least pick the girl up and carry her, throbbing bicep be damned. 'Run, come on!'

Sophie grasped Freya's hand tightly, and at last allowed herself to be led across the burning floor. Once over the threshold Freya tried to close the door behind them.

'Leave it!' Lucy urged, but Freya shook her head.

'It'll spread to the rest of the house!' She was starting to feel light-headed. She swayed, her stomach rolled, and she tasted sour vomit in the back of her throat, mixed with the sooty taste of smoke. She coughed, and her head swam, leaving her blinking and disorientated. She pulled harder on the warped door, but it merely banged against the broken lock and bounced open again, and her right arm had lost all its strength. She was aware that Lucy was alone in the corridor, and that Sophie had fled down towards the stairs. Anger mingled with relief at the girl's safety, but both were muted by this strange, distant feeling that was creeping over her, putting lead in her limbs. Lucy was urging her to run, but she couldn't make her legs move.

She could hear ever-louder crackling as the fire crept closer, and even as she watched, hypnotised, the paint on the window frame began to bubble and drip. There must be some way of securing the door until the fire service arrived. A crash from the far end of the room showed her that part of the ceiling near the window had given way, to reveal a threadwork of narrow pipes, and she wondered again if there was still gas running through them. She turned to ask Lucy, but her answer came in the dull crump from behind her, and in the seemingly solid wall of burning air that flung her face-down onto the floor of the corridor. Her forehead bounced off the hard wood, and a brilliant light flashed behind her eyes ... The world was an ocean and she floundered and struggled a moment, before the waves swamped her and the light went out.

Bill was not in his field, nor in the stable. Tristan looked around the farmyard in rapidly dwindling hope, then climbed back into the field, biting back a ripe curse as he landed on his sprained ankle, and hobbled up the steep field. His ribs and hip were aching as much as his ankle, and it all combined to deepen his anger; Sophie's spiteful lies could be the ruin of everything he loved, including his affection for her, and what did she do? Go riding!

He arrived at Priddy Lane breathing hard and wishing he'd taken the road instead, and climbed slowly over the wall behind the cottages. School was over for the day, but there was a notable absence of noise from the playground up the lane, where some of the younger children usually stayed to play. Someone, somewhere, was burning garden rubbish and the smell lingered in the damp air.

The town was surprisingly deserted too, and there were 'closed' and 'back in an hour' signs, hurriedly hung or stuck haphazardly on shop doors. Penhaligon's Attic sported no such sign, but when he went in he was surprised to see only Teddy there.

Teddy's face was pale, and he was shaking.. 'Thank goodness you're all right!'

'What are you talking about? Where's Freya?'

'She's gone up . . . wait, haven't you heard about the fire?'

Tristan's stomach twisted. 'Fire?'

Teddy told him. 'Freya thought you were up there working,' he finished. 'She told me to stay here with Anna while she went to find you.'

'I'm here now,' Mairead said quickly, seeing the fear on Teddy's face in the same instant Tristan noticed it. 'Go on, the pair of you.'

The two of them hurried up the hill as fast as Tristan's limp could move him, but he could see Teddy wanted to run ahead. 'Go on,' he said. 'Find Lucy.'

'I'm not sure she'll be pleased to see me,' Teddy's face was grim and drawn, more serious than Tristan could remember seeing him. 'But I just want to make sure she's all right.'

'She knows it wasn't your idea to keep anything from her. Go!'

He watched Teddy wrestling with his conscience for a second, and losing, and then he was alone on the road while his friend put on a turn of speed Tristan had never suspected he possessed, and was soon out of sight. He couldn't shake off the newspaper images of the burned-out church at Honiton, and the dread grew, making him feel nauseous.

The grounds of Pencarrack were teeming with little groups of people, pointing at the blazing east wing of the manor house, and speculating about who, or what, had caused it. There was no sign of Freya, nor of Lucy.

'Tristan!' It was Isabel, her eyes huge in a terrified face. 'Is Freya out yet?'

He found his voice, thin and barely audible. 'Out?'

'She went in to find your sister!'

Tristan thought he might black out on his feet. 'Sophie's here too?'

'Freya saw your horse, and ran into the house with Miss Batten.' Her voice trembled, but Tristan pushed away her outstretched hand before it could close on his arm, and reeled away from her. Before he could take more than half a dozen steps, an explosion tore through the east wing of Pencarrack House, raising screams and cries of horror all around.

The strength ran out of Tristan's legs, and he pitched onto his knees. All around him he heard voices, including Teddy's, but he could make no sense of them. The crowd surged forward, people knocked into him and boots scuffed his elbows, but his body was solid rock, his ears filled with a rushing noise that blocked out the tinkling of breaking glass, and the roar of the blaze.

'She's out, old man ... She's safe ...'

Teddy's urgent voice finally broke through the wall of grief and horror. Tristan felt a strong hand between his shoulder blades, rubbing, patting, squeezing the back of his neck, and his friend's voice repeating the phrase, 'They're all safe.'

He finally found the strength to lift his head. Teddy was crouching beside him, and tears stood out in his eyes, so that, for a heart-tearing moment Tristan was certain he must have misunderstood, or misheard. But then Teddy smiled, and the smile turned into a laugh, and the tears began to flow.

'Dashed unmanly,' Teddy said, not bothering to wipe his eyes. 'But who cares, eh?'

'Safe?' Tristan repeated through numbed lips. 'Where?'

'Over there.' Teddy nodded to where a group of people were huddled. 'That explosion was a controlled one; Keir Garvey fetched dynamite from the quarry, and made a ... a fire break, or something, to save the rest of the house.'

'Does Isabel know?'

'She does now. Come on.'

Tristan allowed Teddy to draw him to his feet, and made

his shaky way over to where Lucy and Freya sat on the grass, smoke-streaked and filthy. Freya's feet were bare and pressed into the cool grass, and she was staring at them blankly. She looked up as Tristan approached, and gave him a relieved but weary smile, as he knelt and took her in his arms.

'Oh, my darling girl,' he whispered against her hair. Her arms went around him and he felt the warmth of her tears through his shirt. 'You're the bravest person I know.'

She shook her head against his chest, and held him tighter, and he really thought his heart might break as she abandoned all control and sobbed against him. He caught Teddy's eye, over her head, and mouthed, *where's Sophie?*

Teddy mimed back with his fingers, a figure running. Again. Tristan swallowed his anger as Lucy explained how Sophie had been locked inside the burning gallery, and instead tried to imagine how terrified his sister must have been.

Freya eased herself away from him, and hiccupped her way to a shaky kind of calm. 'I'm sorry,' she said in a low voice. 'I don't know what's wrong with me. I'm not hurt.'

'Miraculously enough,' Lucy put in. Tristan looked at her sharply. 'The gas pipes blew up,' she explained. 'Freya was knocked out, but not for long.' She smiled, and shook her head at Freya. 'She's made of stern stuff, this young lady. We were able to get out of the house before Mr Garvey arrived with the dynamite.' Her light voice hoarsened as she remembered. 'When she fell, I thought . . . I was sure she was dead.'

'Christ.' Tristan's arms went around Freya again; he could hardly bear not to be touching her now, and she made no protest as he pulled her onto his lap. She felt small, delicate, but gloriously solid and real. Her hair smelled of smoke, as did her skin, and her tears had cut streaks through the dirt on her face, but they had stopped now. There was a red mark in the middle of her forehead, that looked set to rise into an egg before too long.

For a while they sat in silence, and Tristan saw Teddy's hand slip into Lucy's, but she removed it, a look of betrayal erasing the relief on her face. She might forgive, one day, but it looked to Tristan as if that day would be a long time coming.

A loud crash from the house made them all jump, and now there were fresh flames licking at the ground-floor window below the gallery – the library. More destruction, doubtless including those months of painstaking research in the form of his, Teddy's and Lucy's notes. His heart ached with it, but he had no time to dwell on the loss.

'How are your feet, Freya?' Lucy asked.

Tristan frowned. 'Your feet? What's wrong with them?'

'My shoes weren't up to the job,' Freya said. 'Things got a bit hot.' She shifted her feet to find a fresh, cold patch of grass, and then took a deep breath and turned them so she could see the soles of both at once. They were red, and clearly horribly sore, rather like a severe sunburn, and her right foot had a blister on the heel but the skin was unbroken.

She gave Lucy a grateful look. 'That thing you did with the magic-maxi, or whatever you called it, probably saved us all. I didn't stop to think how I'd have been able to help Sophie if I couldn't even walk.'

'Where's Doctor Bartholomew?' Tristan looked around, but couldn't see him. 'He ought to be here.'

'He's gone with Dorothy, to see how things are with James,'

Lucy said. 'He must have left before the fire, or he'd have stayed to make sure no one was hurt. Perhaps the mine doctor is here instead, and can tend to Freya.' She started to stand up. 'Shall I see if I can find him?'

'No,' Teddy said quickly. 'You stay here. Tell me what he looks like, and I'll go and ask.'

Lucy gave him a quick, tight-voiced description of Doctor Manley, and Teddy hurried off, no doubt relieved to have something to do that would also excuse his presence.

'Do we know how James is?' Freya wanted to know, and Tristan remembered James was a good friend of her father's.

'I saw them bring him out of the valley,' he said quickly. 'He was in a bad way, but alive.'

I'm sure he's getting the best care.'

'I ought to let Mairead know,' Freya said. 'She might hear half a story, and think the worst. They're quite close, oddly enough.' She looked at Lucy. 'This is not something I ever imagined I would say to a member of the landed gentry, but . . . can I borrow your shoes to walk home in, please?'

'Honestly, Miss Penhaligon,' Lucy sighed, easing them off her own feet. 'You turn up in your silly house shoes, break down my door, and then walk off with my favourite Hook, Knowles.' Her humour was welcome, but obviously forced.

'Are you certain it was Hugh who did this?' Freya asked her, and Tristan looked at them both, astonished.

'Yes,' Lucy said, her voice sad. 'I don't want to be, but I am. He's found out he won't inherit Pencarrack, after all.'

'Poor Hugh.'

'He'll come home when he realises it's not as bad as he'd thought, thanks to your friend with his strange, violent solution.' She gave them both a tired little smile. 'Oh, don't worry, we'll be all right. We've weathered a lot, us Battens. Families do, don't they?'

'Speaking of which, I think I've just worked out where Sophie would have gone.' Tristan shook his head in exasperation. 'I'd better go and talk to her before she makes things even worse.' He stood up and held out his hand to help Freya. Lucy's shoes were a little too big, and Freya winced as her toes slid forward. 'On second thoughts, you ought to wait here. Teddy will be back soon, with this Doctor Manley bloke, and you need to get those feet padded.'

'I will.' She seemed to come to a difficult decision. 'But first, I'm going to talk to my mother. Alone,' she added quietly, and took the sting out of her words by stretching up on tip-toe to kiss Tristan's cheek. 'I'll see you at home in a little while.'

Watching her small, determined figure hobbling away across the grass, favouring her blistered right foot, Tristan was about to follow her, but Lucy caught at his arm. 'When a girl says she's going to talk to her mother alone, you'd be well advised to let her.'

He opened his mouth to argue, then nodded instead. The harsh jangle of bells stopped any further conversation for a minute or two, and they watched the fire engine roll its way up across the grass, disgorging uniformed firemen as it went.

Charles Batten appeared, hot on the heels of Keir Garvey, who was making his hurried way towards the farm cart. 'Garvey! Wait!'

Keir's face took on a wary look when he saw who was calling him. Tristan's own anger came to the fore once again as he thought of the devastation of all those books, not to mention his own notes. Lucy seemed sure her brother was to blame, but Tristan wasn't convinced; Charles Batten had far more to gain from the destruction of his family's history than a disgruntled would-be heir.

'. . . Quick-thinking thing you did,' Batten was saying. 'Where the deuce did a farmer learn to handle dynamite like that?'

'In the gold mines in New Zealand,' Keir said. He shrugged. 'And we had to create fire breaks now and again too, between the forest and the homestead.'

'Well you've saved Pencarrack, and that's the truth. I'd like to offer you a reward. What can I do for you? A job here on the estate? I pay very generously and we could use a resourceful man like yourself.'

Keir studied him for a moment, his head tilted slightly. 'A cottage on Furzy Row.'

Batten frowned. 'I can't imagine that'd make you too popular,' he said at last. 'They're for mine workers only. Besides, there aren't any empty ones, and you wouldn't want to make someone homeless, would you?'

'Certainly not,' Keir said. 'The place isn't for me, and in any case I wouldn't expect you to gift it. It's for one of your bal maidens and her son. She *is* a mine worker,' he pointed out, as Batten frowned.

'Ah, but not underground.'

'Nevertheless.'

'As I say, there's no vacancy. I could create a position for you here, in the stables – I can see you're a keen horseman.'

At the other end of the grounds, the fire crew was tackling the blaze with huge jets of water pumped from the small lake, and the townspeople had moved as close as they were allowed, but Tristan's attention was focused on these two men; one standing at least six feet four in his socks, the other barely making five feet ten; one muscular and broad, the other slender and elegant, yet with a personality that somehow made him tower over taller men. Usually.

Keir was still smiling. 'I'll take the cottage, thanks. You'll invite the widow Ellen Scoble to move into the one until recently rented by her brother and his wife. Currently inhabited by Mrs Scoble's mother, who you will also permit to remain there.'

'Will I, indeed?' Batten's gratitude appeared to be fading fast, but Keir's smile didn't falter.

'One other thing?' His voice was so soft that Tristan barely heard him and had to move closer still. 'Your method of collecting rent from widows has been noted, so I'd think it more proper if you deduct it directly from Mrs Scoble's wage. *Before* the income tax is calculated, of course.'

Batten stared at Keir for a long, tense moment, then he held out a hand. 'Done, Mr Garvey. I hope this Mrs Scoble knows what a good friend she has in you.'

'No, she doesn't,' Keir said, accepting the proffered hand. 'But as long as she knows what a good employer she has, I'll settle for that. Now, if you'll excuse me, I've got to get the farm cart back.'

Tristan caught up with Batten as the landowner strode off towards the fire engine. 'I have to talk to you,' he began. 'To tell you I never had any intention of—'

'Not right this moment you don't,' Batten said grimly. 'In case you hadn't noticed, my home is still on fire.'

Tristan followed Batten's angrily stabbing finger, and his breath halted in his throat. 'There's someone else in there!'

'What?' Batten stopped dead and stared, and Tristan recognised the dark figure in the upstairs window, hands pressed against the glass, at the same moment. 'Hugh!'

Tristan tried to grab at Batten's coat, but the man was too quick for him, and a moment later he was gone, inside the house. Shouts went up, water was redirected, and a moment later Lucy was at his side, clutching at his arm in an agony of fear.

'Why's Father gone in?'

'What's your brother still doing in the house?' Tristan cried, over the commotion that had seized the crowds. 'Didn't he know what was happening?'

'He must have been asleep.' Lucy was shaking, Tristan could feel it through her thin blouse. 'I thought he'd set the fire and run away!'

'How could he have slept through all that noise?' But he remembered Sophie's disgust at Hugh's drunkenness, and realised it had probably not been an unusual occurrence. Not so much asleep then, as in a drunken stupor, and now his life was at stake because of it.

Lucy's eyes were fixed on the window, where her brother was now leaning out to gasp at the cleaner air. She tore herself out of Tristan's grip, but only took a few steps towards the house before she was stopped. 'Father's coming for you!'

There was nothing to do now but watch, and presently a second figure appeared beside Hugh, and drew the young man back into the room – a brief embrace, and then, arms around each other the two of them disappeared from the window. Tristan's heartbeat returned to normal, and he began to breathe more easily, as everyone waited for father and son to emerge from the burning house.

The crash of the collapsing staircase, and the ceiling above it, could be heard above the roar of flame and the hiss of water, and then the sudden, shocked silence of the crowd was broken by Lucy Batten's throat-tearing scream.

Chapter Twenty-two

Penhaligon's Attic

It was earlier than it seemed, with the day darkening outside. Anna kept her eyes closed in order to hold on to the illusion that Matthew lay next to her; she'd discovered during her enforced period of convalescence that, even when he was down at Porthstennack, if she let herself drift a little she could even imagine she heard him breathing. Slow, deep, peaceful . . .

The latch clicked, and Matthew disappeared. Anna lay very still in the darkness, her heart beating fast. No one ever entered without knocking, not even Matthew. A smell drifted across the room, and her nose twitched. Smoke . . . She struggled to pull herself up, and fumbled for the matches to light the candle on her bedside table, wishing the light switch was closer to the bed.

The candle stuttered into life, and Anna saw little Sophie MacKenzie, her face streaked with soot and tears, and her hair in disarray. She looked horrified to have been caught out, and had one hand on the latch ready to leave again, but Anna played the candle light over her, and told her to come and sit on the bed.

Mairead appeared in the doorway, breathless from running. 'I thought it was you, missy! What in the world were you doing, sneaking up the stairs like that?'

Anna held her finger to her lips, and gestured Sophie closer. 'What were you doing at Pencarrack?' she asked, when Sophie had sat gingerly on the very edge of the bed.

'How do you know I was there?'

'Unless there's been a fire somewhere else that I don't know about, the clues are all over your face. Not to mention in your clothes.' Anna wrinkled her nose. 'Are your brother and Freya all right?'

'Freya is. Tristan's not there.'

'Well thank the lord for that at least,' Anna said, letting out a heavy sigh. She put out her hand and took Sophie's, as Mairead crossed to open the curtains, letting in the thin afternoon light. 'I have to ask, why are you trying to hide in *my* room?'

Sophie looked embarrassed. 'Tristan says you're not to be put under any stress.'

'You'll need to explain your reasoning to me,' Anna said, 'because creeping around someone's bedroom in the dark doesn't seem like the best way to keep that person calm. If you understand me?'

Sophie turned beseeching eyes on her. 'It's only that, if Tristan finds me in here, he won't be so cross. Not in front of you. And nor will Freya.'

'Cross?'

'Freya saved my life. And I've been so horrible to them both.' Sophie snatched a quick breath, and a tear rolled from her eye, carving a bright new trail through the smudges of soot.

'Tell me what Freya did,' Anna said. She passed Sophie a neatly squared handkerchief from the little pile on her bedside table. 'How did you come to need saving?'

Sophie hesitated. 'It's a bit of a tale.'

'Well I've nowhere to be.'

'I went to find Tristan, to tell him I'm sorry.'

'For what?'

'For telling lies, to get him to come home.'

Anna and Mairead listened with shared dismay, as Sophie explained how she'd spoken to the Misses Batten yesterday, spilling tales of Tristan's non-existent plan for deception.

'But after I went for a ride, and thought a bit more about it, I realised that it wouldn't only cause a rift between Freya and Tristan, but it would get him into trouble too. People might not buy his books. Miss Batten – the older one – already said he couldn't use the gallery at Pencarrack anymore.'

'Yes, it would have given him a terrible reputation,' Anna said. 'You did a good thing, to try and put it right. I gather you couldn't find him though?'

Over Sophie's bowed head, she saw Tristan appear, his face a mask, and she shook her head minutely, indicating he should stay where he was. His timing couldn't have been more perfect, as the whole story finally came out.

Unable to find her brother, or anyone else for that matter, Sophie had decided to wait for him in the gallery. She'd been sitting in the window, idly kicking her feet against the window seat and watching for him out of the front, and then she saw him leave ... he'd been there all the time! Irritated with herself she jumped up, and was crossing the room when she heard voices coming down the short corridor. Remembering how Tristan would get into trouble for allowing her to be in here, she'd slipped into the alcove, pulling the thick curtain straight just in time.

She stood as still as a mouse, her heart thudding, and waited for whoever it was to leave. One of the men sounded familiar, but she couldn't place him. One of them threw what sounded like a bunch of keys onto the glass-topped case.

'A small one. Very small. Do you understand? Right there, under the middle cabinet.' A pause, and a mutter from his companion, and when the man spoke again his voice was tight. 'For God's sake, man! It's your fault all this is getting out, giving those bloody books to that scrappy little shop!'

'I didn't know ... All right! I'll do it.'

'Good. Wait until I've gone. Then turn the wick up as high as it'll go, and lay a thin – a *very* thin, mind – trail of paraffin to the window. That way someone will see it sooner.'

'But what if someone sees it *too* soon? How will we make sure the books will catch?'

'Start it where I told you, and they'll go up, don't worry.'

'You could just take them, no need to burn them.'

'If I had the key I would.'

'Isn't the key on that chain?'

The first voice sighed. 'Those are room keys, MacKenzie has the only set of cabinet keys.'

The man who sounded familiar, now also sounded desperate. 'Then why not smash the glass, or even just the locks, and take them?'

'Because insurance assessors aren't idiots, and with all our money sunk into that hotel I can't afford questions. Likely as not, that pair will go to prison, once it's established this was no accident. They've got the perfect motive for setting fire to the place, after all.'

Sophie's skin shrank on her bones, but she gripped the curtain tightly and tried to calm herself. She should be able to put out a little fire, then she would run like the wind after her brother, and warn him, and put everything right. She hadn't been able to do enough during the fire at St Michael's, but this time—

'Remember to close the door behind you, so it doesn't spread,' the bossy man said. 'I don't want to lose the whole bloody wing. Then get downstairs and find Dorothy, she wants you to go with her to the infirmary in Truro. There's your alibi, too.'

With that, the door had swiftly opened and closed, and Sophie had heard the familiar man muttering under his breath. It had come to her then, who it was. Doctor Bartholomew. She hadn't dared even tweak the curtain a little bit, in case he was looking in that direction, so she stood still, trying to make her heartbeat slow down, and to stop her hands from shaking in case she made a noise.

There had been the sound of something unscrewing, and then a splashing. Then it sounded as though he was putting the lid back on, but there was a scrape, another, larger splash, and a curse that made Sophie blush, even in the privacy of her alcove. The flare of the match almost made her cry out in shock; some part of her had held on to the belief that he wouldn't really do it, not once the bossy one – Mr Batten – had left.

The roar of the paraffin catching fire made Bartholomew curse again, this time in fearful tones. Then a moment later he left and Sophie was alone in the dark, with those awful sounds a few feet away on the other side of the thick curtain. She waited long enough so she was sure he'd gone, and had just pulled back the curtain, when she heard a key in the lock. No! He wasn't supposed to *lock* it, just close it! Mr Batten must have left his keys where he'd thrown them. Directly in front of her, the wooden frames of the glass cabinets were blazing, and the glass was cracking and turning a cloudy grey. One of them collapsed inwards with a deceptively light-sounding tinkle, and the books beneath it were consumed by hungry flames. Sophie moved towards the window, hoping to open it, to scream for help, but her path that way was blocked by the burning rope of paraffin.

She ran to the door instead, desperately hoping she'd imagined what she'd heard, but it rattled in its frame and would not budge. Sobbing, she looked over her shoulder and saw the flames eating their way across the carpet, and ran back to the cool, comforting depths of her alcove to huddle at the very back. Mr Batten had said someone would see the fire soon, and although the stupid doctor had spilled too much paraffin, they would make sure the room wasn't completely destroyed. All she had to do was wait.

'And so I did,' she said, through hiccupping sobs into the silence of Anna's room. 'I waited and waited ... Then I heard Lucy, and then *she* went away. And then Freya came, with the axe.'

Half Anna's attention was on Tristan, and she watched his face go through all the emotions she herself was feeling. When

Sophie told how she'd already been halfway down the stairs when the gas pipe exploded, and how she was certain she'd been responsible for killing Freya and Lucy, he stepped into the room, and held out his arms. She let out a cry of remorse and went to him.

'Where *is* Freya?' Anna asked.

'She went to talk to Isabel. I didn't want her to go alone, not with her burned feet, but she wouldn't let me go with her.'

Anna didn't want to press him, but her sense of unease returned, and she tried not to think about what might be so important that it couldn't even wait until the girl had had her feet tended to.

They talked quietly for a little longer, and Sophie explained that she'd waited in the crowd until Lucy and Freya had come out, and only then had she run down here, to hide. She knew she shouldn't have left Bill, but she couldn't find him among the horses they'd let out of the stables. Tristan told her Keir had ridden him to the quarry, and that he was safe and comfortable now, and Sophie sagged in relief, her face in her hands.

Mairead received the news of James's attack in silence, but Anna noted the tightness of her daughter's jaw, and saw how her short fingernails dug into her palms. When Tristan assured her, as far as he was able, that James was being cared for, she rose and left the room, and Anna longed to follow, but didn't; some things were better absorbed in the privacy of one's own thoughts, she knew that all too well.

Freya came upstairs around half an hour after her fiancé, quiet and moving awkwardly, and pocketing an envelope she had brought with her. She looked bemused, exhausted, and

357

even more grubby and soot-streaked than Sophie, and Anna realised she had wrapped soft cloths around her feet. She had a strange expression on her face, too, and Anna couldn't place it. It wasn't pain, which came as a relief on seeing those make-shift bandages and the growing lump on her forehead, but it was troubled.

Sophie looked at Freya, her eyes over-bright. 'Why did you do all that to save me?' she asked, in a broken voice. 'I've been so horrible to you, and ruined everything. You might have died.'

'Well, I didn't. ' Freya put her arms around her. 'It doesn't matter what you did,' she said, smoothing the girl's hair as she might a daughter's. 'You're going to be family.' She moved back and held Sophie at arm's length. 'I would do the same thing, and more, for Tristan,' she said, very clearly. 'Do you understand?'

Sophie nodded. 'I do now,' she said softly. 'I'm sorry.'

'Tell me what Keir did,' Anna said, partly to break the awkward quiet that followed this emotional moment, and partly because, with her cousin, it could be anything. When she heard about the explosion that had successfully halted the progress of the fire through the main part of Pencarrack House, she shook her head, bemused. Yes, absolutely anything.

'I expect Charles Batten was grateful.'

'He was. Very. He even offered Keir his choice of reward.'

'And what did he choose?'

Tristan told her about Ellen and the cottage. 'She's to live there along with her mother. In perpetuity.'

'In purple what?' Sophie asked, mystified. Tristan smiled at her, but he was still shaken and pale.

'Does Ellen know yet?' Anna asked, her voice hoarse. God love Keir, he had a heart of pure gold and people were starting to notice it.

'No.'

'Can I be there when he tells her?'

Tristan didn't return her smile. 'I'll leave you to sort that out. Look, I'm sorry, but there's something else.' He took Sophie's hand. 'I know you feel responsible, darling, but you mustn't. Promise me?'

'I promise,' Sophie stammered. 'What is it?'

'There was someone else trapped in the house when it caught fire. Lucy's brother, Hugh. No one knew until his father went in to get him out.'

Freya drew a sharp breath. 'What happened? Are they safe?'

'Hugh is.' Tristan lowered his voice. 'Charles was killed, when the staircase collapsed.'

Anna's heart turned over. She was reminded of her terror during the storm last year, when the Porthstennack house had collapsed around her – how much more dreadful must this have been?

There was a stunned silence in the room for a good while, punctuated by Sophie's soft weeping, and the rhythmic whispering sound of her brother rubbing her back. Freya had slumped in relief at hearing Hugh was safe, but Anna could see Tristan's thoughts parading across his face, and knew he felt even more responsible than his little sister, for what his investigations had led to.

'Don't,' she said to him quietly. 'You couldn't have known. Don't torture yourself.'

Tristan blinked, and she saw how close to the surface his emotions were. 'If I hadn't—'

'Stop it,' Freya said, and limped over to him. He let out a shaking breath to control himself and his voice.

'What's that sticking out of your pocket?'

'Oh, yes. It was with the post.' Freya withdrew the letter. 'But it's addressed to Grandpa Robert. I thought you might want to open it, Anna. I didn't want to upset Papá by giving it to him.'

'Of course. Pass it here, Tristan.'

He reached out to take it from Freya, then paused and angled it towards the light from the window. 'Put the light on, Sophie.'

She did so, and Tristan frowned. 'I thought so. This is from Turner and Mitchell. I recognise the stamp.'

'Who?'

'My publishers.'

'How on earth did they get so muddled as to address it to Robert then?' Anna waved the letter away. 'You'd better open it, it might be important.'

Tristan tore open the envelope, and scanned the paper, and his face at last broke into a real smile. 'The address wasn't a mistake,' he said, and passed the letter to Anna. Mystified, she took it.

Dear Mr Penhaligon

With reference to your letter of December 28th last, and the enclosed children's adventure story written by Matthew Penhaligon. My apologies for the tardiness of the reply. Having discussed this with our partners in the fiction

department, we would very much like to put 'Julia's Gift'
into a book. We feel it would sell very well, especially around
Christmas time.

As it stands, although the story is a beautiful, moving tale,
it is not quite long enough. However, if you could please put
your son in touch with us we would like to discuss lengthening
this story, or, if he has any other work of a similar high
standard, we might talk about publishing a collection.

We eagerly await your response,
Messrs Turner and Mitchell, Publishers.
London. W1.

Anna sat staring at the letter, and only when Tristan cleared his throat did she realise there were two anxious faces focused on her. She read the message aloud, and then looked up to see Freya blinking rapidly.

'But he always thought Grandpa hated his stories!' She wiped at her eyes, half-laughing. 'I'm going to take the news to him now, if that's all right?'

'Of course.' Anna gave her the letter, and watched her struggle to put it back in the envelope with shaking fingers. 'Is there anything else? Anything wrong?'

'No.' Freya shook her head, but Anna didn't believe her. There was another reason the girl was eager to see her father, and she was keeping it locked away. The sooner Anna's blood pressure was under control, the better; it was one thing to have your family around you at last, but quite another to know they were frightened to speak their minds.

'Let me come with you,' Tristan said. 'It's going to be dark soon, and I know how you feel about the beach.'

'No, this is something else I have to do alone. But it's the last thing, I promise.' She smiled, and brushed his jaw with her sooty hand. 'After this, you won't be able to turn around without tripping over me.'

'Good. I could do with some more practice on crutches.'

Freya kissed him. 'Try not to fall down the stairs while I'm out, then.'

'Freya?' Anna felt the first twinge of real apprehension. 'Why won't you tell me what's so urgent?'

Freya paused at the door, and for a moment Anna thought she was going to tell her, but instead she just said, 'Please don't worry.'

When Freya had gone, a strange silence dropped over those who were left, and Anna had the unsettling sense of sands shifting beneath their feet; whatever Freya had to discuss with her father, it was going to change things. That much was certain.

* * *

The road to Porthstennack was busy enough, with the curious and the satisfied returning from the Pencarrack fire, that Freya didn't really notice the repellent push from the beach until she was at its very edge. Her feet felt the rub of her shoes, despite the padding held in place inside her stockings, and her right arm twinged every time she straightened it, but the fresh air, after that awful choking smoke, still tasted like Heaven.

Through the rapidly setting sun, she eyed the encroaching tide with a little tremor of fear, and tore her gaze away quickly; from the corner of her eye she caught sight of the limp, bruised primrose Tristan had plucked for her in lieu of an engagement ring. It was still looped through the button hole of Granny Grace's coat, and the sight of it made her smile, despite everything. She took a deep breath, and put her hand into her pocket to brush her fingers over the publisher's letter. Papá's smile rose to the front of her mind, and her heart lifted a little.

But first there was other news to impart. She followed the road a little further, and rounded the headland, where she saw the *Pride of Porthstennack* moored against the harbour wall. Not long returned from a day's fishing, she was a mass of busy figures, dressed in oilskins and dark blue Guernseys, working around each other with the ease of long familiarity. Papá moved among them, his blond head bobbing in and out of view, his voice now and again raised in command or laughter. Freya watched him for a few minutes, reluctant to break into this routine, his own tribute to the friendship and teaching of Roland Fry, but the time came when she could put it off no longer.

'Papá!' She waved. He didn't hear her, but Ern Bolitho did, and nudged him.

'Here, Skip. The little maid's wantin' you.'

Papá turned, and his face paled beneath the sweat and the dirt.

'Anna's all right!' Freya called out quickly.

Papá braced his hands on his thighs, and lowered his head in relief. Then plunged his hands into a bucket of sea water that stood at his side, and dried them on his shirt before jumping from the trawler.

His eyes went from her to the sea, and back again. 'Then

what brings you here ... are *you* all right?' He sniffed. 'Has there been a fire? God, the shop—'

'Not the shop.' Freya told him about the Pencarrack fire, and assured him everyone he cared for was safe. There would be time to break the news about James later, when they knew a little more.

'But there's something I have to tell you.' She put an arm through his, and nodded in the direction of the end of the wall. 'Down there.'

He frowned. 'Are you sure? The tide's coming in, it's a bit fierce.'

'Quite sure. Only, hold my arm tight, won't you?' The child-like plea was out before she'd known she was going to utter it, and Papá drew her arm close against his side.

'What is it you want to tell me?'

'It's going to be difficult.'

Papá's curiosity and impatience was evident in the tension in his forearm, but he didn't press her, and they walked slowly, and in silence. As they neared the middle, Freya's pace slowed and he drew her to a stop. 'Was it here?' he asked quietly. 'Where it happened, I mean?'

She nodded, her muscles fighting every instinct to run. 'I know it was the most frightening thing I can ever remember, but I think now that perhaps it changed us all for the better. In the end.'

'I think you're right.' He sighed. 'But it shouldn't have taken such a thing, and that's the truth.'

They moved past the place, and presently they came to the end, where the sea surged, and foamed across the stone at their feet. Freya stared at it, her mouth dry, and her limbs shaking. She felt her father's hand, strong on her arm. He didn't speak, but his presence was comforting and after a moment she found she was breathing more freely, and her legs no longer felt as though they might pitch her to the ground. She was able to turn her thoughts to what must be said, instead, and, with her gaze fixed on the swell, she began to tell him.

'You know about Dorothy Batten, and her son Harry. That she had become pregnant in London, and brought him home to Pencarrack.'

'Yes, it's common enough knowledge.'

'No one knew about the boy's father.' She paused. 'You were acquainted with her when you were younger, weren't you?'

'Well, we knew one another a bit ...' He drew a quick breath, and pulled back. 'You can't think she and I—'

'No!' She saw his shocked expression, and flushed. 'Although I'm sorry to say I did think that, for a little while. But then Mama told me the truth. I know you're not Harry's father.'

'Then who is?'

'When we left for London, Mama and me, Dorothy Batten was on her way there too. I remember watching her in the coach, thinking she was so glamorous. When she came home she had a baby boy with her, but ... she wasn't the one who gave birth to him.' She looked up at her father, and spoke as steadily as she could. 'Harry is Mama's son.'

Papá went rigid, and Freya bit back a gasp as his arm clenched tight, trapping her hand. 'I don't understand,' he said at length, just as Freya was starting to be sorry she'd told him after all. 'Who *is* his father, then?' He looked as though he didn't really want to know, only that he had to.

'Charles Batten.'

'Charles . . .' Papá stared at her helplessly. 'This doesn't make sense! How could Isabel hide something like that? And why did *Dorothy* lie? Burdening herself with an illegitimate child when she needn't have?'

'Charles knew about the pregnancy.' Freya closed her eyes, remembering her mother's uncontrolled, bitter tears as she'd tried to explain. 'The night of that storm, Mama said she was visiting a friend in Plymouth, remember? But she was really at Pencarrack, begging Charles to take her in.'

Papá flinched, and Freya saw her own reluctant sympathy for Isabel reflected in his face. 'He refused,' she went on, 'but agreed to let the boy grow up there, as a Batten. Anyway, Dorothy was giving him trouble I gather—'

'She was a proper tearaway,' Papá said, and seemed to seize on that single solid fact as a refuge. 'Her father was at the end of his tether, so the word goes.'

'Well, he apparently decided that this one scandal wouldn't come as a surprise to anyone, and said that, if Dorothy accepted responsibility for Harry, he would leave the estate to her instead of Hugh. Of course, that meant it would go to Harry, eventually.'

'Batten was our landlord,' Papá said, his voice barely audible over the crashing tide. 'He's carrying on with Nancy Gilbert now, and in the same house.' He looked down at her, his expression suddenly fierce. 'Did you ever have to see him? You know, when he was . . . *collecting the rent*?'

Freya took his iron-hard fist in hers. 'I don't remember, but I'm sure I didn't.'

'I ought to go up there and—'

'Papá, Mr Batten is dead.' She told him what had happened, and Papá's expression was unreadable until she'd finished.

'I'd say he's paid up in full then,' he said at length. 'That was a brave thing he did.'

'It was.' A silence fell between them for a minute, then Freya spoke again. 'So Harry's fatherless now. I wonder what Mama will do?'

'If she truly wants him to inherit, she'll keep it quiet,' Matthew said. 'It's odd, I knew there was something familiar about him, something in his laugh.' Then he frowned. 'If she was pregnant when you left here, she must have ... *God*!' He blew out a breath that stirred his hair with its vehemence. He didn't need to finish the sentence, Freya understood; as disappointing as her life had genuinely been, Mama had seized on the excuse his drunkenness had given her, as if it were the answer to all her prayers. *Your papá and I had been strangers for months, mi tesoro* ... There had been no doubt in her mind whose child she was carrying.

'How did she hide it from you?' Papá asked. 'The pregnancy, I mean.'

'I barely saw her that first year at boarding school,' she reminded him. 'I thought Henry Webb had paid for my education, but it was Mr Batten. Rewarding Mama for her discretion.'

'And all this guff about bringing me my stories back?' He gave a brittle laugh. 'She was using them to find a way to young Harry.'

'She told me she's been thinking of him more and more, these past few years,' Freya said. Mama's voice had broken so much, in her telling of it, that Freya had found it hard to make

367

out her words. 'She never intended to tell anyone, but when he went missing today up at Pencarrack she was so distraught, I knew there was more to it than she was telling.' She sighed. 'I'm so sorry. Are you all right?'

He pondered a moment. 'I don't know,' he said. 'It's like I never knew her after all. By the time this happened we had already lost any chance of salvaging our marriage, but still . . .' He shook his head, and was silent for a while, and when he spoke again his voice was hoarse.

'I think I can forgive her. My drinking might have given her the excuse, but it was still a fact: I destroyed her.' He cleared his throat and wiped at his nose. 'But you're the one she really lied to for so long . . . How do *you* feel?'

'When she told me, I wanted to run away and never speak to her again. She's known all my life that I wanted brothers and sisters. Now I discover I've had one for eleven years and she never told me.' She bit her lip, ordering her confused thoughts. 'But I think she's the one who's been the most hurt by it. I think I just feel dreadful for her.'

'That's because you're a kind girl, with a generous heart.' He put his arm around her shoulder and drew her close, and they were silent again, staring out over the water, watching the tide surge against the breakwater.

The wave receded from the beach, and ran into another, on its way in; the crash of their meeting made her jump, but Freya realised, with a little leap of pleasure, that she hadn't shrunk back from the spray that leapt into the air and splattered across the stone, and across her feet. Moreover, she actually felt *calm*; the white-eyed sea-monster that had haunted her dreams for all these years had finally lost the power to weaken her. A smile brushed her lips, and she hurriedly smothered it in case it appeared careless of Papá's feelings, but he was watching her with a flicker of pride on his face.

'I don't think I've ever told you how sorry I am.'

'Sorry?'

'That you've been so frightened all this time, and all because of me.'

'Not because of you ... Well,' she amended, 'because of how much I love you. Which *is* actually your fault, so – apology accepted.'

She was gratified to see his own smile banish the clouds in his eyes, and decided this was the perfect time. She put her hand into her pocket again. 'There's something else I have to show you. It might help, a little bit.'

'What?' He looked wary, but took the letter she handed him. He read it, raised a stunned face to Freya, and then read it again. 'So Ma didn't throw that story away after all,' he said slowly. 'I'm beginning to wonder if I've fallen asleep at sea. First Isabel and Harry, and now this.' He read the short letter a third time. 'I can't believe it.'

'Grandpa's last gift to you, and to Aunt Julia,' Freya said. 'He was prouder of you than any of us ever knew.'

'It seems so.' The wind tugged at the paper in his hand, and he folded it quickly and put it in his pocket. 'It's been quite a year,' he said, after a moment. He sounded a little unsteady at first, but then looked down at her, and smiled. 'Heaven only knows what's in store for us next, but I think we're going to be ready for it, don't you?'

'Yes.' Freya took a deep breath and let it out, and together they watched the grey swell, and listened to the gentle bump and scrape of the *Pride's* hull against the stone of the harbour wall.

There was a comfortable familiarity in that sound, and in the call of hungry gulls wheeling overhead, the shouts and arguments, and occasional laughter, of a working community tending to their daily tasks, but changes were coming. The Penhaligon family, like every other, would be reshaped by them, remoulded, and tested, but Papá was right.

They were ready.

Acknowledgements

I would like to thank my amazing and generous friends – online and 'real' world – for their continued support. You really do keep me going.

Thanks also to my agent, Kate Nash, and to the brilliant team at Piatkus, for putting your faith in the Penhaligons.

A shout-out to my TSAG buddies, as ever. Stay strong, my friends, and keep up the flow of words (and wine, and GIFs!)

To the Keep-it-Real-at-Karaoke Kids: Shelley, Jude, Sue, Holly, John W, John A, Luke, and Nigel. Barry and Freda salute you! Now, who's got the cheesy puffs?

And finally to my family, and my extended family: rightly or wrongly, I feel like this ride is just getting going - hold tight! And thanks for everything so far. x